"So I'd only get hurt if I got involved with you," Cora said.

"Yes. You'd essentially be getting a locked box."

He was being transparent, completely up-front. She was the one who'd set that tone. So it surprised him when she barked out a laugh. "You think you're doing me a favor by staying away!"

He was trying to adhere to the decisions he'd made after that last ugly blowout with Tina. He'd been glad for the peace and balance he'd found since they'd broken up a year ago. But twelve months was a long time to go without a woman… "Essentially."

"Well, you're taking a lot for granted, Mr. Turner. First of all, how do you know I'm going to want you to love me?"

"Experience," he said wryly. "I have yet to encounter the opposite problem."

A NEW-FOUND FAMILY

NEW YORK TIMES BESTSELLING AUTHOR

Brenda Novak

AND

Rochelle Alers

Previously published as *Finding Our Forever*
and *Claiming the Captain's Baby*

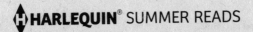
HARLEQUIN® SUMMER READS

ISBN-13: 978-1-335-00829-9

A New-Found Family

Copyright © 2019 by Harlequin Books S.A.

First published as Finding Our Forever by Harlequin Books in 2017 and Claiming the Captain's Baby by Harlequin Books in 2017.

The publisher acknowledges the copyright holders of the individual works as follows:

Finding Our Forever
Copyright © 2017 by Brenda Novak

Claiming the Captain's Baby
Copyright © 2017 by Rochelle Alers

Recycling programs for this product may not exist in your area.

Printed in U.S.A.

HARLEQUIN®
www.Harlequin.com

CONTENTS

New York Times and *USA TODAY* bestselling author **Brenda Novak** is the author of more than fifty books. A five-time RITA® Award nominee, she has won many awards, including the National Readers' Choice, the Booksellers' Best and the Silver Bullet. She also runs Brenda Novak for the Cure, a charity to raise money for diabetes research (her youngest son has this disease). To date, she's raised $2.5 million. For more about Brenda, please visit brendanovak.com.

Books by Brenda Novak

Harlequin Superromance

Sanctuary
Shooting the Moon
A Family for Christmas
Dear Maggie
Baby Business
Snow Baby
Expectations

Dundee, Idaho

A Baby of Her Own
A Family of Her Own
A Husband of Her Own

MIRA Books

Dundee, Idaho

A Home of Her Own
Stranger in Town

Big Girls Don't Cry
The Other Woman
Coulda Been a Cowboy

Whiskey Creek

Discovering You
A Winter Wedding
This Heart of Mine
The Heart of Christmas
Come Home to Me
Take Me Home for Christmas
Home to Whiskey Creek
When Summer Comes
When Snow Comes
When Lightning Strikes
When We Touch

Visit the Author Profile page at Harlequin.com for more titles.

FINDING OUR FOREVER

Brenda Novak

To all lost/hurt boys.
May you find an Aiyana Turner in your life.

Chapter 1

Cora Kelly had never met her birth mother.

The records had been sealed when she was adopted as a newborn twenty-eight years ago. Her adoptive mother didn't even know her birth mother's name, so it wasn't as if Lilly Kelly had ever mentioned it. Cora had had very little to go on. Even with two different attorneys, a website designed to help families reconnect and a private investigator who'd taken her case for free since he was an adoptee himself and did what he could, in his spare time, to help others who'd been through the same thing, it'd taken six long years to glean the information she craved. But here she was, only moments away from coming face-to-face, for the first time since the day she was born, with the woman who'd brought her into this world.

Would she like her mother? Would they resemble

each other more in person than in the one picture she'd seen? Would Aiyana Turner somehow recognize her for who she was?

Those questions churned in Cora's mind, making her stomach churn, as well. But one question weighed heavier than the others: Was she making a mistakte?

Wiping her palms on her slacks, she told herself to calm down. As far as Aiyana knew, they were only meeting to talk about Cora's new job working as an art instructor at New Horizons Boys Ranch, a boarding school for troubled teens, ages fourteen to eighteen, ninety minutes outside LA. No way would Aiyana have any reason to suspect Cora's true identity. And Cora didn't plan to tell her who she was. Not today. Maybe not ever. That was why she'd sought this job—and accepted it. So she'd have the chance to see what she might be getting into before making that decision.

Hopefully, her mother would be someone she could admire, at least. From what she could tell, Aiyana had done a lot to help teenage boys who acted out, some who'd been orphaned as well as many who hadn't. Her work as executive administrator of the school she'd founded twenty years ago seemed to be her one true love. She'd never been married, and she'd never had any more of her own children. According to a newspaper article honoring Aiyana on the anniversary of the date the boys ranch opened, something the private detective who finally solved the mystery of Aiyana's identity had provided, Aiyana had adopted quite a few of the residents who'd come to the school through the years—eight of them, so far. The oldest, Elijah Turner, was now a man in his early thirties. He helped run New Horizons. Cora knew because he was the person who'd interviewed and then hired her. That was why she hadn't yet met Aiyana. Aiyana had been out of town when Cora came two weeks ago.

"I'm sorry it's taking a few moments. Ms. Turner is on an unexpected but important call." The receptionist, a gray-haired woman who had to be in her sixties, smiled kindly as she imparted this apology. "I can't imagine it'll be much longer."

Hauling in a deep breath, Cora smiled. "It's fine. I don't mind waiting." She *didn't* mind, except that she was beginning to fear she'd have a heart attack right there outside of Aiyana Turner's office. Somehow, she had to stem her anxiety…

"Are you too warm, dear? I can turn down the air…"

She glanced up at the receptionist again—and realized she'd been fanning herself. "Um…no. I'm okay, thanks," she said and dropped her hand.

"It's been hot this summer."

"Yes, it's particularly warm today," Cora said, but it was generally worse where she lived in Burbank. Along with Jill, her best friend, Cora rented a small condo just outside of Hollywood, where her adoptive parents still owned the lovely four-bedroom home where she'd been raised.

She felt a twinge of guilt when she thought of her parents, Brad and Lilly. They'd been good to her, treated her just like her brother, who was two years older and their biological child. They wouldn't be pleased that she'd landed this job if they knew the driving force behind it.

Don't think about that. What they don't know can't hurt them. It would be premature to drag them into this, anyway, since she had no idea where it might go.

For all she knew, it wouldn't go anywhere. And maybe that was for the best. Several years ago, when she'd first mentioned that she'd like to find her birth mother, Brad and Lilly had acted shocked and disappointed. They'd taken it personally, didn't understand that they didn't do anything to cause the emptiness inside her and weren't the ones who could fix it. The hole was just there, and Cora felt it would be until she could figure out where she came from, who she was and where she belonged.

She hoped this would help. Her boyfriend—*ex*-boyfriend since she'd broken up with him last month—claimed it was her personal problems that'd destroyed their two-year relationship. He said she needed to let go of her past and move on, that she could be opening Pandora's box.

He could be right. But it was too late to change her plans. She'd already made a yearlong commitment to New Horizons. Today's meeting with Aiyana was merely a formality—an orientation, of sorts. Cora had given notice that she'd be vacating her condo at the end of the month, at which point her friend would get a new roommate and she'd move to Silver Springs, a town of only 5,000 people located slightly east of Santa Barbara.

After spending her whole life in the big city, Cora wasn't sure she'd like living in such a rural area, but if she had to pick a small town, this one wasn't bad. Known for its robust arts community, the renovation of its downtown, its clean water, green energy, recreation and quaint small businesses, there was a lot to recommend it. Life was just slower. Those who didn't grow up here came to retire, raise a family in a "safe place" or enjoy the beauty of the surrounding mountains—

"Ms. Kelly?"

Cora's heart jumped into her throat. The drone of the voice she'd heard coming from the inner office had fallen silent. This was it! The receptionist was about to tell her she could go in...

"Yes?"

"Ms. Turner will see you now."

For a moment, Cora's determination faltered. But when she didn't move, the receptionist—Betty May, according to the placard on her desk—stood expectantly. "It's right through here," she said with a puzzled expression.

Swallowing to ease her dry throat, Cora nodded. "Right. I was just..." *About to run the other way...* Letting her words fall off, since she couldn't readily lay her mind upon a good excuse, she threw back her shoulders and crossed the room to step inside an expansive office with several rows of pictures on the wall—every graduating class of New Horizons.

Those pictures melted into the background as soon as Cora's eyes landed on the diminutive woman with long black hair that fell in a braid down her back. *This* was where she'd gotten the golden color of her skin, Cora thought as she stared. That detail hadn't been quite so apparent in the grainy picture she'd seen with that newspaper article, but her mother appeared to be part Mexican, South American or maybe Native American.

Wasn't that something she should've had a right to know without having to go to all the trouble and expense she did?

Cora had always been conscious of the difference in her skin tone compared to the Kellys. Lilly had blond hair and blue eyes and, like many of her friends, had indulged in a fair amount of Botox and cosmetic surgery. Aiyana, on the other hand, didn't look as though she'd ever altered anything.

"Ms. Kelly, I'm so sorry for making you wait. That call was about another candidate for the school. Considering the mischief he's been in, I figured I should handle it as soon as possible. His poor grandmother, who's raising him, is beside herself."

Cora blinked rapidly, battling a sudden upwelling of emotion. She'd *longed* for this day. And here it was. She was looking at her *mother*.

But she couldn't act strange or she might give herself away. What had Aiyana just said? Something about the wait and the reason for it… "Of course," she managed to respond, dragging what she'd heard out of short-term memory before it could disappear into the ether. "I understand that the welfare of the boys has to come first."

Aiyana's smile as she gestured toward the chair on the other side of her desk suggested she appreciated Cora's response. "Please, take a seat."

Cora could hardly pull her gaze away long enough to sit without missing the chair.

"Eli tells me—"

"Eli?" Cora echoed.

"Elijah," she clarified. "My son."

"Oh right." Aiyana was talking about the incredibly handsome but imposing man who'd interviewed Cora two weeks ago. If only Cora could think clearly, she would've made that connection as instantly as she should have. He'd certainly left an impression.

"He told me you graduated from the University of San Diego with a BA in art education six years ago."

"Yes. I love art, and I love teaching, so…putting the two together seemed like a natural for me."

"You've been working as a substitute since then?"

"That's right. When I first graduated, I was grateful for the flexibility subbing gave me, because I was doing a bit of traveling with my parents. Since then it's been difficult to find a full-time position, given that so many schools are cutting back on their art, music and sports programs."

"I understand. So that's why you answered our ad?"

One of the reasons—though not the most important. Ironically enough, she'd been offered a full-time position for the coming year at the school for which she'd substituted most often, so she'd no longer needed the opportunity. The art teacher at Woodbridge High was retiring and had put in a good word for her. But, to her parents' consternation, Cora had turned it down. Aiyana was *here*. That meant New Horizons offered something no other school could. "Yes."

Aiyana peered at her more closely. "Is something wrong?"

Tears were getting the best of her despite all her efforts to suppress them. "Allergies," Cora explained. "It's that time of year. Fortunately, they don't last long."

"Would you like me to get you a tissue?"

Cora used her finger to remove the tear that was about to roll down her cheek. "No, I'm fine. My eyes are just…a little itchy, that's all."

"Let me know if you change your mind," she said. "I'll get you something if you need it. Meanwhile, I'd like to talk to you about the importance we place on art here at the ranch. Most other schools focus on core subjects, and as an accredited high school, we certainly make that a priority here, too. But it's my feeling that our students cannot excel in those classes—in *any-thing*—if they're too broken to care or try. I believe in healing those who will be healed by showing them the beauty of life and giving them a healthy form of expression. I guess it would be safe to say that, around here, you aren't merely an extra, the first teacher to go when the budget gets tight. You are our most important teacher, which is why I asked to meet with you before you started in a couple of weeks."

"I admire your philosophy." Cora agreed with it, too. But hearing that *she* was the most important teacher at the ranch was intimidating, since this was her first full-time position.

"I want my boys to be educated," Aiyana continued, "but even more than that, I want them to be whole, to find peace."

"Makes sense to me."

"Good. I should warn you that most have never been introduced to drawing, painting or pottery. They think school has to be boring and hard, which is what makes it so rewarding to introduce them to the fun side of learning. Creative endeavors are one of the best tools we have to ease the pain and anger that's inside so many of them."

"Does that mean all of the students here come from a difficult background?" she asked.

"Quite a few. Some have been abandoned. Some have been abused. Some have behavioral issues that can't be blamed on any of those things."

"You mean like autism."

"We have a few autistic students but only those who are highly functioning. More often it's something else—a chemical imbalance, genetic factors. No one can say for sure. Some brains are just wired differently than others."

"Those boys must be the toughest to reach."

"Sometimes we don't reach them at all. But, that said, we're going to reach all we can."

Cora could easily imagine the rich parents of a boy who had behavioral problems being willing to pay a large sum to enroll him at the ranch. But how could orphans afford such a school? "What about the costs associated with coming here—for those who don't have parents, I mean? Does another member of the family pay for it? Or maybe the state?"

"We get some state assistance, we have private benefactors and we do two big fund-raisers a year. As much as thirty percent of our students come here without paying a dime. This year, that equates to eighty students. But as long as we can meet our monthly expenses, I'm satisfied. If we have extra, I'd much rather use it to try to save another boy."

Cora almost felt guilty that she'd be taking a salary. She nearly spoke up to say she could make do with less, but she knew that wasn't the case. In LA, she'd been able to augment her income by waiting tables on the weekends. Chances were, in such a small community, she wouldn't have the opportunity to get a second job. "That's very noble of you."

Aiyana gestured as if she wasn't interested in praise. "I only mention it so that you'll understand what's important to me. It isn't turning a profit—it's making a difference. And I'm looking to work with people who are as invested in the progress of these boys as I am."

"I understand. I'll do my best," Cora said. "But…why

have you focused exclusively on helping boys? Why not girls? Or girls *and* boys? Do you have a strong gender preference or—"

"No. Not at all. I didn't want the added responsibility of mixing the two genders, knew it wouldn't be easy to keep them apart," she said with a chuckle. "The boys who come here have enough to worry about without adding that kind of temptation. This is a time for them to focus on getting their lives in order. Hopefully, as a result, they'll make better husbands and fathers later."

"You're saying it was purely a practical decision."

"Absolutely. Someday, on the opposite side of town, I'd like to open a school exclusively for girls, and do essentially the same thing. Now that I have Elijah handling so much around here, that's more of a possibility than ever before. I just haven't geared up for the push it will require."

"I'm sure you'll do equally well with girls." At least now she knew that her mother hadn't given her up because she didn't like girls. Perhaps that'd been a silly thought to begin with, but Cora couldn't help searching for The Reason. Maybe that was all she really needed to know in order to be satisfied…

"We'll see. Now, I've been told you'll be moving into the housing on campus. But have you seen where you'll be living?"

"Not yet. Mr. Turner showed me the school and some other parts of the property, but he didn't offer me the position until after I got home, so we didn't go inside the faculty housing."

"Well, the cottages aren't big, by any stretch of the imagination, but I like being able to include them in the package we offer our teachers. I figure discounted rent might tempt them into staying for a while." She grinned. "Longer than a year."

This comment revealed that Aiyana was well aware of her arrangement with Elijah. "It's a nice benefit."

"You'll find we're more like a family here than what you've most likely experienced in the past," she said with a wink.

A family... Those two words nearly caused Cora to burst into tears. Aiyana had no idea how literal their connection was.

As Cora followed Aiyana out of the building, she couldn't help thinking back, over all the different ways she'd imagined her mother while growing up. As a drug addict who didn't care about anything except her next hit. As a prostitute eager to rid herself of the child from an unwanted pregnancy. As "the other woman," abandoned by her lover after telling him she was going to have his child. As a businesswoman who refused to allow motherhood to get in the way of her ambition. There were more, but each scenario provided a ready excuse for adoption. She'd never pictured Aiyana like she was—soft-spoken, seemingly wise, well educated, accomplished, stable, kind, loving and devoted to a cause.

Cora had expected that just by meeting her mother so many of her questions would be answered. But she was more baffled than ever. What happened twenty-eight years ago? Why would someone like Aiyana Turner put her only child up for adoption?

Chapter 2

"So...do you like the woman you'll be working for?"

Cora was packing up the kitchen of her condo in Burbank with Lilly when Lilly asked this question. For a second, Cora froze, fearing her adoptive mother had figured out the reason she was moving to Silver Springs. But when Lilly kept wrapping glasses in newspaper and putting them into the box she was filling, it became apparent she was merely making conversation. She *didn't* know—not yet, thank goodness.

"I do." She forced a smile despite the discomfort her deception caused. "She seems really nice." Although Cora had been home for a week, getting ready for her big move, she hadn't been able to quit thinking about Aiyana. She'd spent nearly every extra minute on the internet, doing searches on all of the teachers and many of the students who'd graduated from New Horizons—whatever names she could cull from their website, including a graduate who had turned into a professional football player, one who'd just recently been accused of killing the couple who adopted him when he came to the ranch at fifteen and Elijah Turner, who'd hired her. Only one article had come up on him, but it told a lot. When he was ten years old, he'd been kept in a cage like some animal in the basement of his parents' house, and starved until he was only sixty pounds.

Imagining what he'd been through turned Cora's stomach. What kind of people could do that to one of their own children? And where were those people now? Did he know?

Considering what he'd been through, it was no wonder the man was so guarded, so aloof—and so devoted to Aiyana and New Horizons.

"I can't believe you'll be staying right there on the property," Lilly said.

"The school is about ten miles outside of town, so it'll save me from the daily drive."

"What drive? Ten miles is nothing," Lilly scoffed. "The people in Silver Springs must have no idea how long it takes to go two blocks in LA when the traffic is bad."

"Or they *do* know, and that's why they live there." Cora held up her blender. She made a lot of smoothies and "green" drinks, but her machine was nearly worn-out. Was it worth taking with her—or was it time to get a new one?

Newspaper crinkled as Lilly continued to wrap. "Traffic or no, I could never leave the city."

Brad's office was only a few blocks from their house. He'd been so successful managing other people's money that he could set his own hours. And Lilly did charity work, mostly on nights and weekends. "You two are in the kind of situation that makes it easy to stay. Traffic isn't a huge part of the equation for you."

"Our lives haven't always been so perfect," she said.

Reluctantly, Cora put her blender in the pile for Goodwill. "No. You've worked hard for what you have," she agreed and meant it.

Her mother stopped packing long enough to squeeze her shoulder. "You'll build something, too, honey."

"I hope so." Right now it felt as if Ashton, her brother, was going to be the one to make them proud. Although Lilly and Brad hadn't been too pleased when he left law school to become a movie producer, he already had an indie film out that'd garnered several awards, so they were less critical of his decision than they once were. "From this vantage point, it looks like I have a long way to go."

"It all comes with time."

Cora checked the clock on the wall. Jill, an assistant to a film editor at Universal, would be getting off work any minute. Cora had been hoping to be done by then, so they could meet some other friends for drinks, but there was a lot yet to pack. "Is Ashton going to be able to make it to my goodbye dinner on Sunday?"

"I'm sure he will. Your brother adores you."

"Slightly less than he adores all of the women he's dating," she grumbled.

"That's not true!"

It wasn't *entirely* true, but Cora had been feeling a

little neglected by her brother since he'd turned into such a big shot and become so busy.

The packing tape screeched as her mother closed and sealed the box she'd filled. "Does Aiyana Turner offer discounted housing to *all* the teachers at the ranch?"

The scent of the marker Lilly used to label the box "Kitchen—Fragile" rose to Cora's nostrils. "She can't. There's not enough for everyone—just a handful of small cottages on the far side of the property, away from the school and the boys' dorms."

"So who looks after the boys at night?"

"Each floor has a live-in monitor they call a 'big brother' who makes sure the boys go to bed at lights-out, get up for school, study during study time and clean their rooms."

"Are they teachers, too?"

"No. Most work in town during the day. I was told that some even drive to Santa Barbara. It's merely a way to acquire free lodging, kind of like managing an apartment building."

"How does—what's her name, Aiyana Turner?—decide who gets the other housing?"

"Every teacher has the option to add their name to the waiting list and move in if one becomes available. I just happened to hire on at the right time. The teacher who quit left earlier than planned, and my unit wasn't spoken for—probably because it's so small. It wouldn't be big enough for anyone with kids."

"So where do the other teachers live? In town?"

"I'm assuming they do. Although I suppose some might live in Santa Barbara. It's only about twenty minutes away, not a long commute by our standards."

The packing tape screamed again as her mother built a new box. "But will there be enough of a social life for you in Silver Springs? I mean…if you're living on campus, will you ever get out? How will you meet people?"

"I'll meet the other teachers."

"Who will most likely be older or married."

"I really won't know until I get there."

Lilly straightened and rested her hands on her hips. "There's more to life than work, honey. A year might not sound long right now, but, trust me, it'll seem long if you have no one to do anything with that whole time."

"I can always drive home, visit you guys, Jill, my other friends."

"I hope you come home often. But…what about the man who hired you? Maybe you can get something going with him. Jill told me you said he was hot."

Thank you, Jill. "He *is* hot, but…"

"What does he look like?"

Cora pictured the dark-headed, rather intimidating man who'd shown her around the ranch. He didn't say too much, certainly didn't waste words. But those blue eyes were laser-sharp. They didn't miss a thing. Truth be told, he made her uncomfortable. "Sort of like…a pirate."

Her mother opened another cupboard and started packing the plates. "A pirate? That's a positive association?"

"In this case it is." Mostly… When it came to his physical appearance, anyway.

"How tall is he?"

Cora put her salsa maker, which she'd barely used, in one of the boxes she planned to take with her. If she was going to live in the country, she was going to attend a farmer's market occasionally and make homemade salsa. "*Really* tall. And built."

"He sounds perfect."

"Not perfect exactly." That was what she found most compelling about him—that he was a little rough around the edges. "He's got a fairly big scar on his face." She indicated the line of her jaw. "Right here."

"What's that from?"

"I didn't ask." And now that she'd read the article chronicling some of the abuse he'd suffered, she wouldn't. "As far as I know, he's already married."

"Did you see a ring?"

"I didn't look," she said, but that was a lie. She had looked—and seen no ring. She'd been curious about Elijah from the first moment they met. But she'd also been apprehensive about the fact that she'd had an ulterior motive for applying at New Horizons, had known he probably wouldn't appreciate that she wasn't being fully transparent.

Her mother grinned at her. "You should have."

"Matt and I barely broke up, Mom. I'm not ready to start dating again, especially in a place where I don't plan to stay." Besides, she wasn't sure she'd be capable of taking on a man as complex as Elijah. There was no telling what kind of scars his upbringing had created, and she wasn't referring to the one on his face, although that could easily be part of the legacy his parents had left him.

"So you're only staying there a year?" her mother said.

"That's right."

"I can't tell you how happy I am to hear it's temporary." Lilly bent to give her a hug. "I love you, you know."

Cora *did* know. And she was grateful. She could easily have gone to a family who weren't so kind and accepting—a family like Elijah had known. "I love you, too," she said and tried to ignore how selfish she felt for doing what she was doing in spite of the fact it would hurt Lilly if—or when—she found out.

Elijah Turner was brushing down his horse when Aiyana found him. At the sound of her footsteps, he didn't need to turn in order to see who it was. If he didn't come for dinner when she invited him, she tracked him down. She always acted as if she had some official reason, some business question to ask him, but he knew she was simply assuring herself that he was okay. Whenever he complained that he was too old for that kind of coddling, she'd say it didn't matter, that he'd always be her boy.

"How was your ride?" she asked.

He lifted Atsila's foot and used a pick to gently clean his horse's front left hoof. "Relaxing."

"Cora Kelly arrives tomorrow."

"I know."

"Is the cottage ready?"

He moved on to the other front hoof. "Of course."

"Are you ever going to explain that decision to me?"

"What decision?" he said, but he knew what she was going to say before she explained.

"To hire Cora Kelly. You knew, as well as I did, that Gary Seton, from right here in Silver Springs, was waiting for that job to open up."

"I interviewed Gary, too—gave him a chance."

"And…"

"I thought Ms. Kelly was better suited for the position."

"She's pretty."

"That had nothing to do with it."

"Let's say that's true—you're not worried that she might be a distraction to the boys?"

"You're saying I should've discriminated against her because she's attractive?"

She gave his shoulder a little shove. "Stop it."

"You were talking about her looks!"

"Because I wanted to see if you agreed with me."

"That she's pretty? I'd have to be blind not to see that."

"So…do I surmise a bit of interest on your part?"

"None. I'm not the marrying type. You should know that by now."

"I'd like grandkids at some point."

"You have plenty of other sons to give you grandkids."

She sighed as if he was being purposely stubborn. "Fine. Obviously, you don't like talking about this subject."

He didn't argue. There were moments he wondered if he truly wanted to be alone for the rest of his life. But he also saw nothing to be gained from allowing his happiness to hang on the love or will of another person.

"You missed dinner tonight," his mother said.

"You said to come by if I was hungry."

"You should've been hungry. It's nearly eight."

"We've talked about this before," he responded. "I'm too old for you to worry about."

"You'll *never* be too old for me to worry about. And you know why? It's called caring."

His problem was that he had the tendency to care too much, to be *too* intense. "I'm fine." He started on Atsila's fourth and final hoof. "I'll grab a bite while I'm in town tonight."

She leaned against the fence post. "Whoa, don't tell me you're leaving the ranch for a social outing. You don't do that very often."

He gave her a look that let her know he didn't appreciate the sarcasm.

Unperturbed, she smiled. "Your dark looks don't frighten me the way they do everyone else."

"They should."

"Why? I know you love me, even if you rarely say it."

"What good are words?" His parents used to claim they loved him, but they only loved themselves and the twisted joy they received from tormenting him. "Words are empty, meaningless."

"Hopefully, someday, you'll regain your trust."

He winked at her. "Don't hold your breath. But... I am very grateful for everything you've done for me. I hope you know that."

"Stop!" She started to walk away.

"What?" he called after her.

"That wasn't a leading statement. I'm not looking for your gratitude."

She wasn't comfortable with it, either. "You want me to fall in love."

"I want you to be *able* to fall in love. I want to see

you lose your heart—and not be afraid to let it go. Then I can rest easy, knowing you're completely fulfilled."

"*You* never married," he pointed out, but she offered the usual lame excuse.

"Because I'm married to this place."

Knowing that was all he'd ever get out of her on the subject, he studied her retreating figure. "Yeah, well, so am I."

Chapter 3

Cora was using her Bluetooth to talk to Jill when she passed through the wrought iron arch at the opening of the school, her car packed full of her belongings. "I'm here," she announced as she wound slowly around to where she'd be living.

"That didn't take long. What time did you leave again?"

She'd gone in to hug her friend goodbye, but Jill, dead asleep, had mumbled something about missing Cora, promised to call and dropped back onto the pillows. "Six."

"That's not even two hours ago."

"See? I'm not that far away." Although…it almost seemed as if she'd moved to another planet; Silver Springs was nothing like LA.

"I should've come with you," Jill said.

"How?" Cora asked. "You have to be to work in an hour."

"I could've called in sick. You need someone to be there to help you unpack."

"No, I don't. My mother would've been hurt if she found out I let you come, since I told her I preferred to organize everything on my own." Cora had definitely not wanted Lilly on the ranch. She knew Lilly had never met Aiyana, that the whole adoption had been handled through an agency. According to the documents her private investigator had uncovered, Aiyana had demanded absolute secrecy. But that didn't change Cora's need to keep the two women apart. "I can handle this. The cottage is furnished. And everything I'm bringing fits into my car. It's not as if I'm towing a trailer."

"Still, I'm curious."

"About…"

"The ranch, for one thing. What does it look like?"

"Your basic high school, but with horses and cattle—and some dorms and a machine shop. You'll see it when you come visit me."

"I've been to Ojai but never Silver Springs. How does it compare?"

"The towns are similar, which makes sense. Silver Springs is located in the same valley, has some of the same mission-style architecture. Only they've added a few murals in Silver Springs, like they've done in Exeter."

"Where's Exeter?"

"Central part of the state." Cora pulled into the drive that would be *her* drive for the next year and cut the engine. "My mom took me there once to show me the murals, thought I'd be interested because of my art degree."

"I'm not that big on murals," Jill said. "I've seen some pretty bad ones."

"I've seen a lot that are worse than the ones they have here. The man who painted the one downtown interviewed for my job. I'm still surprised they didn't hire him instead."

"They told you who you were up against?"

"Aiyana and Elijah didn't. When Aiyana showed me the house, she got a call on her cell, leaving me to speak with a neighbor. He said Gary Seton was a friend of his and was really disappointed."

"Why *didn't* they hire him?" Jill asked.

Cora gazed at her bungalow, trying to imagine calling this place home for the next twelve months. "I'm not sure. I would've guessed they'd prefer a local."

"Could it be that Elijah wanted *you* to come to town?"

"No. I didn't get those vibes at all."

"So you think he's married?"

"Not married." There was too much sexual energy surrounding him for him to be in a committed relationship. She could tell he found her attractive—couldn't help finding him attractive, too. A woman would have to be dead not to feel a *little* sizzle when a man like Elijah Turner came around. "Just completely closed off."

"I've seen you approach guys before. You've never been afraid of a challenge."

In this situation, she was. She had a lot to cope with already, didn't need to add a romantic relationship into the mix. Even if she could manage to gain Elijah's attention, she doubted she'd be able to keep it for long. He was too remote. "I'm only here for a year."

"That could prove to be a very *long* year if you plan to remain celibate the whole time," she joked.

"I'll survive." Although…she was already missing certain aspects of her relationship with Matt and, if she was being honest, sex was one of them. "It'd be kind of odd to hit up the man my mother adopted."

"Why? You're not related by blood. You didn't even grow up together. For all intents and purposes, you're part of a different family. You're a Kelly."

Cora dug through her purse, searching for the house key Aiyana had provided her. "On paper."

"More than on paper! You've spent your whole life with the Kellys."

"I was talking from a strictly literal perspective. But that reaction right there is part of my problem."

"What do you mean?"

"Am I being ungrateful simply by wanting to know my birth mother? That tears me up inside, because I *am* grateful. I love my parents dearly."

"It's the same with regular parents. All kids should be grateful and aware of their parents' sacrifice."

"No, it's not the same. There's a sense of entitlement with children who've been kept and raised by their biological parents that doesn't extend to me. Anyway, let's not get caught up in all of that. Bottom line, people would look askance at Elijah and me if we ever admitted to having the same mother."

"You wouldn't admit that, because you don't have the same mother."

Cora groaned to show her frustration. "It's murky. You have to give me that. Regardless, Elijah makes me jealous." So did the other boys Aiyana had accepted into her life. That Aiyana would give Cora away and then take in eight other children left Cora feeling hurt, baffled. "He holds such a prominent place in Aiyana's heart that it makes me wonder why she wanted him and not me."

"We've talked about this."

She climbed out of the vehicle and circled around to grab the suitcase that held her essentials. "You believe she feels the need to fix things—fix people."

"You told me he had a rough childhood. The other boys probably did, too."

Other than her ex-boyfriend, Jill was the only person she'd confided in about her search for her biological mother, her true purpose in coming to Silver Springs, and the background of the man who'd hired her. "No doubt. Elijah's defies imagination. Which only makes me feel worse. When I think of what he's been through, I can't even be jealous without an avalanche of guilt. Considering the emotions he dredges up, I doubt he and I should even be friends."

Jill ignored her uncomfortable laugh. "There were a number of years between the time Aiyana gave you up and adopted him. Her situation must've changed, that's all."

Since both hands were full, Cora used her hip to close the car door. "Maybe that's it."

"You can't always assume the worst."

"It's hard not to. Especially now that I see how functional she is. I mean…if she were a down-on-her-luck prostitute, I could point to that and say, *Makes sense*."

"The fact that she isn't a down-on-her-luck prostitute is why you're interested in getting to know her. There's promise there. You believe she might be someone you'd like to have in your life. That's what scares you. You're afraid she'll reject you a second time."

Cora had to set her suitcase down to let herself into the house. "Do you have to be so frank?"

"It's important to know when fear's doing the talking—to keep things straight in your head."

"It could be a while before *anything*'s straight in my head—another reason I'd be crazy to get involved with Elijah, even if he were open to a relationship, which I can tell he's not."

"Fine. You won't listen to me, anyway. You're too busy throwing up roadblocks."

Cora wasn't sure she felt any better now that Jill had conceded. She sort of liked it when Jill was arguing the other side. Maybe that was because she *did* find it hard not to think about Elijah. Even though she'd been almost completely focused on the fact that she'd just found her birth mother when she had that interview with him, she couldn't help wondering what was going on behind those inscrutable eyes... "You were never given up for adoption. You grew up in a big, boisterous, happy family. You can't relate."

"I've tried to be understanding," Jill said.

"I'm sorry," Cora responded. "I don't know where that came from. It was uncalled for."

"You're angry. That's where it comes from. And I can see why. But I'm on *your* side."

Cora opened her mouth to say she believed that, but before she could formulate the words, she heard a car engine and turned. What she saw wasn't a car; it was a silver truck. And Elijah was behind the wheel. As he parked in front of her house and jumped out, she felt her pulse leap. "I've got to go," she told Jill.

"Why? What's up?"

She ducked her head so she could speak without being overheard. *"He's here,"* she whispered and clicked the button on her Bluetooth that would disconnect them.

Cora was wearing a silky orange tank with a pair of white linen shorts that showed off her long, tan legs. As Elijah approached with the orientation materials he'd brought, he found those legs to be distracting. But she was a teacher at New Horizons. That meant he couldn't get involved with her, even on a casual basis. Contrary to what his mother seemed to believe—and probably everyone else who was surprised he hadn't hired Gary—he hadn't offered her the position because he had any romantic interest in her. He'd been impressed with her portfolio. Each piece—a sculpture, a painting, a photograph and a piece of pottery—moved him in some way. He liked that she could make *him*, someone who knew very little about art, feel something. Gary Seton's work simply hadn't been the same.

One piece that Cora had brought, the conceptual sculpture of a mother cradling a child, affected him deeply. When she'd unveiled it during their interview, it'd been hard for him not to stop and stare. He'd wanted to keep it—not because he felt *he* needed that kind of love. No one would ever be able to hurt him again. He wanted the boys here at the ranch to experience the safety and security that piece inspired, and he wanted to give them a teacher who could not only depict that emotion but understand it, *feel* it.

Because he knew Gary was disappointed, he hoped he'd made the right choice. Fortunately, the sensitivity he saw in the large brown eyes staring up at him as he drew closer reassured him. She'd wanted the job even worse than Gary. He wasn't sure why—if she'd needed to get out of whatever situation she was in or was on her last dollar—but he'd been able to feel her eagerness during their interview and he'd responded to that. Maybe this woman would never be able to teach the boys how to create a decent picture or vase, but she should be able to entice them to see the beauty of the world. She *was* part of the beauty of the world. And she seemed open and vulnerable to the point that he almost felt he should warn her to be careful or life would chew her up and spit her out. After what *he'd* experienced, that she could get so far without learning that lesson was a bit of a shock to him.

"Hello," she said.

"I see you made it safely."

"Yes."

He motioned toward the older BMW X3 sitting in the drive. "Can I give you a hand with anything?"

"No, it's okay. I was careful when I packed—didn't make the boxes too heavy. I can grab it."

"Are you sure?"

She nodded, so he handed her the orientation manual he'd brought over. "I doubt you'll care to read *all* of this. Watching paint dry would be more interesting. But there's a table of contents. I figured you could glance through, check out any topics you're curious about and become familiar with how we do things around here."

"I'll take a look at it." When she hugged it to her

ample chest, he decided her body was partly what he found so attractive about her. She wasn't as skinny as some of the girls he'd dated. She was curvy—looked soft, comfortable, sexy.

He searched his pocket for the more important part of what he'd come to give her. "Here's a key to the high school, as well as one to the art and ceramics rooms. With school starting next week, you'll be eager to set those up."

"Definitely. Thank you."

"You bet. You received the group email about the staff meeting tonight?"

"I did. That's why I came a few days earlier than I would have otherwise."

"Great. I'll see you there." He started back toward his truck. "Everyone is eager to meet you."

"Mr. Turner?"

"Call me Eli," he said as he turned.

"Okay, Eli it is. Where, exactly, is the meeting tonight? You showed me the library when we toured campus the day I interviewed, but I'm a little turned around at the moment."

He went back and flipped past the syllabus he'd given her to the campus map on the next page. "You're here," he said, and drew a line from her house to the library so she could easily find her way.

"Thank you."

"Sure," he said. But instead of leaving, he went over to her SUV and began unloading the boxes. He just couldn't leave a woman to do that alone, not when it would be so much easier for him.

"Whoa, I can get those," she said, hurrying out to him. "Really."

"There's no need for you to carry all of this stuff by yourself. Just point to where it should go. It'll only take me fifteen minutes."

As promised, in a short time, he had her vehicle completely unloaded.

"Thank you," she said as he put down the last box.

"See you later." His conscience appeased, he started toward his truck.

"Eli?"

He stopped again. "Yes?"

"I—I have a boyfriend. Sort of."

He felt his eyebrows slide up. Then he almost laughed. She was assuming he had an ulterior motive for helping her. "I'm sorry if I gave you the wrong impression," he said. "I was only trying to make your move a little easier."

Her cheeks bloomed red. "Right. Of course you were. I'm sorry."

Cora's face burned as she watched Eli drive off. "What's wrong with you?" she muttered to herself. "Of course he was just trying to help. It's not as if he asked for your number."

That blunder actually said more about her than it did him, she realized. *He* hadn't been anything but circumspect. *She* was the one who'd had a difficult time keeping her eyes off him. She was so aware of him on a sexual level that it was hard to act as if she wasn't, which was odd. She couldn't remember having such a strong reaction to any other man. That was the reason she'd suddenly tried to throw up a barrier. She'd been hoping to give him a reason to look at her differently—or stay away entirely—and wound up making a fool of herself instead.

"I *told* you I didn't need your help," she grumbled to him even though he was gone, and cringed at the prospect of having to face him at the staff meeting in a few hours.

"You had to do that on your first day here, Cora?" she said as she started to unpack.

Her phone dinged to let her know she'd received a text, and she paused to pull it out of her pocket.

Jill. What'd "dark and brooding" have to say?

Dark and brooding. How apropos. But since she was still writhing with embarrassment, Cora didn't want to talk about Eli, so she scowled at the clock. Aren't you at work?

You know I am. I was talking to you while driving here.

I don't want to get you in trouble for being on the phone. I'll call you later.

Is that a dodge?

Yes. But as long as her friend was willing to risk getting caught on a personal call at work, Cora figured she might as well break the news. He said he's not interested in me.

What? Seriously?

Seriously.

But...you just got there.

Cora shoved a hand through her hair as she recalled his startled expression. Yeah, it came up quick. Thanks to her…

How? He couldn't have come by just to let you know he's not interested.

Again Cora hesitated, but when she didn't respond her friend sent her a question mark, so she typed, I brought it up.

At that point, texting fell by the wayside. Jill called to make her explain the whole thing.

"Oh jeez," she said when Cora was done. "I should never have let you go there without me. I could tell you were rattled, nervous."

"I'll get my feet underneath me. I'm just…not myself at the moment. The prospect of rubbing elbows with my birth mother has me…floundering a bit. I was expecting *that* to be difficult, but when I started this whole thing, I was *not* expecting my mother to have adopted a son who…"

"Who…" Jill pressed.

She pictured the muscles that bulged in Eli's arms as he hefted box after box into her cottage. She really wanted to touch the smooth curve of his biceps. But it was the size of his broad chest and wide shoulders that *really* made her short of breath. "Who somehow gets under my skin!"

"To whom you feel an immediate attraction, you mean."

"He's good-looking. That's all," she said, hoping to minimize it.

"That's why you told him, out of the blue, that you have a boyfriend as if you were accusing him of hitting on you? Because he's good-looking? What were you thinking?"

"I don't know! I was merely attempting to wall off the possibility. So I wouldn't even consider it. That's not *too* weird, is it?"

"You might've gotten ahead of yourself, but... I'm guessing you succeeded. I doubt he's hoping for anything now, so you can relax."

Cora took a deep breath. Jill was right. Maybe she hadn't done it gracefully, but she'd put Elijah Turner on notice that she wasn't a romantic possibility. Even if he hadn't considered her one to begin with, establishing certain boundaries was important to *her*. She needed to focus, to keep her life simple while she was here so that she could do a good job for the kids at the ranch while getting to know Aiyana. If she decided she wanted to be part of Aiyana's life, she'd eventually have to determine if Aiyana wanted to be part of hers—and break the news. Imagine how awkward it would be if the answer to that question was no and yet she was seeing Eli!

"It's better that we covered it early."

"If you say so. How's the cottage?"

"Small but cute." She wandered over to a Mason jar filled with wildflowers that someone had left on her table. It was a thoughtful touch, one she hoped Eli wasn't responsible for...

"I can't wait to see it." Jill suddenly lowered her voice. "I've got to go. My boss is here."

Cora wasn't even sure she said goodbye when they

disconnected. Her attention had switched entirely to a small card she found beside the flowers.

Welcome to New Horizons. We are so excited to have you here.

Aiyana

Bending slightly, Cora put her nose to one of the delicate yellow poppies that made up the bulk of the arrangement. "I hope you'll be just as glad once you learn who I am," she said as she exhaled.

Chapter 4

"So *you're* the new art teacher."

Cora smiled at the middle-aged man with thick glasses who sat on her right side. "Yes."

"Ah. Makes sense at last."

"What makes sense?" she asked, but he didn't get the chance to answer—or even introduce himself. Aiyana stood near the circulation desk and called the staff to order. Cora felt she knew where the man had been going with that comment, anyway. Everyone thought she'd gotten the job based on her looks. Otherwise, Gary Something-or-Other would've gotten it.

"Thank you all for coming," Aiyana said. "Although we had a few of you here during the summer, handling one program or another, classes were limited. So I hope, now that the rest of you are back, you feel refreshed, because I'm anticipating one of the best years in ranch history."

As Aiyana spoke, Cora glanced around. There were thirtysomething people in the room, an assortment of teachers and support staff, but she couldn't see anyone even close to her own age. Half the people seemed to be in their forties, the other half in their fifties. A few looked even older.

She was beginning to believe Jill and her mother were right: the next year was going to be terribly lonely...

"Before we get started, let's go over a few of the changes that have occurred in the past two and a half months. First, we will have 256 students when we start classes on the twenty-eighth, up from 223 last year. That's a significant increase, so we'll have to watch out for the newcomers and help them feel at home. We also have a new football coach—Larry Sanders, who played in the pros thirteen years ago. Larry couldn't be here tonight due to a family commitment, but he's been practicing with the boys for over a month. I believe he'll be a real asset to our sports program—at least that's what Elijah tells me. As most of you know, Elijah is our athletic director in addition to many other things—basically whatever he needs to be in order for the ranch to operate smoothly."

Cora's neighbor leaned over. "Someone with real experience, huh? Maybe we'll finally win a game," he muttered.

Cora didn't respond; she was too interested in witnessing the pride on Aiyana's face when she looked at her adopted son. They were close. That was obvious without either one of them having to say a word—but as nice as that was for Elijah, Cora found it a bit disheart-ening. Was there any room in Aiyana's heart for her?

Cora didn't get the impression there was, but she didn't have the chance to think about it for too long. Aiyana was moving on.

"Not only do we have a new football coach, we have a new art instructor." She stretched out her hand in in-vitation. "Cora, will you please stand?"

Elijah's eyes seemed to cut right through Cora as she got to her feet. Why she could feel the weight of his gaze and not anyone else's, she couldn't say, but she'd been struggling to ignore him since she walked into this meeting.

After a nod to acknowledge all the smiling faces that were turned to see the new art instructor, she sank back into her seat.

Aiyana was talking about how they were going to allow student government to run the assemblies from now on when the man next to her leaned over again. "Where have you taught before?" he asked.

After his earlier comment, Cora almost provided the name of the high school that had offered her a permanent position a few weeks ago, but a quick word with Aiyana or Elijah would too easily reveal the truth, since she'd been honest with them. "I've never had a permanent position."

"You're a *brand-new* teacher?"

"Relatively new," she admitted. "I've been subbing for six years."

"Do you have any idea how difficult some of the boys who come here can be?"

Aiyana hadn't given the bad behavior Cora was likely to encounter much emphasis. But Cora had known from the beginning that this school wasn't for the well-adjusted. "I understand that most of the boys come from a very difficult background," she replied. "But it shouldn't be *too* much of a change. You should see how some regular students treat substitutes," she joked.

The man laughed but quickly sobered. "Subbing isn't easy. Kids will get away with whatever they can. Still, for an attractive young woman of your age—"

"I'm nearly thirty," she broke in, but she had to wonder—in her hurry to get close to Aiyana, had she given what she might face here enough weight?

"Still," the man said. "It won't be easy. I hope you haven't gotten in over your head."

When Cora glanced up, she happened to catch Elijah watching her. He didn't look away, as she expected him to; he continued to measure her with those enigmatic eyes. Was he experiencing any doubts about having hired her?

Possibly. *Probably.* She hated to even consider that. But if she had to fight to find her place in the world, she'd do it. She supposed, in that respect, she wasn't much different from Elijah or the other boys who'd come through here, or were still attending.

"I'll be fine," she said—and hoped it was true.

"I see you met Sean Travers."

Cora recognized Elijah's voice even before she turned to see him standing at her elbow. Why he'd put her through the discomfort approaching her was bound to cause, however, she couldn't say.

"The guy who was sitting next to me?" she asked.

"Yes. Our science teacher—or ranch pessimist, depending on how well you know him."

She nibbled at the cookie she'd just snagged from the refreshment table. "He doesn't think I'm capable of teaching here. I guess I look too young and delicate to handle the boys who act out."

"Does that shake your confidence?"

"I admit I'm a little worried. Everyone seems to believe the job should've gone to a man named Gary…"

"Seton," he filled in as he handed her a cup of punch. "Because he's local—they know him."

"But…"

"It wasn't their decision," he said simply.

She couldn't help envying him his long, dark eyelashes. She knew she had pretty eyes—guys told her that all the time—but she felt his were prettier. "No. It was yours. So…can you tell me why?"

"Why I chose you?"

"I know it isn't what they all seem to think. You made that clear earlier."

He took a sip of his own punch. "As far as I'm concerned, your competition has no…vision."

"Am I supposed to understand what that means?"

His massive shoulders lifted in a shrug. "I wasn't impressed with his work."

"You were impressed with *mine*?"

"You're talented," he said evenly. "Perhaps more than you know."

"I'm *teaching* art, not selling it. I'm guessing he was at least proficient."

Elijah finally shifted that unnerving gaze away from

her. "You have to understand certain concepts to be able to teach them."

"What concepts are you specifically referring to?" she asked, but someone else approached him at that moment, interrupting, and he turned away without answering.

Since Eli fell deep into conversation with a woman who looked sixty or so and was concerned about a particular student Cora had no way of knowing, she felt awkward standing there waiting for the chance to speak to him again. So she gave them some privacy by carrying her punch over to the corner. She was looking for an unobtrusive vantage point from which to observe her birth mother. Aiyana was mingling with the staff. But then Cora saw the science teacher who'd sat next to her approach Aiyana and knew, when they both glanced in her direction, that they were talking about her. Sean Travers was expressing his reservations.

Disgruntled that this man she'd barely met would jump to conclusions based on her age and gender, and start to advocate against her, Cora finished her punch, dropped the paper cup in the wastebasket and left the library. Her phone kept vibrating in her pocket anyway, making her feel as if someone really needed to reach her.

When she got outside and felt she could check, caller ID indicated it was her father.

Gazing up at more stars than she'd ever seen in the sky before, she wandered around the campus as she spoke to him. Most of the students were away, at home if they had a home to go to, for a quick holiday before classes started in earnest, so the campus was quiet, especially this far from the outdoor basketball courts and the dorms.

"So are you going to like it there?" her father asked.

She tried to let the energy in his voice help lift the depression that had set in. "It's definitely going to be a change."

"A positive one, though, right?"

"Sure," she said, kicking a small pebble across the sidewalk.

"Whoa. Is something wrong?"

"It's just different, that's all. I'm not used to smelling manure at night. Or seeing stars that shine so bright."

"The manure can't be pleasant, but the stars sound nice."

"They are nice. And the manure isn't all that bad, not if I stay away from the livestock pens. I guess it's more that... I'm beginning to wonder what made me think I could handle teenage boys who have significant behavioral issues." She'd mostly been thinking of her own emotional issues, not the responsibility she would feel to be a guiding light to teenage boys who'd lost their way. Was she bound to disappoint Aiyana and Elijah and let her students down?

She couldn't abide the thought of failure.

"Don't make it too complicated, babe," her father said.

"In what way?"

"Everyone responds to love."

"I have to do more than love them, Dad. I have to *teach* them. And what if they won't let me?"

"If you love them, they'll trust you. Love and trust come first. Then you'll be able to teach. I promise you."

She thought of Gary Seton. Maybe he had no "vision," whatever Elijah meant by that. But she was willing to bet he'd be firmer when it came to meting out discipline. *She* didn't want to punish anyone. "I'm not sure why these people hired me," she grumbled.

"They must've seen what your mother and I see in you."

"And that is…"

"You can do anything."

Tears filled her eyes. She was tired, which made her emotional. But she was also experiencing a little culture shock, and she missed her family already. "Maybe I was a bit hasty making the decision to come here, Dad."

"It's only for a year, honey. Do your best. That's all anyone can ask. And come see us when you can."

She wiped her cheeks as she told him she loved him. But she felt even worse after she disconnected. She had good parents. The conversation she'd just had with her father proved it yet again. So why was she betraying them?

The moment she got back to her cottage, Cora went straight to bed. She had a lot of unpacking yet to do, but she figured that could wait. She needed sleep, knew it would help her cope with all the recent changes—as well as the uncertainty.

Fortunately, she felt a lot better when she woke up. She spent the morning unpacking the rest of her belongings and stacking the cardboard from the boxes in her SUV so she could take it to a recycling center. Then she decided to go into town to look around, have lunch and buy a few groceries. Someone—she guessed Aiyana since Aiyana had also been responsible for the flowers—had put a few essentials, like eggs, bread and milk, in her fridge, but the cupboards needed to be stocked.

Cora was halfway to town when she saw a man on horseback galloping down a dirt road off to her right. She would've thought nothing of it—she could only see the rider from the back as he wove in and out of the trees between them—but she recognized the man. It was Elijah Turner!

She pulled over and angled her head to see through the passenger window, trying to get a better look. He was something else. A puzzle. What drove him? What did he want out of life? Had he put the past behind him? How did he feel about the boys who came to the ranch? Did he see himself in each one? Where were the people who'd abused him? Did he have any contact with them? Was his work enough to fulfill him? Or was he seeing someone?

Maybe he was dating around...

Cora was also curious to learn how he'd gotten that scar on his face—but equally afraid to find out. What she'd read about him scared her. She didn't want to imagine him going through any more pain and suffering than what she'd been forced to imagine when she'd read that article about him. She wondered if other people had the same reaction—if they shied away from him for fear they might have to walk into that darkness.

Movement behind him caught her eye, and she realized that he wasn't alone. He had three boys with him. It looked as though he was taking some New Horizons students out for a ride...

She glanced into her backseat. She had her camera, had brought it to take some pictures of Silver Springs she could send to Jill and her family. She still planned to do that, but her fingers itched to take a few shots of him and those boys first. She'd never seen a man sit so comfortably in the saddle as Elijah. And she loved the way he kept looking back at the boys, like a mother hen checking her chicks.

This wasn't about admiring Aiyana's adopted son so much as it was about the symbolism she saw here, she told herself as she cut the engine. He represented a man who'd not only survived tremendous difficulty but risen above it. Someone who'd conquered his demons. And now he was helping others battle theirs. There was a great deal of artistic beauty in that, and she had to capture it.

She couldn't get a clear shot from the roadside, however. There were too many trees in between.

After hiking down the embankment, she wove through the forest to get close enough. Luckily for her, or she never would've caught up with them, Elijah and the boys had stopped and were laughing and talking while drinking from a canteen Eli passed around.

She fastened her heavy telephoto lens to the expensive camera her parents had given her for Christmas last year and clicked away, using a fast shutter speed so that the pictures wouldn't turn out blurry. In one picture, she captured Elijah laughing. She'd never seen him smile, not so easily. He was in his element out here, and he cared about the boys he was with. Those two things were readily apparent; she could see it in both his body language and his expression.

Cora was disappointed when he put the lid on the canteen, slung it over his body, where he'd been carrying it before, and charged up the next hill, making it impossible for her to get any more pictures of him.

As the boys whooped and hollered in their efforts to keep up with him, she hiked back to her car. They were having a blast. She could easily imagine any problem they had disappearing while they were out enjoying the beautiful scenery and the equally beautiful weather.

Witnessing the impact Elijah was having on the students at the ranch—by taking enough interest to guide them on a ride even during their "off" period—inspired her. He was embracing the spirit of his job. Like Aiyana, he was doing it for the right reasons. And so could she. She had a lot of love to give. Who needed it more than abused, neglected and angry teens?

How are you doing today?

Her father's text came in just before Cora started her car. Better, she wrote.

Because...

Because coming here was no longer only about her. I feel like I could make a real difference with this job.

That's the spirit!

Cora responded by sending a smiley face, put her phone down and headed into town, where she took quite a few pictures. It was a great way to investigate her new surroundings. Those were the ones she posted on Instagram and sent to family and friends who were eager to see where she'd moved. But it was the photographs of Elijah and the three boys that she downloaded onto her computer when she returned that night. She spent over an hour experimenting with different filters and other bells and whistles on Photoshop. In her favorite photograph, one where Elijah was smiling at the boy to his left, the lighting was perfect as it came through the branches of the trees.

She could win a contest with that shot...

"Hail to the conquering hero," she muttered before she set her computer aside and turned off the light so that she could get some sleep.

Chapter 5

Over the next few days, Cora put her classroom in order by making sure the large, commercial-sized kiln and sixteen throwing wheels in the pottery room were clean and in good repair. She also took stock of the clay and other supplies. The teacher before her had done a respectable job caring for the equipment and maintaining the necessary inventory, so it wasn't too overwhelming of a job. She obtained permission to order some glazes she'd been hoping to get, as well as a new set of colored pencils and paintbrushes for each student, so she'd at least have the supplies needed to start the year off right.

By the end of the week, Cora was feeling pretty encouraged about beginning school on Monday. She'd been running into more and more students as the boys returned to the ranch and was looking forward to meeting the rest. Other than texting and calling her old friends and her brother, who promised to come out and see her soon, she'd had virtually no social life since she arrived, so she figured more distraction, work and activity would help fill that gap. The neighbor opposite to Sean Travers, Doug Maggleby, a math teacher at the school, chatted with her whenever he caught her out and about. But she'd started to avoid him, where possible. The more he talked, the more uncomfortable he made her. He liked to rave about politics, and she rarely agreed with his opinion. He'd also mentioned taking her to the movies even though he was clearly too old for her. She wasn't looking forward to having to say no, but knew that was coming. So instead of visiting with him in the evenings like she had the first few nights, she'd sneak out of her bungalow and walk down to the pond to watch the sunset or stop by the horses' pen to say good-night. If Mr. Maggleby happened to be in his yard working in his fall garden, however, she'd settle for having a glass of wine in her cottage and reading a book or going over her lesson plans.

She'd seen very little of Elijah since taking those photographs of him horseback riding with the boys. Although she wasn't pleased by the fact, she'd developed a habit of looking for him whenever she was out. Occasionally, she'd spot him at a distance and couldn't help admiring what she saw. But he seemed extra busy getting the ranch ready for the fall semester, so she was fairly certain she was the last thing on *his* mind.

Aiyana had been especially busy, too. Since Betty May had handled the purchase requisition for the art supplies, Cora had had no interaction with her birth

mother—not until Friday afternoon. She was in the cafeteria between lunch and dinner, nibbling on a chocolate
chip cookie while she finished reading the orientation
materials she'd been given, when Aiyana came in, poured
herself a cup of coffee and walked over to join Cora.

"Hello." Instantly self-conscious, Cora closed the
manual as her "boss" sat down.

"How are you holding up, dear?" Aiyana asked.

"Good." She cleared her throat. "Great."

"I'm relieved to hear it—and glad to find you here.
This time of year is so crazy for me. I apologize that
I haven't had the chance to check on you. Did you get
the supplies you requested?"

"Not yet. But last I heard they've been ordered, so they
should arrive soon. Thanks for giving the okay on that."

She took a drink of her coffee. "I told you how I feel
about art. That isn't where I choose to skimp."

"I have to admit your attitude is refreshing. I'm not
used to art being much of a priority."

"The practicalities of running a school can often get
in the way of even the best intentions," she said. "Fortunately, right now, we've got some wealthy benefactors
who are giving us the support we need." She winked.
"Makes a difference when we have a fair number of
students with rich—and sometimes famous—parents."

"Are we talking movie stars?" Cora hadn't considered that possibility, but she supposed, since they
weren't far from LA, it was logical.

"A few. Others are the children of producers and
movie execs, attorneys, doctors, that sort of thing."

"Are the wealthy kids ones who are typically loved,
or…"

Her lips curved into a rueful smile. "Oh, they're

loved, just a little more generously than would probably be best. From what I've seen, being given too much can be as difficult as being given too little."

"Doesn't that create quite a disparity? I mean…you mentioned taking in orphans who have no one to support them."

"We have some of the richest *and* some of the poorest students in the state. But we make it clear from the beginning that everyone is on an equal footing here at the ranch. There is no favoritism, no bending of the rules because of who their parents are."

"I can't imagine that goes over very well—not for people who are used to receiving preferential treatment."

"I've lost several students over that policy," she admitted. "All parents agree to it when they enroll their child—but can change their minds once they want or need special treatment." She pushed a strand of loose hair out of her face. "Regardless, I won't bend. To me it's a matter of integrity. And, if a parent will stand behind me, their son usually settles down and begins to learn the lessons they were hoping we'd teach him."

Cora swallowed another bite of her cookie. "How does that play out in a social setting—for the kids, I mean?"

Aiyana took another sip of coffee. "Depends. We take a hard line on bullying, too—watch carefully for it. Most get the message early on that the rules are firmer here, but fair to all, and life falls into a sustainable rhythm. I don't think we're too terribly different from other high schools—all schools have some behavioral problems."

"But you've taken on the behavioral problems other

schools can no longer cope with. Doesn't that ever make you feel...intimidated?"

"I wouldn't want to go back and start over—I can tell you that," she said with a mirthless chuckle. "But now that we're up and running, and I've got the momentum that comes from doing this for so long, it's easier than it was. Still, I couldn't continue without the community support I've received, not to mention the devoted teachers we have here—and Elijah, who has such a knack for communicating with these boys. Even if I can't get one to behave, he usually can."

Cora pictured Aiyana's son on top of that horse. "Elijah's your secret weapon."

"Absolutely."

She studied Aiyana's face. Her mother was so pretty despite the lines that were beginning to appear around her eyes and mouth and the ribbons of gray in her hair. "I hope you don't mind me asking, but..."

"Ask me anything," she said.

"I was wondering what nationality you are."

She seemed surprised by the question—that Cora would have any interest in that—but not put off. "My mother is a Nicaraguan immigrant. My father was a white farmhand in the Central Valley."

"Are they still alive?"

"They are. But my mother is no longer with my father. He was an abusive man, so I don't have any contact with him, either. For many years now she's been with the farmer who employed them both and has been so much happier. What about you? What nationality are you?"

Cora thought it might be too coincidental if she were

to say she was part Nicaraguan, but that was good to know—filled in one of the many blanks in her life. Aiyana had said her father was white; from her skin tone, Cora assumed hers was, too. "I'm a mix, I think."

"And your parents? Where are they?"

"In LA. My father's a financial planner. My mother's sort of a…socialite."

She smiled at that. "Do you have siblings?"

"An older brother who's larger than life and terribly handsome. Like a lot of people in LA, he's a movie producer. What about you?"

"I have one older brother and two younger brothers, but I don't see my younger brothers very often."

She seemed noticeably saddened by that. "They don't live close?"

"My brothers are all over California. One owns a winery in Napa. One is in banking in San Francisco. The oldest runs the farm for my mom and stepdad in Los Banos, where I grew up."

"Are they all married?"

"Yes. With kids. What about your brother?"

Suppressing her curiosity about why Aiyana had never married, Cora answered the question. "Still playing the field."

"Sounds like my sons."

"Where are they all? I mean, besides Eli, of course."

"Gavin, my second oldest, has a house in town but works here. He's a handyman, can fix anything."

"Really?" Cora had been around for five days, yet she couldn't recall ever seeing a handyman. "Was he at the meeting on Monday?"

"No. He's not someone who likes to get involved in

the administration aspect of the ranch. He prefers to remain in the background, which is why he lives in town."

"How old is he?"

"Twenty-eight. I adopted him three years after I adopted Elijah. Then there's Dallas. He's twenty-five and a mountain climber, so he's usually off, traveling to remote destinations all over the world. I don't get to see him much." She seemed to regret that but moved on. "Seth is twenty-three. He recently graduated from UC Berkeley, wants to be a sculptor. That's one of the reasons I love art so much," she confided. "I'm not sure what I would've done with him if I hadn't been able to reach him in that way..."

"He has...emotional issues?"

"Anger issues, mostly. I seem to gravitate to the most damaged of the boys. I can't help trying to make them whole."

Did Aiyana always accomplish that? Or were some of her sons *too* damaged? "Let's see—Elijah, Gavin, Dallas and Seth. That's four sons, but I heard you have eight," Cora said. "What about the others?"

"Ryan and Taylor are twins. Well, they're not actually *related*, but we call them twins because they're the same age and have done just about everything together since they met here at the ranch. They're still in college. Ryan wants to be a planetary scientist, and Taylor has set his sights on becoming a theoretical physicist. They're both too brilliant for their own good," she added. "Now that they're actually applying themselves."

"Where do they go to school?"

"MIT. Then I have Liam and Bentley, who go here. Liam's a senior. Bentley's a sophomore."

"I wonder if I've seen either one of them around."

"Not yet. They've been with Dallas at Yosemite the past ten days. He's teaching them how to climb."

"That's nice of him."

"They *live* to spend time with their older brothers." She lowered her voice. "He better not let them get hurt, though."

"It's a scary sport." Cora dusted the cookie crumbs off her "boyfriend" jeans. "Would you ever consider adopting more?"

Finished with her coffee, Aiyana pushed the cup aside. "I keep telling myself I need to stop. But every couple of years, it seems as if there's at least one more I'm dying to take home with me."

"That means…maybe?"

"I guess. It'll depend on the circumstances."

So she would take in another boy if she felt he needed her that much, Cora decided. "Did you always want a big family?" she asked and then held her breath. She thought this might be the most revealing question yet, that it might give her some clue as to why Aiyana hadn't wanted *her*, but Aiyana's face grew shuttered as she shook her head.

"No. Never thought I'd have any kids."

Cora was dying to ask why, but there was something so forbidding in the sudden change in Aiyana's expression and body language that she could tell it would be too intrusive. Aiyana had essentially slammed the door shut on that subject, and she didn't stick around long enough to give Cora much of a chance to talk about anything else.

"I'd better go." She reclaimed her empty cup as she

stood. "It's been wonderful having a chance to chat, but I've got a lot to do before the pizza party tonight. You're coming, right?"

Cora had found a flyer taped to her door when she got back to her cottage last night announcing a Kick-off Party for all the teachers at a place called Moon-struck Pizza in town. "I haven't made up my mind, to be honest."

"Oh, don't miss it," she said. "The entire staff gets together the Friday before school starts to celebrate the end of summer and the beginning of a new year. It's a tradition."

"And the students? They stay on campus?"

"Yes. The floor monitors keep an eye on them. So come to the party. It'll give everyone a chance to get to know you. And there'll be plenty of pizza and beer—and karaoke, if you sing."

"I sing a little," Cora said, but that was an understatement. She sang a lot. She and a handful of friends liked to compete in various local contests, enjoyed standing behind a mic. And she really needed to get out and have some fun. She just hoped Doug Maggleby wouldn't be too determined to monopolize her time. She could easily imagine spending the evening trying to dodge him.

"So you'll be there?" Aiyana seemed eager for her company.

At that point, Cora didn't feel as if she could refuse—not if it might afford her a few minutes more with her birth mother. "Sure. Why not?" she said, but as soon as she agreed, she began to wonder if Elijah would be part of the festivities. Then she chided herself for having the desire to see him. She was letting herself get quite a "thing" for Aiyana's handsome son, even though she barely knew him and he'd made it clear he wasn't interested in *her*.

He *was* there. Cora spotted Elijah as soon as she walked into the pizza parlor and hated herself for suddenly being so glad she'd come. She didn't need to get her heart broken; she was trying to mend it by moving here, to finally get over the sense of rejection her adoption had engendered.

But she figured she shouldn't be *too* hard on herself. She didn't yet know anyone other than the staff she'd been introduced to at the school, so it wasn't all that surprising she'd fixate on the one man she'd met who was in her age bracket—especially when she factored in how darned handsome he was.

She couldn't get hurt if he never responded, anyway. His disinterest made the attraction safe. So she figured she might as well enjoy the view he provided, maybe even indulge in a few harmless fantasies. If allowing him to fuel her imagination helped pass the time and made her stint in Silver Springs more enjoyable, why not?

Feeling slightly empowered by the fact that she had no expectations, she smiled widely when he looked up. Once she found a seat and everyone went back to chatting and drinking their sodas and beer, she even winked at him, since he was still watching her.

He didn't wink in return—or even smile. But he didn't look away, either. He studied her that much more closely, as if he was trying to figure out what she was up to.

Since Doug Maggleby insisted on crowding as close to her as possible, she was glad when the pizza finally arrived. Doing her best to keep interaction with him to a minimum, she focused on the female English teacher on her other side, a recent divorcée with two kids, neither of whom was with her now because her ex had picked them up for the weekend.

Cora also kept an eye on Aiyana. She hoped to speak to her mother again—at some length, if the opportunity presented itself. She now knew that she had living grandparents and uncles and where they all lived and what they did for work! It was a revelation, considering the dearth of information she'd had until six months ago. There were a lot of other things Cora wanted to know—but Aiyana was always surrounded by an eager group of teachers or other staff.

Everyone who worked for her liked her, Cora realized. They all seemed to bask in whatever attention she gave them. Thanks to that, there was no chance for Cora to approach her while they waited for the pizza, and Aiyana left shortly after it came, before the karaoke even started.

"Are you leaving, too?" Cora asked Darci Spinoza, the English teacher she'd been chatting with most of the night, when another group from their party started to say goodbye.

"No way," she replied. "You said you were going to sing. Since I don't have a voice, and wouldn't have the nerve to perform in front of a crowd even if I did, I'm waiting to hear you."

"Me, too," Doug chimed in.

Although Cora was grateful that Darci would be

staying, she wished Doug would find other friends. Her other neighbor, Sean, sat in the corner with a couple of people. Why couldn't Doug go over there? He was drinking too much, which made him feel free to touch her…

Briefly, she considered going home herself, to avoid him, but she hated to miss her chance to sing. And Elijah was still there. He stood with his back against the wall and a beer in his hand, talking to a man she'd never met. Because that man was somewhere close to their age, was part of the group from the school and seemed so comfortable around Elijah, she guessed it was Gavin, the handyman Aiyana had mentioned and Elijah's younger brother. Tall and thin, he had a beard and several tattoos on his arms. He was handsome, but not nearly as handsome as Elijah.

Once the karaoke started, Cora tried to ignore the bothersome, overbearing and balding Doug and went to the mic to sing "Jolene." On subsequent trips she performed "I Hope You Dance" and "Wrecking Ball." After that, Darci, Doug and several others kept prodding her to get up again. Some people even made requests— and a table of four men, who hadn't been part of their group but had come in later, started sending her drinks.

"Those guys are really into you," Doug said. "But of course they would be. Who wouldn't like a gorgeous woman like you?"

Cora couldn't help leaning away from his sour breath. He was getting so close when he talked it felt as if he was trying to look down her blouse.

Catching her recoil, Darci gave her a nudge. "I think

it's time for Doug to go to bed, but…he can't drive in that condition."

No, he couldn't. Someone had to see that he got home safely, and Cora was the obvious choice. They lived right next door to each other, after all—and Sean had already left. "Is there any way we could call him a taxi or even an Uber?" she whispered back.

Darci laughed at the question. "Not in this small of a town. There's no such thing here. But if you'd rather not take him, I will."

Cora couldn't ask her new friend to go twenty minutes out of the way. Darci had already told her that she lived in town. "No, I'll do it. Just…help me get him to my car, okay?"

"Sure, I can do that."

They had no trouble persuading Doug that he shouldn't drive, not once he learned he'd be riding with her—and that she'd bring him back to get his car in the morning. At that point, Cora forgot about Elijah. She was too intent on stopping Doug from copping a feel as she and Darci helped him outside. She'd just unlocked her car so they could put him in the passenger seat when Elijah came out of the pizza parlor along with the man she'd guessed was Gavin.

Darci said good-night to them, so Cora looked up and said the same. She expected the brothers to go on their way, possibly to a bar if they weren't ready to go home for the night, but "Gavin" waited on the curb while Elijah came around to where they were trying to get Doug in the car.

"Here, I'll take him." Slipping Doug's arm around his neck, Eli started to cart the math teacher off.

Cora was so relieved she almost couldn't hide it. "Are you sure?"

"Why would I go home with you when I could go home with *her*?" Doug protested, his voice overloud and his expression bordering on belligerent.

"Because I'm not giving you any choice," Elijah said, and that was the end of it. Cora was fairly certain Doug knew better than to balk, that he'd be stupid to try to stand up to Elijah, because he didn't object again. "Gavin" met his brother and took hold of Doug's other arm, and Cora was left to drive home alone.

"That was nice," she said on a long exhale.

Darci smiled as if she was holding something back. "What?" Cora asked.

"Eli could tell you weren't comfortable, that you didn't want to take Doug home."

She straightened. Of course she didn't want her drunk octopus of a neighbor in the car with her. But Darci was intimating something more than that. "What do you mean? Elijah was clear across the room. How would he know anything?"

"You're kidding, right? He's been watching you all night. Every time I glanced up, he had his eyes on you. I've known him for a year and have never seen him so focused on a woman. I think Doug got a little too close to what Eli wants himself."

"That's not true," Cora argued. "Eli was simply being a stand-up guy by putting me out of my misery—knew he was better equipped to handle Doug in his current condition than I am."

"If you say so." Her singsong voice indicated she didn't believe that at all, but she didn't belabor the point.

"It was great spending time with you," she said. "I'm glad you've come to town. What with the divorce and dealing with my ex since I moved here, it's been hard to make friends. And now it's too late to be that new girl who gets introduced around. So... I'm happy to meet someone who's starting fresh and might be open to getting to know me."

"I'm definitely open to that," Cora said.

"Even though I'm quite a bit older than you?"

Cora waved her words away. "Age doesn't matter when it comes to friendship."

"That takes care of that, then. Now maybe I'll have someone to do something with when the weekends roll around and my kids are with their dad."

"I'm sure I'll be looking for a chance to get off the campus." She waved as Darci walked down the street to her car, but her mind wasn't on her new friend. She kept mulling over what Darci had said about Elijah, and realized she was right. Elijah wasn't just being a good guy in general when he took Doug off her hands. He was looking out for her—*specifically.*

Chapter 6

Elijah found Cora leaning up against the side of his truck when he came out of Doug Maggleby's house.

"Thanks for putting my neighbor to bed for me," she said as he walked toward her. "I was not looking forward to that."

He could tell. She didn't like Doug touching her, and he hadn't liked it much, either. "No need to thank me. He's not your responsibility."

"He's not yours, either."

He shrugged. "It's not like I was going out of my way."

She tucked her long brown hair behind her ears. "So you didn't do it for me?"

He *had* done it for her, but he preferred to downplay that part. "No."

He assumed she'd let it go at that, but she gave him a skeptical once-over.

"What?" he said.

"You're so full of it."

He felt his eyebrows go up. He wasn't sure he'd ever had another woman say something like that to him before. "Excuse me?"

"You're acting like you're not interested in me, but…"

This new girl was nothing if not unpredictable, Elijah decided. She didn't play by the usual rules—at least not the old-fashioned rules he'd grown accustomed to living out here in the country. Problem was…she was right. He *was* interested in her. But he couldn't let himself act on that interest. "What makes you think so?" He rested both hands on the truck, one on either side of her. He figured if she was going to challenge him, he was going to challenge her right back.

But she didn't flounder for a response, didn't back down. She wasn't intimidated in the least, even though he had her penned between his arms and virtually towered over her.

Her gaze lowered to his mouth. "The way you look at me."

He tensed with the desire to press her up against his truck and kiss her soundly. She was baiting him, trying to see what he would do, which left him torn. Part of him felt she deserved to get a bit more than she bargained for. The other part knew better than to let things move in that direction. He'd been keeping his distance from her for a reason.

"*You're* the one who said you had a boyfriend," he

said. "Maybe you've forgotten the other day. I was carrying in your boxes, you were acting all concerned, as if that might mean you owed me something, and then you said—"

"I remember," she broke in.

"So…what's up with that? Where'd your boyfriend go?"

She lifted her chin defiantly. "I broke up with him over a month ago."

"You lied?"

Still, she didn't back down. "Basically."

"Because…"

For the first time her confidence seemed to waver. "I don't know. It doesn't make sense. I… I felt something I didn't want to feel. And I panicked."

He was so astounded by her honesty he wasn't sure how to respond. So he went with the obvious—what he'd been using to warn himself off since she'd arrived in Silver Springs. "I'm your boss, Cora."

"*That's* what's holding you back? Professional integrity?"

"One of the things, yes. This school—the boys here—are important to me."

"One doesn't necessarily cancel out the other."

"I hired you because I thought you'd be the best teacher for the job." He'd also thought he'd be able to ignore how alive he felt whenever he was around her, but he'd never expected her to confront him so directly. That forced the issue out in the open, made the attraction more difficult to ignore. "I'm sure my mother wouldn't thank me for giving her new art instructor reason to quit and leave."

That brief moment of insecurity he'd noted before seemed to fall by the wayside. "You're sure dating me would go in that direction?"

His ex-girlfriend said he walled himself off, refused to give anything emotionally. And she probably had the right of it. The shrink Aiyana used to send him to said a lot of the same stuff. Dr. Anderson told him he needed to learn how to open up, which sounded good in theory but he couldn't figure out how. He'd finally refused to continue therapy. He wanted to close the door on his past and make sure it was never opened again, not re-hash those painful memories.

"It's not like I've never been down this road," he said. "I've been in a number of relationships. Enough to know my limitations."

"*All* those relationships ended badly?"

He'd been taught to believe he was so terrible, so *unacceptable*, that he'd been painfully shy around girls growing up. He hadn't even started dating until he was twenty, and he'd only had three fairly seri-ous—and fairly short—relationships since. "Let's just say… I don't have a high success ratio when it comes to women."

"You and Aiyana are *very* close."

"That's different."

"Love is love. You had to decide to trust her at some point."

"Not everyone has her patience," he said. "She was so determined to love me, I had no choice."

"And those other women?"

The scent of her perfume rose to his nostrils. He liked the way she smelled, wanted to touch all that soft-looking skin. The temptation to slide his hand up her shirt burned through him like hard liquor. "As I said, it's not the same thing."

"Because it involves physical intimacy? What, exactly, are your 'limitations'? Are you saying you can't have sex?"

He was pretty sure she was goading him. At least, he hoped she was, that she didn't really believe he was incapable. Either way, he was eager to put the question to rest. "My body works fine. It's my inability to make you feel loved and 'validated.' I think that was the word."

"So I'd only get hurt if I got involved with you."

"Yes. You'd essentially be getting a locked box."

He was being transparent, completely up front. She was the one who'd set that tone. So it surprised him when she barked out a laugh. "You think you're doing me a favor by staying away!"

He was trying to adhere to the decisions he'd made after that last ugly blowout with Tina. He'd been glad for the peace and balance he'd found since they broke up a year ago. But twelve months was a long time to go without a woman… "Essentially."

"Well, you're taking a lot for granted, Mr. Turner. First of all, how do you know I'm going to want you to love me?"

"Experience," he said wryly. "I have yet to encounter the opposite problem."

"You're in such high demand that you've grown arrogant?"

"Failure hardly makes me arrogant. It does, however, make me want to avoid running into the same brick wall."

"I see. Well, you don't have to look out for me. I'm a big girl."

"Which, of course, you'll say until our relationship doesn't progress. Then you'll quit your job and go back to LA."

She rolled her eyes. "I'm only here for one year. No matter what happens, I'm not going to quit my job."

Was she as resilient as she pretended? He couldn't help getting his hopes up. He was already starting to imagine her on her back, her hair falling across his pillow… "Then you have a decision to make."

"What kind of decision?"

"Are you up for a strictly physical relationship? Because if that's all you're after, I'd be happy to accommodate you. I have no doubt I could satisfy you there."

She studied him. "That's all *you're* interested in?"

"Yes. I'm sorry." He wasn't about to go down the same road he'd been down before. But he wasn't sure why he was apologizing, since she sounded almost… relieved by this news.

"You're *sure*? *I* could never hurt *you*?"

"No. I'm too good at keeping my gloves up." He'd been trained from a young age…

She nodded slowly. "Okay. I'll think about it."

That didn't sound as though she'd make up her mind as quickly as he was hoping. "Any chance you could think fast?"

He wanted to kiss her so badly; the way she chewed on her bottom lip made him sort of light-headed. "We should probably give it a few weeks. See how we feel," she replied.

"*Weeks?* Does it have to take that long? Because I've already made up my mind."

She seemed uncertain. "There is something I should probably tell you…"

"And that is…"

More lip nibbling. "I've never had a strictly physical relationship."

He shifted his gaze from her lips to her eyes. "Not even a one-night stand?"

"No."

"*What?* You're from LA!"

Her expression changed to one of outrage—until she realized he was joking. "Don't even start with those stereotypes," she grumbled. "Or I'll go for the country bumpkin stuff."

Somehow, he'd underestimated her. She wasn't making it easy for him to ignore the attraction he felt. He liked her spunk. "Can you at least tell me what my chances are?" he asked, leaning a little closer.

"*I'm* the one who approached *you*, so… I'd say they're pretty decent."

"What made you approach me?" he asked, because that was a game changer. Otherwise, he would've continued to skirt around her indefinitely.

"There's just something about you."

All the things he could say to coax her, to convince her she wouldn't regret spending the night with him rose to his lips. But he knew it wouldn't be fair to put any pressure on her. She could *easily* regret the arrangement he proposed. And he didn't want that.

Taking her hand, he held it to his chest so that she could feel how hard his heart was beating. Maybe he couldn't promise her forever, but she wanted him. She'd just said so. And he wanted her.

Her hand moved slowly over his pectoral muscles in a curious caress that made him hard as a rock. He almost kissed her, was tempted to use his body to convince her if he couldn't allow himself to use his voice. But as soon as he dipped his head, she seemed to understand they were only seconds away from "too late." Once they crossed that line there would be no going back. One spark could cause them both to go up in flames.

"Like I said, I'll think about it." Pulling away, she started up the drive.

Disappointment bit deep. He stood there without reacting for several seconds, trying to overcome the letdown. Then he said, "Wait."

She didn't come back to him, but she turned, so he walked over and held out his hand. "Where's your phone?"

When she pulled it from her pocket and handed it to him, he put in his number and gave it back to her. "In case the answer is yes. Maybe it won't take as long as you think."

Cora stared at Elijah's number for at least an hour after he left. She switched between the contact information he'd put in her phone and the picture she'd taken of him out on that ride. She loved that picture so much. And yet…they'd never really spent any time together. It was ridiculous that she'd feel so compelled to call him.

She was just lonely, she told herself. She'd made a big change, was out of her element. She needed to forget about him and concentrate on what she'd come here to do, which was to teach and get to know Aiyana. She was part Nicaraguan. She had grandparents. She had uncles. These were the things she'd hoped to seek out. Her plans didn't include Elijah.

But she couldn't have anything serious with Elijah, anyway. Not without telling him that she was Aiyana's biological daughter. And she wasn't ready to do that. So he'd offered her the perfect solution: the chance to fulfill the desire he evoked without expectation.

After another ten minutes spent pacing around her small cottage, she decided to walk over to the pond. She thought sitting on the dock with the moon shining down on the water might help calm her mind. But even there, she was restless—too restless to remain on the jetty. Eventually, she made her way over to the horses' pen where she hoped, with the animals, she wouldn't feel quite so alone.

"There you are, big boy," she crooned, petting the nose of Elijah's giant horse when it ambled over to see her. "Looks like you're not getting much sleep tonight, either."

"You okay?"

Startled by the sound of Elijah's voice, Cora turned to see a dark figure sitting on the fence of the llama pen not far away, in the shadow of the nearby barn.

She pressed a hand to her chest to compensate for the shock he'd given her. "How long have you been there?"

"Since before you came out."

"You saw me, and you didn't say anything?"

"I was considering it."

"It took you a while to decide!"

"I wasn't sure you wanted to be disturbed."

Somehow it seemed like fate that they would run into each other again tonight. Or maybe she'd been subconsciously hoping for that, hoping for another opportunity, without actually having to call him. Although she'd never seen his house, she knew he lived on this part of the ranch, near the animals. She was hesitant to admit it, but, deep down, she was fairly certain that was why she'd come over here so often already. She'd been hoping to see him all along. "What are *you* doing out here?" she asked.

"Same thing you are, I suppose."

"You can't sleep."

"I have something on my mind."

"And that is…"

"You."

Cora squinted across the distance between them, trying to make out his expression. He was lonely, too, she realized. As much as he tried to pretend otherwise, he had to be. He was so aloof, so careful to warn most everyone away. She was no psychologist, but after what he'd been through, that had to be a defense mechanism. And what he'd said about Aiyana seemed to prove it. By his own admission, Aiyana had only busted through his reserve because she wouldn't take no for an answer.

Maybe that was what getting close to him required— the ability to love without expectation, without measuring or demanding anything in return. Cora could understand why that might be the case. He was tired of disappointing the women he dated, tired of feeling inadequate when they became disappointed. She'd sensed that in what he'd had to say earlier. There'd been a degree of fatalism, as if he'd given up.

His previous girlfriends had probably wanted to establish a regular relationship, one that escalated toward marriage. So they had an agenda, of sorts. Cora, on the other hand, had no agenda. She wasn't looking for a long-term relationship, couldn't have one with him, anyway, not without a very honest conversation she wasn't willing to have.

So…what if she just gave him someone to be with while she was here, some meaningful intimacy that was warm and supportive without pushing him for anything more?

"Sounds like you could use a massage," she said.

There was a moment of silence. Then he said, "Are you offering to give me one?"

She could tell he wasn't really asking about a massage, just as she knew he understood her answer wouldn't be strictly limited to one. "Sure."

"Tonight—or do I have to wait a few weeks?"

She chuckled. "Don't push your luck."

The darkness made it difficult to tell for sure, but she was fairly certain she'd gotten a smile out of him.

"You wouldn't be out here if you weren't as taken with the idea as I am," he said.

"You have a point, I suppose."

"You're not going to pretend otherwise?"

"No. Should we go to your place—or mine?"

He hopped off the fence and came toward her. "Mine."

"Any particular reason?"

"I don't have neighbors."

"Mr. Maggleby does tend to keep tabs on me."

"Mr. Maggleby is probably down for the count, but my house would still be better."

Cora drew a steadying breath as he advanced. She'd be spending the night with him. She'd just made the commitment, wouldn't feel good about backing out now.

Fortunately, she didn't want to. But her motives weren't *entirely* altruistic. She'd been craving the opportunity to touch him since the first day she'd met him.

And now she was going to have her chance.

Chapter 7

Elijah's small A-frame was the most isolated house on the ranch and the hardest to reach, which suited him well, Cora thought as he showed her inside and closed the door behind them. He had plenty of privacy here. She got the impression that few people were ever invited inside, and that included the students he cared so much about. This was his place of retreat where he could put some distance between him and other people, since people were what he probably considered to be the biggest challenge life had to offer. Everything else seemed to come easy for him.

"Would you like a drink?" he asked.

Cora shook her head. "No. I'm good."

"Are you sure? Maybe a glass of wine?" Now that he had her inside, he was treating her as if she might bolt if he wasn't careful or courteous enough. That was another thing that made her wonder if he wasn't quite comfortable with having company. She got the impression he almost didn't know what to do with her—how to get from where they were in this moment to where he hoped to go, which wasn't in keeping with how he behaved in every other circumstance she'd noted so far.

"Okay." She relented, thinking that might help. "I'll have a glass of wine."

While he opened a bottle and poured, she wandered around his living room, which was very utilitarian—so utilitarian that the walls were completely bare. She couldn't find one thing that defined him as a person, nothing that spoke of who he was or what he liked, even on the shelves or counters. She'd never seen a house stripped down to the bare essentials before. The men she'd known had a tendency to decorate sparsely, but still.

Was it just that Elijah didn't know how to make a house a home? Or was the ability to reveal even that much of himself also locked inside the "box" he'd mentioned?

"Aren't *you* going to have one?" she asked when he handed her a glass and stood back to watch her drink it.

"No."

So much for letting a drink ease them into the evening… "Why not?"

"I'm not interested."

He was too single-minded to drink right now, Cora decided. He knew what he wanted, and it wasn't wine. But he was trying to wait his turn. "So you were merely being polite by offering me one."

"I thought you might enjoy it."

He seemed to feel as if he needed to take certain steps for her sake, as if he'd memorized a set of "rules" for how to be successful in such situations—and that included putting whatever *she* wanted first.

Setting her glass aside, she stepped up to him. She could tell he was dying to touch her, saw his hands curl into fists and his muscles tense as he wrestled with his self-control. For some reason, he was trying to let her make the first move. She supposed he wanted some reassurance that she wasn't going to suddenly change her mind. Or maybe he merely wanted to be confident he wasn't pressuring her into anything. Regardless, he was far more wary now that they were alone and behind closed doors than he'd been at his truck earlier. But they'd never had any real chance of getting intimate there, so maybe that was why.

What'd happened to him in the past had influenced *everything*, even the way he approached sex, she realized. He didn't trust other people, didn't trust *her*. "How long has it been for you?" she asked.

"Since..."

"Since you've been with a woman."

"A year."

No wonder he watched her like a wolf chasing a rabbit. That was a long time to go without for a man his age—at least it would be a long time to the men she knew in LA. But Eli lived in a small town and had the reputation of the ranch to consider—and she knew the pain that hid behind that handsome face. As normal as he came off, every once in a while there was something in his eyes that reminded her of an animal that'd been beaten so often it growled or showed its teeth even when someone tried to be kind. He craved what she was offering, couldn't bring himself to skirt around her and continue on his way, as he most likely preferred. So he was waiting for the perfect moment—when he could safely snatch it away. Were he anyone else, she felt certain he would've reached for her already...

"These encounters don't come with a script," she said.

"Meaning..."

"You don't have to serve me wine, or...or check anything else off a list."

"I'm merely trying to make sure you get what you need. I may be sort of...limited in what I can offer you, but I'm not a *completely* selfish bastard. If you'll tell me what you want, what you like, I'll give it to you."

"I don't have a punch list, Eli. That's what I'm saying. But I'm pretty sure we can figure out what we *both* like." His nostrils flared when she lifted his hand to her breast. "Does this help?"

Elijah wished it was easier to go without human touch. His life would be so much simpler. But nothing else felt like a woman. He tried to hold himself in check, to remain in control. He didn't want to overwhelm or frighten Cora, had been trying to be measured and kind. But once she put her mouth on his, and he could feel the weight of her breast in his palm, something snapped. She didn't have to do anything more. He started kissing her so hungrily that he could hardly catch his breath. And, within moments, he was peeling off her clothes, so anxious to get to bare skin that it felt like he couldn't wait another second.

He thought she might be put off. On some level, he knew he was being pretty aggressive, probably *overly* aggressive. But she had her hands in his hair and clung to him as if she was just as caught up in him as he was her. So if she was put off, he couldn't tell.

He hoped it wasn't something he'd learn about in the morning. To prevent that, he promised himself he'd take their lovemaking slower as he carried her down the hall to his bedroom.

Once there, he made an honest effort to do just that, but her kisses were so hot and wet, and she was sucking on his neck and licking his nipples. She was even biting him, just not so hard that it hurt.

Although his shirt was already on the floor, he still had his jeans on as they rolled around in his bed. Since everything he touched felt so damn good, he forgot about taking it slow and gentle. If anything, he felt the compulsion to make everything go harder and faster.

Fortunately, she seemed to be perfectly happy. With a promising smile, she unzipped his pants.

He gasped as her fingers closed around him and, only moments later, he was naked, too.

To his credit, he took a moment to admire her full breasts, small waist and the appealing flare of her hips. She had no hair *anywhere*, which, coming from LA certainly didn't surprise him, but he'd never seen a woman so bare. He liked the way she looked lying beneath him in the moonlight streaming through his window. She was as beautiful and soft as he'd expected.

Dimly, he thought about all the things he could do to

bring her to climax. He planned to do every single one before he took his own pleasure. He wanted to make sure she was glad she'd agreed to be with him tonight. But once he began to suckle her breasts, she arched into him as if she craved him inside her.

"Okay. Hang on. Let me…let me take care of you first," he said.

"I'm ready," she gasped when he slid his hand between her legs.

He groaned as he encountered the slickness he was hoping to find. She *felt* ready. But burying himself inside her, this soon, wouldn't be slowing down.

"Do you have a condom?" she asked.

Fortunately, he did—in the nightstand. But he barely managed to roll it on before she pulled him on top of her and wrapped her legs around his hips—an unmistakable invitation and one he couldn't refuse.

He felt shaky as he pushed inside her. She was so wet, so tight he had to hold himself still. Otherwise, he wouldn't have even half a chance of making her come. He didn't want to be the only one who was fulfilled tonight. Then he wouldn't have done *anything* right.

"God, you feel good," he murmured, running his mouth up her neck.

"So do you," she said. "I guess it's true what they say about guys with big hands and big feet."

That comment took him so much by surprise that he almost laughed, but she didn't give him time. She grabbed hold of him—to pull him deeper inside her—and encouraged him to thrust.

"Give me a minute." He could hardly recognize his

own voice it sounded so hoarse. "You're going to be disappointed if you don't."

Crooking her arm around his neck to bring him closer, she pulled his bottom lip into her mouth. "Quit *thinking*," she whispered.

He shook his head. "You don't understand. It's been a long time for me. I'm not going to make it."

"So what? Let go. Do it any way you want." Her breath, hot in his ear, was followed by her tongue.

Her words, the freedom she gave him, sent a fresh deluge of testosterone through him, which did nothing to help his control. But if she wasn't going to help him hold out, he figured he was facing a losing battle. So he closed his eyes and drove into her with an abandon he'd rarely allowed himself before, and felt the pleasure of each thrust escalate to the point that his whole body shuddered when he hit climax.

"Goose bumps," she said as she ran a hand down his arm. "That must've been a nice one."

He stared down at her while trying to catch his breath. "It was. But I know it was too fast for you. I'm sorry."

"I enjoyed watching you," she said. "I think you needed to let loose."

Suddenly, he was *so* tired. "Give me an hour or so, and I'll redeem myself. I promise," he said as he curled around her. But he fell into such a deep sleep that it was morning when he woke up, and by then she was gone.

Elijah had a hard time being selfish. That was the most significant fact Cora had learned about him while she was in his bed. As she drove to town the following morning to meet Darci for breakfast, she couldn't help chuckling as she remembered how he'd tried to rein himself in—and how guilty he'd felt when he couldn't. Of course, she'd enjoyed urging him on, had wanted to see what Elijah Turner was like when he threw off all of that restraint. Not only was it gratifying to her that she could have such an effect on him, she figured that was the best way to discover his true personality—when he wasn't closely monitoring everything he said and did. Although he came off as remote, she was beginning to understand that he was actually quite sensitive. He also seemed honest and intrinsically fair.

Her phone rang. Assuming it would be Jill, or maybe Darci, since she was running a few minutes late, she answered using her Bluetooth. "Hello?"

"Cora? It's Aiyana. How are you?"

She froze at the sound of her birth mother's voice. Had Aiyana learned that she and Elijah had spent the night together? Cora had slipped out of his place while it was still dark so that no one would see her. They were both consenting adults; she didn't think what they'd done should be a *really* big deal, at least to anyone else. They did work for the same school, however. So, of course, that would be frowned upon.

Was she about to be confronted about her behavior?

A honk from the car behind her reminded her that it was her turn to clear the intersection. "Um… I'm fine," she said as she gave her SUV some gas. "How are you?"

"Great." Aiyana covered the phone as someone spoke to her in the background. "Sorry about that," she said when she came back on the line. "We just got a new shipment of books for the library."

"From what I've seen, we already have an extensive collection."

"I won't skimp on the library, either."

What *did* she skimp on? Nothing, not when it came to the school. Cora had the impression she worked 24/7 to make sure the boys had everything they could possibly need. "Are you a big reader?"

"I am. I read more nonfiction than anything else, but I stock a lot of action-adventure, sci-fi, mysteries and thrillers for the boys. I encourage them to read by giving them books they're going to like. Feel free to take a look and borrow anything that catches your fancy."

Cora had an e-reader, which was well-stocked, but she didn't say so. She didn't want Aiyana to feel as though her offer wasn't appreciated. "I will. Thank you."

"I hope you'll be able to adjust to living here in Silver Springs," she said. "I know it might require a bit of an adjustment."

"Living out here is…different," Cora admitted. "But it's not without its attractions." She winced as those words came out of her mouth. She thought Aiyana would instantly guess that Elijah was the biggest and brightest of Silver Springs' "attractions," at least where she was concerned. But Aiyana didn't seem to clue in—thank God.

"Your supplies should be in on Monday. I checked, wanted to let you know."

Cora pulled in front of Lolita's Country Kitchen, where Darci had asked to meet for breakfast. She had to admit that it was wonderful to find ample parking—

that rarely happened in LA. She wouldn't even have to pay for it. "Wow. How nice of you to follow up."

"No problem. But…that isn't the only reason I called. If you have a minute, I'd like to talk to you about something else."

Oh boy. Maybe she *did* know about Eli. Cora turned off the car but didn't release her seat belt even though she could see Darci waving at her through the window of the diner. "Sure, I've got time. What's going on?"

"One of the other teachers mentioned to me that Doug Maggleby was making you uncomfortable at the pizza parlor last night."

"It wasn't…all that bad," she hedged.

"He was drinking, which I'm sure didn't help. Anyway, I'm sorry. I'll speak to him. I definitely don't want him scaring you off."

"No, don't bother," she said. "He didn't get *too* out of line." Thanks to Eli, he didn't get much of a chance…

"Are you sure?"

"Positive."

"Well, I'll let this incident go, but only because he's had a rough few years. He lost his wife to cancer and is just now getting over it and hoping to find someone else."

"He might have better luck looking for someone closer to his own age," Cora said.

"Yes. If necessary, I'll mention that to him."

"I appreciate your support."

"Of course. That's what I'm here for." She was about to hang up when, impulsively, Cora stopped her.

"Aiyana?"

"Yes?"

"To tell you the truth…" She searched for the right

words to express what she had to say and came up empty.

"Have you changed your mind about having me talk to Doug?" Aiyana asked.

"No. This is…something else."

"What is it?"

She tapped her fingers on her steering wheel. "Um… I wanted to make sure you wouldn't be…angry or—or disappointed if I ever…you know…"

"What?" Aiyana prompted.

"Showed interest in your son," she blurted out.

"Elijah?"

Cora squeezed her eyes closed. She had no idea what the heck she was doing. She just hated the feeling that she might be letting Aiyana down by going behind her back, needed to know how serious of an infraction it would be if she were to continue to see Elijah. She had no idea how *he* felt about last night, but she definitely wanted to get to know him better. "Yes. I've seen Gavin but haven't actually met him."

There was a long pause. Afraid of what Aiyana might say to discourage her, Cora hurried to fill the silence. "I realize we both work for you, at the same school, but in the high schools where I've taught, if two teachers happen to go out once in a while, it's pretty much ignored."

"I'm not so concerned about two employees dating…"

"And yet you sound hesitant."

"He bears some unique scars, Cora."

Letting her breath seep out, Cora finally opened her eyes. "I'm aware of that."

"Do you realize that what he's been through will

probably always be part of him? How a background like his could affect a relationship?"

Darci was now at the door, watching her with a confused expression, so Cora lifted one finger to indicate she'd be just another minute. "Here's the thing. He's fine the way he is. I'm not asking for anything serious. I think I could be a good friend to him."

More silence. Cora didn't get the impression Aiyana was *against* her seeing Elijah—it was more that she seemed to be weighing certain reservations in her mind, trying to figure out if she should say more.

Cora bit her lip. "I shouldn't have said anything. It wouldn't be serious, like I said. I guess I just…needed to know you wouldn't be too upset if…if we ever hung out."

"I wouldn't be upset. I'm just worried that…well, because he's so hard to get to know, it may not seem as if he can be hurt—"

"Anyone can be hurt."

"*Especially* him," she said. "I guess that's my point. His heart is so big."

"Trust me—it's not like that. You have nothing to worry about."

"Well, if that's the case, no one can have too many friends," she said, and they both laughed at her quick reversal.

"Okay. Great. Can I ask for one more favor?"

"Of course."

"Don't tell him we had this conversation?"

"Trust me—I won't. He wouldn't like the idea of me getting involved, so to be honest, I'm hoping you won't mention it, either."

"I won't. This will be our little secret. And now I'll let you go."

"Cora?"

She pulled her phone back to her ear. "Yes?"

"Relationships, even friendships, can be unpredictable at times. So protect your own heart, too."

"I will." As Cora disconnected, she felt as if a huge weight had been lifted off her shoulders. Maybe she hadn't come *totally* clean. She wasn't willing to go that far. But at least she knew she wouldn't be doing anything that would upset Aiyana if Aiyana found out about it. As attracted as Cora was to Elijah, she didn't want to kill any chance she had of being part of her biological mother's life—if she ever decided to go for that.

Chapter 8

"Thanks for being willing to get together," Darci said.

Cora was a little self-conscious about the fact that she hadn't had a chance to shower this morning. When Darci called, she'd rolled out of bed and thrown her hair into a ponytail. She was still tired after being up until the wee hours with Elijah. "I'm glad you reached out," she told Darci.

"I almost didn't, but with school starting on Monday and my kids coming home tomorrow, I figured this would be the best time to get together."

"It's perfect. I haven't had a chance to eat in Silver Springs yet." Cora noted the number of filled tables. "This seems like a popular place."

"It's one of the best cafés in town, not that we have a

lot of them," Darci added with a laugh. "Do you know if Elijah got Doug home okay last night?"

Cora took a drink of water from the glass the waitress had delivered to her a moment earlier. "He did. I saw him as he was coming out of Doug's house."

"Did he say anything to you?"

She opened her menu, pretending to be preoccupied by choosing her meal. "Not really." After what Darci had said about the way Elijah was looking at her last night, Cora didn't dare admit to anything. Her face was heating up, threatening to give her away as it was.

Fortunately, someone walked by that Darci knew, drawing her attention. "Hello, Cal!"

"Cal," a handsome, middle-aged man who wore a cowboy hat and boots, stopped, a look of pleasant surprise on his face. "Darci! I didn't even see you there. How are you?"

She got up to give him a hug. "Better. Thanks."

"That ex of yours isn't still giving you trouble, is he?"

"Things seem to have settled down for the moment." She slid back in the booth. "He's met someone else, so that helps."

He shook his head. "You've had a rough year."

"It's been a rough *twelve* years. But the divorce would've been worse without you."

"I didn't do much." He glanced at Cora. "Is this a new friend?"

As Darci introduced them, she told Cora that Cal Buchanon owned a big cattle ranch not far from town. "He supplies New Horizons with beef, gives Aiyana a heck of a deal. Actually, he helps *everyone*," she said emphatically. "Silver Springs wouldn't be what it is without him."

"Stop!" he said, obviously embarrassed. "I do my part, like everyone else. It's very nice to meet you, Cora."

"Likewise," Cora said.

He chatted with Darci for several more minutes before tipping his hat to the both of them and heading to the cashier to pay his bill.

"Cal's superrich," Darci whispered. "And he uses his money to do so much for the community. I was serious when I said Silver Springs wouldn't be the same without him."

"You seem to know him well."

"I do. He has a couple of houses on his ranch that he typically rents to his hands. He let me stay in one *for free* until I could get on my feet. Wouldn't take a dime for six months."

"Is that why you came to Silver Springs? You knew him from before, and he made you that offer, or…"

"No. I came to teach at New Horizons, like you. But the house that was supposed to open up in the faculty housing—the two-bedroom so that I'd have room for my kids—didn't, and I couldn't afford anything in town."

"So how'd you meet him?"

"Through Aiyana. She jumped in to make other arrangements when the faculty housing didn't work out for me."

"How nice of her."

"She's generous, like Cal. And, from what I've heard, Cal has been in love with Aiyana for years, almost since the day she came here. I believe he took me in for her sake. But he's been kind enough to befriend me, too."

"He's never married?"

"Not to my knowledge. He doesn't even date. He's waiting for her."

"He reminds me of Sam Elliott with that gravelly voice and weathered face. Doesn't she care for him in return?"

"I'm convinced she does. The way she looks at him… it's as if he hung the moon. But she's very private about her love life. If you ask her about Cal, she'll make some glib comment about how he's a great guy but she's too old to get married for the first time."

Aiyana was only forty-nine. Cora knew that from the documents provided by the private investigator who'd taken her on pro bono. "Do you ever see them together?"

"I run into them all the time. He supports anything her boys participate in so he comes out to the ranch a lot. And he sends her flowers or chocolates at least once a month. I wish I could find a guy as devoted to me as he is to her," she added wistfully. "My ex only cared about himself."

Cora had no business asking, but she was so curious about her birth mother that she couldn't stop herself. "Do you think they're sleeping together?" she asked, lowering her voice to a whisper.

Darci's mouth twisted as she considered the question. "Don't know, to be honest. When I lived out at his place, she never stayed over, not that I could tell. And I've never known him to sleep at New Horizons. But that doesn't mean it hasn't happened. Like I said, Aiyana's very private about that sort of thing. She'd never let on, even if they were intimate."

"There must be some reason they're not an official couple. What's missing?"

"I couldn't tell you." She made a signal to let Cora know the waitress, who'd introduced herself as Missy, was coming to take their order.

"Sorry to put such an abrupt end to the conversation," she said after she'd ordered pancakes and eggs and Cora had ordered a Spanish omelet. "I was afraid Missy might overhear us. Everyone knows everyone else around here—and even if they don't, most everyone knows Aiyana."

"No problem. I understand."

Difficult though it was, Cora let the conversation drift away from her birth mother to the school and what the coming year would entail. They also discussed some of the more troubled boys.

"How do you deal with those who won't behave?" Cora asked.

"Easy," Darci replied. "I threaten to send them to Elijah."

Cora put down her fork and took a drink of her orange juice. "Why not Aiyana?"

"Elijah tries to spare her anything difficult, anything that might upset or disappoint her. He prefers we get him involved if we need help."

"Elijah's the enforcer."

"Sort of."

"What methods does he use for discipline?"

"The threat of being sent to his office is usually enough. If they do something wrong, they don't want him to find out about it. They care about his good opinion, about getting the chance to be with him for various activities."

"Surely there have been a few who *haven't* cared enough to behave."

"Of course. He barred one boy, Ricky Peterson, from playing sports and attending the dances and assemblies until he brought up his grades. But then he studied with Ricky for an hour a day. After a few weeks, Ricky was doing better than ever before."

Considering they were talking about a man who called himself a "locked box," Cora thought that was interesting. Apparently, he had plenty of love for the boys—but she'd already noted that when he was on the horseback ride.

She opened her mouth to ask if Darci had ever heard anything about the various women Elijah had been with but caught herself. She couldn't show that much interest, didn't want to give Darci any indication that there was something going on between them. Since they weren't serious, she preferred to keep it on the down low. So she asked about Darci's marriage and divorce, and then she tried to offer some support. But in the back of her mind she couldn't quit thinking about Elijah and the role he played on the ranch. Aiyana remained on her mind, as well. Her biological mother was such an enigma. Why wouldn't she marry Cal?

Cora had just stepped out of the shower when she heard a knock at the door. Assuming it was Doug, since he'd caught her when she got back from breakfast to say he had some fresh vegetables he planned to gather from his garden and bring over, she groaned and started to grab some clothes so that she could get dressed. Then she realized she'd have a much better excuse not to invite him in if she answered in her robe.

Prepared to thank him and quickly send him on his way, she pasted a smile on her face and cracked open the door. But it wasn't her neighbor, it was Elijah. He stood on her stoop in a pair of faded jeans, his tan, muscular arms stretching the sleeves of his red New Horizons T-shirt as he tossed his keys from hand to hand.

"Hello," she said, blinking in surprise.

His gaze lowered to her robe. "Just getting up?"

"No. I met Darci in town for breakfast and didn't have time to get ready beforehand, so I just showered." She'd also done a conditioning treatment on her hair, given herself a mani-pedi and rubbed her whole body with some vanilla-scented lotion. She told herself she wanted to look and feel her best to start her new job, that she was doing this as a matter of routine. But she knew Elijah had more to do with it than she cared to admit.

His lips curved into a devilish smile. "Then I'd say my timing is perfect."

Not only was he smiling freely, he was smiling at *her*. "For…"

"I owe you a little something, remember?"

Slightly concerned by how easily he could make her knees weak, since she was supposed to be keeping some emotional distance in this relationship, Cora drew a steadying breath. "You don't owe me anything."

He reached out and tugged on her belt to loosen it, so she stepped back to let him inside. The last thing she needed was for someone to drive by and see them. "You don't think it's too risky to come to my house during the day? If you're not careful the whole school will be talking about us."

"What do you mean? It's much safer to come during the day. Then it doesn't look like we're trying to hide anything."

That made sense, but the fact that her robe was coming open also made it difficult to think. He continued to pull on her belt—slowly so she'd have time to stop him if she wanted. But she didn't stop him, and soon the belt fell to the ground.

Suddenly nervous, she wet her lips as she stared up at him. "So now it's my turn, huh?"

"Unless you have other plans for the next hour or so…"

Cora felt she should come up with something. Put this off, at least until she could regain her perspective. She shouldn't be this excited.

On the other hand, she'd just spent two hours getting ready to see him—and here he was.

Dipping his head, he kissed her long and slow as he slid his big hands inside her robe and gripped her waist.

He wasn't holding back today. Last night had convinced him that she wasn't skittish, wasn't going to bail out too easily. "I take it you don't want to…to talk first," she said.

"No. I'm not interested in talking."

Cora found it quite erotic that she was naked while he was fully dressed. She also liked his level of focus. "So there'd be no point in putting on my clothes."

"Why make me take them off again?" He hoisted her up onto the dining table, putting her on her back.

She caught the lapels of her robe so it wouldn't fall *completely* open. The soft terry cloth was beginning to feel like a safety blanket. But he pulled the fabric out of her grasp and ran his fingers over her bare stomach and breasts.

Cora shuddered as a ripple of pleasure went through her.

"You like that?" He continued his light touch, skimming up her neck to her face, where he ran his thumb over her bottom lip. "You're so beautiful."

The compliment surprised her. He wasn't much for that sort of thing. She told herself not to take him too seriously, but at the same time she caught his hand and pulled his thumb into her mouth.

His pupils flared as her tongue moved over his skin, and he lowered his mouth to her breast.

Every nerve seemed to fire at once; she'd never been more aroused.

"Now I see how convenient a Brazilian makes everything," he said as his mouth moved down her stomach. "Easy access. I like that."

Cora couldn't even speak. His hands were on her hips, and he was pulling her toward him, spreading her legs so he could fit between her knees. "Maybe… maybe we should wait until we know each other better for this," she said, finding her voice.

"Because…"

"Because it…it makes me *really* self-conscious."

"You don't have to be self-conscious with me."

He bent his head. When she felt his tongue, she nearly jumped off the table.

"It's okay," he murmured, his breath warm. "Relax. This is going to be fun."

The next few minutes were more than fun; they were mind-blowing. Cora drew in a deep breath and closed her eyes as he used his mouth in a way she'd never experienced before. The sucking motion was so subtle, so gentle and so incredibly effective that her legs began to quiver. She felt his hand rub one of them, as if in encouragement, before that hand slid back up to her breast.

She was seconds away from the best climax of her life. Cora felt the escalation, the compulsion of her body to reach that pinnacle.

Then the doorbell rang.

Trying to force her sluggish brain to work as it usually did, she started to get up. She thought Elijah would stop so she could deal with her guest, especially because his truck was outside. They couldn't be caught doing something like this. It wouldn't look good. But he muttered a gruff, "No!" and held her that much more tightly as he continued his ministrations.

He was so insistent that she let her head fall back and reached for the sides of the table. She had to hold on to something...

"Cora, you there?"

Doug. Of course. He *would* show up at the worst possible moment.

"The door!" she whispered emphatically, but Elijah wouldn't let Doug take this away from her. She felt his beard growth on her thighs as he shook his head in refusal.

Fortunately, the climax she'd been chasing burst

upon her soon after, despite the fact that Doug knocked again.

After Elijah heard her gasp and felt her body jerk, he straightened in satisfaction. He'd given her one hell of a climax. She could tell that had been his goal, but he didn't seem pleased. "Damn him," he grumbled, his voice low as he scooped her off the table, set her on her feet and bent to retrieve the belt to her robe.

"What should we do?" Her mind scrambled to decide how best to explain Elijah's presence, her disheveled appearance and their delay.

After a brief hesitation, he took charge. "She's in the shower," he called out, turning her toward the bedroom and giving her a little push.

As she hurried down the hall, he headed for the door.

"When I got here, she yelled for me to come in," she heard him say as soon as she was safely behind the closed door of her bedroom. "But I've been waiting for fifteen minutes, and she's not out yet. So you might want to leave those here or come back later. I'm going to come back myself."

Doug said something in reply. Cora couldn't make it out. His voice wasn't as strident as Elijah's. Then there was silence, and when she peeked out, they were both gone.

Smooth move, she texted to Elijah.

What I did with Doug or before? came his response.

Although she could tell he was teasing, his words let her know he was still very much fixated on what had occurred—and she couldn't blame him. She was having a hard time forgetting about it herself, and she was the one who'd at least been satisfied. Pretty proud of yourself, huh?

That felt good—even to me.

Lol. I won't lie. You could win an award with that technique.

Glad to hear it. Then maybe you'll see me again tonight.

She could only imagine how aroused he'd been when he'd had to leave. Being interrupted at that point was never fun. But she wasn't sure they should continue what they'd started. She'd been thinking of this fling in such a harmless way. She'd presented seeing Elijah to Aiyana in a harmless way. And yet…spending more time with him was beginning to feel dangerous.

Can't. Going to LA to see my folks.

Until that moment, she hadn't planned on returning home. She was essentially running away. But she knew where she'd spend the night if she didn't get out of Silver Springs, and she needed to put on the brakes, gain some perspective, rethink what they were doing. The tenderness she felt at any thought of him frightened her. This wasn't nearly as casual as she'd imagined.

When will you be back?

Tomorrow night.

Call me when you get in.

Okay, she wrote back. But she didn't return until it was late—too late to consider seeing him before school started the following morning.

Chapter 9

Eli had never had trouble concentrating. Not since he'd overcome what he'd been through as a child and grown into an adult. He was so focused on his job and the boys he served that there were days when he almost forgot to eat. Work was what he enjoyed, what kept him going and looking forward to each new day. He was especially busy this time of year, when there was so much to do in order to get the semester started off right.

On top of that, his two youngest brothers were back, and Dallas, the middle brother who'd taken them climbing in Yosemite, was temporarily visiting. The following week, Eli spent most of his evenings with them, which he enjoyed, but he often found his mind drifting when it shouldn't. He kept remembering what it had been like to make love to Cora, felt such a strong craving to be with her again he couldn't help watching for her whenever he was on campus. She'd texted him when she left LA last Sunday night but only to let him know she'd be getting back too late to see him. With Dallas in town, Eli hadn't thought much of it. He'd told her to let him know when she'd be available, which indicated he wanted to see her again, but he hadn't heard from her in six days. He wasn't sure what she was thinking. Although she'd smile and wave if she happened to bump into him—she wasn't *un*friendly—she'd turn away right after, wouldn't really meet his eyes. And she never called him or reached out to him, even at night. Since Dallas was staying at the big house with Aiyana, Liam and Bentley, they *could've* seen each other despite Dallas's presence on the ranch, if she'd acted interested.

Eli had almost stopped by her place a dozen times. He would have at least called her, but he could tell that something was different. She'd withdrawn. He wanted to believe she was just busy. Being a new teacher, *any* teacher, the first week of school was stressful. He needed to give her time to settle in, couldn't expect to take priority over her work. From what he could tell, she was dedicated to her students and intent on getting to know them. Since he was the one who'd hired her, and he'd chosen her over a candidate most others had expected to get the job, he wanted her to excel. He'd heard from several of the boys that she was already well liked, which gave him hope. But when he saw her at their first football game last night, and she still didn't reach out to him afterward, like he'd thought she might with the weekend before them, he knew it was more than her job that was keeping her away.

She'd decided she wouldn't see him again. Why? What had made her change her mind? Had she decided a strictly physical relationship wasn't worth it? Had she gotten back with her boyfriend? Or...what?

"Hey, where are you tonight, man?"

Eli blinked and drew his attention back to Dallas and Gavin, who'd dragged him to the bar. He didn't come here often, was careful about how much he drank. Although drinking could wipe out the painful thoughts and memories that plagued him, it could also rob him of his functionality. And he was determined to show the boys he worked with how to overcome that temptation, not fall right into it.

"Sorry, what'd you say?" he asked Dallas, who'd broken into his thoughts.

Dallas finished his last swallow of beer. "You're a million miles away. I was wondering what you were thinking."

Eli lifted his own glass. "I'm thinking Freddy Nance deserves to play ahead of Jason Peachtree."

"Do you have any idea what the heck he's talking about?" Dallas looked to Gavin for an explanation.

"Cougar football," Gavin replied. "Freddy and Jason are both hoping to make first-string quarterback at New Horizons."

"Jason's so gifted," Eli said. "But Freddy's willing to work twice as hard. That counts for more, in my book."

Dallas shook his head. "I swear, big brother. You need to get off that campus a little more often. Look at the chicks here, man. Have some fun."

Dallas's childhood hadn't been any better than Elijah's. After a relatively normal life, he'd watched his father come unhinged and shoot his mother and his sister, and attempt to shoot him before he managed to run out of the house. When the police came, they found that his father had turned the gun on himself. While Eli used work to anesthetize him from his past, Dallas deadened the painful memories he carried with sex when he wasn't climbing and adrenaline when he was. Eli was fairly certain, of the three of them, Aiyana worried about him the most. Eli did, too. Although Gavin had been abandoned at six years old in a park, he seemed to cope better with life.

Or maybe he just pretended to.

"I try to leave the women alone," Eli said.

"Because…"

"Because I'll wreck their life. I should come with a warning label."

"It's only sex, man. As long as it's consensual and doesn't get too crazy, sex never hurt anybody."

"You forget," Eli said drily. "This is a small town. There's no way not to run into the same woman over and over."

"You can't do that sort of thing here," Gavin grumbled in agreement.

"Then you *both* need to get off that ranch a little more often. Drive to LA."

"If we slept with as many women as you do—" Gavin started, but Dallas cut him off.

"You'd have some fun for a change."

Eli rolled his eyes. "Or wind up with a disease."

"Not if you're careful."

"I don't get the impression you're as careful as you should be—about anything," Eli joked, but if Dallas answered, he didn't hear it. He felt his smile wilt the second he glanced up and saw Cora walk into the bar with Darci Spinoza.

She didn't notice him, not at first. But it didn't take long. Those wide, innocent eyes of hers, busy scanning the tables along the periphery of the dance floor as she looked for a place where they could sit down, stopped the second they encountered him—and recognition dawned.

To her credit, she and Darci walked over to say hello. Actually, Cora didn't really have any choice—neither one of them did. He was their boss, after all. It would've been rude to ignore him.

Fortunately, Darci didn't seem to know anything had ever happened between him and Cora. "Hey." She grinned at Dallas. "Look who's in town—trouble!"

"You know me already," Dallas responded. "It's great to see you again. You're Darci, right? The English teacher?"

They'd met at the school Christmas party. Aiyana insisted that the entire family get together for the holidays—no matter what they had going.

"Yes," Darci replied. "It's great to see you, too."

Dallas slid off his stool and stood, his gaze shifting to Cora. Eli could tell he found her attractive. "I don't believe I've ever seen *you* before."

"I noticed you at the football game last night, down on the field with Eli."

"If only I would've known *you'd* be in the stands," he said.

Darci introduced Cora, and Cora smiled politely as she shook first with Dallas and then Gavin. "Nice to meet you both."

"You must know Eli," Dallas said.

"Yes. Eli hired me."

"I can see why." Dallas pulled over a stool and began

looking for a second one. "Any chance you'd like to join us?"

Cora started to decline. She looked as though she couldn't get away fast enough. But Darci didn't seem to be paying any attention to her discomfort. She overrode Cora's response with an eager, "Sure. Why not? We were looking for some entertainment."

Gavin pulled over another chair while Dallas gave her a bow. "We're happy to provide that, aren't we, boys?"

Darci took the seat closest to Dallas, which left the stool between Eli and Gavin for Cora. She sat down, but Eli got the impression she was being careful not to touch him, even incidentally.

Darci and Cora ordered a drink. Then they all talked for an hour—about Dallas's climbing, the places he'd visited, that he'd be leaving in three days, the fact that Seth, another brother who was a sculptor, had secured a gallery showing in San Francisco, one he'd been working hard to parlay into a second and third showing in Chicago and New York, which was why he hadn't visited this summer as he'd originally intended.

Darci brought up her kids and her divorce and how much better she was feeling now that she was getting beyond it, but Cora didn't say much. She mostly listened— and focused on Dallas or Gavin, anyone but him. When Dallas asked her to dance, she agreed, but Eli had a difficult time watching. He didn't care to consider the reason.

Eventually, while they were having a second drink, she mumbled something about having to go to the bathroom and crossed to the far side of the bar, where the restrooms were located. Eli held off for a few seconds, so it wouldn't appear as if they were going together.

Then he followed her and waited in the hallway until she came out.

She took one look at him and stopped.

"Have I done something to offend you?" he asked.

"Of course not."

"Then why haven't I heard from you?"

"No reason," she said. "I've been…busy. I figured you were, too."

He shoved a hand through his hair. He was so confused by her abrupt reversal. "You didn't get back with your boyfriend when you went to LA last weekend…"

She shook her head. "Didn't even see him. I went to my folks'."

"So…what is it?" he asked. "*Something*'s different."

"Nothing. Not really. I just… I think you were right."

A trickle of foreboding went through him. "About…"

"You're my boss. It isn't wise to get so intimately… *involved* when we work together."

That wasn't the reason she'd stepped back; he could tell. "So… I screwed up somehow. You don't want to see me anymore."

She rubbed her forehead. "You didn't screw up."

"I must've done something, because I thought everything went…well. Better than well. *Great*." He lowered his voice in case someone else happened upon them. "Maybe I came too soon that first time and disappointed you, and you have every right to be frustrated that I wouldn't be more sensitive to *your* pleasure, but I hadn't been with anyone in a long time. That isn't how I usually behave. Trust me. I'll make sure it doesn't happen again."

"I'm not like that, Eli. I *wanted* you to come—to do

whatever you were compelled to do. That first time has nothing to do with it."

"Then there's something else…"

She said nothing, so he stepped closer.

"I'd really appreciate it if you'd take two seconds to explain, so I don't have to keep wondering why everything was fine and then…"

After tucking her hair behind her ears, she lifted her chin to confront him. "Being with you *did* go well. *Too* well. Every night before I go to sleep, you're all I can think about—the way you touched me, the way you kissed me. Even the way you *smell*."

"So why are you stonewalling me?" he asked, stunned.

"I'm trying to do us both a favor, okay?"

He spread out his hands. "By rejecting me?"

"By adhering to our original agreement! You wanted to keep it strictly physical."

"So did you!"

"Yes, but—"

"Physical means we touch each other."

"Except I *feel* something! I know it's crazy. We just met. But you were right in the beginning. I can't do it," she said and brushed past him.

Cora wished she could go home. Sitting next to Eli, talking and laughing with his brothers, certainly didn't make her want him any less. She'd thought her admission in the hallway would scare him away, or at least make her feel so exposed *that* would douse the flames. But the way he watched her only made her crave his hands on her body more with each passing second. Sexual energy all but crackled through the air between them like electricity.

How could she become infatuated with someone so quickly? Especially when she'd only ever been luke-warm with her previous partners?

Her ex-boyfriend would've given *anything* to be able to make her feel even half as much...

Her response to Eli was a mystery—an ironic mystery. After being so cavalier with him that night when he brought Doug home, she was getting what she deserved, having to eat her words. And, to make it all worse, she couldn't slip out of the bar to escape the tension between her and the man sitting next to her. Forcing Darci to leave when she was having so much fun would be too selfish. After what Darci had been through, this was the kind of thing she needed. A night that was carefree and fun. The chance to talk and laugh and forget the difficulties of the past year. Darci was enjoying every moment and didn't seem to notice that Cora sat on pins and needles.

"Dance with me."

Dallas had danced with her twice before, but this was Eli. He hadn't danced with anyone yet, and because he'd asked in front of his brothers, she didn't feel as if she could refuse him.

"Go dance!" Darci said before she could respond, and she got up and let him lead her onto the floor.

Rihanna's "Stay" was playing as he looped his arms around her back. She tried to resist getting too close but gave up on that the moment his hands slid up her back. He was coaxing her to relax, which made it impossible to resist the temptation to melt into him.

"Why are you doing this?" she asked as they swayed to the music.

"Why am I doing what?"

His breath was warm against her ear. "Tempting fate."

"Because it's too late to back away now. We're already in this."

"It's not too late."

As he brought his head up, his lips brushed her neck. To the casual observer that move probably looked inadvertent, but *she* understood he'd done it on purpose—and felt a corresponding sizzle zip through her.

"You think we're going to be able to fight what we feel for a whole year?" he murmured.

What else could they do? He was Aiyana's son! The only reason she'd let herself go as far as she did was because she'd assumed she'd be able to remain somewhat objective. Now that she'd spent some time with him, however, she had to acknowledge that it wasn't going to be easy come, easy go.

"We can try."

"As far as I'm concerned that'll be a frustrating exercise in futility," he said. "I'm already going crazy."

She hated that she'd started something and was refusing to finish it. That didn't seem quite fair. Maybe she needed to let this play out. She'd never gotten involved in a relationship that was more physical than anything else. That meant the attraction might be explosive at first, but would eventually burn itself out, didn't it?

If so, she was worried about nothing.

"To be honest, so am I," she admitted. "So...where can we go?"

"You mean later? What's wrong with my place?"

"I mean *now*," she told him.

He pulled back to look at her. "Are you serious?"

She could already taste his kiss, had committed every detail about him to memory. "Do you have a problem with that?"

"Absolutely not," he replied. "Make your way out back. There's a side patio where smokers go that should be fairly deserted. I'll be there in a few."

Since they didn't want to be caught together, this was a risky endeavor. That she was willing to take such a gamble surprised Cora. It wasn't like her. But nothing she'd done with Elijah so far had been like her and, in this instance, the need for privacy couldn't outweigh the urgency to feel him inside her. After battling that desire for a whole week, she was more than ready to surrender.

When Eli returned to the table, Darci looked up at him in surprise. "Where's Cora?"

"She went to the bathroom."

"Again?"

He shrugged as if he hadn't asked for details, and, as soon as she was distracted by something Dallas said, he nudged Gavin. "Why don't you ask Darci to dance?" he murmured.

Gavin seemed startled by this atypical request, but Eli had spoken low and used a tone that suggested he not question it, and Gavin didn't.

As soon as Gavin and Darci walked away, Eli leaned close to Dallas. "I'm going out back," he said. "Keep Darci occupied, will ya?"

"Keep her occupied?" Dallas repeated.

"Make sure she doesn't go looking for Cora."

Dallas sat up straight. "What are you two going to be doing?"

When Eli didn't answer, his brother swore under his breath. "No way! I've been flirting with her all night, with zero results. You dance with her once, and she goes outside with you?"

"It's not like that," he said.

"Then what's it like?"

Eli lifted his beer. "None of your business. Just take care of Darci, okay?"

"Sure. What are brothers for?" he replied. "But isn't Cora your new art teacher? Is that okay? Because I'll step in for you if it isn't," he joked.

"Like hell you will," Eli grumbled and tossed back what was left in his glass before making his way to the door leading to the patio and the parking lot beyond.

Cora was waiting for him near the vine-covered trellis. Two guys were smoking on the far side of the patio, but they were so deep in conversation they weren't paying any attention. Taking Cora's hand, he quietly led her to the back of the building, which faced nothing except a wide expanse of farmland.

"On second thought, maybe this is a little reckless," she said as he pressed her up against the building.

It had taken him long enough to join her that she'd grown nervous. He could tell. "Apparently, you need a little recklessness in your life."

"Because..."

He kissed his way up her neck. "It's exciting."

"Being reckless is a good way to get burned."

Threading his fingers through hers, he held her hands above her head. "Like I said, we're in it now."

"And if someone comes out?"

"They won't."

"How do you know?"

"I told my brothers to see to it."

Her eyes widened. "You did *what*?"

"I didn't want you to worry about Darci."

"But…what must your brothers think?"

"It doesn't matter."

"It does to me!" she said. "I'm embarrassed!"

"I'm sorry. It was either that or risk having Darci come looking for you. I figured that would be *more* embarrassing, and I knew I could trust my brothers to make sure that didn't happen."

He was afraid she was going to leave. He held his breath as she stared up at him, and bit back a curse when she pulled away. But after taking a few steps, she turned back and grabbed him by the shirtfront, pulling him up against her again. "This is crazy. Look at us! We're behind a *bar*. And somehow that's not enough to stop me. What you told your brothers isn't enough to stop me, either. Because I've never wanted anyone like I want you."

He let his breath go in relief. "Hallelujah. Then I suggest you relax," he said and slid his hand up her skirt.

Cora told herself that she should care more about the fact that Dallas and Gavin knew what was going on—and that Darci could easily figure it out. But the kiss Elijah gave her was so achingly sweet that the last thing she wanted to do was walk away. This was a new side of him, one she hadn't seen before.

"I *love* the way you touch me." She'd anticipated coming together in the same heady rush they'd experienced before. They'd both felt the same chemistry on the dance floor. But tonight Eli was taking his time.

"Then you needed this reminder. Maybe it means you won't ignore me this week."

"You could've called *me*," she said as his mouth found her earlobe.

"I was getting signals that precluded that."

"I don't remember sending any signals."

"You wouldn't even look at me."

"Because I knew where it would lead."

"To this."

"Yes."

"Is that a problem?"

She sighed as he kissed her again. "It doesn't feel like one right now."

His fingers hooked the thin fabric of her thong and began sliding it down her legs. "Why hold back? Like I told you before, I'll give you whatever you ask for."

Except his heart. He'd made that clear. But, considering the situation, did it really matter? She was only here for the year. And once he found out she was Aiyana's daughter—if she ever decided to tell him—she couldn't imagine he'd be pleased that she'd allowed them to get so intimate without disclosing her true identity.

"Great. Then give me this," she said and undid his pants.

Chapter 10

Cora had never had sex outside of a bar or any other public place. She'd heard of other women doing things like that, but she'd never dreamed *she'd* be one of them. It was humbling to learn she could be that girl, but... what'd changed? What'd made her do such a thing?

It was Eli. He had such a profound effect on her. That animal magnetism, the immediacy of what they'd done, had been potent. She'd been so aroused, so sensitive to his every touch that she'd been able to climax when he did, making the fifteen minutes they spent outside quite an experience. She'd never forget him holding her up against the building, the moon full overhead as he drove into her, the only sound she could hear above the music filtering out of the building that of their own labored breathing—and then her groan at the end, which he'd quickly smothered with another kiss.

She was having a torrid affair—with her boss. Her ex-boyfriend would be shocked. Her parents would be shocked. Heck, *she* was shocked. She and Eli hadn't even used a condom. They hadn't had one, hadn't come prepared because they hadn't expected anything to happen. They'd been forced to use the withdrawal method.

"Where've you been?" Darci asked once Cora had righted her skirt, smoothed down her hair and returned to the table.

Cora hoped it was too dark to see the blush heating her cheeks. "It's so hot in here." She slid over as Eli joined them. He'd purposely let her go in first so that they wouldn't come back at the same time. "I stepped out for some fresh air, and there were a couple of guys outside, smoking. We got into a conversation."

"Oh. You were gone so long I was about to come looking for you." She lifted her glass to catch the attention of the waitress.

Fortunately, Darci didn't seem suspicious, but Dallas wasn't about to let Cora off quite that easily. "Wasn't it every bit as hot outside?" he asked with a grin that left little question he was messing with her.

Eli shot his brother a warning glance, but there was nothing he could do or say in front of Darci, who turned to look at her in expectation of her response.

"It was…a little warm," Cora said, but the waitress Darci had called over appeared. As soon as Darci turned to speak with her, Cora leaned closer to Dallas. "Actually, after it was all over, I could've used a cigarette myself!"

Dallas burst out laughing and slapped his older brother on the back. "Damn, I like her. She's *definitely* hooking up with the wrong Turner."

"What'd you say?" Darci asked as the waitress left. "Something Turner?"

Dallas clinked his glass against Cora's. "Not Turner, *learner*. I said Cora's a fast learner."

Darci blinked in apparent confusion. "What'd you learn?" she asked Cora but Eli dragged Cora onto the dance floor to save her from answering.

Cora was fairly certain she'd never had more fun. On some level, she knew she was screwing up her life. She was so taken with Eli, too taken for it to be safe. But she could hardly feel bad about what she was doing when she was still in the middle of it. She, Darci and the Turner boys talked, laughed and danced until the bar closed. Then Eli drove them all home, since he'd had much less to drink—barely two beers. Although Cora wasn't much of a drinker herself, she'd been feeling more carefree than usual. After her stint outside with Eli, she'd quit holding back and simply cut loose. If she was going to regret this night, she figured she might as well go all the way.

Eli dropped Darci and Gavin off first, since they both lived in town. Cora would have to reclaim her SUV in the morning, but she was so happy and tired when she got home that she wasn't worried about that or anything else.

After Eli pulled into her driveway, he walked her to the door. Dallas was probably watching from the truck as he kissed her, but she didn't care about that any more than anything else tonight—and just to prove it, she pulled Eli back and kissed him a second time before letting him go. "You are *so* hot!" she said.

"And you are so drunk," he responded with a laugh.

"I'm not drunk. I mean…not *that* drunk."

"Yeah, you are."

"I'll never forget tonight."

A thoughtful expression claimed his face as his gaze moved over her. "Neither will I," he said. "But you'd better go inside if you don't want your neighbors peering out to see what you're up to."

She let him go, but once she was inside, she twirled around the living room, reliving the evening before falling onto her bed. "What a night," she said aloud. She thought Eli might come back after he took Dallas to Aiyana's. She wanted him to. But if he tried to knock, she didn't hear it. She fell asleep before she could even take off her clothes, and when she woke up, it was late morning.

Reluctant to roll out of bed, she checked her phone—and found she'd missed several calls since she'd paid any attention to that sort of thing last, which was before she'd gone to the bar. Her brother. Her mother. Jill. She'd even missed a call from Aiyana.

Expecting a nasty headache to hit as soon as she sat up, she moved gingerly at first, but she wasn't as hungover as she'd thought she might be. She deserved worse.

With a yawn, she shoved her hair out of her face and put her phone on speaker so she could listen to her messages with minimum effort while sitting on the bed.

Her mom: "Call me when you get a chance, honey.

I found the cutest dress for your birthday, but it's expensive so I'd like you to try it on before I buy it. When will you be coming home?"

Cora smiled in affection. Her birthday wasn't for six months, but her mother bought her stuff all year long.

Her brother: "Just calling to see how my baby sister's doing. I'll be in New York for a few weeks trying to line up the financing for my next film, so don't panic if you don't hear from me. I'll check in when I get back."

She hated that she'd missed his call. Ashton was always so busy these days.

Jill: "So how's Silver Springs? I was hoping to come visit you next weekend, like we talked about, but Todd's grandmother will be celebrating her ninetieth birthday in Palm Springs, and he wants me to go with him. Give me a call so we can set another date."

She'd never told Jill that she'd slept with Eli. She'd decided it didn't make sense to tell anyone since she wasn't going to be with him again.

So much for that...

Aiyana: "Hi, Cora. Sorry for the late notice, but I was wondering if you'd be able to join the boys and me for dinner tomorrow. I'd love the opportunity to get to know you better."

Cora hungered for the opportunity to get to know her better, too. But by boys, did Aiyana mean Eli and possibly Gavin and Dallas? Or was she talking strictly about the two youngest Turners—the ones living at home?

Cora sighed as she stared at her phone. She hesitated to put Eli in an awkward situation by showing up at his family dinner, but... Aiyana was the whole reason she'd come to Silver Springs. She wanted to accept the invitation.

After mulling it over, she texted him. Your mother has invited me to dinner today. Will you be there?

His response came almost right away. Yes.

Is it okay if I accept?

Why wouldn't it be?

Because she wouldn't be attending in the capacity they thought—as merely a new teacher at the ranch. She was excited to see how Aiyana lived, felt Aiyana's house and the items in it might reveal more about who her biological mother was and what her life had been like. At a minimum, she'd probably be treated to pictures of her grandparents and uncles, maybe even some of the places Aiyana had lived in the past.

But Eli didn't know that her interest extended beyond what she'd stated in her interview.

I don't want to intrude on your time with your family.

You won't be intruding.

She thought he'd leave it at that, but he texted her again a few minutes later.

When do you want to get your car?

In an hour or so? I was about to take a shower.

No problem. I can wait.

She put her phone on the nightstand only to hear it signal another text.

This was from Eli, too: Better yet, why don't I join you?

Aiyana must've said something to Doug Maggleby, even though she'd said she wouldn't, because he'd been less intrusive the past week. Or maybe he was getting the hint. Regardless, Cora was relieved that Doug wasn't there hoping to talk to her every time she walked out her front door, but she still didn't want him to see Eli's truck sitting outside. You can't park in front. We'll have to be more careful or people are going to get the wrong idea.

You mean they might get the right idea.

She couldn't help laughing. Basically.

Well, we can't have that. I'll walk over and slip in. No one will see me.

Oh boy. She was about to sink even further into her "torrid affair." But there wasn't a darn thing she could do about it. Even if she said no now, she knew she'd say yes later.

I'll leave the back door unlocked.

"Damn, I'm glad I hired you," Eli joked as they dropped onto her bed after thirty minutes of the best shower sex she'd ever had. "But since we seem to make love in a vertical position more often than not, I'd better spend more time at the gym. My arms feel like they're about to fall off."

She leaned on one elbow so she could smile down at him. "You didn't seem to be struggling."

"Are you kidding? You weigh a ton."

The twinkle in his eye confirmed that he was teasing her. "You said you like my body! You said it was the hottest body you've ever seen."

"Heat of the moment," he scoffed, but one finger traced her breast as if he'd meant every word.

"Fine." She knocked his hand away. "I guess I'll have to find someone who's more…appreciative of my physical appearance."

In a quick, easy motion, he rolled her onto her back, straddled her hips and pinned her arms above her head. "No way. You're mine for the entire year, remember? And I plan to make the most of it."

He'd already proved that… "Do you think we're really going to be able to pull this off?" she asked. "Without people finding out, I mean? Without it turning into a big deal that…that comes to the attention of your mother?"

He bent his head to nuzzle her neck. "No doubt there will be talk."

"You're not concerned?"

Slowly, he kissed his way up to her mouth. "Not concerned enough to stay away."

"So what do you propose we do?"

"Ignore it. As long as we're both performing at our jobs, we shouldn't have any problem."

"Maybe I should go on the pill..."

He lifted his head at her abrupt change of subject. "Would you mind? I'm willing to be responsible for birth control, but I admit I'd love to be able to come inside you."

She hated the way her heart seemed to beat in double time as she gazed up at him. She was getting in too deep. He'd told her he wasn't capable of opening up, of making her feel loved and validated.

Was she about to learn what his other girlfriends had learned?

"Cora? Would you mind?" he repeated eagerly.

She drew a bolstering breath. "No."

A bead of sweat rolled down between Cora's shoulder blades as she stood on the wraparound porch of the large, two-story ranch house that belonged to Aiyana. A gusty breeze tossed her hair around, and she'd worn a light, flowery sundress, so she wasn't overly warm; she was battling nerves.

"Relax," she muttered as she knocked. She'd seen Aiyana's home before, from a distance. Although built on the periphery of the ranch, it wasn't far from the administration building.

Aiyana answered the door. Eli's truck was already in the drive. Cora saw him the moment Aiyana showed her in, but she barely allowed her glance to skim over him as Aiyana introduced her to Dallas and Gavin, both of whom she'd met, of course, and Liam and Bentley. Cora had Liam as a student in one of her classes, so she was familiar with him, too. A tall, gangly boy with a bit of acne, he excelled in basketball, from what she'd heard. She'd only ever seen Bentley, who was African American, on the football field.

She handed the wine she'd brought to Aiyana as she said hello to everyone else.

Eli offered to pour her a drink, but she declined. After imbibing so much at the bar last night, she wasn't interested in more alcohol. She accepted a bottle of water instead while listening to Liam complain about how much trouble he was having with the self-portrait he'd been assigned in her class. After some small talk with the others, she went up to his room to help with it while Aiyana put the finishing touches on dinner.

Leaving the kitchen and dining area gave Cora a chance to see more of the house. As she would've expected, every room was clean and tastefully decorated. Aiyana had pictures of her boys all over the place—senior portraits, family portraits and candid shots from their various sports. She saw a few of Eli. Like Bentley, he'd played football. But it wasn't until after she'd helped Liam and set him to finishing the rest of the assignment on his own that she was able to look over those pictures more carefully.

She wandered down the hall, eventually winding up in the living room. She could hear Aiyana banging around in the kitchen and the boys watching TV in the great room but wasn't in any hurry to return to the group, especially when she spotted the family photograph she'd been hoping to see of Aiyana with her parents and brothers. It was framed and sitting on an old 1960s piano.

She'd just picked up that picture when she heard someone come into the room behind her.

She turned to see Eli.

"You're all finished with Liam?"

"I am. He's still upstairs working, but I figured I should make him do as much as possible." She almost put down the photograph. She felt guilty snooping around but was too curious about the people in that photograph, and her connection to them, not to take advantage of the opportunity. "These are your grandparents?" she asked, indicating the couple in the middle.

"Yeah. Hank and Consuelo."

"Your mother mentioned that Consuelo is a Nicaraguan immigrant."

"That's true. She had one son when her husband left her to come to America. He promised he'd make a better life, then send for them."

"And?"

"She never heard from him again."

Cora felt her jaw drop. "He moved on without her?"

"He was killed trying to swim across the Rio Grande to reach Texas. She came looking for him as soon as she could cobble together the money. But she couldn't find him. It was two years before she learned what happened. By then she was living in a small shack on Hank's farm with her son—German, who was six at the time—picking fruit."

"And Hank fell in love with her?"

"Eventually. Consuelo married two other guys first, Aiyana's father, who was an abusive jerk, and another man with whom she had her last two boys. That didn't work out, either. He walked out on her or something."

"Then she married Hank. So Hank's her fourth husband?"

A fond smile curved Eli's lips. "Yes. She finally got it right."

"How'd they get together?"

"He says he fell in love with her cooking first. Her third husband wouldn't pay his child support, so, to get by, she'd make homemade tortillas and tamales to sell on the weekends. Hank would come to her stand first thing Sunday morning, which was her only day off, and buy almost everything she had."

"Wow. He *must've* loved her cooking."

"That wasn't all there was to it. He couldn't have eaten that many tortillas and tamales. Once they started dating, she found he had a whole freezer full."

Cora laughed. "What a story!"

"I've never seen a man adore a woman more than Hank adores Consuelo."

His wistful expression caught Cora's attention. He loved them almost as much as Aiyana. "So…these three must be your mother's brothers." She pointed at the other men in the photograph.

"Yes." He fingered the one with the darkest skin. "None of the children actually belong to Hank, but he claims them all and loves them as if they do."

For which they should all be so grateful. Eli didn't state that, but the subtext was clear, and that subtext made it difficult for Cora not to bristle. She'd heard a lot of that type of thing herself. "Aiyana's name is unusual. Is it Nicaraguan?"

"Consuelo claims it's Native American for eternal flower. A woman who was part Cherokee came to her rescue one night when she was so hungry and tired she was ready to collapse. German was crying. Neither one of them could go a step farther. So she hid in a barn, hoping to rest before pushing on—only to be discovered by this woman whose name was Aiyana. Consuelo thought she'd be reported or turned out, but Aiyana fed them dinner and gave them a bed to sleep in. To this day, Consuelo says Aiyana was an angel sent from God, that she wasn't really human."

"That's a beautiful story, too."

"Consuelo's lived a challenging but interesting life. Fortunately, other than old age, her worries are behind her. Hank takes care of her every need. Grandma Sway, as we called her growing up, is the one who gave me my horse," he added.

"Atsila?"

"Yeah. Apparently, the Aiyana who helped her had a horse by the same name, which she gave to Consuelo so that Consuelo would have some mode of transportation, and so that German wouldn't have to walk anymore. Without that horse, Consuelo swears she and German would not have survived the next two weeks. Not long after, she had to sell it, which broke her heart, but she claims she would've starved without that money."

"How kind. What does Atsila mean?"

"I don't know. I tried looking it up once but couldn't find anything definitive—other than that it has Native American roots." He came closer and took the picture from her to look more carefully at it himself. "I figure the real meaning doesn't matter, anyway. To me, it means compassion."

"I bet the original Aiyana would be proud of her namesake," Cora said. "Your mother seems to be very generous herself."

"Yes. Not only has she helped me and my brothers, she's helped so many."

After what Eli had been subjected to, he'd deserved his own "angel." So did the others. And yet Cora couldn't help feeling rejected, jealous, left out, overlooked...*something* that felt like a knife to the heart. "Has she said why she's never had any biological children?"

"No. I've always assumed that maybe she couldn't."

Cora stood as living proof that Aiyana wasn't infertile. But, of course, she couldn't say anything to refute the assumption. "Darci told me that Cal Buchanon has been in love with her for years."

"They spend a lot of time together, more than she lets on to me or anyone else, if she can help it."

"She must care for him, too."

"I'm pretty sure she does."

"What gives?"

He scratched his neck. "She's afraid of getting hurt, or feels as if devoting herself to a relationship like that will take away from her work or something. I can't figure it out myself. And she won't talk about it." He put the picture back on the piano. "Why does this stuff seem to mean so much to *you*?"

Only then did Cora realize she was being too transparent. Straightening, she forced back the frustration and disappointment, as well as the curiosity she'd manifested so far, and conjured a polite expression. "I didn't mean to give you the impression it was overly important. I was curious, that's all."

Fortunately, he didn't get the chance to question her further. At that point, Aiyana called them to dinner.

Chapter 11

During the meal, Dallas tried to tease Cora about last night with a few carefully placed innuendos. But it seemed to Eli that Cora was too distracted and preoccupied to focus on Dallas or what he said, even when he made reference to what'd happened outside the bar. She'd smile or laugh where appropriate, but only Aiyana could claim her full attention. By the end of dinner, after Cora had helped Aiyana put the leftover pot roast, vegetables, mashed potatoes and cheesecake in the fridge and do the dishes, Eli was feeling a bit neglected. He got the distinct impression that she'd come to see his mother, that he had nothing to do with her desire to join them, especially when, instead of watching TV with everyone else, the two women went into the living room and talked for over an hour.

When he got up to fetch a glass of water, or he simply made an effort to listen, he could hear various bits and pieces of their conversation. Most of it was about the ranch—Aiyana's philosophy for the school, the fact that she'd chosen to place New Horizons in Silver Springs because it had wide-open spaces but wasn't too far from a major population center, why she'd adopted each one of her sons and which students she was concerned about this year.

He thought he might finally get a few crumbs of Cora's attention when they rejoined the group—even if it was only a quick, private smile. Instead, as soon as they finished visiting, Cora said she should go, that she had to get ready for her classes in the morning.

They'd made crazy, impromptu, almost animalistic love outside at the bar last night and then again in the shower this morning, but she'd hardly given him the time of day since coming to dinner.

"Thanks so much for having me," she told Aiyana. "You have a lovely home and a wonderful family."

"You're welcome. It's nice to have a little estrogen in the house," she said with a laugh. "You must join us again next Sunday. Dallas won't be here. He leaves on Tuesday. But Eli, Gavin, Liam and Bentley will."

"I'll do that, but only if you let me bring the dessert or another dish."

"I'm sure I could be persuaded," Aiyana told her.

"It was really great to meet you," Cora said to Dallas. "I'm sorry you have to leave town so soon."

"There are mountains to climb," he joked as he got up to hug her goodbye. Eli got off the couch, too, and was standing close enough to hear Dallas whisper something like, "Take good care of my brother."

Whether that was really what Dallas said or not, Cora turned and gave him a dutiful hug, one no different from the kind she'd imparted to everyone else. "Again, thank you."

"Eli, why don't you walk her out?" Aiyana piped up as Cora grabbed her purse.

Eli wasn't sure if that suggestion was as random as Aiyana pretended, but he didn't care. He was eager for a few minutes alone with Cora, so he was grateful his mother had tapped him instead of one of his brothers. "Sure."

"Dinner was wonderful," Cora said as they strolled down the drive side by side, without touching. "Now that my brother and I are adults, my mother doesn't bother to cook anymore. She's very generous about inviting us over for carryout, or taking us to a restaurant, so I'm not complaining. But a big Sunday meal from scratch? That's almost unheard of these days."

"It's not like it was a sacrifice to have you. You can come back next Sunday. You heard my mom."

"I'd like that," she said, but he didn't get the impression he was the reason she'd like it, and that bothered him.

"Are you really going home to get ready for classes?" he asked as he opened her car door for her.

"Yeah. I promised my students we'd start ceramics this week. Now that I'm more familiar with their skill level, I need to figure out the ideal project and how much time it will require on the throwing wheel."

He almost said, *And if I'd like to see you again?*

but he got the distinct impression that something was causing her to distance herself from him and he'd be stupid to push.

"You look incredible in that dress," he said instead, which was the truth. Ever since she'd arrived, he'd had difficulty looking anywhere except at her.

He was glad he'd told her that when, at last, she focused on him—and smiled. "Thank you," she said, but she didn't try to set up their next meeting, didn't ask if he'd call, didn't say a word about getting together with him again. "Good night," she added, and that was his signal to close the door.

The TV played in the background as Cora curled up on her couch and thumbed through the file the private investigator had, after much searching, provided on Aiyana. There wasn't a great deal in it, just some basic background information—where and when Aiyana was born, where she grew up, a couple of articles on New Horizons. Thanks to California's adoption laws, Cora had been unable to get the records that were sealed by the court. She'd had an attorney working on that, but because of various details her adoptive mother had let slip—like where and when she was born and at which hospital—the private investigator had come through first. So she'd given up on pursuing the court order. Several states had unsealed their adoption records. She hoped California would soon follow suit. Then maybe she'd be able to find out who her father was—if his name was on her original birth certificate. Adoptees had access only to their ABC or Amended Birth Certificate, which not only facilitated the change in the name of the parents but could list a different place of birth. In some instances, agencies even altered the *day* of birth. Fortunately, Cora hadn't been given a new birthday. Otherwise, chances were she never would've found Aiyana.

Or…maybe that would've been for the best. She'd spoken to several other adoptees, online and otherwise, who'd told her to be careful what she wished for. They'd been disappointed in their birth mothers, but she was not. She respected Aiyana, admired her and wished she could be part of her life in a more significant way than merely working for her. But she couldn't see how she'd ever be able to do that if she was still sleeping with Elijah.

Regardless of Elijah, did she dare—or even have the right—to upset Aiyana's life by announcing her true identity? Would Aiyana be happy to have found her?

That would probably depend on the reason Aiyana had given her up, and there was no file, attorney or private detective who could provide that information. Perhaps her grandmother could shed some light on the matter, but even that wasn't guaranteed. It was possible Consuelo had never been made aware of the pregnancy. Aiyana had had Cora when she was twenty-one, so she'd been an adult but not a well-seasoned one. Maybe Consuelo hadn't approved of the relationship that'd left Aiyana pregnant, and that was part of the reason Aiyana had acted as she did.

After staring at the grainy picture in the newspaper clipping that'd given Cora her first glimpse of Aiyana, she put down the file and picked up her phone. She hadn't yet returned Lilly's call. She needed to do that, didn't want her adoptive mother to feel as if she was being neglected.

"There you are!" her mother exclaimed as soon as she answered. "How are you, sweetheart?"

Cora rubbed her left temple with her free hand. "I'm doing great. How are you, Mom?"

"Missing you. It's not the same without you here. I have no one to go shopping with," she said in a pouty voice that Cora knew was a joke.

"I'll go shopping with you when I visit next."

"Yes. We'll have you try on that dress I found. You're going to love it."

"I'm sure I will."

"Your father and I thought you might come home again this weekend, we're sad when we didn't see you. What'd you do?"

Cora considered mentioning that she'd had dinner at Aiyana's but decided it wasn't necessary. "I've met a new friend—another teacher here at the school named Darci. We went out last night."

"How nice. I'm so relieved you're adjusting. I was afraid you wouldn't like it, and this year would prove long and miserable. I was surprised when you decided to go there instead of accepting the position at Wood-bridge. But you don't regret it?"

"No. Not at all," she said, and that was mostly true. If nothing else, the rabid curiosity that'd nearly driven her mad over the years had been appeased, to a point. As she finished talking to her mother she had to admit, however, that she had no idea if she'd regret what she was doing in the end.

Chapter 12

Cora knew she shouldn't have accepted when Eli texted her while she was at lunch the following day to see if he could take her horseback riding in the evening. After having dinner at Aiyana's, she was more aware than ever that she was putting them all in a difficult position. She'd decided to back away, had assumed she still had the fortitude—until she heard from him this afternoon and had thrown all of that out the window with a "one more time" excuse.

When he'd explained where to meet him, she'd guessed he was taking her to the same place he'd taken the boys—not that she intended to reveal the fact that she'd seen him here before. He'd been so carefree that day, so...unguarded. That memory was the one thing she planned to take away from this place when school let out—probably because she'd only seen Elijah like that once or twice since, when he was so caught up in their lovemaking that he dropped the aloof mask he wore otherwise. She felt like those moments were the only ones where she got to see the vulnerable heart beneath that rugged chest.

A silver truck towing a white trailer turned off the highway and parked in the clearing where she'd left her car. When she stepped out of the trees and greeted Eli, he responded with an uncharacteristically wide smile, one that suggested he was happy to see her, which made her glad she'd come. He usually kept his emotions more carefully concealed.

"Have you ever ridden before?" he asked as he pulled on a pair of leather gloves.

"Once. In Mexico. It was a four-hour-long trail ride with my family on the beach, and it was beautiful. But my horse was only allowed to walk slowly behind the horse in front."

"That's not really riding."

"After the first hour or so, it got boring," she admitted.

"You'll like this better."

She expected him to be towing two horses, but when he opened the trailer, she saw only Atsila. "We're riding together?"

"Is that okay? I figured if you're not familiar with horses, you might feel more comfortable riding double."

Since all she wanted to do was touch him—didn't care if they ever left the clearing—she had no reason to complain. "No problem."

"Great. I'll let you take the reins whenever."

He led the horse out and lifted Cora into the saddle before securing the truck and the trailer. Then he walked over and swung up behind her.

The warmth of his body made her wish she could turn and kiss him. They'd trained their bodies to expect such contact when they saw each other. She wasn't even sure what they were doing here. She liked the idea of riding, but it felt as if they were wasting what little time they could spend together.

They traveled mostly in silence. Cora got the impression Eli didn't care to talk. He'd answer if she asked a question, but only with a simple yes or no, if possible. There were a few minutes when she took the reins, but as soon as they came to a narrow pass that she wasn't confident in navigating, he took over.

"What made you ask me to go riding?" she asked as they continued to climb the mountain.

"You'll see," he replied, and that was it. Apparently, she was waiting for something. She didn't find out what until they crested the top of the mountain, where the trees thinned, revealing a stunning red-and-gold sunset.

"Wow," she murmured.

He pulled the horse to a stop. "Have you ever seen anything more beautiful?"

If she were being objective, some of the sunsets she'd seen at the beach and around the world were as spectacular. Cognitively, she knew that. But he'd brought her out here because he wanted her to enjoy this, and that made it the best darn sunset in the world. "Not with you," she said.

"What does that mean?"

"It means I'd like it even if it wasn't nearly so beautiful."

One hand came up to catch her chin as he finally kissed her. She wasn't entirely sure how everything went from there. Somehow, in a matter of minutes, they were off the horse and on the ground, their clothes open and askew, kissing and exploring and enjoying what they'd wanted from the first moment they met up.

"You can't be comfortable out here," he said with some regret, as if he hated to stop but felt too much guilt to continue. "I'll take you back down."

"No." Cora wasn't ready to leave. Not yet. When he pulled away to get up, she pressed him onto his back. Then she nibbled at his neck and his bare chest as she moved down—and heard him draw a sharp breath as she took him into her mouth.

They drove home separately, just as they'd come, as if they hadn't been together. Because Eli hadn't said anything about meeting up later, Cora assumed their ride—and what had occurred on it—was the end of their time with each other for today. She spent the next couple of hours getting ready for her classes tomorrow while trying to build up her resistance to him—so she wouldn't melt so quickly when he called or texted her the next time—only to have him surprise her by showing up at her door as she was getting ready for bed.

He didn't explain why he'd come; he didn't need to. He stepped inside as if he had every right and pulled her into his arms. Then it was like the ride earlier, when they couldn't pull each other's clothes off fast enough. She managed to remove his shirt and toss it aside before he kissed her again. Then he lifted her into his arms and she wrapped her legs around his narrow hips and let him carry her into the bedroom, where they fell onto her bed and made love.

On some level, Cora knew their affair was getting out of hand. They couldn't seem to stem the desire they felt for each other—the more he touched her, the more she craved his touch, and he seemed to be every bit as caught in the same web.

What happened to getting satisfied and moving on? she asked herself when it was all over and he was dozing beside her. That had been the original plan, but the opposite seemed to be taking place. Just watching him sleep made her feel so much tenderness it frightened her. She was losing her heart to a man who'd told her he wasn't to be trusted with it.

What am I going to do?

She reached over to push the hair off his forehead, and he opened his eyes. Since it was nearly eleven, she thought he'd get up and leave. They both had to work in the morning. Instead, he drew her into the curve of his body and, after a kiss on her bare shoulder, drifted off again.

Apparently, he didn't feel any pressure to get home at a reasonable hour. Or he was enjoying being with her too much to put an end to it. She preferred to believe the latter, but feared she was building things up in her head—a dangerous practice in its own right.

She wondered where he'd parked his truck, and guessed that he'd left it at home and walked over. He wasn't stupid, wouldn't be that obvious.

Slowly, she allowed herself to succumb to the comfort and satisfaction of having him there next to her. She was going to be hurt; she had little doubt about that. But it wasn't going to be tonight. She'd merely take their relationship moment by moment, she decided—and the next thing she knew, her alarm was going off the following morning, and Eli was still in her bed.

Since he hadn't reacted to the alarm, she reached over to touch his shoulder. He needed to get out of the house before everyone on campus was up and moving around. But before she could even touch him, someone knocked on the front door.

That brought his head up immediately. "Doug?" he said without preamble.

She bit her lip. "It's only seven. I can't imagine he'd pop over so early."

He scrubbed a hand over his face. "Maybe he has more vegetables."

"He hasn't brought any since the last time. He's been much better about leaving me alone," she said as she got up and hurried to don a robe. She had to answer the door. Whoever it was would know she was home. Her car was in the drive. "Your mother must've spoken to him even though she told me she wouldn't."

"*She* didn't speak to him—*I* did," he said.

She paused to gawk at him. "What did you say?"

"Nothing. I just told him to keep his distance."

She laughed. Of course it would be that simple for him. No glossing over anything, no mincing words. Just the bottom line: *stop*.

"What's so funny?" he asked.

"Nothing." She pulled the belt of her robe tight. "My hair's not *too* crazy, is it?"

He grinned.

"That must be a no."

Whoever was at the door knocked again, causing her to glance toward the living room.

"You look like you've had a busy night," he said, that grin slanting to one side, "but I wouldn't want to make you self-conscious."

"Thanks for doing just that," she whispered in mock outrage but couldn't help betraying herself with a smile of her own. Maybe he wasn't capable of trusting her enough to give her his heart, but he was incredibly good in bed, especially now that they were becoming more comfortable with each other. She also liked these little moments when he revealed that he *did* have a playful side.

"It's a great look on you," he said.

She didn't take the time to answer. "Stay here. And don't make any noise," she said as she left the bedroom.

Once she reached the door, she tried to smooth her hair down one final time as she peered through the peep hole.

It wasn't Doug; it was Aiyana. Cora wanted to alert Eli to the fact that his mother was standing on the stoop, but she'd delayed too long already and couldn't call back for fear Aiyana would hear her through the panel.

Cora could only hope she hadn't come here looking for her son... "Hi," she said as she opened the door.

Aiyana's lips curved into a pleasant smile. "I'm sorry to bother you so early."

"It's no trouble," she said but couldn't help wondering why this couldn't have waited until she was in her classroom. "I was rolling out of bed, anyway."

"I figured you'd be up, what with school starting in little over an hour. There's a guy who looks like he's had a pretty rough night at the administration building, asking for you. I tried to reach you on your cell but couldn't get an answer. Apparently, he's been trying to reach you, too."

She hadn't taken her cell out of her purse last night to charge it. "The battery must be dead. Did this man say who he is?"

"He said you broke up with him when you left LA."

Matt? *Damn*... "I—I'll... Sorry about the random visit. Let me get showered and I'll be right over."

"Would you rather I send him here?"

It was going to be hard enough for Eli to get out of her house without being seen. "No. Um...have him wait there. I'll come as soon as I can."

"Okay." Her gaze shifted to something behind Cora. "Tell my son I said good morning," she added and left.

Cora pivoted to discover Elijah's shirt on the floor. Shoot! Now there would be no pretending that she and Eli were only friends.

Eli came to the doorway, wearing nothing. "What'd she say?"

Cora picked up his shirt and handed it to him. "She said to tell you hello."

To Cora's surprise, he didn't seem to be upset by that. He scratched his head and said, "I mean before that."

"My ex-boyfriend is at the office." Looking like he'd been up all night. *Why?* Cora hadn't spoken to him since moving to Silver Springs.

"What does he want?"

"I have no idea," she replied but realized her phone might provide the answer. She plugged it in and waited for it to charge while Eli dressed. She was just listening to the many messages Matt had left when Eli walked out of the bedroom again.

"You're not coming back to me? I thought we loved each other. But you must never have cared for me the way I cared for you."

Instead of heading to the door, Eli walked over to the counter and listened to Matt's next message along with her.

"You're not going to answer your phone? Seriously? I can hardly breathe now that you're gone. Whatever I did wrong, I'll fix it, okay? I'll change. Just…give me another chance."

Cora clicked away from her voice mail. She figured Eli had heard enough.

"He wants you back," he said.

"Apparently."

He raked his fingers through his hair. "How do *you* feel?"

"I feel bad that I've hurt him."

She knew that wasn't the answer Eli had been looking for, but she didn't care to address anything else. She had to shower, hurry over to see what she could do for Matt and get to class—all before eight thirty.

"You're upset he's here."

"I'm upset that your mother knows about us."

"Because…"

Because Aiyana was her birth mother, and now, if she ever decided to have that conversation, it would be even harder. She was ruining any hope she had of re-uniting with Aiyana as the daughter she was! But she hadn't planned on Aiyana having an adopted son she couldn't resist. "I respect her. I don't want her to think poorly of me."

"She doesn't think poorly of you. She likes you."

For some reason, that simple statement nearly made

Cora burst into tears. He'd spoken so casually, as if he was saying, "Why would you matter much to her either way?"

Aiyana was her *mother*. She wanted more than the courteous treatment other teachers received.

When she started to blink fast, trying to hold back the tears, he walked over and rested his hands on her shoulders. "I'm sorry I stayed over. If you'll still see me in the future, I'll be more careful."

"I'm not blaming you. This has nothing to do with you." She could've asked him to go at any moment, but she hadn't—because she'd wanted him to stay right where he was. Her emotional reaction to Aiyana's appearance was about something else, something he couldn't even begin to guess because he, most likely, didn't know his mother had ever had a child of her own.

"Then it's your ex that has you upset."

She dashed a hand across her cheek. "Matt? No. It's nothing."

She could tell he wasn't sure what to say next. "I'm fine," she added.

"I'm sorry," he said again, as if he hated to see her like this, especially because he suspected he might be part of the cause.

"It's nothing, like I said."

"Okay." He had to get to school, too, and she knew it. Although he acted reluctant to walk away at this juncture, he seemed to understand there was nothing more he could do. After pressing a kiss to her forehead, he left.

Chapter 13

The day seemed to last forever. Knowing that Matt was sleeping at her house, waiting for her to get out of school, made Cora glance at the clock—and grind her teeth—over and over. Time seemed to be standing still. She didn't want her ex-boyfriend in Silver Springs, couldn't believe he'd come down here.

As soon as the lunch bell sounded and the students filed out of her classroom, she considered going home. She had thirty minutes or so she could use to talk to Matt. But she preferred to wait until she could sit down with him at length and hash out whatever he felt he needed to go over. Then maybe she could send him on his way knowing that was the end, once and for all.

While she was standing at the window, watching the

students who'd already finished their lunch mill about campus, Eli walked in.

"Hey."

She turned and straightened. He'd never come to her room before. "Hi."

"I didn't see you in the cafeteria so... I thought I'd bring you some lunch." He lifted a brown sack.

She'd eaten an apple from her desk drawer. She hadn't had it in her to face him or Aiyana, in case either one of them happened to be in the cafeteria. "I've had too much to do here."

The fact that she'd been staring outside, doing nothing, contradicted that statement, but he didn't point it out. He carried her lunch over to the desk. "You feeling okay?"

"Yeah."

"What happened with Matt?"

"Nothing. Yet. I had to get to my first class, and he looked like he wasn't feeling great, so I told him to sleep until I get out of school."

He rubbed a hand over his smooth-shaven chin. "You'll talk to him when you get home."

"Yes." She peered into the sack to find a turkey sandwich, some celery and carrot sticks and a big chocolate chip cookie. "This is very nice of you. Thank you."

"No problem."

He didn't seem to be in any hurry to leave.

"Did your mother say anything to you about this morning?" she asked as she broke off part of the cookie.

"We've been too busy."

"*Will* she say something?"

"I doubt it. For the most part, she's pretty good about minding her own business."

Cora wondered about his biological mother. Did he ever hear from her? Did he care about her—*could* he care? "Aiyana seems really great."

"She is." He checked his watch. "I've got to go."

"Thanks for stopping by."

He hesitated at the door. "Will you call me when Matt's gone?"

"I don't know," she admitted.

"Nothing's changed, Cora," he said.

What was he talking about? *Everything* had changed. She was falling in love with him, which was exactly what he'd warned her not to do. And Matt knew about Aiyana! If she didn't handle him carefully enough, he could tell everyone what she was *really* doing in Silver Springs. "There have to be other girls you can…be with. You might have to drive to LA once in a while, but someone like you…you'd have no problem getting laid."

He winced as if she'd slapped him. "I never said the person I was with didn't matter—that it could be anyone. And I hope I haven't treated you that way."

He hadn't. He'd been a dream lover—as considerate and kind as she could ever expect him to be. He'd also been clear about his limitations. Despite all her big talk, *she* was the one who couldn't seem to live up to their agreement.

She opened her mouth to apologize, but it was too late. He was gone.

Cora's stomach was twisted into knots by the time school let out and she was able to hurry home. Part of her wished Matt would simply be gone—that once he'd sobered up he'd been embarrassed and eager to get out of Silver Springs. She'd said everything she wanted to say to him when they broke up. And, because of him, she felt as if she'd somehow hurt, frustrated or disappointed Eli.

But Matt wasn't gone. He called out to her from the bedroom the moment he heard her come through the door.

Since she had such a small place, and only one bed, he was in it. After having shared that same bed with Eli only the night before, seeing Matt there felt so strange. But she hadn't invited Matt to New Horizons. She was merely being kind—and cautious—by giving him a place to rest until they could discuss whatever he'd come here to discuss.

"How was school?" He propped himself up with her pillows as she walked into the room and put her purse on the dresser.

That he was just rousing indicated he'd slept since she'd been gone, which answered *that* question. She hadn't missed an opportunity to get rid of him. "Today? Tedious."

"You don't like teaching here?"

She sat on the edge of the bed. "Normally, I do. But I was on pins and needles knowing you were waiting for me. What's going on?"

"What do you mean?"

"Why did you drive down here? Show up unexpectedly—and at least partially intoxicated? You could've killed yourself or someone else, driving that way."

"I wasn't drunk!"

She suspected he'd started out that way. He was lucky he hadn't had an accident, and that he hadn't been picked up. "You were disheveled and smelling of alcohol."

"Because my mother was just diagnosed with Alzheimer's, Cora. If you'd been staying in touch at all, you'd know that."

Cora clasped her hands together. "I'm sorry. I know that you were afraid…that you suspected something was wrong, but…"

"One day last week, she forgot we broke up. Asked when you were going to come see her."

"I'm sorry," she said again. She felt terrible about what was happening to Matt's mother. Sara was a lovely woman, certainly didn't deserve something like this. But there was nothing Cora could do about his mother's condition, wasn't sure what he expected. "I'll stop by to see her next time I'm in town."

"Next time you're in town," he echoed. "You say that as if you don't really care about her."

"Of course I care. I've always liked your mother."

"Well, she *loved* you. She thought you'd become her daughter-in-law, would've offered you all the love you feel as if you've had to live without, being adopted."

"It's not that I feel as if I haven't been loved, Matt. You don't understand at all, if that's what you think. I appreciate my parents—"

"Then why are you here instead of in LA with us?" he broke in. "Can't you tell how much I'm struggling without you? You haven't called me, haven't texted me. You haven't responded to anything I've posted on social media."

She hadn't viewed his social media, had quit doing that sort of thing even before she started seeing Eli.

"I thought you'd be back once you realized we had a good thing," he went on. "There's nothing better out there, you know."

In ways, what she had with Eli was better. They didn't have a label for what they were to each other, had no commitment, but she'd never felt so love drunk in her life than when she saw him or felt his hands on her body. "I've been moving, starting a new job. That takes focus," she responded lamely.

"It can't take up every minute. You don't even know anyone down here. Aren't you lonely?"

"I've made a few friends."

"So you've kissed all your old friends goodbye."

She got up. "Not at all. I'm staying in touch. But we weren't *friends*, Matt. We were more than friends, and now we're broken up. Why would I confuse you or… or give you any reason to hope by remaining in contact? Maybe later, in a few years, when we've both had a chance to move on, we can reconnect. But it's too soon right now."

He shoved himself into a sitting position. "What are you saying?"

She threw up her hands. "What I told you before. I'm really sorry, especially about your mother. I don't want her to suffer. I don't want you to suffer, either. But I can't reciprocate what you're feeling. I don't know a nicer way of putting it, except to be honest. You're a wonderful guy, and I'll always care about you, but—"

"Who's going to treat you better?" he interrupted, his eyes snapping with challenge.

"No one! I have no complaints about the way you treated me. I said you were a great guy—"

"But you think your birth mother is somehow going to make your life better."

"Meeting Aiyana has already answered so many of my questions," she said. "The curiosity I felt was half the problem."

When he got out of bed, she was relieved to see that he was still wearing all his clothes. "So you're glad you did it."

That would depend on what happened from here. She had to admit that things weren't looking good, not with a one-sided relationship developing between her and Eli and Aiyana showing up to find his shirt on her floor. But she couldn't say she regretted coming to Silver Springs, because she didn't. She was glad she'd met Aiyana, glad she knew where she came from and what her birth mother was like. She was also glad she'd met Eli. Otherwise, she might never have experienced the kind of passion he could evoke. Everyone deserved to encounter that magical feeling at least once in a lifetime. The fact that she hadn't been more passionate about Matt only confirmed that she'd been right to break things off with him. "I did what I needed to do."

"That doesn't answer the question."

"Then, yes, I'm glad."

His face fell. "You don't care about me anymore."

Not in the way he wanted her to. Hadn't she said that—many times? "I'd like to be friends—when you're ready," she reiterated.

Dropping his head, he rubbed his temples. "You're making a mistake, Cora. We are meant to be together."

She let her breath go in a sigh. "I can't change how I feel."

He folded his arms as he studied her. "Fine. Then… can I just ask for one last favor?"

"Of course."

"Let me stay here a few days? I need some time away from LA—to get my head around this and come to terms with my mother's diagnosis."

"I don't see how that will help."

"I'm telling you I can't go back. Not yet. You say you care about me. Let me hang out for a while, talk things through."

She didn't want him to stay. As far as she was concerned, he couldn't hit the highway fast enough. But she did feel terrible about his mother's diagnosis. And she thought having Matt around might finally stop her from seeing Eli. So there was that, too. If Matt got his way, at least in that regard, maybe he'd believe she really *did* wish him well and would leave peaceably, without saying anything that would give her away to Aiyana or anyone else.

"I have only this one bed," she said. "You'll have to sleep on the couch. You realize that. I won't get physical with you. There's not even a remote chance."

"Fine. I understand. I'm happy just to be able to spend some time with you to sort of…grow accustomed to our new roles. I mean…if you're sincere about being friends."

"Of course I'm sincere!"

"What happened before was too abrupt."

"I got that. You can stay until Friday," she said. "But I doubt you'll really care to hang out that long. I'll be at work most of the time, and you'll be sitting around here alone, bored stiff."

"At least we can spend our evenings together. Let me stay until Saturday, though, okay? My aunt's in town to visit my mom, and I don't really want to see her. You know we butt heads. Being out of town gives me a good excuse to avoid another argument with the old curmudgeon."

"So long as it's Saturday *morning*," she said. And she hoped it would be early, before the day could really begin, so she'd have the rest of the weekend to herself. She was already looking forward to that.

"Okay," he said.

She forced herself to return his smile. She supposed, after two years together, she could give him that much. What was three or four days?

"What's wrong?"

Eli blinked and then focused on his brother Gavin. They were sitting at the bar on Friday, listening to the music and watching the people who were dancing—had gone out at his request because he'd needed the distraction. The football team had a bye this week, so he didn't even have that to think about this weekend. "Nothing, why?"

"You're not the same tonight."

He took a sip of his beer. "I don't know what you're talking about."

"You're preoccupied, quiet."

Because he couldn't help remembering what'd happened here the last time. "I'm tired."

The waitress stopped to gather Gavin's empty bottle and to see if she could get him another beer. "No, thanks," he told her. "So how's Cora?" he asked as she walked off. "Everything going okay with her?"

It wasn't going at all. Eli hadn't heard from her since he delivered her lunch on Tuesday. He'd looked for her in the cafeteria and on campus since, but if he happened to find her and catch her eye, she'd look away and leave the area soon after.

He kept telling himself he didn't care. That she'd decided to quit seeing him, which saved him from having to break things off later. Every romantic relationship he had came down to that eventually...

But this was different. She'd quit on him long before he was ready to let her go. The thought of her in that small house with her ex-boyfriend made him sick inside. He kept going over and over their time together, remembering the way she'd smile when he came toward her, the way she'd laugh if he said something funny, the way she made love without coming off so needy that she wound up making him feel cornered and desperate to get away.

And then he'd wonder what more he could've done to make her want to continue seeing him. "I guess. She's been busy."

"Meaning...what? You haven't seen her?"

He gripped his bottle that much tighter as a vision of her pressed up against the back of this very building filled his head. "Not recently."

"But you guys were so hot for each other when we were here last. I had to dance with Darci half a dozen songs in a row to keep her occupied."

Eli mustered a faint smile for Gavin's sacrifice, hoping that would finally put an end to the conversation. But Gavin went right back after it.

"Does that mean it's over?"

"Do we *have* to talk about this?" he finally snapped.

"Whoa! Okay. I see how it is."

Irritated that Gavin would even bring her up, Eli threw a few bucks on the table and stood. "Let's go. I should never have suggested we come here."

"God, you've been a bear the past couple of days," Gavin complained. "I've never seen you in such a sour mood. I'm not trying to piss you off, big brother—I'm just trying to figure out what's wrong. So cut me some slack!"

"Nothing's wrong. I don't know how many times I have to say…" The door opened, and he let his words trail away as Cora walked in with a tall, thin guy who had long, curly brown hair, a goatee and glasses. He would've finished his statement, but he could no longer remember what he'd been about to say.

This was Matt. Eli had known he was still in town. He'd walked over to Cora's a time or two and spotted the additional car in her drive.

Gavin followed his gaze. "Shit. She's with someone else now? *Who is that guy?*"

Eli couldn't make himself look away. "Her ex-boyfriend's in town."

"They're back together?"

He didn't know what the situation was. She hadn't told him, and he hadn't approached her to ask. He'd been trying to give her the space she seemed to want, had been hoping that by not pressuring her, she'd miss him the way he was missing her and come around again. "I guess."

"Ah! Finally, it all makes sense!"

"What makes sense?" Eli growled.

"You really liked her."

He said nothing.

"I've never known a woman to get under your skin before, but she's managed to do that, hasn't she?"

"You don't know anything," he grumbled.

Cora couldn't have seen his truck outside, because Gavin drove. Eli was waiting for her to realize he was there—and watched her nearly trip over her own feet the moment her eyes landed on him. She hesitated for a moment. Then she said something to Matt and they changed direction, walking around the perimeter of the bar to the other side.

"You okay?" Gavin asked while Cora and Matt found a table.

"Yeah. Sure." Eli tossed back what was left in his bottle. "Let's get out of here," he said, but he received a text while Gavin drove them home that only made his night worse.

"That her?" Gavin asked when Eli pulled out his phone to look at it. "Cora, I mean?"

Eli felt his stomach knot as he stared at the message. "No." He wished it was Cora. Maybe he wouldn't feel quite so terrible if she'd asked him to come back to the bar, or requested a few moments to talk.

Gavin gave him a funny look. "So…is it Mom?"

Not the mother Gavin meant and not the mother Eli claimed. But that was the name by which she called herself. "It's nobody," he said. Nobody to *him*, anyway.

Determined to ignore this message like those that had come before, he slid his phone back into his pocket.

Chapter 14

"Who was that guy?" Matt asked as Eli and Gavin headed for the door.

Cora's cheeks ached from clenching her jaw. She preferred to ignore that question, but she had to say *something*. The way Eli had stared them down as they came in had made an impression on Matt. She should never have brought him here. She wouldn't have, if she'd had any clue that Elijah would be here, too. She'd just been looking for some way to entertain him, to help the time pass until he left tomorrow.

"Cora?" Matt pressed when she didn't answer.

"My boss," she replied.

"He didn't look happy."

For good reason. Eli had to be wondering if she'd taken her ex-boyfriend back. She planned to talk to him; she just couldn't do it while Matt was in town. She wanted to make sure their paths never crossed.

"What do you think's wrong with him?" he asked.

"He's under a lot of pressure," she replied.

"But if you work for him, why didn't he say hello?"

"I doubt he even saw us."

"*What?* He was staring at us the whole time we were trying to find a table."

Desperate to escape this conversation, Cora came to her feet. "I like this song. Let's dance."

They danced a lot, and Matt drank a lot, which distracted him enough that he didn't ask anything else about Eli. He seemed to be having fun, but Cora was just biding her time, couldn't wait for this interminable night to end. She kept him at the bar until she thought everyone at the ranch would be settled in for the night. Then she drove him back to her place.

"What time will you be heading out in the morning?" she asked as she turned off the highway onto the narrow road that led, after another two miles, to the school.

"*Tomorrow?*" He acted as if this was the first he'd heard of his going.

She gripped the steering wheel that much tighter as they rolled under the high arch at the front entrance. "Yeah. I said I'd let you stay until Saturday morning."

"But you've had to work the whole time. Why don't I leave on Sunday? That way, we can do something fun tomorrow."

"Matt, you said you needed some time to pull yourself together, and I've given you that. I've even let you stay long enough to avoid your difficult aunt."

"And I appreciate it. But what's the rush?" he asked. "We've been having a great time, haven't we?"

No. She couldn't take another day. "I'm done," she blurted.

"What does that mean?"

"I'm ready for you to go home."

She was afraid this would provoke a fight, but she'd run out of patience. He thought *he* was having a difficult time; well, she was having a hard time, too. She'd felt nauseous ever since she'd seen the look on Eli's face at the bar.

Matt opened his mouth to reply but she let out an involuntary gasp that silenced him.

Eli's truck was parked in front of her house.

Eli couldn't believe he was doing this. He'd never felt the need to chase after a woman, but Cora was driving him crazy.

Matt got out of the car when she did and came around by the trunk. Eli noticed his surprised expression but refused to let the fact that Matt was there get in the way. He strode over to Cora. "Can we talk?"

He'd taken her off guard; he could tell. She paused for several seconds as if searching for the best way to respond before she said, "Um...tomorrow, okay? Tomorrow would be better for me."

She didn't understand that he was desperate or he wouldn't be here. "I don't want to wait." He needed her, needed...something with the power to divert his thoughts and ease the rage burning like acid inside him. His biological mother had been texting and calling him relentlessly since he'd left the bar, saying she was in a bad way and needed his help. But she was a psychopath and a drug addict, so she was always in a bad way. He wasn't going to let her back into his life. He wasn't the person to call even if she had straightened up, not after all the cruelty he'd suffered at her hands.

He'd finally left his phone at his place and gone out for a drive, traveled aimlessly around the valley for two hours before making the decision to allow himself to go to Cora's. He had to resolve at least *one* thing that was bothering him. Otherwise, it felt like his head would explode. Although his birth mother had contacted him once or twice before, she'd never been quite so insistent.

You know it was that damn Tim I married who treated you so bad. Wasn't me. I wasn't involved in any of that.

She'd had the nerve to send such a text—a blatant lie—as if he hadn't been fully aware of exactly what happened, and who was responsible. They'd been in it together, one feeding off the other. But it wasn't just that. He wasn't himself, wasn't in control, not since seeing Cora at the bar.

"This isn't… I mean, you're her boss," Matt said. "This isn't personal, right?"

Eli ignored him. He was wound up, on edge, afraid he'd bash him in the face if he so much as acknowledged his presence. His birth mother triggered too many painful memories, a surfeit of emotion. Eli felt like there was a monster growing inside him that was about to bust out at any moment.

Fortunately, since Aiyana had taken him in and he'd worked through most of his issues—the ones he *could* resolve—he hadn't allowed his frustration to erupt, hadn't let it get the better of him.

But it'd been a long time since he'd been this raw.

"I asked you a question," Matt said.

Eli leveled a glare at him. "If you know what's good for you, you'll go inside."

Eyes wide, Matt stumbled back as if he'd just caught a glimpse of the rage lurking inside Eli, but before he could do anything else, Cora grabbed his arm and pulled him toward the house. "Give us a few minutes. Will you? Please?"

Unwilling to make it that easy, Matt looked from her to Eli and back again. "Don't tell me... You guys are seeing each other, aren't you!" He glared at her as if she'd cheated on him. "There's no way you'd start dating Aiyana's son! Not without—"

"Matt, if you say another word I'll never forgive you!" she broke in.

Without what? Eli had no clue and didn't get the chance to ask before she shoved her ex toward the house with more force. "Matt, please. If you value our friendship *at all*, you'll go inside this minute."

He cursed but accepted the keys she tossed him and finally did as she asked.

Once he was gone, a profound silence fell.

Suddenly, Eli was no longer sure what he'd hoped to achieve. His eyes were beginning to burn as badly as his gut, and a lump the size of a baseball rose in his throat, making it impossible for him to speak normally.

What the heck was he doing? He'd been a fool to come here. He was only making matters worse.

Without another word, he turned on his heel and

opened his truck door. He intended to get in and drive off before she could realize how close he was to breaking down, but she grabbed hold of him.

"What is it, Eli?" She looked concerned as she dragged him around to face her, but that only made it harder for him to maintain his composure. He jerked away, didn't want her to see him like this. But she refused to let him go. She caught hold of him again, this time with a stronger grasp.

"*Talk* to me!"

"It's okay. I'm sorry. I shouldn't have come here." He managed to mutter that much without having his voice crack—thank God—but she didn't act like she heard him. She stared into his face, trying to read what he was feeling. Then she wrapped her arms around his waist and pressed her cheek against his chest. "What is it?" she asked, clinging tightly. "Tell me."

He lifted his hands to her shoulders. He intended to push her away, couldn't believe he'd allowed himself to need her. He should've gone home like he was about to do now. He couldn't rely on her, on anyone, no matter how tempting it was to believe otherwise. But she wouldn't let go—and the next thing he knew his arms slid around her, securing her against him instead of breaking off the embrace.

"It's okay," she said.

He knew she could probably feel how badly he was shaking, but there was nothing he could do about that now. "Where've you been?" he asked.

Her hands slipped up the back of his shirt, and he felt her press her palms against his bare skin—a move he found both satisfying and intimate. She wasn't merely offering him a light "you'll be okay" pat. She was making it clear that she cared about him and wouldn't let him down. "It doesn't matter. I'm here now."

Burying his face in her hair, he gripped her that much tighter, and they stood like that until he could overcome all the terrible feelings that had him so twisted up inside. "Come home with me," he said at length, his mouth at her ear.

When she hesitated, he feared she'd refuse. She had Matt in the house, after all. He was asking a lot for her to leave her guest, but he needed to hear her say yes, needed to know that *he* came before Matt.

And, in the end, she murmured, "Okay."

Cora promised herself she'd tell Eli. Tonight. She had to. She didn't see how she could continue sleeping in his bed without divulging her connection to Aiyana. But, despite what he'd indicated at her place, Eli wasn't interested in having a discussion. That she'd go home with him was all that seemed important at the moment.

On the drive over, when she asked him what was wrong, he said he didn't want to talk about it. So she let the conversation lapse, but the ensuing silence wasn't awkward or upsetting. It was more like everything that'd been so wrong was now right, just because they were together.

The moment they reached his house, he tugged her inside and, without so much as turning on the light, began to let her know how badly he'd missed her. He wasn't *un*willing to communicate, she realized. He just preferred to speak to her in a different way, one in which he felt more capable of expressing himself.

She did get four words out of him—"I'm glad you're back." But that was all, and she wasn't willing to push. Something significant was going on between them that he didn't seem capable of putting into words, and she didn't need him to. She could feel the difference in the way he touched her.

His thick eyelashes rested on his cheeks as he ran his tongue across her lips. "*You're* what I need," he said, surprising her by speaking again.

What'd happened tonight? He'd been so upset at her house he'd been trembling when she slid her arms around his waist. Just the memory of it made her defensive of him. She knew simply seeing her with Matt wasn't enough to cause a reaction like that. So what was it?

Regardless, she could feel that he was doing much better. His fingers curled and locked through hers as he bent his head to kiss her.

"You can kiss like no one else," she told him, relaxing as the desire he so easily evoked began to rise inside her once again.

"It's not difficult to kiss good when the person you're kissing tastes like honey," he told her and pulled back to look at her, seemingly content just to have her back in his house.

Cora might've been embarrassed to be the subject of such close scrutiny. She couldn't hide how deeply he affected her, so there was a certain vulnerability that came with holding his gaze. The fact that she did hold it, however—that she let him see she wasn't unaffected—appeared to be what he was looking for. His lips curved into a rather boyish smile and he kissed her again, even more softly, before leading her into his bedroom.

"Will you undress for me?" he asked as he sat on the bed.

Cora was tempted to derail that request by closing the gap between them. There'd be so much less risk in what they were doing if she could accelerate their love-making to the point that neither one of them was thinking clearly. Doing it with such *intention*—it almost felt like this was the first time they'd ever been together.

In a way it was, she realized. He was taking her more seriously, investing more time, effort and emotion. But…dared she take this step? *Before* telling him who she was?

"Relax. It's just me." He wanted her to trust him, to act confidently, but by not telling him who she was, she was sort of lying to him…

Although she hesitated, in the end she couldn't bring herself to ruin this moment. She'd slept with Matt for two years and never experienced what it was like to make love in such a cerebral fashion, one in which her heart and mind were as active and involved as her body. Now she understood how many times she'd merely gone through the motions, either for her own physical release or simply to be a good partner and satisfy Matt.

Eli was much deeper than the women he'd been with had given him credit for, she decided. He had a tender heart; he merely protected it well. That he would reveal his sensitive side was making her fall that much harder.

Slowly, she removed her clothes.

"Gorgeous," he said, his expression rapt. "It's been *such* a long week."

His nostrils flared as she stepped closer. "At least it's going to end well," she said and guided his head to her breast, stroking his cheek as he suckled her.

His hands slid to her waist, then moved over her hips and around to the back, at which point he lifted her easily onto the bed before removing his own clothes.

"Do we need a condom?" he asked.

She'd been on the pill for a week. "According to what I've read online, we should be safe."

His teeth flashed in another smile. "I get to come inside you," he said and, when they both reached that pinnacle, Cora couldn't help but acknowledge that she'd never enjoyed making love to anyone more.

After an experience like that she wasn't willing to have the talk they needed to have about Aiyana. That would ruin everything, destroy the memory. So she promised herself she'd tell him in the morning and faded off to sleep, her arms and legs entwined with his.

Chapter 15

"What are you going to do about Matt?"

Cora pulled herself out of the last vestiges of sleep so that she could answer Eli's question. He'd begun to stir several minutes ago, but she'd been reluctant to reach full consciousness, knew she'd have to face all that awaited her when she did. "I hope he got up and left," she mumbled. "He was supposed to leave this morning."

"What's he been doing here?"

She heard the caution in Eli's tone, could tell he was prepared for an answer he didn't like. "Sleeping on the couch."

"You didn't get back together with him."

"No."

He seemed so relieved when he reached for her that she smoothed her hand over his bare chest in a comforting fashion as she rested her head on his shoulder.

"What did he want, then?" he asked.

"He wanted to reconcile, but I wasn't interested."

"So why didn't he leave?"

"He asked if he could stay—to show me what I was missing, I suppose."

Eli lifted his head. "And you let him?"

"It's complicated."

"I can't imagine it would be that complicated to me."

Because he didn't know everything. She'd let Matt stay mostly to appease him. She'd been trying to end their relationship in such a way that he wouldn't cause trouble. With what he and his mother were going through, she'd also wanted to be supportive and prove she was sincere about maintaining a friendship. "We were together for two years. He said he was having a hard time getting over me, so I figured I owed him a few days to come to terms with our new relationship."

"Wouldn't being around you only make getting over the breakup harder?"

"I told him that. He argued that he needed to get used to our new status, and I thought it might give him the closure he seemed to be missing if I didn't rush him out the door."

"He didn't know about me."

That had been apparent in Matt's reaction last night. "Of course not. I haven't told anyone."

He dropped his head back. "Even your family at home?"

She understood what that would likely indicate to him—that she wasn't taking the relationship seriously. But she wasn't supposed to be taking the relationship seriously. "No. Why would I? You told me not to expect anything."

"You've certainly taken that to heart," he said wryly.

"I don't want to get hurt any more than you do."

"And now?"

"Has that changed?"

His fingers slipped through her hair. "You can't tell?"

She could tell last night. But there were still a lot of blanks to be filled in. She leaned up on her elbow to be able to see into his face. "What is it you want from me, Eli?" she asked. "Specifically."

He thought for a moment. Then he said, "I want to be with you while you're here."

"And what would that entail? A night together every once in a while?"

"I'm asking for a little more than that."

"But more equals…what? Would we quit trying to hide the fact that we're seeing each other?"

He sat up against the headboard. "Why not? That hasn't been the best-kept secret in the first place."

She pulled the sheet with her as she came into a sitting position, too. "What about dating other people?"

"We won't date other people." He spoke quickly enough to suggest he knew his mind on that matter without even having to think.

"We'd be exclusive."

"Yes, and we'll see each other a lot. Okay?" He lifted a hand to run a thumb down her jawline. "This past week just about killed me."

She assumed he was joking, so she chuckled, but he didn't laugh with her. He seemed serious. "You mean that," she said, sobering.

"I hated every minute of it."

"So…we'll be exclusive and see each other a lot—and then?"

"We'll deal with that when the time comes."

"No promises."

His eyebrows came together. "I told you I'm not good at this. I'm hoping I'll get better at it. But, either way, it's too early to try and decide what might come later."

He had a point. But she had a secret. Now that they had an understanding of sorts, would she be a fool to divulge that? What if she shared the circumstances surrounding her birth and he insisted she tell Aiyana? The deception could make Aiyana angry. Or there could be some reason Aiyana wouldn't or couldn't be around her. In that case, she'd lose her job, which wouldn't be the best thing for her or the school, not midyear. She liked it here, liked being with Elijah.

So, once again, she ignored her better judgment—put what she felt now above what she'd probably be feeling at the end of the school year—and decided to wait.

Fortunately, that was made easy when Eli's phone began to buzz, drawing their attention. He was getting a call or text. When he reached over to grab it, she thought he'd answer. But after checking the display, he cursed and tossed the phone back on the nightstand as if it had burned his hand.

"Who is it?" she asked.

Closing his eyes, he leaned his head against the wall again.

"Eli?" Whoever it was, he didn't like them—or wasn't happy they were trying to reach him. "It's not Aiyana…"

"No."

Of course not. Cora couldn't imagine he'd be unhappy to hear from one of his brothers, either. So… maybe it was an old girlfriend.

When she said nothing more, he opened his eyes and looked at her.

"What?" she said.

Instead of answering, he reclaimed his phone and showed her the text he'd received—How can you be so selfish? I only need $50.

She noted the name associated with that text. "*Maleficent's* texting you?"

"Jo Seifert. My mother."

"Maleficent's a Disney character, right? From *Sleeping Beauty*?"

"An evil character. Maleficent means doing harm."

His mother. She was tempted to touch the scar on his chin—she still didn't know how he'd gotten it—but refrained. "Seems fitting."

That he would change his mind and share this with her suggested he was making an effort to be more open, to have some semblance of a real relationship, despite what he'd termed his "limitations." She would've smiled at that but she didn't want him to think she was smiling at the fact that he was upset.

She leaned forward to peck him on the lips. "Are you going to give her the money?"

"Hell, no."

"I don't blame you." She started to get up, but he caught her arm.

"That's it?"

"What do you mean?"

"You're not going to ask me a million questions about Jo?"

God knew she wanted to. She was *so* curious about his biological family and background. But she figured he'd talk about his past when he was ready. She wouldn't try to force him to share things that were painful for him. "No."

"Because…"

"I already know the most salient points."

The old guarded expression claimed his face. "You're aware of what happened to me?"

She wished she could erase all the pain he'd suffered. She hated the people who'd hurt him, even though she'd never even met them. "I did an internet search."

"On *me*?"

"I was attracted to you from the beginning."

"My childhood is *on the internet*?" he asked with a scowl, obviously too fixated on that to react to anything else.

"You've never Googled yourself?"

"Why would I?"

"Some people do, just to see what comes up."

"I guess I've never been interested in seeing what's out there. Everyone around here knows me, so it didn't seem important until now. What'd you find?"

"An old article from when Aiyana first opened this place. They cited you and your…um…background as an example of the type of boy she hoped to help."

"Oh. Right." He relaxed a bit. "I have seen that article, now that you mention it. Although it's been a while."

"She probably needed the publicity to stay afloat."

"She tried to keep me out of it, but…there's no controlling what some reporters dig up."

"It made for a sympathetic story—a heartbreaking story—so it had to have helped with donations."

"I wouldn't know. I was just a freshman then. But… what you read about me, it didn't raise more questions?"

"It did," she admitted, "but I'm not going to pressure you for details. If you want to talk about that period of your life, I'm here. If not…let it go—if you can."

His mood lightened instantly. "Hallelujah," he said. "Let's get some breakfast."

Cora smiled to think letting him avoid that conversation would bring him so much relief. "At Lolita's Country Kitchen?"

"If you like that place."

She thought it would be a nice change to go out with him, to forget about trying to hide the fact that they were romantically involved. "Sounds good to me. But… what about Matt?"

He grimaced. "Don't tell me we have to invite him. I don't like him very much."

"No, we don't have to invite him," she said, laughing. "But I should at least go over and talk to him, tell him goodbye." And see what she could do to minimize the damage she might've caused by running out on him last night…

"Do that if you have to—then call me when you're ready," he said and tugged the sheet away to get a final look at her before rolling out of bed.

Eli's phone buzzed just as he was about to turn on the shower. He assumed it would be Jo again, but the screen showed Gavin's number, so he answered. "'Lo?"

"It's me. You on for basketball with the boys this morning?"

"Not today."

"Why not? It's Saturday. What else you got going?"

"I'm about to have breakfast with Cora."

A strained silence ensued. Then his brother said, "The same Cora who was at the bar last night with her ex-boyfriend?"

"Yeah."

"You don't find that a little strange?"

He leaned against the door to the bathroom while he talked. "They're just friends, Gav."

"I thought you were going to say *you're* just friends. That's the type of thing you normally say when I ask about a woman."

"Cora's different."

His voice changed, grew more somber. "Eli, I just passed Doug Maggleby a few minutes ago—out in his yard. He said her ex has been staying with her."

"I'm well aware of that."

"In a small house with only one bedroom…"

"Stop it. She has a couch."

"I'm just being real with you, man."

Eli started the shower so the water would get hot. "They're *friends*, like I said."

"How do you know?"

"She told me."

After another brief silence, during which he seemed to be weighing whether to continue the argument, Gavin said, "Breakfast with Cora it is, then. I guess basketball can't compete."

"You could join us."

"No. One of us needs to show up at the court. The boys will be disappointed otherwise. But…can I say one more thing?"

"I have the feeling you're going to do it regardless."

"I'll take that as a yes. Besides the fact that Cora's had another man in her house for several days, are you sure you're doing the right thing, getting involved with one of the teachers here?"

"I'm not sure at all," he admitted.

"But you're doing it, anyway."

Eli remembered how he'd felt last night, right before she agreed to come home with him—and how having her say yes had changed everything. When he was with her he could more easily put his childhood into perspective, more easily remember the present and what his life was like now. "I can't help myself."

"That's freaking terrifying," he said.

Eli drew a deep breath. "Yeah, I know. I guess we'll see how it goes."

Matt was gone. Hallelujah! The dread in the pit of Cora's stomach eased considerably when she saw that his car was no longer in her drive. She still feared she'd find a nasty note waiting on her dresser, but at least she wasn't facing a confrontation.

After she let herself into the house, she held her breath as she wandered around. She was afraid he'd only stepped out to buy milk or something and planned to return. But everything that belonged to him was gone. And he hadn't left her a message or anything else to indicate that he was upset with her. While on the way home, she'd briefly considered the possibility that he might've dumped out her drawers, ransacked her personal belongings or thrown away her birth control...

Fortunately, all looked as she'd left it.

A ping signaled an incoming text message, so she reached into her purse to retrieve her phone.

Everything okay? Eli wanted to know.

Fine, she wrote back. She didn't think of her ex-boyfriend as particularly vengeful, but she did know he'd always been a little threatened by her search for her birth mother. He probably blamed the fact that she'd found Aiyana and was planning to move to Silver Springs as the reason she broke things off with him. It was easier to believe that than the truth—that she just wasn't fulfilled in the relationship.

Matt's not giving you any trouble? He's leaving?

He's already gone, she told Eli.

Great. Then I'm going to swing by the basketball court and play hoops for a while—until you're ready to go, okay?

The students were going to love seeing him. Okay. I'll walk over there when I'm done.

She set her phone to charge, since it was almost dead after going all night, and peeled off her clothes. Then she paused to stare at herself in the mirror.

"I hope you know what you're doing," she mumbled and turned on the water.

Chapter 16

Jo tried to call three times and texted twice while he was at breakfast with Cora. Eli had believed, if he ignored her long enough, she'd simply go away. Now he wasn't so sure. His birth mother seemed determined, adamant—was desperate to get some money out of him. But she had no right to come to him in the first place.

"Have you thought about changing your number?"

The question caused him to glance up. Cora had seen him check his phone numerous times but, true to her word, she hadn't asked any intrusive questions. Although this one made it clear she knew who kept interrupting their meal, it still respected his privacy regarding the details of his past and his feelings toward his biological mother.

"I have."

"And?"

He set his phone aside. "Seems pointless to go to all that trouble."

"If hearing from her upsets you…might be worth it."

"I don't believe a new number would really get rid of her, not for any length of time. She knows where I work, could do the same thing she did before."

She drank a sip of her orange juice. "Which was…"

"She called the office, got hold of Betty May, gave a false name and claimed to be interested in making a large donation to the school. She even went so far as to claim that Aiyana Turner recommended she speak to me. After hearing Aiyana's name, Betty was so eager to make sure this 'donor' got through, she suggested Jo call my cell."

"Yikes."

"Exactly." He still hadn't had the heart to tell Betty she'd screwed up. He didn't want anyone to know that his past had come back to haunt him. He'd thought he could handle it, was determined to bear that burden alone so Aiyana wouldn't have to feel any added empathy or concern. She dealt with enough of that type of thing as it was.

"Has she ever come by—tried to see you in person?" Cora asked.

"Not yet. The last time she asked for money, she wanted me to use an app to transfer it. I doubt she has transportation."

"Where does she live?"

"I haven't even asked. I'm guessing LA, but it could be anywhere. Maybe she's out of state. I'm not sure what her situation is, to be honest. But chances are it's not good. It was never good when I was a child. I have no reason to believe that's changed, since it's obvious *she* hasn't."

He had to have raised more questions than he'd answered with the information he'd conveyed so far, but Cora simply said, "I see," and went back to eating.

"It can be so confusing," he admitted, watching her.

Her chewing slowed, and she swallowed. "What part?"

"All of it, but—" he pointed to his phone "—most especially what to do about her now."

"Parent/child relationships—even bad ones, *especially* bad ones—can be complicated," she said.

His food was getting cold, so he shoveled in a bite of his bacon-and-egg omelet. "Are you speaking from experience?"

"To a point."

"Care to elaborate?" he asked, waiting before taking another bite.

"Not really. I haven't experienced anything like what you have, which is why I hesitate to offer any advice. I don't appreciate it when people tell me what I should do or how I should feel about certain things when they've never been in the same situation."

He respected her for not being too heavy-handed with her opinions and remarks. That was what made it possible for him to talk to her even though he had so much trouble talking to most other people. He didn't have to worry that she wouldn't back off if he indicated he'd had enough. "I can appreciate that."

Cora put some jelly on her toast. "Does Aiyana know your birth mother's been trying to get in touch?"

"No. And I'd rather she not find out."

"Because…"

"Why upset her? There's nothing she can do about it, anyway."

"Do you ever hear from your father?"

"My biological father died in a motorcycle accident shortly after I was born, but he wasn't together with my mother, anyway. He probably wouldn't have been a big part of my life." Although… Eli had always wondered if it would've made a difference, had his father lived. "The man who married Jo and was there while I was growing up is in prison for sexually abusing his daughter."

She put down her toast without even taking a bite. "He had a daughter? Did she live with you?"

"No. Stayed with her mother, only came to visit once, maybe twice a year. But if she hadn't said something about me to the next-door neighbor—and that neighbor hadn't called the authorities—I might never have escaped my…situation."

"Seems more likely she would've told her mother about you. That didn't happen?"

"She was quite a bit younger than I was. Who can say how much she really understood or conveyed about what was going on at my house? The way I heard it, she said something about her father having a *boy for a dog*—as if it wasn't a big deal—which shows you right there that her understanding was limited. Anyway, Jenny's mother never did anything, even if she did know. I'm guessing she ignored what she could, felt the less she had to do with Tim and his life, the better."

"I bet she'd like to kill him now."

He turned his water cup around, making circles in the condensation. "That makes two of us."

"I don't blame you. Are you still in contact with Jenny?"

"She's married, lives in Virginia, so I don't see her often, but we've had lunch once or twice."

"And Tim?"

"Nothing from him, thank God. I wish my mother would follow suit and leave me the hell alone. I have a new life, am an entirely different person. I don't want anything to do with her."

She waited for the waitress, who'd come around with a pitcher, to fill her glass and leave. "So…what are you going to do?"

He picked up his phone. "I'm going to tell her to beat it. *Again*." He did that, but turning her away wasn't as easy as he was leading Cora to believe. Part of him— the part that admired the mother/child sculpture Cora had brought into his office when they'd first met—still craved an apology, an explanation he could understand, some sense of closure, even a little contrition, if not a full acknowledgment of what she'd done. She owed him *something*.

Whatever that something was, however, he'd never get it. She was too narcissistic to feel the slightest bit of remorse. How could she feel bad about what she'd done when she claimed no responsibility?

As difficult as it was, he had to learn to live with the reality that she wasn't a fully functioning individual, that she never loved him and never would.

Some things just were what they were, he told himself.

"Is she or Tim responsible for the scar on your face?" Cora asked.

He fingered it, remembering. Late one night, he'd managed to get free of the cage they kept him in, but instead of running—he was too weak from lack of food—he tried to get something to eat. Tim caught him going through the pantry and slugged him so hard he'd flown across the kitchen, right into the door frame, splitting open his chin. There'd been so much blood, yet they'd never taken him to the doctor, which was why the cut had healed so badly. "Yeah."

Cora reached across the table to take his hand. "Bastards. I hope they rot in hell."

He couldn't help smiling. He'd never heard her use that kind of language before. "I like being with you," he said as if it was a revelation, because it was. Not only was she refreshing, she was *healing*, knew how to be supportive without being too overbearing. He felt like a whole new person when she was around, and that didn't happen with just anyone.

He expected her to say the same to him, but she didn't. "Who wouldn't?" she said and that enabled them to climb out of the mire of his past—to shove it all away—with a laugh.

Cora was invited back to Aiyana's for dinner on Sunday night. She'd been looking forward to it ever since she'd left Aiyana's house last week. Only this time she'd be going as Eli's girlfriend, which changed the way she'd be viewed by everyone else at the gathering. She knew Aiyana, and Eli's brothers, would be watching her in a different way. She'd also be that much more conscious of what she was hiding from them.

As it turned out, however, she didn't mind the extra attention. Gavin teased her quite a bit more and the younger brothers gave her shy smiles as if they were excited to think Eli had a romantic interest, but Aiyana treated her as kindly and politely as ever, almost as if she was determined to ignore the change. It was Eli who surprised her the most. He touched her freely and at every opportunity, despite the presence of his family. He could be so withdrawn and difficult to read, she hadn't expected him to be this demonstrative.

"How are your classes going?" Aiyana asked after they'd shooed the men from the kitchen so they could clean up without threading their way around so many big bodies.

Cora liked having this time alone with Aiyana, liked puttering around, helping with such mundane tasks. "They're going well."

Aiyana filled the sink with hot water. "You're not having any behavioral issues, are you? I remember you were worried about that."

"The new student—Zack Headerly—is giving me some trouble, but from what Darci says, he's acting out in English class, too. I think it's a general problem and not specific to me."

Aiyana lowered her voice in concern. "You know his parents were killed in a plane crash last year..."

"Yes. Eli told me. My heart breaks for him. That's why I haven't sent him to the office. I've been trying to gain a rapport with him, hoping the relationship we establish will encourage him to settle down."

"How's that going?"

Cora put plastic wrap over the cauliflower au gratin she'd made and contributed to the dinner. "It's too early to tell, but I remain hopeful."

"Let me know if you need help."

"I will. I was thinking that maybe Eli and I could take him and a friend riding this week. I feel as if some one-on-one time might help calm and reassure him. He needs to know that there are people who are still invested in him and his life."

Aiyana tossed Cora an approving smile. "That's the real secret," she said, her hands deep in suds. "I've invited him to have lunch with me tomorrow, so I'm trying to do the same thing."

Cora began loading the dirty silverware into the dishwasher. "Do you spend one-on-one time with all the boys?" That would be a daunting task, she thought, in addition to running the school and taking care of such a big family. Aiyana still had two high schoolers at home, who had homework every afternoon along with sports, but Cora supposed living on campus made a big difference.

"Just the most troubled," Aiyana replied. "I wish I had time to get to know them *all* on the same level, but the logistics are such that…"

"It's impossible," Cora finished.

"Sadly, yes." She raised a wet, soapy hand. "But enough about New Horizons and what's going on with the school. You're here to relax and have a good time. Why don't you tell me a little more about your family? I'm guessing you're missing them by now."

Cora did miss her family, although, once she got

beyond that first night she'd been too caught up in adjusting to her new situation, fighting her attraction to Eli, making friends with Darci and feeling guilty for keeping her true identity a secret to get *too* homesick. "I've already been back to see them once. And I hear from them regularly."

"You're close to your parents, then?"

Cora hesitated before putting the glasses in the dishwasher along with the silverware. "Yes." Otherwise, she wouldn't feel so guilty for wanting to include her birth mother in her life.

"How's your brother doing?"

"He's been out of town. Claims he's going to come see me when he gets back, but…he's always busy. Keeps putting it off. So we'll see. I'd love for you to meet him." In a way, that was true even though Cora knew she'd probably never introduce them—not with the way things stood now.

"I'm looking forward to that." She indicated the leftover carrot cake. "Any chance you'd like to take that home?"

Aiyana had obviously taken note of how much Cora had loved the dessert. "Sure. If you don't want it or want to keep it for the boys."

"We all get plenty of sweets as it is."

A ruckus broke out in the living room—Eli and Gavin wrestling with their younger brothers, who'd been teasing and goading them to get them to do just that. The loud noise and the rattle of dishes and other furnishings caused Aiyana to roll her eyes. "Boys."

"They seem to get along well," Cora said.

"Every family has its moments, but for the most part,

they've been very good to each other. They are all wonderful people."

"They're lucky to have you."

Aiyana turned to face her wearing such an intense expression that Cora feared she'd given away too much with the longing in her voice. But when Aiyana spoke, she realized that Aiyana's thoughts were moving in a different direction. "On the phone just after you came here, you mentioned wanting to become friends with Elijah."

Cora swallowed with some difficulty. "Yes…"

"It appears the relationship has moved beyond friendship."

Feeling on the spot, Cora could barely refrain from wringing her hands. Like most all of the students and staff, she loved Aiyana, didn't want to displease her. "We are…we are dating, if that's what you mean."

"It's serious?"

"We haven't put a label on it. It's too soon."

"But you're open to getting serious with him."

When she flailed around, searching for the best answer, Aiyana dried her hands and moved closer. "I owe you an apology, Cora. This is none of my business, and Eli would be furious if he knew I was getting involved. It's just that I've never seen him like this. His eyes follow you wherever you go, and I think I indicated on the phone that as tough and unreachable as he may seem, at times, his heart is so fragile…"

After clearing her throat, Cora met her gaze. "Well, I'm just as concerned for my own heart, if that tells you anything."

Aiyana's face creased into a big smile. "For you, it

wasn't quite as obvious to me, probably because I don't know you as well. So… I'm glad I asked," she said and pulled Cora into her arms for a warm embrace.

Cora breathed deeply, taking in the scent of her biological mother. She was hugging the woman who'd given her birth, a woman she was coming to love and respect more than she ever dreamed possible.

She probably hung on a little too long. When Aiyana tried to pull back, Cora couldn't quite let her go, but she didn't seem to mind. She kissed Cora's cheek—and then Eli interrupted by poking his head into the room.

"What's going on in here?" he asked.

Aiyana turned back to the dishes. "I just gave Cora the rest of the carrot cake, and she was thanking me."

"You gave her *all* of it? No way! I get half," he said, and later, once they were at his house, he decided to claim his share. But Cora didn't mind, since he ate it off her body.

"Were you really hugging my mother because she gave you the cake?" he asked as he licked a final drop of frosting off her nipple.

She caught her breath as he made sure he'd gotten it all, wondering if now might be a good time to tell him who she was. He'd just given her the perfect intro—and yet she couldn't bring herself to do it. What if their fledgling relationship couldn't withstand the shock wave?

She didn't want anything to come between them. Not only that, but Aiyana was so pleased they were together. Why risk ruining everyone's current happiness when she had all year? "Yes."

He dropped onto the bed beside her, seemingly sated and obviously tired. "Wow. You really like carrot cake."

"I really like your *mom*," she said softly.

"Doesn't everybody?" He propped his head up with his hands. "What's yours like?"

"She's...different from Aiyana. Not quite so socially conscious, but she's also a nice person. She did a great job raising me."

"You don't have any complaints about your childhood? The way you were talking at the restaurant, I thought maybe there'd been some problems."

"No big ones." Her mother's vanity could wear on her. Lilly could be a little materialistic, but Cora couldn't say anything derogatory about her. She already felt too disloyal just by being here—and getting involved in Eli's life and Aiyana's life...

"I'd like to meet her."

Cora wasn't about to invite Lilly to the ranch. She planned to keep this new world separate from the one she'd left in LA. Otherwise, she'd feel even guiltier. "She's really busy."

"Doing what?"

"She's a big philanthropist, always involved in one community event or another."

"That makes her sound caring."

Except that she sometimes gave the impression she did charity work more because she was bored and liked the positive attention it brought her. "She is caring. It's complicated, completely harmless. No one is all one way or the other, you know?"

"She doesn't have a job?"

"Doesn't need to work. But she has lots of friends

she goes out with for…for brunch and movies and what have you. And she golfs," she added weakly.

"Ah, I can see she's completely buried."

Cora heard the sarcasm but pretended she hadn't. "She is."

"We're not that far from LA," he said.

"Yeah. She'll come visit. Sometime."

He lifted his head to give her a funny look. "I mean we could go there any weekend you choose."

"Maybe for Christmas," she mumbled since the holidays sounded a long way off.

He didn't say anything. He got up and went into the bathroom to turn on the shower so they could wash off the sticky residue of the frosting, and she leaned over to check her phone. She'd tried to reach Matt earlier, before going to the basketball courts to find Eli for breakfast, but he hadn't picked up. He hadn't responded to her text, asking him if he got home okay, either. She thought he was just going to write her out of his life, and was happy to have him do that. But when she took a moment to listen to the voice mail her mother had left while she was having dinner at Aiyana's, her blood ran cold. In a voice choked with emotion, Lilly asked her why she hadn't told them she'd gone to Silver Springs to meet her biological mother.

"Oh God," Cora whispered. Matt hadn't told Aiyana and Eli why she'd sought out a job at the ranch—but he had told Lilly.

Chapter 17

"What did you say?" Eli poked his head out of the bathroom to see Cora grabbing her clothes off the floor and hurrying to get dressed.

"I said I have to go."

"But…you're sticky."

"I'll rinse off at home. There's been a—a family emergency."

Feeling a fissure of concern, he hooked his arms above his head using the lintel of the doorway. He would've helped gather her things, but she already had her clothes and there wasn't much he could do to help her dress. "What kind of emergency?"

"My mom…she's upset about something. I have to go home."

He turned off the shower. "Would you like me to drive you there?"

"No. It's fine. I'll go alone. I don't know when I'll be able to come back so…so you should stay here."

"Then…do you need someone to cover your classes tomorrow? If I can't get one of the other teachers to combine, I can always show them a movie or some-thing—act as babysitter, at least."

Cora couldn't conscionably leave her students in the lurch and make him step in, not when this wasn't the type of emergency Eli assumed. No one had been hurt or killed; no one was in the hospital. This was merely the consequences of the fact that she hadn't been able to let certain things go—things that some adopted kids, maybe even a lot of them, could do with apparent ease. "No. I'll be here."

"It's already eight o'clock!"

"The drive's only two hours. I can get there and be back before morning."

"After being up all night, will you be in any condi-tion to work?"

"I'll muddle through. School doesn't last that long."

"I'm willing to help you," he said. "Just tell me what's wrong."

When she looked up at him, she had tears in her eyes, which brought him out of the bathroom. "Cora…"

"I'm fine." She put up a hand to ward off the com-fort he'd hoped to offer. "I… I need to go. I'm sorry," she said and hurried out.

Eli stared after her. Just when he felt as if he was get-ting close to her, closer than he'd ever been to a woman, she seemed to retreat behind some invisible wall.

For a change, it wasn't him. But that didn't mean it wouldn't turn out to be a problem.

* * *

The silence in the kitchen felt tangible—like a thousand pounds of sand bearing down on Cora's shoulders, so heavy it was hard to bear up beneath it. Both of her parents were sitting at the table across from her, but neither seemed to have much to say. Lilly had cried a lot, and Brad acted confused, as if he was still trying to piece together why she'd needed more than what they'd provided when they'd given raising her their best effort.

"It isn't anything you've done," Cora reiterated. "You've been wonderful parents, and I'm grateful for everything."

He lifted his gaze to meet her eyes. "Then…why?"

She didn't get a chance to answer before her mother broke in, "Does your brother know? Did he help you?"

"No," she replied. "I only told Matt and Jill, because they were so present in my life during the past two years."

"And we weren't present?" she said.

Her father glanced at his wife as if he wanted to comfort her but was uncertain as to how to go about it.

"Of course you were," Cora said. "That's not what I meant. I would've told you, but every time I brought it up, you acted so…resistant to the idea—as if it would be a personal betrayal."

"So you did it, anyway," her mother said, fresh tears in her eyes.

"Not because it would hurt you! I never wanted to hurt you. I love you both. Why can't you understand? I *had* to meet Aiyana. A part of me has always been insatiably curious about her."

"What about your birth father?" Brad asked. "You're not curious about him?"

"I am but... I don't have any information on him. Unless Aiyana is willing to tell me the circumstances surrounding my conception, I have no hope of ever finding him."

"Will she give you that information?" he asked.

"I don't know yet. I haven't told her who I am. No one knows down at New Horizons." When she thought of Matt, she wanted to punch him. He had no business causing this wreckage. He'd only told Brad and Lilly to strike out at her, to hurt her for breaking up with him and having the audacity to find someone else.

"So when are you going to do that?" Brad asked. "And why haven't you done so already?"

"Because... I felt I should tell you first, for one. But the timing hasn't been right. There are moments when I think I'll never tell. At least I've seen my biological mother. At least I know who she is and what she's like."

Her father scratched his head, making his hair stand up. "I understand the questions you've had must've been...difficult," he said, making an attempt to be conciliatory.

"They were! I wasn't even certain of my nationality, Dad! Such a simple thing most others take for granted. I hated being so in the dark. I have only a partial picture now, but at least it's *something*."

"It's the deception I'm struggling with." Lilly glowered at her beneath wet eyelashes, but Cora wasn't convinced her "deception" was the root of it. Fear of losing Cora's affection was the real problem, which was probably why Cora had found her birth mother in spite of

Lilly's resistance. She knew Lilly had nothing to fear. There wasn't any way her adoptive mother could ever lose her affection.

"I lied because there was no way of knowing whether Aiyana would be anyone I'd be willing to associate with. If she wasn't, I was going to leave things as they are now. I didn't see any point in upsetting you if I ended up walking away."

"But you're not walking away. You adore her!" her mother said. "You talk about her like she's Mother Teresa!"

"I admit the fact that she's such a good person makes everything a bit more...complicated, but it doesn't change how much you both mean to me. *You* will always be first, Mom. You were the one who stood by me when she walked away."

Fresh tears confirmed that Cora's comments had hit the real target.

"Mom, stop," she said, getting up to hug her. "How could you question my love for you? We've always been close, haven't we?"

"*I* thought so. I did my best by you, but I'm not the kind of person Aiyana has turned out to be. I'm no champion of orphans and abused boys."

"What are you talking about? You're always working on one fund-raiser or another," she said. "You do a lot of good. Besides, that type of thing doesn't matter. You've been everything I need. I have no complaints, so don't let Matt tear us apart. That's exactly what he intended when he called you. He's angry that I'm not getting back with him, so he's hurting me by hurting you."

Lilly wiped her cheeks, smearing her mascara. "I know he wasn't trying to do any of us any favors…"

"Have you thought about Aiyana and how *she* might feel about all of this?" her father asked.

"Of course!" Cora replied. "Why do you think I haven't approached her? I'm not attempting to force myself into her life—or anyone else's. I'm just trying to figure out who I am and where I came from."

"But Matt said you went home with her son last night!" Lilly said.

"Her *adopted* son. As far as I can tell, I'm the only child she's ever had."

"So that makes it okay to date him?"

"It's not ideal, but there's nothing really wrong with it. It's not like we're truly related."

Lilly accepted the tissue Brad got for her. "Then you're not worried about how *he* will feel when he finds out you deceived him,"

"Like I said, I'm not even sure he has to find out."

"That's not realistic," Brad said. "This is all leading *somewhere*, Cora."

And there it was—what scared them all, even her.

She took her father's hand. "Can you tell me why my birth mother gave me up, Dad?"

"No. They provided us with no information, Cora. We've told you that before. We were just glad to get you."

"And we didn't mind not knowing," her mother added. "We were excited to be your parents—your *only* parents. Having that blank canvas meant…it meant we didn't have to consider the fact that you weren't actually born to us."

"But the fact that I didn't come out of your womb doesn't matter, right? You've told me before. Only love matters."

"That's true," Lilly admitted. "You'd think that would be enough, that you wouldn't have to go searching for someone who could…who would possibly ruin our lives."

"Aiyana can't ruin our lives if we don't give her that kind of power," Cora insisted. "The woman I've come to know would never want to hurt us, anyway. She'd step out of the picture before she became a problem."

"That's how you see her now, but you never know what she may be like once she feels entitled."

Cora rubbed her tired and burning eyes. "I'm sorry. I wish I could've been satisfied with not knowing. Maybe for some people, it's easy not to look back, to only move forward. But it hasn't been like that for me. I went to a lot of time, effort and expense to find Aiyana, and I wouldn't have done all of that if I hadn't felt compelled, from when I was just a little girl, to find out who my biological parents were—and why they gave me away."

Brad shook his head. "You hardly ever said anything!"

"Because I knew it would go like this!" she said.

"We would've tried to understand," he argued.

"Then try to understand now, Dad. Please? Wherever this is going, does it *have* to be somewhere bad? Can't I satisfy my curiosity, fill in the gaps that most people don't even think about so that I can feel satisfied? At peace? Can you trust my love enough to let me navigate my way through this?"

"Do we have any choice?" her mother asked.

"I guess not, since I've already done it," she said with a sigh. "But I'm an adult now. I feel like I should have the right to these answers. You know where you came from. Why can't I?"

They didn't answer.

"Still, I'd like your blessing, because I *do* love you and care about how you feel." She stared at them both imploringly. "Please?" she said again.

"You're *my* daughter. I don't want to share you!" her mother burst out. "Especially with some…some saint I can't compete with!"

Brad took Lilly in his arms and Cora stood so that she could hover over her mother and rub her back. "But that's just it, Mom. You won't have to compete. *No one* can threaten your place in my heart. Ever."

"You're down there with her, aren't you?" Her mother's words were muffled—they'd gone into her father's shoulder—but Cora could understand them in spite of that.

"Only for the year." She sought her father's gaze and, when their eyes met, she could tell she'd managed to convince *him*, even if she hadn't been able to completely assuage her mother's fears.

"I want you to be happy," he said. "We both do."

"Then don't be mad at me for this."

"I don't want Aiyana in our lives!" her mother insisted.

"Mom, you'd really like her—"

"That only makes it worse!"

"Give your mother some time to come to terms with this," her father said softly, indicating that Cora should back down.

"Okay." She checked the time on her phone. "It's nearly two. I have to head back."

Letting go of Brad, Lilly whipped around to face her. "You're leaving? *Now?* But you can't drive for two hours. You haven't had any sleep!"

Cora wished Matt would've at least waited until the following weekend to sabotage her relationship with her parents. That slight adjustment in timing would've made it so much easier for her to recover. "I have a job, Mom. I have to teach."

Her mother grabbed her and pulled her into a tight embrace. "Don't go. I'm afraid you'll fall asleep at the wheel and crash."

"After such an emotional conversation, I'm pretty amped up. I'll be fine." Perhaps it would be hard to get through the day tomorrow, but she figured, with enough caffeine, she'd manage…

Her mother cupped her face. "So you really like Aiyana's son? You told me he was intimidating."

"I didn't know him very well when I said that."

"And now?"

She smiled. "I like him. I like him a lot." *Too much*…

The promise of a possible romance seemed to check some of her mother's more negative feelings. She'd been after Cora for some time to settle down and get married so they could have grandchildren, since it didn't seem as if Ashton was in any hurry to provide them. "Will I get to meet him?"

"If you can be careful not to let on to what I'd rather they not know at this point…"

"I won't say a word," she promised. "That's up to you."

Cora slung her purse over one shoulder. "Then I'll bring him home with me next time I come—if he's available."

Her mother sniffed and used the tissue in her hand to dry her face again. "Make sure he's available," she said.

Cora chuckled at her sulky words. "Okay. He'll be my peace offering."

Cora was just getting her purse to head to the cafeteria to meet Darci for lunch when Eli ducked into her room. "Hey," he said. "How are you feeling?"

"Tired," she admitted, but smiled, anyway. She loved the way he looked in the worn denim jeans and soft T-shirt he wore. Because he was so involved in the school's athletics program—as well as caring for the school's animals—unless he had a business meeting he dressed more casually than the other administrators she'd known. But he did such a good job helping Aiyana run the school, and he fit in so well with both the faculty and the students, no one questioned what he wore.

"You got back late?"

Although he'd tried calling her around one to see if she was safe, she hadn't checked her phone until she was on the drive home and by then she felt it was too late to respond. "After four."

"Then you're running on almost *no* sleep."

She covered a yawn as she checked the clock on the wall. "I'm halfway through the day. I can make it."

He didn't pull her into his arms and kiss her like she was hoping he would. When he stopped halfway to her and leaned one shoulder against the wall, she was shocked by the degree of her disappointment, which only alarmed her further.

"So…what's going on?" he asked.

She busied herself straightening her desk so that she'd have a good excuse not to look at him. "What do you mean?"

"With your family. You seemed pretty upset when you ran out of the house yesterday."

"It was nothing," she said. "Just the usual stuff."

When he made no rejoinder, she glanced up.

"Stuff that you don't care to share with me."

Cora caught her breath. Was she being unfair to continue keeping her secret? Part of her was tempted to tell him, to completely unburden herself and let it out. But she was too frightened by what could change. He meant so much to her—already. And she couldn't begin to guess how it would affect Aiyana; she had no idea why Aiyana hadn't wanted her in the first place.

Surely there would be a better time to try to explain her situation—and that "better" time always seemed to be *later*. "Matt called my mother and tried to make trouble for me."

"By telling her you went home with me."

She cleared her throat. "Yes."

"And that caused a problem?"

"Matt and I were together for two years. She cares about him."

"She's hoping you'll go back to him."

Cora stacked some self-portraits she had yet to grade in the box of stuff she took home with her at the end of each day. "Not necessarily. It's just that… I've only been here a month or so. She was concerned that I might be jeopardizing my job." Part of what she said was true, at least. Her parents were concerned about what she was doing in Silver Springs—they were just concerned for different reasons than she'd given him so far.

"By hooking up with your boss."

"Yes."

"Does the fact that you're on the rebound have anything to do with it?"

"I'm not on the rebound," she said. "I'm over Matt." Sadly, she was over him before she even broke up with him. "But we were together long enough that my mother wasn't convinced of that. She expected us to get married one day."

He pushed off the wall and came toward her. "Why didn't you marry Matt? I bet he'd pop the question in a heartbeat if that was what you wanted."

"I wasn't ready. And I didn't love him as much as I felt I should."

He picked up the blown glass paperweight that had been an end-of-the-year thank-you gift from a class she'd substituted for and tossed it from hand to hand. "So did she calm down? Is everything okay?"

"Once I promised to bring you home for dinner."

No longer interested in the paperweight, he put it down as he came around the desk to where she was standing.

"Are you still interested in visiting LA?" She arched her eyebrows in challenge as he drew close. He'd mentioned driving her home to see her folks when they were in bed together yesterday afternoon, but meeting her family said something a bit more in this context.

They both understood she'd be bringing him home as "her new man."

Her skirt moved up to her thighs as he lifted her onto the desk and stood between her knees. "What do *you* think?" he asked and pressed his lips to hers in a hot, wet kiss.

His hand slid up under the silky material while his tongue mated with hers.

"Eli!" she gasped when his thumb found its way beneath her panties. "Not here!"

"Shh…it's okay," he whispered. "Give me two seconds. Everyone's at lunch. Your back's to the door, anyway. The worst anyone will think we're doing is kissing."

That was bad enough.

"Meet me at my place after school, okay?" he said as he found and stimulated her most sensitive spot.

She could hardly think straight. "You mean after dinner? You usually work until six."

He ran his nose up her neck, breathing deeply. "Coach Sanders can get football practice started without me, for a change. I've got better things to do today."

"That will be okay? He—" she moaned as a finger joined his thumb "—won't mind?"

The way his pupils dilated and his body tensed made her worry he might try to take this further, but he didn't. "He won't mind. But you're right. I'm only making this harder on both of us." Pulling his hand away, he set her back on her feet as if he had to put her out of reach while he still had the presence of mind to do so. "I'll come up with some excuse," he said. "Then I'll join him for the rest of practice and let you nap. Knowing you're naked in my bed, waiting for me, will get me through the rest of the day."

Which meant he'd also come home to her after. Whatever she'd started with Eli, it seemed to be accelerating very fast.

Chapter 18

Cora enjoyed getting to know her students over the next several weeks, despite facing some difficulties when it came to Zack Headerly. With Aiyana's help, she muddled through the challenge he presented and was actually glad for the opportunity to have something important to speak to her biological mother about. Trying to turn a specific boy around was a project they could work on and feel good about together.

The passing time brought other good things, too. She admired Aiyana more and more as the days went by, and she spent every extra minute she could with Eli. When they weren't together, she looked forward to his calls, texts and lunchtime visits. He often stopped by her classroom if he could. And, true to her word, in early October she took him to meet her folks, which went over well, except they liked him enough that they grew more worried instead of less about what might happen when he found out she hadn't been entirely truthful with him.

"That man's in love with you," Lilly would warn whenever they talked on the phone. But Cora would stubbornly refute that.

"He hasn't said anything about love," she'd argue. Although she longed to hear him speak those three words—had choked them back time and again herself—she was also sort of relieved. As long as he didn't make that verbal commitment, she could justify what she was doing by pretending their relationship wasn't that serious, that they were merely enjoying each other while she was in Silver Springs.

Jill agreed with her parents. "What do you mean he doesn't love you?" she'd scoff. "Of course he does! Maybe he doesn't come right out and say it, but he shows you in so many ways."

Jill, who'd seen them together twice and heard all the details of their relationship over the phone, was right. Cora had his full attention whenever they were together. He never acted like he didn't want to see her. They spent every night together, except for when he'd go out with his brothers or do something with his mother—or she was with Darci, Jill or her big brother, who met her in LA between trips to New York. Even when they split up for various commitments, he'd check in with her often and slip into bed with her after. In addition to all of that, he took her with him to Sunday dinner at Aiyana's every week. He even invited her along when he did extracurricular activities with the students, all of whom had come to view them as a couple. Some jokingly called her Mrs. T—or warned any new student that he'd better not flirt with "Eli's girl."

It was Thanksgiving almost before she knew it, and she and Eli were trying to figure out how to split their time between both families, just like a married couple. They ended up doing Thanksgiving dinner with Aiyana, the Turner boys, Aiyana's parents and one of her brothers—who were all so wonderful to meet—on Thursday and driving to LA to have dinner with her parents on Friday, since Ashton was hung up in New York and couldn't get back until then, anyway.

"He's quiet, but I love the way he looks at you," her mother said as they finished cleaning up after the big meal. Although Eli had helped with the dishes, too, he was now in the living room, watching football with her father and brother.

"You're making more of it than it really is," she said. "We enjoy each other. But we know it's only a short-term affair."

Her mother stopped scrubbing the big roasting pan she'd used to cook the turkey. "You're still planning on moving back at the end of the year?"

"Of course."

"What about Aiyana?"

Cora did her best to act as though she had everything under control. "I've decided not to say anything—to just…let it go. That solves everything, right?"

"Does it?" she countered. "After everything you did to find her?"

Surprised that it was Lilly who was pressing the issue, Cora nibbled at her bottom lip. This almost sounded as if Lilly would *encourage* Cora to tell Aiyana the truth, even though doing so came with the obvious risk that Aiyana would accept Cora into her life and Lilly would no longer be Cora's only mother. "She didn't want me for a reason, or she wouldn't have given me up. And she must not regret her decision because she hasn't come searching for me."

Lilly turned on the sprayer to rinse the suds from the pan. "You don't know that she hasn't tried. Do you?"

"She could've found me. I found her, didn't I? And I had a lot less resources to work with."

"Maybe she's afraid you won't be happy to see her— that she'll disrupt your life. Or that she'll be stepping on my toes."

"I was facing similar questions and concerns, and I still fought to find her."

"I know, but from what you've told me, she's pretty focused on her work. Perhaps she *will* come looking for you someday when…when she's not so busy."

"I doubt it. Let's face it, 'busy' is an excuse. If I weighed on her mind as heavily as she once weighed on mine, she would've acted by now. Instead, no one even seems to know that she ever had a child." She stood on tiptoe to return a bowl she'd dried to the cupboard. "I guess, when you put all of that together, I have my answer. She *still* doesn't want me. But…at least we're friends. At least I know her. That fills in some of the blanks and helps to… I don't know…anchor me in some way." It especially helped that they thought well of each other. That was so huge, Cora couldn't regret having gone to such great lengths to find Aiyana. Thanks to the sacrifices she'd made, she'd had the opportunity to meet her grandparents and her oldest uncle yesterday, all of whom had been so nice.

"But you haven't been able to ask her about your father," Lilly said. "Or learn why she put you up for adoption. Both of those questions were important to you."

Those questions had helped fuel her curiosity, but she only had herself to blame for her current predicament. Although, in the beginning, her plan had seemed so clever, it had turned into a far-reaching lie that she was now hesitant to expose. "I've made such a mess of everything. I guess I deserve to remain in the dark. I should've been up front—with you, Dad and Aiyana—from the start. I was trying not to hurt anyone. I wanted to test the water first, but then I met Eli, and everything just…spiraled out of control."

"Have you heard from Matt since he called us?"

"To tattle on me?" She grimaced. "Yes. But just a couple of nasty texts."

"He sent you some nasty texts?"

"Only after I called him a jerk for telling you guys," she admitted.

"What'd he say?"

"That I'm not the woman he thought I was. Blah, blah, blah. He also said I should've told you to begin with. He's right about that one."

"But if you'd handled this any differently, if you hadn't applied for a job there, you would never have gotten to know Eli. Maybe you would never even have met him."

"That's what Matt regrets," Cora grumbled. "He's mad that I've found someone else."

Lilly, who'd wrung out the rag and started washing down the counters, turned to face her. "I think you should tell Eli, Cora."

"About Aiyana?" She shook her head. "No. I've considered that many times, but I'm fairly certain she's never told him that she ever had a baby. I don't have the right to reveal something that personal about her life, in case…in case it will somehow hurt her or what she's established." She retrieved the dish towel she'd been using before and started drying the wineglasses. "Besides, if I tell him, he'll feel like he has to share that information with Aiyana, for my sake if not hers, and I'd rather he not get involved, not be making those decisions for me." She heard a soft *ding* as she set another cup on its bell-shaped top. "So, no matter how I look at the situation, it comes down to the same thing."

"And that is…"

"I need to keep my mouth shut."

Her mother pursed her lips. "What if your relationship with Eli continues to progress? What if someday he asks you to marry him?"

"He won't," she said.

"How do you know?"

"Because he's a confirmed bachelor!"

A skeptical expression claimed her mother's face. "Surely, he'll want a family at some point."

"Why? A family isn't for everyone. He's told plenty of people that he'll never marry."

"Because he doesn't want to need anyone, doesn't want to be hurt again, right? But it's too late to protect his heart. He needs you. And if he doesn't know that yet, he will soon."

She waved her mother's words away. "That's not

true. The students at the ranch are his family. He's got his mother and brothers, too. And look at him—he could have about any woman he wanted if…if he was hungry for that sort of thing."

Her mother gripped her shoulders so that she had to look up. "I think you're underestimating him."

"You don't know what he's been through, Mom."

"Yes, I do," she said quietly. "You've mentioned a few things, so…your father and I looked him up on the internet."

Cora fell silent.

"It's tragic," her mother added in a whisper. "Does he ever hear from the people who…who were so unkind?"

"He hears from his biological mother every once in a while."

"He has a relationship with her?"

"No, he doesn't want anything to do with her. But she hits him up for money when she gets desperate." Jo hadn't called or texted him since he'd told her to leave him alone the last time, but how long would that last? She'd contact him again in the future. He said she reached out every once in a while, when she was desperate for financial support or she felt the need to justify her actions. He said she always tried to convince him that she wasn't to blame.

"How could any mother be like that?" Lilly asked.

"It's tough to imagine."

"Turned my stomach to read about it. But look how he's turned out in spite of them. I'm so proud of him."

Cora felt the same warmth pour through her she experienced whenever she saw him or thought about him. "So am I."

Her mother pulled her into a tight embrace. "I believe you were brought together for a reason, honey. That it was meant to be."

"And Aiyana?" Cora asked.

Lilly released her. "I guess I'm finally coming to terms with the idea of sharing you."

She smiled wryly. "You just like Eli and know he wouldn't be part of our lives if I hadn't gone in search of Aiyana."

Her mother chuckled. "I admit that's part of it. Acquiring a son-in-law helps soften the idea that I might lose part of my daughter. But I've been doing some thinking—about you and me and the situation."

"And?"

"I've decided that I need to trust love," she said.

"What are you doing?"

Eli glanced up to see Gavin scowling at him for stopping so abruptly. They'd just finished breakfast, were walking down to the hardware store to pick up some parts Gavin needed to repair a sink in one of the dorms when Eli'd noticed they were passing H & G Jewelers. Sight of all the sparkling diamonds on display had caught his attention and caused him to fall out of step.

"Nothing." He pulled his gaze away from what was behind the glass so he could catch up, but turned back almost immediately. He wasn't ready to leave yet; he wanted to look some more. "I've been trying to come up with a good Christmas gift for Cora," he explained.

"You're thinking jewelry?"

"Most women like jewelry, don't they?"

"All the ones I know," Gavin agreed.

Eli gestured toward the door. "Do you mind if we stop in here for a few minutes?"

"Not at all." His brother followed him inside. "What kind of jewelry are you looking for? A necklace? Earrings?"

It was the engagement rings that'd captured his attention. He'd begun to think about Cora in a different way. As easy and natural as their relationship had been, he'd felt the shift several weeks ago. He'd tried to fight it by giving himself all the reasons he'd be stupid to try to make it permanent. But no matter what he told himself, he couldn't seem to regain his enthusiasm for bachelorhood.

The simple truth was that he'd never cared for anyone the way he cared for her, never enjoyed someone so much. She didn't seem to mind that he couldn't verbalize his emotions or talk about his past, didn't take it personally. That helped, but there were other things about her that made her unique, too. She seemed more relaxed, more confident, more easygoing than any of the women he'd dated before. They just fit together somehow, and although she was still talking as if she planned to leave in the spring, he was beginning to dread the thought of going on without her.

"Eli?" Gavin prompted when he didn't respond.

"I don't know yet," he replied as a sales associate— a woman wearing a Santa hat—made her way over.

"Can I help you?"

"I'm looking for something special to give my girlfriend for Christmas," he told her. "Do you have anything you might suggest?"

"We have a lot of pretty things." She showed him a

thick chain bracelet, a ruby heart necklace, some black onyx earrings and several other items. She had a good eye—he thought Cora would like any of the items she'd singled out. And yet his attention kept straying to that case of engagement rings he'd seen in the window.

Once he walked over there, the sales clerk quickly followed and smiled coyly when he met her eager gaze. "Or, if you really want it to be a nice Christmas, you could go for one of *these*," she said.

Gavin gestured dismissively. "Those are wedding sets."

"I know what they are," Eli said.

His brother blinked at him. "And you're still interested?"

Was he? For years he'd been adamant that he'd never tie the knot. But the four months he'd known Cora had been the best four months of his life. He'd never felt more whole or healthy in a psychological and emotional sense. The thought of presenting her with a diamond ring that showed he was not only willing but eager to spend the rest of his life with her was exciting.

It was also a little terrifying, given his past. He'd be launching out into uncharted territory. Would he be able to make her happy? Or would there come a time when things wouldn't be as easy or fun as they were now?

"Yes, I am," he told Gavin and, shaking his head at how quickly he'd fallen for her when he thought he could avoid love altogether, he pointed at a ring featuring a large round solitaire. "That one looks like her."

"Are you kidding?" Gavin cried. "That's a big diamond! It'll cost you ten thousand dollars, at least!"

The sales associate handed it to Eli, and he looked it

over carefully. Unfortunately, the price was as high as Gavin had predicted, so he let his brother talk him into putting it back until he could devote some more thought to whether he really wanted to make such a purchase.

But over the next week, all he wanted to do was go back and buy that ring.

"Are you sure she'll say yes?" Gavin asked when Eli brought it up again while they were lifting weights one evening at the school gym. "Because every time I talk to her, she seems dead set on leaving Silver Springs as soon as school gets out. I mean, if she won't even stay here and teach another year…"

Eli had been a little worried about that, too. He knew she liked New Horizons and the area. She liked Aiyana, the rest of the staff, the students, too. And when she was with him? He got the feeling he meant a lot to her. Sometimes, just the way she looked at him seemed to speak volumes—especially when they were making love. But she'd never tried to commit him, never talked as if they had a future together. "I called the store this morning. The owner knows Mom, said I can surprise Cora with the ring and then return it if she says no."

"So you want to risk it."

He finished loading the barbell he was about to use. "The idea of proposing to her—of marrying her—has somehow taken hold of me, and I can't get it out of my head."

Gavin studied him closely. "You love her."

With a groan for the physical strain it cost him, Eli did eight clean and jerks before dropping the barbell. "Yeah, I do," he responded and realized that was the first time he'd ever said it out loud.

Chapter 19

A week later, when Eli got up to play basketball on Saturday morning, Cora fell back asleep, so she was totally out of it when she heard a knock at the door. Eli didn't get many visitors. He gave so much to the school during the day that when he retired to his "cave," as Cora fondly called it, he demanded absolute privacy, and everyone knew it. That was what made it possible for her to stay with him so often. No one made a big deal about her almost living there because no one was privy to what he did, or who he spent his time with, after he disappeared from campus. Aiyana was about the only person who ever came over. Even Gavin and Eli's younger brothers typically called or texted him rather than showing up. So Cora wasn't surprised when she peered through the peep hole to find his adoptive mother on the stoop.

"Shoot," she whispered and waited, hoping Aiyana would realize he wasn't home and leave. Aiyana knew they'd been sleeping together, of course, but seeing Cora standing in *his* living room, wearing *his* T-shirt made it all a bit more...brazen, especially because he didn't welcome a lot of people into his house and she was becoming a regular fixture.

But Aiyana didn't leave. Another knock sounded.

Accepting the fact that she wasn't going to get out of this encounter, Cora used her fingers to comb down her hair and answered the door. "Hi," she said, squinting against the sunlight. Although Christmas was only a week away, the weather felt more like March or April.

Aiyana grinned as her eyes swept over Cora, then took in what she could see of the living room.

Nervously smoothing the wrinkles from Eli's T-shirt, Cora turned to follow her gaze. "What?"

"I've never seen this house look so...homey. My son actually has a Christmas tree—probably for the first time since he moved out of my house. And look, there're photographs of the two of you, and art you've created. Even a few plants. Wow. Who knew so much could change in such a short time."

"I tend to fill my space with the things I love," she said but flushed immediately after because this wasn't "her space."

"This place was pretty barren," she added lamely.

"So was his soul. Fortunately, that's changed, too," Aiyana said, but she didn't allow Cora any time to comment. "Can I come in?"

"Of course. Except Eli's not here. He's—"

"At the basketball court. I know. I tried calling you, but you didn't pick up so I decided to walk over."

Cora didn't get the impression she'd first tried the faculty housing. Aiyana had known right where to find her. "Are you…upset about something?" she asked as she stepped out of the way so that Aiyana could come in. Her mind raced through the past several days, searching for any incident in her classroom that might've warranted a visit from her "boss."

"Not at all. I'd like to go Christmas shopping today and was hoping you'd be interested in going with me. That's all."

Cora felt her eyes widen. "You mean…the three of us?"

"No. Just you and me. Eli's not much fun to take on an extended shopping trip. He's tolerant, if you know what you want and are just going to pick it up. But wandering around, admiring lights and decorations and such?" She shook her head. "Not particularly."

Cora laughed. She'd taken him to Rodeo Drive the last time they visited LA, since he'd never been there, and found that to be true. He was far more interested in seeking out places to eat or heading to the beach to play sand volleyball or go body surfing than shopping. "True."

"I thought maybe we could make a day of it, go to lunch, too. There's a delicious Thai place in Santa Barbara that I'd love to treat you to."

"I'd like that," Cora said.

"Great. How soon can you be ready?"

"Thirty minutes?"

"No rush. Just come over to my place when you're done."

"Sounds like fun." Cora was so excited about having the opportunity to be alone with her biological mother for hours—Christmas shopping, no less—that she grabbed Aiyana and hugged her on impulse. "I love you," she said. "You are *so* wonderful."

Although Aiyana permitted the hug, Cora could tell she was taken aback. When Cora let go, Aiyana searched Cora's face wearing a bemused expression. But then she smoothed the hair out of Cora's eyes and smiled. "I'm so glad you came to us," she said and kissed her cheek, just as she might've done had they been together when Cora was just a child.

Cora's heart was pounding when Aiyana left. She couldn't even make herself get ready. She sat on the couch, remembering every minute of that exchange. There was a moment when Aiyana was staring into her face that Cora had almost told her. She'd come *so* close...

She was still sitting on the couch in a bit of a daze when Eli walked through the door a few minutes later.

"Hey. What are you doing out here?" He used the bottom of his T-shirt to wipe the perspiration from his forehead as he spoke.

Cora summoned the energy to stand. "Nothing."

His eyebrows came together as he dropped his shirt, which was now stretched and wrinkled as well as sweaty. "Was I gone too long? Have you been waiting for me?" He checked the clock on his phone, which he'd left on the counter. "I thought I'd wake you up when I got back. You usually sleep until nine or ten on weekends."

"I wasn't getting impatient. Your mother came by and woke me up."

He crossed to the kitchen to get a glass of water. "What for?"

"To invite me to go shopping with her."

"Does she want me to go, too?"

"No. Just me." That was the beauty of it. Aiyana had sought *her* out. She wasn't merely a tagalong because she was dating Eli.

"Really." He eyed her speculatively. "Do you want to go?"

"I'd like to—if you wouldn't mind me skipping out on whatever we might've done today." They didn't have any specific plans, but they'd started to spend all their weekends together, so she knew the expectation would be there.

"Of course I wouldn't mind, not if you think it'd be fun." He downed his water. "So it's a girls' day, huh?"

"That's how she presented it."

"With as much as you admire my mother, I bet you'll enjoy that. I don't get *any* attention when we go over there on Sundays," he joked.

"You get plenty of attention—always." He was almost all she could think about. If only he knew how drastically he'd impacted her in every way. "But you're right, I'm excited to spend some time with her."

He walked over, took her hands and straightened the rings she wore on three different fingers so that the jeweled parts no longer slanted to the left or right. "What is it about her?"

"Nothing," she lied. "I just…like her."

"I'm glad, because she likes you, too. Anyway, I'll take some of the boys riding. I promised those who scored the highest on Mr. Travers's chemistry test that I'd take them out one day."

Cora flinched beneath the guilt she felt for continuing to keep such a secret. "Perfect time to fulfill that promise."

Being careful not to get her sweaty, he leaned in for a kiss. "I'll miss you."

"I have a few minutes," she said with a promising grin and pulled him into the bathroom so they could shower together. She needed something powerful to help her forget the confrontation she knew was coming—eventually.

The day seemed so boring without Cora. That he missed her even more than he thought he would told Eli how much he was coming to rely on her company, which made him a little nervous. Would that turn out to be a bad thing?

If she insisted on leaving Silver Springs at the end of the school year it would…

He held off contacting her until it was almost dinnertime, hoping she'd get back. But then he texted her.

How much longer are you going to be? You guys are taking forever.

We're on our way home.

Have you eaten? Should I turn on the barbecue and

grill a couple of burgers? He'd been waiting to eat with her.

No. I'm bringing you sushi. We had Thai for lunch but ended up staying so long we went to sushi for dinner. It was a great place. You're going to love it.

Did you get all of your shopping done?

Most of it.

What'd you get me? he teased.
Nothing. I already had your present, she wrote back with a winking emoji.

Where is it? I'll go take a look.

You'd better not snoop around! You'll see it at Christmas.

He imagined how surprised *she* was going to be. I've got yours, too. Picked it up today.

I have no clue what it could be.

And she'd never guess. What he didn't know was whether she'd like it.

Christmas morning dawned to dark skies and rain. Cora listened to the soft patter hitting Eli's house as she watched him sleep. She cared so much about him, had never been so in love—and that meant she had to tell him the truth. Every minute they grew closer under false pretenses was a minute she feared he might one day hold against her. Aiyana, too. She'd been sleeping with him for *four months*. That was such a long time to perpetuate a lie, so long she'd definitely struggle to explain why she didn't speak up sooner.

But when she looked back, she couldn't isolate a point in time when she could definitively say, *That's when I should've said something.* As soon as she picked a point like that, she'd realize what the truth could've cost her—Sunday dinners at Aiyana's, the nights she'd spent in Eli's arms and the days she'd spent looking forward to them, the shopping excursion she'd enjoyed with her biological mother last week, being invited to Aiyana's for Christmas Eve. If she'd told the truth from the beginning, most of that, maybe none of it, wouldn't have happened.

Choosing the path she did had enabled her to create some beautiful memories. But if she lost Eli and Aiyana, mere memories would never be enough...

Eli opened his eyes and smiled the second he realized that she was awake. "Morning."

She returned his smile. "Morning."

"Merry Christmas."

"Same to you." She tucked her hands up under her pillow as she studied him. "Would you like to open your present?"

He covered a yawn. "We're not going to wait until we have dinner at your parents'?" They'd spent Christmas Eve with Aiyana and all his brothers last night so that they could join her family today.

"I'd like to give it to you now." Because it was something she hoped would speak to, and comfort, his inner child, she didn't want him facing an audience when he opened it.

"Okay." He sat up. "Let me have it."

She slipped out of bed to grab the box she'd put under the tree after they'd returned from his mother's house last night. Until that time, she'd hidden it in a closet at her place.

"It's heavy," he said as she put it in his lap.

"I hope you'll like it." She sat nervously on the bed beside him as he tore off the paper. "I mean…it's not something the typical guy would probably like, but… I don't know. It seemed to me as if…"

His expression changed, grew less anticipatory and more reflective, as he lifted her sculpture out of the box. Although it was conceptual, she hoped he could tell that it depicted a man holding the hand of a little boy.

"Wow," he murmured. "You made this?"

"I did. I admit I'm not as good as I want to be, but I was trying to create something for you that represented the difference you are making here at New Horizons— in so many lives."

"I love it," he murmured. "I've often stared at that sculpture you created of a mother cradling her child. That piece is the reason I hired you. I've always loved it."

"I've noticed. That's why I attempted this. If you like that one better, you can have it. I just thought it was more important to focus on what *you* are giving others." And not highlight the fact that he didn't at first have the kind of mother who would nurture him as a mother should.

"I don't even know what to say, Cora. This must've taken you hours and hours. I couldn't love anything more."

He seemed so sincere that she let her breath go in relief. "I'm glad. I struggled so long with the way their hands come together. That was the hardest part. It still doesn't look right to me."

"Are you kidding? That part—all of it—is perfect." He studied her gift for several more seconds before setting it reverently to one side. "And now I have something for you."

"You're going to give me your present now, as well? You can wait until we go to dinner, if you want."

"No, I think this is the right time."

"Okay." She felt such excitement. He'd bought her plenty of things so far—lots of meals and treats and even a few clothes when they'd happened upon a blouse or something she liked. She'd bought him stuff, too. But this was their first formal exchange. She thought maybe he'd purchased some art supplies or the painting she'd fallen in love with at the boutique off the beach they'd found last time they went to LA. But what he retrieved from his drawer was far too small to be either of those things.

It was jewelry. Clearly. But what kind?

She grinned at him as she tore off the tiny bow and the pretty wrapping. Inside she found a box with a lid. Under the lid was another box, this one the velvet type. "I never would've expected you to get me jewelry," she said. "We've never even looked at it."

He said nothing, just watched as she opened the lid. Her jaw dropped the moment she saw the ring, and she blinked several times, trying to decide what it might mean. "This is…this is stunning!" she said. "Literally. I don't know what to say. It must've been *so* expensive. And…" And it looked like an engagement ring! She searched his face, trying to figure out if it *was* an engagement ring as he took her hand.

"Will you marry me, Cora?"

Cora could hardly breathe. This was a proposal— nothing she'd expected to come from Eli. Not this soon. He'd convinced her that he would never take that step, that he couldn't trust enough to take that step. Somewhere in the back of her mind, she'd always hoped he'd find his way around that barrier. But now? She wasn't prepared! She still hadn't told him the truth!

"You keep talking about moving away after next semester," he said. "But I hate the thought of that. I hope you'll stay here, with me. You gave me that statue to symbolize what I'm trying to do here at New Horizons—"

"What you *are* doing," she broke in.

"But you're doing the same thing—making a difference in the lives of young people who need you. *I* need you, too, even though I'm not so young," he added with a grin.

Her gaze met and locked with his. "Are you saying you *love* me, Eli?"

"How can you even ask that? Nothing else could ever make me take this risk. You've changed my life, Cora. Made me whole," he added softly.

Tears filled her eyes as she stared down at the big diamond he'd bought. "This is gorgeous."

He leaned in to catch her eye. "I was hoping you'd simply say yes. Don't you love *me*?"

"I do. Without question. I just…" She wiped her cheek with the back of her hand. "I have to tell you something before I can accept this. I wasn't going to do it on Christmas—I didn't want to ruin the holidays. But… I'm afraid I've put it off too long already. And now you'll hate me, which will make this ring a moot point."

Lines of consternation appeared on his forehead. "What are you talking about?"

She shook her head. "You won't believe it. And what makes it all worse is that I don't even know if I have the right to tell you. I feel like this should come from Aiyana, since you're her son. But…but it hasn't come from her. No one seems to know about me. And once I met you, I couldn't resist you. I tried. Lord knows I tried. Anyway, here we are."

He got off the bed. "That just confused the hell out of me. What are you talking about?"

"Aiyana's my biological mother, Eli." There. She'd said it.

For a moment, she wished she could snatch those words right back. She was so terrified of what they might destroy. But she couldn't continue to live a lie. That wasn't fair to Eli, which meant she didn't really have a choice.

"That's impossible," he said.

"I assure you it's *not* impossible. It's true."

"She had a child." His words rang with disbelief.

"Yes. One she gave up for adoption twenty-eight

years ago—to a couple in LA. Brad and Lilly, both of whom you've met. I'm that child."

"But…why would she give you up? Was she too young? Unable to care for you? Aiyana loves children!"

"I can't provide the reason. She was twenty-one, so not outrageously young. That's the thing. I've always wondered why she didn't want me. That's what drove me to come here—that and wondering what my biological mother might be like."

"Does *she* know who you are?"

"No."

He shoved a hand through his hair. "Holy shit."

"I'm sorry. I would've told you sooner, but…it's all been so complicated for me. Once the private investigator helped me locate Aiyana, and I saw that she ran New Horizons and was looking for an art instructor, I believed it was meant to be. What an opportunity, right? I thought I'd apply and hope to land the job so that I could get to know her a bit before…before divulging my identity. I felt if I could only learn more about her, I might understand why she gave me away and be able to determine if she might welcome me back. That's all. I wasn't trying to trick anyone, not in a harmful way. And I certainly wasn't planning on falling in love with you."

He began to pace. "That's why you wanted the job so badly."

She nodded.

"And that's why you were so set on leaving at the end of the year."

"Yes. I didn't see any other choice." She sniffed to keep her nose from running. "As I said, it was never my intent to hurt anyone. That's partly why I haven't spoken up. Once I got to know Aiyana, I realized that there must be a good reason she cut me out of her life. But I've been afraid to find out what that reason is—even while curiosity eats me alive every day. Why would someone like Aiyana walk away from her own baby? It's been nearly thirty years—why wouldn't she come looking for me? And why has she never mentioned that she once had a child—*to anyone*? No one seems to know about me, which is why I feel guilty telling you. It feels disloyal to reveal all of this, as if I'm divulging her most intimate secret—even though it's my secret, too."

His chest lifted as he drew a deep breath. "Are you going to tell her who you are?"

"I don't know. I go back and forth on that every day—another reason why I never told you. I didn't want to burden *you* with the same uncertainty, didn't want you to wonder if you were being disloyal to your own mother by not telling, if that's the way you decided to go. So… I'll ask you the same thing—are *you* going to tell her?"

He sat on the edge of the nightstand. "I feel like I should—like we should do it together."

"What if she's not happy to have me back, Eli?"

"How could she not be happy about that? Look at you! You're gorgeous and so smart and good. What mother wouldn't be proud of you?"

At that point, the emotion Cora had been struggling to hold back got the best of her. As tears began to run down her cheeks in earnest, he walked over to scoop her into his arms. "Don't cry," he murmured. "It breaks my heart to see you cry. Everything's going to be okay. We'll figure it out together."

"You don't hate me?" she asked.

He laughed as he kissed the tip of her nose. "No. If this is the worst thing we ever have to get through—I mean between us, I understand it's been very difficult for you and I'm not making light of that—we're going to be okay."

"So are we getting married?" she asked. "Do I get to keep the ring?"

He reached over to get it. "Absolutely," he said as he slid it onto her finger. "Do you like this setting, or do you want to take it back and pick another one?"

"I want this one," she replied. Somehow it meant more that he'd gone to the trouble of finding what he thought was just the right thing for her.

"I'm glad you like it." He held her chin while he kissed her. "Merry Christmas."

Chapter 20

Eli was so happy that he and Cora were to be married that he tried not to let the little detail of her maternity bother him. He could see why she hadn't told him that she was Aiyana's daughter, so he didn't find it hard to forgive her. Being in love for the first time made him hesitant to let *anything* destroy the excitement they were feeling. He knew how wonderful Aiyana was, couldn't imagine her reacting negatively to the news, so he figured they'd wait until the holidays were over and sit down with her and explain everything. He told Cora that Aiyana probably didn't have the support she needed, so she'd made the decision to go with adoption because she thought it would be the best alternative for Cora—and had simply been too engrossed in helping others to search for her.

But the more he mulled over the situation, the more he began to think there had to be other factors he should be taking into consideration. Cora kept saying that the woman she'd come to know would not have walked away from her child unless she felt she had to. So, why did Aiyana feel she *had* to resort to adoption? And how could they find out before dropping a bombshell that could either make her incredibly happy, or bring up a part of her past she preferred to leave buried, even if it did include a child?

He didn't dare approach his grandparents or uncles with the conundrum he and Cora faced. Like Cora had said, it felt wrong to bring *anyone* in on this, especially Aiyana's family, since they didn't have her permission. But there was one other person Eli trusted, one person who also loved Aiyana with all his heart.

"Sorry for the delay," Cal said as he walked into his wood-paneled office, where Eli had been waiting for the past ten minutes.

Eli smiled as they shook hands. He believed Cal to be one of the finest men he'd ever met—and still it felt awkward to speak to him about something so personal. Maybe it would be easier if Cal's relationship with Aiyana had been more clearly defined over the years, if Eli felt as if he could look at him as a father figure instead of just a particularly generous friend of the family. But as much as Cal loved Aiyana, and Aiyana seemed to love Cal, the relationship had never progressed—a mystery in and of itself. "Thanks for seeing me."

"You said it was important."

"It is."

"What can I do for you? Do you need food, equipment, money for the school? If so, you came to the right place."

"Thank you, but...this has nothing to do with New Horizons."

Cal's ruddy face showed concern. "Then what's it about?"

"My mother."

A frown tugged at the corners of his lips. "I should warn you that might change my position. I care about you a great deal. I hope you know that. But my first loyalties will always lie with her."

Eli let his breath go in relief. "Thank you for confirming your devotion. That's why I'm here—because I knew I could depend on that."

"I don't understand."

"You've met Cora." Eli knew he had; Cal and Cora had joined them for several of the Sunday dinners they'd had at Aiyana's over the past few months.

"Yes. A very nice woman. You chose well."

"Thank you." News of their engagement had obviously spread, but Eli wasn't here to talk about that. He scooted forward. "I'd like to ask that what I'm about to say doesn't leave this room. If anyone is going to tell Aiyana about...what I plan to reveal, it should be Cora. Can you give me your word?"

"As long as whatever you're keeping from her isn't harmful to her."

"That's what I'm hoping you can help me decide."

Cal, more somber than Eli had ever seen him, leaned back in his seat and clasped the wooden arms of his leather swivel chair. "What is it?"

As Eli explained, Cal sat motionless, listening.

"You know Aiyana as well as anyone," Eli said when he was finished. "You love her, too. Should we tell her?"

"No."

Eli blinked in surprise. Cal hadn't sounded the least uncertain when he gave that answer. At a minimum, Eli had expected a bit of deliberation. "Because…"

"I'd rather not say."

Another surprise. "You need to tell me. Otherwise, I won't know how to protect *both* of the women I love."

"I'm glad you came to me before…proceeding. I'm sorry for Cora. She must've come to Silver Springs hoping for a happy reunion with her mother, but I'm afraid it's not that simple."

"Why?" Eli lowered his voice. "Was it rape? That's where my mind keeps going. What else explains such secrecy? Was Aiyana brutally attacked? Is Cora's father some scumbag rapist who's spent time in prison?"

"I think it would be easier for Aiyana if that was the case. Maybe then she'd be able to forgive herself. As it stands—" he shook his head "—no amount of atonement seems to be enough."

Eli's heart leaped into his throat. "Forgive herself for what?"

He didn't answer, was obviously still wrestling with his reluctance to break a confidence.

"Cal, as you've no doubt heard, in June Cora will become my wife. Please help me to understand the seriousness of this situation. Trust me to guard the secret as carefully as you have."

"I would if I thought it would help Cora to know…"

"But if she doesn't have a good reason not to, she'll eventually tell Aiyana who she is! The closer they become, the safer she'll feel to do that. And, as my wife, I can only imagine they will get close. That's already happening."

Cal dropped his head into his hands. "Aiyana will never forgive me."

"She'll never know. I swear it."

"Even if she learns, I care more about her than I do myself," he said on a fatalistic sigh. "So…if this might possibly protect her, I'll do it."

Eli could feel his heart pounding in his chest. "What happened?"

"When Aiyana was just a teenager, maybe eighteen, she fell in love with her stepfather."

A sick feeling crept into the pit of Eli's stomach. This was not what he'd been expecting. "She *what*?"

"He took advantage of her youth and inexperience, touched her where he shouldn't, convinced her they were meant to be together—and, eventually, she gave in to his entreaties and ran off with him."

"You've got to be kidding."

"I wish I was. She realized almost immediately that she'd made a terrible mistake, but by then the damage was done. She felt she could never go back. She'd betrayed her mother and taken away the father of her two younger brothers, was positive Consuelo would never be able to forgive her."

"So she stayed with him?"

"She had no choice, had nowhere else to go. They rambled around from town to town, picking up odd jobs and living in motels and dumpy apartments. Before too long, she was so miserable she began to search for a way out and finally met a girlfriend who offered to help.

But when she tried to leave Dutch—Dutch Pruitt was his name—he came after her, made all kinds of crazy threats against them both. Your mother was so afraid he'd act on those threats, and hurt someone besides her, that she went back to him and, for the next year or so, was treated as more of a captive than anything else."

Eli's throat had gone so dry he could scarcely swallow. "How did she eventually get away from him?"

"She got a waitressing job. The owner of the place was a retired cop by the name of 'Murph' Matheson, and he and his wife took a shine to her. They helped her get a restraining order against Dutch, let her move in with them and their children. They even insisted she start college and helped with the expenses."

"And the pregnancy?"

"Your mother realized she was going to have a baby a month after she moved in with the Mathesons. But she knew if she kept the baby, she'd never really be rid of Dutch. He'd be part of her life forever, and because she was convinced he wasn't completely sane she didn't want him around the baby. She also knew her mother would never be able to accept the child, would never be able to love it, if they ever reconciled, which was something she was beginning to hope for. So…"

"She gave it up."

"That's right."

Leaning back, Eli took a deep breath. "Did Dutch ever find out about the baby?"

"No. But he would have had she kept it. It took another three years for her to get rid of him altogether. He was a truck driver by then and took his own life by driving his semi over a cliff."

Eli sat rubbing the beard growth on his chin as he attempted to process this information. "Wow..." he said on a long exhale. Even a saint like his mother had a skeleton in her closet, and that skeleton had quite a stigma attached to it.

Cal came to his feet and circled the desk. "Eli, I hope you won't let this damage your opinion of your mother. I would feel terrible if it did. Regardless of her past, I've never met a better person. I don't think she should be defined by that one mistake."

He lifted a hand to signal that Cal had nothing to worry about. "I'm not judging her," he said. "My mother has proven who she is many times over." This just confirmed, once again, that no one was perfect.

But what did he do with the information now?

While Eli was gone, Cora cooked some Cajun pasta sauce for their dinner from a recipe she found on the internet. She was trying to stay busy, but she often found herself staring off into space, wondering if Cal might be able to answer some of the questions that'd nearly driven her mad over the years—and if Eli was getting him to talk. Would Cal know that his beloved Aiyana had had a child? And, if so, had Aiyana told him she'd put that child up for adoption?

Even if he *didn't* know, if the news came as a complete surprise, would he suggest they tell Aiyana who she was—or not?

Cora would've gone to see Cal along with Eli, so that she could take part in the discussion. She really wanted to be there. But Cal was so protective of Aiyana, she and Eli both felt that Eli had a better chance of getting him to open up without her—which left her to wait and worry.

Although Eli was gone for only a couple of hours, it felt like forever. The second Cora heard him at the door, she turned off the stove, left the Cajun sauce in the pan and hurried to meet him. "How was it?" she asked as he came in.

That Eli didn't seem to be relieved or excited made Cora's chest constrict to the point that she could barely breathe. She tried to read his thoughts and feelings as he grimaced and rubbed his forehead.

"It wasn't good," she surmised.

He pulled her over to the couch. "I think maybe you should sit down."

She did as he suggested but perched on the very edge, too nervous to relax. "Cal didn't know anything about me?"

"Actually, he did."

She wanted to feel some hope, but Eli's manner didn't warrant any. "And…"

"It's complicated—difficult to know how to proceed without hurting Aiyana as well as…others."

"Others?" she echoed in surprise.

"That's the thing. This could affect more than just you and her."

"Do you mean Lilly and Brad? Because they're okay with me telling Aiyana. They weren't at first. They felt threatened, to a degree. You know that. But they've begun to understand that I'm an adult now, and I should have the right to know where I come from. They also know it won't change how I feel about them."

"I'm not talking about Brad and Lilly, Cora."

She drew a deep breath and clasped her hands together to stop them from trembling. "Then who?"

He wore a sympathetic expression as he reached over to slide a strand of hair out of her eyes. "Remember how you had trouble telling me that you were Aiyana's child because no one knew she even had a child and you thought you might be revealing something too personal?"

Cora curled her fingernails into her palms. "Yes..."

"That's how I feel right now. What happened to Aiyana, what she did, would be hard to...to cope with. She's not completely to blame—she was so young—but she made some bad decisions that got her into a situation no one would ever ask to be in."

"She was raped?" Cora had wondered that before, many times. If Aiyana had been raped, Cora could understand why she might not care to live with the reminder, so she was surprised when he shook his head.

"No. Cal said, and I agree, that if it had been a random attack, something where she wasn't also culpable, she might've been able to get over it by now."

"You're saying she's *not* over it."

"Not from what I can see. If she was, I believe she'd be married to Cal. Instead, she's pushing him away, denying herself any hope of that kind of happiness and fulfillment."

"She's punishing herself because of *me*?"

"Not because of you. Because of guilt. Because of regret. Because she hurt someone she loves. Cal told me she doesn't believe she deserves to be happy, which is why we see her giving so much to everyone else while continually denying herself."

"*Cal* said that?"

"Not in so many words. But once he explained the situation, I understood. Aiyana's rejecting his love because she doesn't feel she deserves it."

Forcing her hands open, Cora rubbed her sweaty palms on her denim-clad thighs. "But if it wasn't rape, how bad can it be? And if it *is* that bad, why would Cal ever open up about it?"

"Trust me, he was reluctant. He just didn't have much choice, not with you living here and marrying me."

"Your mother wouldn't want me here if she knew who I was. That's the bottom line, isn't it?" She'd told herself she'd accept whatever Eli came back with, take it well. She'd been lucky enough to have Lilly and Brad. But she couldn't stem the bitter disappointment that flooded through her.

"*I* don't believe that, no. And it took some convincing, but before I left Cal agreed with me. As painful as it might be, confronting the truth is the only way you'll be able to have the relationship with Aiyana that you deserve, and then maybe she can finally heal. Sometimes things have to get worse before they can get better."

Those were harrowing words. "So what is it?" Cora asked. "You're going to tell me, right? What happened?"

Eli seemed to have trouble getting started. Whatever Aiyana had done was obviously not something he wanted to expose.

"Eli?" she prompted.

Finally, he managed to explain what'd happened nearly thirty years ago. He did so as diplomatically and kindly as possible, but what he had to say still shocked Cora.

"Wow," she said when he was finished.

"She was young, confused," he added for the second or third time. "What she did is so unlike her. There must've been some extenuating circumstances that we're not aware of."

Cora's mind raced as she tried to imagine how a situation like that could've developed and the damage it would cause. "My heart aches for her as much as it does Consuelo and her younger brothers. No wonder Aiyana doesn't have much of a relationship with those two."

"I'm guessing Consuelo has forgiven her. But I feel like those two brothers might be harboring some resentment, which is why I've hardly ever seen them."

"So what did you mean, it's time for the truth to come out? We can't tell your mother who I am, Eli. If not for me, she'd be able to leave the past in the past, which is something she's proven she's desperate to do. I love her, too. I didn't come here to bring her misery and unhappiness."

"That's just it," he said. "Once you sit down and tell her who you are—"

"No! Aren't you listening? I don't want to serve as a constant reminder of—of all that."

Eli scooted closer. "Hear me out. Why not tell her and leave it there? I mean, just because you both know doesn't mean *everyone* else has to know."

Her mind raced as she tried to comprehend what he was getting at. But she was still processing The Terrible Secret in which she played such an integral part. "You're suggesting we tell her but not the extended family?"

"Or anyone else. Why would we have to? You'll soon be her daughter-in-law as well as her daughter. If she loves you, spends a lot of time with you, calls you her little girl, no one will think twice about it, even Consuelo or my uncles. From what Cal told me, Consuelo never knew about the pregnancy. Aiyana went through those nine months, and the delivery, alone. She made the decision to put you up for adoption alone, too. Then she did her best to move on and build something out of her life—and she did that alone, too, until she could reconcile with her family, which didn't happen until about five years after you were born."

"She didn't tell *anyone*?"

"Only Cal, and that well after she was back in touch with her family. He said she couldn't talk about those years or the adoption without breaking down. She was too ashamed. And she didn't want to hurt her mother and brothers any more than she already had by announcing the fact that she'd had a baby by her former stepfather."

Cora nibbled at her lip as she pictured what having such a discussion with Aiyana might be like but eventually shook her head. "I can't. I can't tell her if she'll only be sad that I found her. That's not why I came here."

"Cora, listen to me." He took her hands. "Imagine how she must feel when she thinks of you. She gave you up because she was convinced she had to, which means, not only did she lose her family, at least for a while, she lost her only child. That *has* to be painful. She feels she deserves the pain, which is why she's tried so hard not to look back and hasn't taken up a search for you. But if you were to come to her, and it didn't hurt her mother, her brothers or anyone else, I have to believe it might finally fill the hole in her heart. Don't you see? Finding out that her baby had a good upbringing, one in which she was treated well, and has turned into such a beautiful, fully functioning young woman would *have* to erase some of that terrible guilt. It would also make her proud. Having you back... I believe she'd feel complete—at last."

Cora's eyes began to burn with unshed tears.

"You *have* to tell her," he said. "Only you can bring her peace."

Cora almost turned around a million times. If not for Eli's words, his strong belief that she was doing the right thing, she would have. Instead, early the following Sunday, after a sleepless night she spent alone at her own house, she kept walking toward Aiyana's. At least she knew that Liam and Bentley wouldn't be there, that she and her biological mother would have the house to themselves. When Eli had called Aiyana to set up this appointment, he'd asked if the boys could spend the night with him. According to the good-luck text she'd just received from him, Liam and Bentley were still sound asleep. She knew Eli would run interference for her until he received the "all clear."

Everything was ready—except her.

"How am I going to say it?" she muttered as she trudged along, hugging herself against the early morning chill.

Fortunately, the campus was deserted. She was grateful for that, wasn't sure she'd be able to fake a smile if she happened upon a student or fellow teacher. She was close to tears, and she hadn't even arrived yet.

When she did reach Aiyana's, Aiyana answered the door immediately. Cora could tell she'd been waiting and watching for her. Aiyana knew something serious was up; the concern in her eyes proved it.

"Thanks for…thanks for allowing me to come over," Cora said.

Aiyana stood aside and waved her in. "Of course. You're welcome here anytime. I hope you know that."

"I do."

Aiyana led her into the living room where that picture of Hank, Consuelo and family graced the old piano. Cora felt a niggle of doubt when she glanced at it. Once she said what she had to say, there'd be no taking it back. But she knew she'd come too far to change her mind. For better or worse, it was time for the truth.

"Why all the secrecy?" Aiyana asked as they sat, facing each other, on the sofa. "I'd assume it was because you want to arrange a surprise for Eli, maybe for the wedding, but he's the one who asked me to set this time aside and insisted on taking the boys, so…that doesn't seem to fit."

"No, it's not that kind of surprise."

"So he knows what you're about to say."

"He does. Cal does, too. And my parents. They all felt you and I should address this at a time when we could be alone and weren't likely to get interrupted."

Her eyebrows knit above her dark, searching eyes. "*Cal's* part of this?"

"Yes. And my parents, as I said. But it's a very small, tight circle, and we all want what's best for you. This is no one else's business but our own."

The color drained from Aiyana's face as she stiffened. "You're giving me the impression this is bad news. You and Eli haven't changed your mind about the wedding. You're not leaving New Horizons."

"No. I love Eli more than I've ever loved anyone. I hope I'll be able to make him happy."

"I know he feels the same about you. You've taught him to trust again. I've been waiting for a woman to come along who had the power to do that. So…"

Cora couldn't help wringing her hands. "Aiyana, I… I'm…" She tapped a hand to her chest as if she could force out the rest of the words, but that was as far as she got before she choked up and couldn't speak.

Sympathetic tears filled Aiyana's eyes. "What is it, Cora?" she asked. "You can tell me anything."

"It's something I've been trying to tell you since I came here. Since the private investigator who…who helped me first find you."

With a gasp, Aiyana covered her mouth. She knew. In that moment, she knew, but Cora spoke, anyway.

"I'm the child you gave up."

"Twenty-eight years ago," she whispered, her eyes filled with nostalgia and pain. "Twenty-nine on February 21."

"Yes. I—I hope you're not upset that I went to such great lengths to find you. And that I didn't tell you from the start. I'm not here to remind you of anything that might be painful or to bring you any unhappiness. I just… I've always craved a connection. And now that I have one, I'm glad. You are everything I ever hoped you would be!"

She sprang to her feet and backed away as if Cora had slapped her. "No, you have no idea who I really am. What I…what I did."

Cora stood, too, and caught hold of her hands. "That's just it, I *do* know. And it doesn't change anything."

A tortured expression claimed her face. "But I'm so ashamed—"

"Don't be," Cora broke in. "Let it go. All the people you know love you in spite of whatever you did in the past. I want to share my life with you as the daughter I am. But as far as I'm concerned, your mother, the rest of your family, everyone else can know me as your daughter-in-law."

"I won't ask you to lie for me," Aiyana said.

"You're not asking me to lie. We'll keep this to ourselves for their sakes. Why would they need to know? Why open that old wound? They never knew I existed in the first place, so they aren't missing anything. I'm perfectly satisfied with that and would be thrilled if only…if only you could forgive yourself and let yourself love me in return."

"I *do* love you," Aiyana said. "I have never forgotten the day you were born. I can't tell you how many millions of times I've thought of you and wished…wished I could at least know where you were, if you were happy, if you had what you needed."

Which was why she'd made it her life's mission to love every orphaned child she could, why she'd adopted so many. Cora could easily see the correlation—her attempt to compensate. "The past is the past. It can't be changed. Just don't deny us a future. Please?"

"I never would." Aiyana squeezed her hands. "I can't believe I have you back, that nearly thirty years of wondering and worrying has come to an end."

Cora smiled through her tears. "Thank you."

"No, thank *you*." She pulled her into a tight embrace. "I'll never let you go again."

Epilogue

"What do you think of this?"

Cora turned to see Aiyana holding a lovely teal bridesmaid dress. Although she'd done most of her wedding shopping in LA with Lilly—who'd made it her new life's mission to throw the most spectacular wedding in the world and had dived in as if they'd given her only six weeks instead of a full six months to plan everything—they'd been unable to find the right bridesmaid dresses. Cora had been hoping to visit Santa Barbara to see if she could find anything different, so she'd invited Aiyana to drive over with her and have lunch.

"Oh my gosh! That's it!" she exclaimed. "Finally! Do you know how many shops I've visited?"

"More than ten?"

"More than twenty!"

"Lilly must've loved such an in-depth hunt."

Cora smiled at the sparkle in Aiyana's eyes. They both knew how much her adoptive mother enjoyed shopping. "She did. I'm sure she'll be slightly disappointed that we came up with this on our own."

"I'll have to tease her about that," Aiyana joked.

"It's a good thing she likes you."

"I never realized that by getting my daughter back, I'd also be getting such a good friend."

They checked the price, sent Lilly a picture and, after receiving her exuberant reply, ordered one in the appropriate size for Jill, Darci, an old childhood friend who Cora kept in touch with every few months, two other friends from high school and a teacher she'd met while substituting at Woodbridge High.

"Well, it's exciting to finally meet with success, but finding the dress so early cuts our day short," Cora said as they left the boutique. "I didn't expect to buy from the first shop we visited."

"We can start searching for something else on the list. What's left?"

"My shoes. I haven't yet found a pair that's both pretty and comfortable. But the restaurant's just down the street, so let's eat before we do any more shopping. I'm starved."

"Me, too." As Aiyana linked her arm through Cora's, Cora felt such a tremendous rush of love and admiration. Her relationship with her biological mother was every bit as good as she'd ever dreamed it could be.

"Thanks for taking the time to come with me today," she said.

"I love being included, love having you in my life. I can't wait for the wedding."

Cora covered her mother's hand as they sauntered down the sidewalk. "We could always make it a double wedding, you know."

Aiyana pulled Cora to a stop. "What are you talking about?"

"Me and Eli—you and Cal."

A blush suffused Aiyana's cheeks. "What makes you think I'd ever marry Cal? We're just friends."

"It's hilarious you'd even try to say that!" Cora said, laughing. "I know you stayed over at his place last Friday, when we had Bentley and Liam."

Her cheeks, already red, turned crimson. "I got home late, that's all."

Cora couldn't quit grinning. "Uh-huh."

"How'd you know?" her mother asked.

"Liam forgot something, so we dropped by the house. Your car wasn't there."

"Liam doesn't know I slept at Cal's, does he?" she said with a gasp.

"He didn't even seem to notice that your car was gone. He was too preoccupied with getting the video game he wanted. And Eli and I didn't talk about it until later, after the boys were asleep."

"I can't get away with anything," she grumbled.

Cora laughed again. "Which brings me back to the idea of a double wedding…"

Seemingly flustered, Aiyana waved her off. "Don't even suggest that! We would never horn in on your happiness."

"You wouldn't be 'horning in.' We'd be thrilled to share the limelight."

"You're jumping to conclusions." Aiyana started to

walk away from her, picking up the pace as if she could outdistance the conversation, too. "Let's not even talk about it."

Cora hurried to catch up with her. "He loves you, you know." And the two of them had grown so much closer in the last few weeks. Eli had noticed the same thing.

"I'm too old for that sort of thing," she insisted.

"That's what you always say. But I think you should reconsider your stance—to allow yourself to be happy at last."

Aiyana stopped again and pivoted to face her. "He's mentioned it," she suddenly admitted, sobering.

Cora felt her eyebrows slide up. "And?"

"I'm not ready. But—" her lips curved into a rather shy smile "—maybe soon."

"That's wonderful!" Cora cried.

She lifted a hand. "Like I said, let's not talk about it now. Your wedding comes first. After that's over, in another year or so, I don't know. We'll see."

Aiyana had already revealed far more than Cora had expected, so she let her retreat behind her usual curtain of privacy and they talked about other things as they walked the final block. Just before they entered the restaurant, however, Aiyana stopped Cora and, to Cora's surprise, hugged her. "Eli's so lucky to have found you."

Cora stared up at the beautiful spring sky visible over her mother's shoulder, grateful that she was finally satisfied and not still questioning, wondering and searching. "And we're both lucky to have you."

* * * * *

Since 1988, national bestselling author **Rochelle Alers** has written more than eighty books and short stories. She has earned numerous honors, including the Zora Neale Hurston Award, the Vivian Stephens Award for Excellence in Romance Writing and a Career Achievement Award from *RT Book Reviews*. She is a member of Zeta Phi Beta Sorority, Inc., Iota Theta Zeta Chapter. A full-time writer, she lives in a charming hamlet on Long Island. Rochelle can be contacted through her website, rochellealers.org.

Books by Rochelle Alers

Harlequin Special Edition

Wickham Falls Weddings

Home to Wickham Falls
Her Wickham Falls SEAL
The Sheriff of Wickham Falls

American Heroes

Claiming the Captain's Baby

Harlequin Kimani Romance

The Eatons

Sweet Silver Bells
Sweet Southern Nights

Sweet Destiny
Sweet Persuasions
Twice the Temptation
Sweet Dreams
Sweet Deception

Kimani Arabesque

The Wainwright Legacy

Here I Am
Because of You

Hideaway

Secret Vows
Eternal Vows
Summer Vows

Visit the Author Profile page at
Harlequin.com for more titles.

CLAIMING THE CAPTAIN'S BABY

Rochelle Alers

Chapter 1

Mya Lawson sat staring out the window in her home office as she waited for the pages she had revised to fill the printer's tray. She was still amazed that she had come up with yet another plot for her fictional New England series. What had begun as a hobby for Mya was now a vocation since she gave up her position as college professor to become a stay-at-home mother.

The sound of the printer spitting out paper competed with the incessant tapping of rain against the windows. It had begun raining earlier that morning and had continued nonstop throughout the midafternoon. Mya knew it was an indoor play day for Lily once she woke from her nap. An unconscious smile parted her lips when her gaze lingered on the oak tree shading the backyard. Mya lost count of the number of times she and her sister hid

behind the massive trunk or climbed the thick branches
once they were older while playing hide-and-seek with
their mother. Although aware of their hiding places,
Veronica Lawson elected to play along much to the delight of her rambunctious daughters. But as they grew
older the game stopped because Veronica claimed she
did not have the energy to chase after them.

An expression of melancholy sweeping over Mya's
features replaced her smile. She and seven-month-old
Lily were the last of the Wickham Falls Lawsons. What
she found ironic was that neither she nor Lily shared
DNA with their namesake ancestors. Graham and Veronica Lawson, after more than twenty years of a childless marriage, had decided to adopt. They adopted Mya,
and then two years later Samantha joined the family.

Mya exhaled an audible sigh. Her parents were gone,
Samantha was gone, and now there was only she and
her niece.

Her sister wanted Mya to raise Lily in Wickham
Falls—a small town with a population of little more
than four thousand residents—even though Samantha
had complained about growing up in a small town and
couldn't wait to grow up and leave to see the world.
She got her wish once she began her career as a flight
attendant and got to visit many of the cities and countries she had fantasized about.

Sammie, as Mya always called her, had died a month
ago and Mya was still attempting to adjust to the loss
and her life without her sister. Sammie had returned
to Wickham Falls for a rare visit with the news that
she was six weeks pregnant. She told Mya of her affair
with a New York City businessman, and despite using

protection, she'd gotten pregnant. Her sister refused to disclose the name of her lover or tell him about the baby because he had been adamant when he told her he wasn't ready for marriage or fatherhood.

The sudden ring of the telephone shattered her reverie. Unconsciously her brow furrowed when she recognized the name of the law firm that had handled Sammie's will. She picked up the receiver before the second ring.

"Hello."

"Ms. Mya Lawson?"

Mya nodded before she realized the person on the other end of the line could not see her. "Yes. This is she."

"Ms. Lawson, I'm Nicole Campos, Mr. McAvoy's assistant. He'd like you to keep your calendar open for next Thursday because he needs you to come into the office to discuss your daughter's future."

Her frown deepened. "Ms. Campos, can you give me an idea of what he wants to talk about?"

"I'm sorry, but I cannot reveal that information over the telephone."

Twin emotions of annoyance and panic gripped her. She did not want to relive the anxiety she had experienced before the court finalized her adopting her niece. "What time on Thursday?"

"Eleven o'clock. I'll call you the day before as a reminder and follow-up with an email."

Mya exhaled an inaudible sigh. "Thank you."

She hadn't realized her hand was shaking when she replaced the receiver in the console. Leaning back in the desk chair, she combed her fingers through a wealth of brown curly hair with natural gold highlights, holding it off her forehead.

There never had been a question that she would lose Lily to the foster care system because her sister had drawn up a will that included a clause naming Mya as legal guardian for her unborn baby.

A week after Sammie gave birth to a beautiful dark-haired infant, she handed Lily to Mya with the pronouncement that she wanted Mya to raise her daughter as her own. At first she thought Sammie was experiencing postpartum depression, but nothing could have prepared her for the reality that her younger sister was terminally ill.

Sammie had been diagnosed with an aggressive form of breast cancer. Mya put up a brave front for her sister because she needed to be strong for her, but whenever she was alone she could not stop crying. The young, beautiful, vivacious thirty-two-year-old woman who was in love with life was dying and there was nothing she could do to help her.

Gurgling sounds came from the baby monitor on a side table. Mya glanced at the screen where she could observe her daughter. It was after three and Lily was awake.

Pushing back her chair, she rose and walked out of the office and down the hall to the nursery. Lily was standing up in her crib. She'd sat up at five months, began crawling at six and now at seven was able to pull up and stand, but only holding onto something. It was as if her precocious daughter was in a hurry to walk before her first birthday.

Months before Lily's birth, Mya and Sammie spent

hours selecting furniture and decorating the room that would become the nursery. The colors of sage green and pale pink were repeated in blankets, quilts and in the colorful border along the antique-white walls.

"Hey, doll baby. Did you have a good nap?"

A squeal of delight filled the space when the baby raised her chubby arms to be picked up. The instant she let go of the railing, Lily landed hard on her bottom but didn't cry. Mya reached over the rail of the crib and scooped her up while scrunching up her nose. She dropped a kiss on damp, inky-black curls. "Somebody needs changing."

Lily pushed out her lips in an attempt to mirror Mya's expression. Mya smiled at the beautiful girl with long dark lashes framing a pair of large sky blue eyes. Lily looked nothing like Sammie, so it was obvious she had inherited her father's hair and eye color.

She placed her on the changing table and took off the damp onesie and then the disposable diaper. At thirty-four, Mya had not planned on becoming a mother, yet learned quickly. She'd read countless books on feedings, teething, potty training and the average milestones for crawling, walking and talking. She had childproofed the house—all the outlets were covered, there were safety locks on the kitchen cabinets and drawers, wires secured off the floor, and all furniture with sharp edges were placed out of the way.

She gathered Lily in her arms and pressed a kiss to her forehead. "You're getting heavy."

Lily grabbed several strands of Mya's hair as she carried her down the staircase to the kitchen. "If you keep pulling my hair, I'll be forced to get extensions." She had made it a habit to either style her hair in a single braid or ponytail because her daughter appeared transfixed by the profusion of curls resembling a lion's mane.

She entered the kitchen and placed Lily in her high chair. Opening the refrigerator, she took out a bottle of milk and filled a sippy cup. Lily screamed in delight when handed the cup.

Mya felt a warm glow flow through her as she watched Lily drink. Her daughter's life would mirror her biological mother's and her aunt's. She would grow up not knowing her birth mother, but Mya had started a journal chronicling the baby's milestones, photographs of Sammie and a collection of postcards from the different cities and countries her sister had visited. Once Lily was old enough to understand that her aunt wasn't her biological mother, Mya would reveal the circumstances of her birth.

"Giles, Brandt is on line two."

The voice of Giles Wainwright's administrative assistant coming through the intercom garnered his attention. He had spent the past twenty minutes going over the architect's rendering and the floor plan of six three-bedroom, two-bath homes on an island in the Bahamas he had recently purchased for the international division of Wainwright Developers Group.

He tapped a button on the intercom. "Thank you, Jocelyn." He activated the speaker feature as he leaned back in the executive chair and rested his feet on the corner of the antique desk. "What's up, cousin?"

"I'm calling to let you know Ciara and I have finally set a date for our wedding."

Brandt "The Viking" Wainwright's professional football career was cut short when he broke both legs in an automobile accident. Sidelined for the season and confined to his penthouse suite, Brandt had had a revolving door of private duty nurses before no-nonsense Ciara Dennison refused to let him bully her. In the end, Brandt realized he had met his match *and* his soul mate.

"Finally," Giles teased. "When is it?"

"We've decided on February 21 at the family resort in the Bahamas. It's after the Super Bowl, and that week the schools are out for winter break. And if adults want to bring their kids, then the more the merrier."

Giles smiled. "I'm certain you won't find an argument from the kids who'd rather hang out on a tropical beach than ski upstate."

Brandt's deep chuckle came through the speaker. "You're probably right about that. Ciara's mailing out the Save the Week notice to everyone. If the family is amenable to spending the week in the tropics, then I'll make arrangements to reserve several villas to accommodate everyone."

Giles listened as Brandt talked about their relatives choosing either to fly down on the corporate jet that seated eighteen, or sail down on the *Mary Catherine*, the Wainwright family yacht. Giles preferred sailing as his mode of transportation, because two to three times a month he flew down to the Bahamas to meet with the broker overseeing the sale of two dozen private islands now owned by Wainwright Developers Group International, or WDG, Inc.

The conversation segued to the news that there would be another addition to the Wainwright clan when Jordan and his wife, Aziza, welcomed their first child in the coming weeks.

Giles lowered his feet and sat straight when Jocelyn Lewis knocked softly on the door and stuck her head through the opening. She held an envelope in one hand.

Giles beckoned her in. "Hold on, Brandt, I need to get something from my assistant."

"I know you're busy, Giles, so I'll talk to you later," Brandt said.

"Give Ciara my love."

"I'll tell her."

Giles ended the call, stood up and took the letter from Jocelyn's outstretched hand. He thought of the woman as a priceless diamond after he had gone through a number of assistants in the four years since he'd started up the overseas division. Within minutes of Giles interviewing her, he had known Jocelyn was the one. At forty-six, she had left her position as director of a childcare center because she wanted to experience the corporate world. What prompted Giles to hire her on the spot was her admission that she'd taken several courses to become proficient in different computer programs.

He met the eyes of the woman who only recently had begun wearing makeup after terminating her membership with a church that frowned on women wearing pants and makeup. The subtle shade of her lipstick complemented the yellow undertones in her flawless mahogany complexion. "Who delivered this?" he asked, when he noticed that the stamp and the postmark were missing. Personal and Confidential was stamped below the addressee, while the return address indicated a Wickham Falls, West Virginia, law firm.

Jocelyn's eyebrows lifted slightly behind a pair of horn-rimmed glasses. "George brought it up. He said it came with this morning's FedEx delivery."

Giles nodded. "Thank you." All mail for the company was left at the front desk. The receptionist signed for documents requiring a signature, and then she alerted the mail room where George logged in and distributed letters and packages to their respective departments.

Jocelyn hesitated and met her boss's eyes. "I just want to remind you that I'll be in late tomorrow morning. I have to renew my driver's license."

He nodded. Jocelyn had saved his department thousands when she redesigned the website from ordinary to extraordinary with photos of Bahamian-Caribbean style homes on private islands with breathtaking views of the Atlantic Ocean and others with incredibly pristine Caribbean beaches.

Waiting until she walked out of the office and closed the door behind her, Giles sat down and slid a letter opener under the flap of the envelope. A slight frown settled into his features when he read and reread the single page of type. He was being summoned to the reading of a will. The letter did not indicate to whom the will belonged, but requested he call to confirm his attendance.

Picking up the telephone receiver, he tapped the area code and then the numbers. "This is Giles Wainwright," he said, introducing himself when the receptionist identified the name of the law firm. "I have a letter from your firm requesting my presence at the reading of a will this coming Thursday."

There came a pause. "Please hold on, Mr. Wainwright, while I connect you to Mr. McAvoy's office."

Giles drummed his fingers on the top of the mahogany desk with a parquetry inlay.

"Mr. Wainwright, I'm Nicole Campos, Mr. McAvoy's assistant. Are you calling to confirm your attendance?"

"I can't confirm until I know who named me in their will."

"I'm sorry, Mr. Wainwright, but I cannot disclose that at this time."

He went completely still. "You expect me to fly from New York to West Virginia on a whim?"

"It's not a whim, Mr. Wainwright. Someone from your past indicated your name in a codicil to their will. If you choose not to come, then we'll consider the matter settled."

Giles searched his memory for someone he'd met who had come from West Virginia. The only person that came to mind was a soldier under his command when they were deployed to Afghanistan.

Corporal John Foley had lost an eye when the Humvee in which he was riding was hit by shrapnel from a rocket-propelled grenade. The young marine was airlifted to a base hospital, awarded a purple heart and eventually medically discharged. Giles prayed that John, who had exhibited signs of PTSD, hadn't taken his life like too many combat veterans.

He stared at the framed pen and ink and charcoal drawings of iconic buildings in major US cities lining the opposite wall. A beat passed as he contemplated whether he owed it to John or his family to reconnect with their past.

"Okay, Ms. Campos. I'll be there."

He could almost imagine the woman smiling when she said, "Thank you, Mr. Wainwright."

Giles hung up and slumped down in the chair. He had just come back from the Bahamas two days ago, and he was looking forward to sleeping in his own bed for more than a week and hopefully catch up on what was going on with his parents and siblings.

Most days found him working in his office hours after other employees had gone home. It was when he spent time on the phone with his Bahamas-based broker negotiating the purchase of several more uninhabited islands. Other days were spent in weekly meetings with department heads and dinner meetings in the company's private dining room with the officers and managers—all of whom were Wainwrights by bloodline or had married into the family.

Wainwright Developers Group was the second largest real estate company in the northeast, and everyone associated with the company was committed to maintaining that position or bringing them to number one.

Swiveling on his chair, he sent Jocelyn an email, outlining his travel plans for the following Thursday. Giles had no idea where Wickham Falls, West Virginia, was, but in another week he would find out.

Giles deplaned after the jet touched down at the Charleston, West Virginia, airport. A town car awaited his arrival. Jocelyn had arranged for a driver to take him to Wickham Falls. She had also called a hotel to reserve a suite because he did not have a timetable as to when he would return to New York.

The trunk to the sedan opened, and seconds later the driver got out and approached him.

"Mr. Wainwright?"

Giles nodded. "Yes." He handed the man his suitcase and a leather case with his laptop.

When he'd boarded the jet, Giles had experienced a slight uneasiness because he still could not fathom what he would encounter once he arrived. He had racked his brain about possible scenarios and still couldn't dismiss the notion that something had happened to John Foley.

He removed his suit jacket, slipped into the rear of the car, stretched out his legs and willed his mind blank. When Jocelyn confirmed his travel plans, she informed him that Wickham Falls was an hour's drive from the state capital. Ten minutes into the ride, he closed his eyes and didn't open them again until the driver announced they were in Wickham Falls. Reaching for his jacket, he got out and slipped his arms into the sleeves.

"I'm not certain how long the meeting is going to take," he said to the lanky driver wearing a black suit that appeared to be a size too big.

"Not a problem, Mr. Wainwright. I'll wait here."

Giles took a quick glance at his watch. He was thirty minutes early. His gaze took in Wickham Falls's business district, and he smiled.

It was the epitome of small-town Americana. The streets were lined with mom-and-pop shops all sporting black-and-white awnings and flying American flags. Cars were parked diagonally in order to maximize space. It was as if Wickham Falls was arrested in time and that modernization had left it behind more than fifty years before. There was no fast-food restaurant or major drug store chain. To say the town was quaint was an understatement.

He noted a large red, white and blue wreath suspended from a stanchion in front of a granite monument at the end of the street. A large American flag was flanked by flags representing the armed forces. Giles knew it was a monument for military veterans.

He strolled along the sidewalk to see if John Foley's name was on the monument. There were names of servicemen who'd served in every war beginning with the Spanish–American War to the present. There was one star next to the names of those who were missing in action, and two stars for those who'd died in combat. Although he was relieved not to find the corporal's name on the marker, it did little to assuage his curiosity as to why he had been summoned to Wickham Falls.

As he retraced his steps, Giles wasn't certain whether he would be able to live in a small town. He was born, grew up and still lived in the Big Apple, and if he wanted or needed something within reason, all he had to do was pick up the telephone.

He opened the solid oak door to the law firm and walked into the reception area of the one-story, salmon-colored stucco building. He met the eyes of the middle-aged woman sporting a '60s beehive hairstyle, sitting at a desk behind a closed glass partition. She slid it open with his approach. His first impression was correct: the town and its inhabitants were stuck in time.

"May I help you, sir?"

Giles flashed a friendly smile. "I'm Giles Wainwright, and I have an appointment at eleven to meet with Mr. McAvoy."

She returned his smile. "Well, good morning, Mr. Wainwright. Please have a seat and I'll have someone escort you to the conference room."

He nodded. "Thank you."

Giles did not bother to sit on the leather sofa, but stood with both hands clasped behind his back. He had sat enough that morning. First it was in the car heading for the airport, then all through the flight and again during the drive from the airport to Wickham Falls. He had altered his normal morning routine of taking the elevator in his high-rise apartment building to the lower level to swim laps in the Olympic-size pool.

Swimming and working out helped him to relax, while maintaining peak physical conditioning from his time in the military. Going from active duty to spending most of his day sitting behind a desk had been akin to culture shock for Giles, and it had taken him more than a year to fully adjust to life as a civilian.

"Mr. Wainwright?"

He turned when he recognized the voice of the woman who'd called him. "Ms. Campos."

The petite, dark-haired woman with a short, pixie hairstyle extended her hand. "Yes."

Giles took her hand and was slightly taken aback when he noticed a small tattoo with USMC on the underside of her wrist. He successfully concealed a smile. It was apparent she had been in the Marine Corps. *"Semper fi,"* he said sotto voce.

Nicole Campos smiled. "Are you in the Corps?"

He shook his head. "I proudly served for ten years."

"I was active duty for fifteen years, and once I got out I decided to go to law school. I'd love to chat with you, Mr. Wainwright, but you're needed in the conference room."

Giles always looked forward to swapping stories with fellow marines, yet that was not a priority this morning. He followed her down a carpeted hallway to a room at the end of the hall.

His gaze was drawn to a woman holding a raven-haired baby girl. Light from wall sconces reflected off the tiny diamond studs in the infant's ears. The fretful child squirmed, whined and twisted backward as she struggled to escape her mother's arms.

He smiled, and much to his surprise, the baby went completely still and stared directly at him with a pair of large round blue eyes. She yawned and he was able to see the hint of two tiny rice-like teeth poking up through her gums. He couldn't pull his gaze away from the baby girl. There was something about her eyes that reminded him of someone.

His attention shifted from the baby to the man seated at the head of the conference table. His premature white hair was totally incongruent to his smooth, youthful-looking face.

Giles smiled and nodded. "Good morning."

"Good morning. I'm Preston McAvoy. Please excuse me for not getting up, Mr. Wainwright, but I'm still recovering from dislocating my knee playing football with my sons." He motioned to a chair opposite the woman with the baby. "Please sit down."

Giles complied, his eyes meeting those of the woman staring at him with a pair of incredibly beautiful hazel eyes in a tawny-gold complexion. He wondered if she knew she looked like a regal lioness with the mane of flowing brown curls with gold highlights framing her face and ending inches above her shoulders. A slight frown appeared between her eyes as she continued to stare at him. He wondered if she had seen him during his travels in the Bahamas, while Giles knew for certain he had never met her because she was someone he would never forget; she was breathtakingly beautiful.

Preston cleared his throat and opened the file folder on the table. He looked at Giles and then the baby's mother. "I'm sorry when my assistant called to ask you to come in that she was bound by law not to tell you why you'd been summoned." He removed an envelope from the folder and withdrew a single sheet of paper. His dark eyes studied each person at the table. "This is a codicil to Samantha Madison Lawson's last will and testament."

Giles went completely still. The name conjured up the image of a woman from his past who had disappeared without a trace. Now it was obvious he had not come to West Virginia for an update about a fellow soldier, but for a woman with whom he'd had an off-and-on liaison that went on for more than a year.

"Ms. Lawson, before she passed away," Preston continued, "made provisions for her unborn child, hence named Lily Hope Lawson, to become the legal ward of her sister, Mya Gabrielle Lawson. Ms. Lawson, being of sound mind and body, instructed me not to reveal the contents of her codicil until a month following her death." He paused and then continued to read from the single page of type.

Giles, a former marine captain who had led men under his command into battles where they faced the possibility of serious injury or even death, could not still his momentary panic. A tense silence swelled inside the room when Preston finished reading.

He was a father! The woman sitting across the table was holding his daughter. He had no legal claim to the child, but his daughter's mother sought fit to grant him visitation. That he could see Lily for school and holiday weekends, Thanksgiving, Christmas and one month during the summer, while all visitations would have to be approved by Mya Gabrielle Lawson.

Giles slowly shook his head. "That's not happening." The three words were dripping with venom.

"What's not happening?" Preston questioned.

"No one is going to tell me when and where I can see my daughter."

"You've just been told." The woman holding the child had spoken for the first time.

Chapter 2

Mya was certain the rapid pumping of her heart against her ribs could be heard by the others in the room. She hadn't been able to move or utter a sound when the tall, black-haired man with piercing blue eyes in a suntanned face walked into the conference room. It had only taken a single glance for her to ascertain that the man was Sammie's ex-lover and Lily's father. He continued to glare at her in what was certainly a stare down. However, she was beyond intimidation because legally he had no claim over her daughter.

"That's where you're wrong," Giles countered in a low and threatening tone. "As Lily's biological father, I can sue for joint custody."

"If you do, then you will surely lose," Mya countered.

Preston cleared his throat. "I'm afraid Ms. Lawson's

right, Mr. Wainwright. Legally, you have no right to the child. But look on the bright side, because it was the baby's mother's wish before she passed away that you could have a relationship with your daughter."

Giles's eyes burned like lasers when he turned to glare at Preston. "You fail to understand that a woman carried my child and neglected to notify me about it. Even though she's gone, you're allowing her to become the master puppeteer pulling strings and manipulating lives from the grave?"

Preston shrugged shoulders under a crisp white shirt. "Ms. Samantha Lawson must have had a reason for not informing you about the baby. I'm going to leave you and Mya alone, and I suggest you work out an arrangement that you both can agree on. Please keep in mind it's what's best for the baby." Reaching for a cane, Preston rose to his feet and limped out of the office.

Lily began squirming again, and Mya knew it was time to feed her and then put her to bed. "We're going to have to put off this meeting for another time because I have to get home and feed Lily."

"I don't have another time," Giles said. "The sooner we compromise, the better it will be for all of us."

A wry smile twisted Mya's mouth. Spoken like a true businessman. She wanted to tell him it wasn't about compromising. The terms in the codicil did not lend themselves to negotiating a compromise. "That's not possible now because I'm going home."

"Then I'll go with you."

Mya went completely still, and she stared at Giles as if he had taken leave of his senses. Did he actually expect her to welcome him, a stranger, into her home as if she had offered him an open invitation? "You want to come home with me?"

He cocked his head at an angle. "I don't hear an echo."

Her temper flared. "You cocky, arrogant—"

"I know I'm an SOB," he drawled, finishing her outburst. "Look, Ms. Lawson," he continued in a softer tone. "Up until a few minutes ago I had no idea that I was a father. But if Samantha had told me she was carrying my child, I would've made provisions for her and the child's future."

Mya scooped the diaper bag off the floor and looped the straps over her shoulder. "In other words, you wouldn't have married Sammie, because you weren't ready for marriage and fatherhood. She wouldn't tell me your name, but she did open up about your views on marriage and children." Mya knew she had struck a nerve with the impeccably dressed businessman when he lowered his eyes. Everything about him reeked of privilege and entitlement. His tailored suit and imported footwear probably cost more than some people earned in a month.

"What's the matter, Mr. Wainwright? You see a little girl with black hair and blue eyes and suddenly you're ready to be a father? What happened to you asking for a paternity test?"

Giles's eyes narrowed. "I don't need a paternity test because Lily looks like my sister."

"If that's case, then you can save some money," Mya mumbled under her breath. Suddenly she realized she wasn't as angry with Giles Wainwright as she was with her sister. Sammie had completely blindsided her with the codicil.

Giles rounded the table and took the large quilted bag off Mya's shoulder. "Please let me help you to your car."

Mya resisted the urge to narrow her eyes at him. At least he'd said please. She walked out of the room, Giles following as she cradled Lily to her chest. Fortunately for her, the baby had quieted. She had parked the Honda Odyssey in the lot behind the office building.

Pressing a button on the remote device, she opened the door to the minivan and placed Lily in the car seat behind the passenger seat. She removed the baby's hand-knitted sweater and buckled her in.

"We'll be home in a few minutes," she crooned softly as Lily yawned and kicked her legs. She closed the door and turned around to look for Giles. He was nowhere in sight. Where could he have gone with the diaper bag?

"Are you looking for this?"

She turned to find him standing on the other side of the vehicle, holding the bag aloft. Bright afternoon sun glinted off his neatly barbered inky-black hair. Closing the distance between them, she held out her hand. "Yes. I'll take it now."

Giles held it out of her reach. "I'll give it back to you when you get to your house."

She didn't want to believe he was going to hold the bag hostage. Mya bit her lip to keep from spewing the curses forming on tongue. She wanted the bag, but more than that she needed to get her daughter home so she could change and feed her and then into her crib for a nap.

She knew arguing with the arrogant man was just going to delay her. "Okay," she conceded. "Follow me."

She flung off Giles's hand when he attempted to assist her into the van. The man was insufferable. She couldn't understand how Sammie was able to put up with his dictatorial personality. It was as if he was used to giving orders and having them followed without question.

Mya hit the start-engine button harder than necessary. Lily's father was definitely working on her very last frayed nerve. She maneuvered out of the parking lot, not bothering to glance up at the rearview mirror to see if he was following her.

Mya's fingers tightened around the steering wheel at the same time she clenched her teeth. She knew the anger and frustration she'd unleashed at the man who'd just discovered he was Lily's father was the result of Sammie keeping her in the dark as to her child's paternity; repeated attempts for her to get her sister to disclose the identity of the man who'd gotten her pregnant had become an exercise in futility. It was a secret Sammie had taken to her grave.

And why now? Mya mused. What did Sammie hope to prove by waiting a month after her death to disrupt not only her life, but also Lily's and Giles Wainwright's? She decelerated and took a quick glance in the rearview mirror to see a black town car following her minivan.

Giles closed his eyes as he sat in the back of the sedan. Samantha was dead and he was a father! What he found incredulous was that they'd never made love without using protection. And to make certain he would not father a child, Giles had always used *his* condoms, because he did not trust a woman to claim she was using birth control when she wasn't. And while he had been forthcoming when he told women he'd slept with that he wasn't ready for marriage and fatherhood, he never said he did not want a wife or children. It was just that the timing wasn't right, because after serving his country for ten years as a captain in the Marine Corps, he found difficulty transitioning to life as a civilian.

Giles opened his eyes and stared out the side window. Towering trees growing close to one another nearly blotted out the sunlight, while a series of waterfalls washing over ancient rocks had probably given the town its name. The mountainous landscape appeared untamed, forbidding. It was a far cry from the skyscrapers, crowded streets, bumper-to-bumper traffic and the sights and sounds that made his hometown so hypnotically exciting. He sat straight when the driver turned off into a long driveway behind Mya's minivan.

He leaned forward. "Don't bother to get out," he ordered the driver. "I'm not certain how long I'm going to be inside."

"I'll wait here, Mr. Wainwright."

Giles reached for the colorful blue-and-white-patterned diaper bag. He was out of the town car at the same time Mya had removed Lily from her car seat. The baby's head rested on her shoulder.

Looping the straps of the bag over one shoulder, he gently gathered Lily from Mya's arms. "I'll carry her." He met Mya's brilliant catlike eyes, not seeing any of the hostility she had exhibited in the law office.

"Thank you."

He followed her up the porch steps to a house he recognized as a modified Louisiana low-country home. As a developer, he had gotten a crash course in architectural styles and he favored any residential structure with broad porches welcoming the residents and callers with cool shade. Tall shuttered windows and French doors were representative of the French Colonial or plantation style.

Admiring the house with twin fans suspended from the ceiling of the veranda, the white furniture, and large planters overflowing with live plants did not hold as much appeal as the small, warm body pressed to his chest. He lowered his head and pressed a kiss on her silky curls. The distinctive scent associated with babies wafted to his nose, a pleasing fragrance that reminded him of the times he'd held his nephews.

His previous declaration that he wasn't ready for fatherhood no longer applied, because the child in his arms was a blatant reminder that he had to get ready. He and Samantha engaging in the most intimate act possible had unknowingly created another human being. Even before sleeping together, he and Samantha had talked about marriage and children and he was forthcoming and adamant that he wasn't ready for either.

And when he'd walked into the conference room and had seen the infant for the first time, there was something about her that reminded him of someone, and within minutes of the attorney reading the contents of the codicil, Giles knew that someone was his sister. Lily had inherited Skye's raven-black hair and blue eyes. Giles, his mother, his sister and his cousin Jordan were the dark-haired anomalies among several generations of blond Wainwrights.

He watched Mya as she unlocked the front door;

she tapped several buttons on the wall to disengage the house's security system. He stared at her delicate profile, wondering what was going on behind her impassive expression. She and Samantha may have been sisters, but there was nothing physically similar that confirmed a familial connection. Samantha had been a petite, curvy, green-eyed blonde, while Mya was tall, very slender, with a complexion that was an exact match for the gold strands in her chestnut curls.

She held her arms out for the baby. "I'll take her now."

Giles handed her the sleeping infant and then the bag. "What are you going to do with her?"

"She needs to be changed, and then I'm going to give her a bottle before I put her to bed."

A slight frown appeared between Giles's eyes. "It's lunchtime. Aren't you going to give her food?" he asked. Mya had mentioned having to feed her.

Mya shook her head. "No. I'll give her a snack after she wakes up. The bottle will hold her until then. Make yourself comfortable in the family room. I'll be back and then we'll talk about what's best for Lily."

Giles felt as if he had been summarily dismissed as he stared at Mya's narrow hips in a pair of black tailored slacks. He walked over to a pale-pink-and-white-pinstriped sofa and folded his tall frame down.

Everything about the space was romantic and inviting, beckoning one to come and sit awhile. He admired the floor plan with its open rooms, high ceilings and columns that matched the porch posts. French doors and windows let in light and offered an unobstructed view of the outdoors. Wide mullions in the off-white kitchen cabinet doors were details repeated in the home's many windows. The tongue-and-groove plank ceiling, off-white walls, kitchen cabinets, cooking island and break-fast bar reflected comfortable family living.

Family. The single word reminded him that he now had a family of his own. A hint of a smile tilted the corners of his mouth when he thought of his daughter. Then within seconds his smile vanished when he real-ized he had no legal claim to her. The lawyer had indi-cated Samantha was of sound mind and body when she drew up her will and then added the codicil, but Giles wondered if she actually had been in her right mind. It was obvious Samantha had died, and he wondered if she had known she was dying?

Giles knew he could challenge the will and authenti-cate his paternity. He had the resources to hire the best lawyers in the country to sue for sole or joint custody with Mya. Lily may be a Lawson, but she was also a Wainwright. And Giles wasn't above using his family name and wealth to claim what belonged to him.

He rose to his feet when Mya reappeared. She had exchanged her slacks and man-tailored blouse for a pair of skinny jeans and an oversize University of Chicago T-shirt. Thick white socks covered her bare feet. She had brushed her hair off her face and secured it in a po-nytail. Giles found that he couldn't pull his gaze away from the small, round face with delicate doll-like fea-tures. He retook his seat after Mya sat opposite him on a chair.

"How old is Lily?" he asked; he decided he would be the one controlling the conversation.

"Seven months." Her eyebrows lifted slightly. "How well did you know my sister?"

Giles was taken aback by Mya's question. "What do you mean by how *well*?"

Mya crossed her arms under her breasts at the same time she crossed her outstretched legs at the ankles. "I know you were sleeping with her, but what else did you know about her?"

"Apparently not enough," he countered flippantly. "Maybe I was mistaken, but I thought she told me she was from a small town in Virginia, not West Virginia."

"You were mistaken because we've never lived in Virginia. What else do you know about her? Did she ever talk to you about her parents or her family?"

Giles cursed under his breath. He wanted to be the one to interrogate Mya, yet unwittingly she had turned the tables on him. "She told me her parents were dead, but nothing beyond that. Most times we talked about the places she had visited as a flight attendant, while I wasn't very forthcoming about my time in the military because I did not want to relive some of what I'd seen or done."

Mya's expression softened as she angled her head. "Were you deployed?"

He nodded. "I managed to complete a couple of tours in Afghanistan."

"Thank you for your service."

Giles nodded again. Suddenly he was reflective. Now that he thought about it, there wasn't that much he had known about Samantha Lawson, except that he enjoyed whatever time they had spent together whenever she had a layover in New York, which wasn't that often.

"Samantha and I did not spend a lot of time together," he admitted. "She would call me whenever she had a layover in New York and there were occasions when we'd just go out for dinner. She loved the theater, so if she had a few days to spare, I'd purchase tickets for whatever play she wanted to see."

"But you did sleep with her."

"Yes. And I always used protection."

Mya lowered her arms. "Sammie told me you did. But we both know the only form of birth control that is one hundred percent foolproof is abstinence."

A wry smile twisted Giles's mouth. "I'm fully aware of that now." He sobered. "You claim that you and Samantha are sisters, yet you don't look anything like her."

"That's because we were both adopted. Our parents couldn't have children, so they decided to adopt. They adopted me first, and then two years later they adopted Sammie. My sister spent all of her adult life searching for her birth mother and that's probably the reason why she wanted me to adopt Lily, so I would be able to tell her everything she would need to know about her mother. When she found out she was having a girl, she selected the name Lily Hope, after her favorite flower and Sammie's hope she would someday find her mother. My sister spent hours writing letters to her unborn baby and making recordings so Lily could hear her voice."

Sadness swept through Giles as he attempted to deal with all that his former lover had planned for their daughter. "Please answer one question for me, Mya?"

"What is it?"

"Did Samantha know she was dying?"

Mya averted her head. "Yes. When she discovered

she was pregnant, she was also diagnosed with Stage IV breast cancer. Chemotherapy couldn't be given during throughout her pregnancy, so she had to wait until after the baby was born for radiation and hormonal therapy. However, during her second trimester she did undergo a mastectomy, but by the time she delivered Lily the cancer had spread to her liver and lymph nodes. Even though she never complained, I knew she was in pain. In the end, I hired a private duty nurse to take care of her because she refused to go to hospice. The nurse made certain to keep her comfortable, and several days after Lily turned six months old, Sammie passed away. And when she's older, I'll show Lily where her mother and grandparents are buried."

Giles felt as if someone had reached into his chest and squeezed his heart, making it nearly impossible for him to draw a normal breath. He hadn't found himself in love with Samantha, yet if he had known she was sick, he would have been there for her even if she wasn't carrying his child. "I'm so sorry."

Mya exhaled an audible sigh. "She's at peace now."

He leaned forward, hands sandwiched between his knees. There was something he had to know before he decided his next move and he hoped Mya didn't construe it as heartless. "Was Samantha of sound mind and body when she drew up her will?"

"Are you thinking of challenging her will because you don't believe she was in her right mind?"

"That's not what I'm saying," he argued softly.

"That's exactly what you're saying," Mya said in rebuttal. "There was nothing remotely wrong with Sammie when she drew up her will. She refused to tell me who had fathered her child, and I didn't understand her reasoning until Mr. McAvoy mentioned your name. Sammie did reveal that she was sleeping with a wealthy New York businessman, and when I finally heard the name Wainwright I understood her reluctance to tell me, because you probably would've talked her into having an abortion so as not to besmirch your family name when the word got out that you had a baby mama."

Giles covered his face with his hand, unable to believe what Mya was saying. "Is that what you really think?" he asked through his fingers.

"It's not what I think, but how Sammie felt. I know she withheld the fact that she had your child, but in the end she did redeem herself with the codicil. She didn't want Lily to spend her life looking for her father as it had been with her and her birth mother."

"What about you, Mya? Do you intend to raise Lily as your daughter?"

With wide eyes, she stared at him. "I *will* raise her as my daughter. I'm not only her legal guardian, but also her adoptive mother. I'm the only link between Lily's past and her future, so if you're thinking about suing me for custody, then I'm prepared to fight you tooth and nail for *my daughter*."

Giles went completely still. He had underestimated Mya. There definitely was fire under her cool demeanor. "There's no need to fight each other when we both want what's best for Lily."

"And that is?"

"For her to grow up loved and protected."

"And you don't think I'll be able to love and protect her, Giles?" Mya asked.

He smiled. "I don't doubt you will, but she needs to grow up knowing she has a father."

"She will, because Sammie has granted you visitation."

"How many times a year? And don't forget a month in the summer."

"Being facetious will definitely not endear you to me, Giles."

"I don't intend to be facetious. I'm just repeating the terms of the codicil."

Mya closed her eyes. The verbal interchange was beginning to wear on her nerves *and* give her a headache. Not only was Giles strong-willed but he was also relentless in his attempt to undermine her sister's decision to conceal her pregnancy from him. The Wainwright name was to real estate as Gates was to Microsoft, and Samantha, knowing this, had attempted to make provisions for Lily that would prevent her from becoming a legal football between the Lawsons and Wainwrights.

"I'm not your enemy, but if you keep pushing me then I'll become your worst nightmare. I'm willing to grant you more liberal visitation than what Sammie stated in her will. And that means I'm not opposed to you taking Lily to New York to meet your family, but not without me. Wherever she goes, I go along."

"I don't have a problem with that."

Mya was mildly shocked he would agree to her terms. "You'll have to let me know in advance because she has scheduled doctor's appointments."

"What about you, Mya? What about your work schedule?"

"My schedule is flexible, because I'm now a stay-at-home mother. I resigned my teaching position once Sammie moved back home."

"What and where did you teach?"

"Comparative literature at the University of Charleston."

He mentally filed away this disclosure. "Do you miss teaching?"

"A little, but I love being with Lily." Mya didn't tell Giles that working at home allowed her to pen her novels in her spare time. "When are you going back to New York?"

A beat passed. "Tomorrow morning. Once I get back I'll have to rearrange my work schedule before I return. I'm going to give you several numbers where you'll be able to reach me. Jocelyn Lewis is my administrative assistant. So if you call my office, make certain you identify yourself and she'll put you through to me."

Mya stood, Giles also rising with her. "I'm going to get my phone so you can program your numbers into it."

Reaching into his shirt pocket, Giles handed Mya his cell phone. "You do the same with your contact info."

Her thumbs moved quickly over the keys as she tapped in her name, address, cell and landline numbers, along with her email address. She retrieved her phone from where she had left it on the dining room table and gave it to Giles.

"How many numbers do you have?" she asked when he took an inordinate amount of time tapping keys.

"Three. I'm giving you my cell, the number at the office, and the one in my apartment." Glancing up, he winked at her. "You can always send me a text if you need me for anything. And I do mean anything."

Mya stared, momentarily speechless. The warmth in his voice and the tenderness in his expression made her fully aware of why her sister had been taken with him. Not only was he urbane, but also unquestionably charming when he chose to be.

She smiled. "I'll keep that in mind if I do *need* you for something."

Giles returned Mya's phone to her. "I'll call you once I make arrangements to return. You don't have to see me out," he said when she made a move to walk him to the door.

Mya met eyes that shimmered like polished blue topaz. "Safe travels."

He inclined his head. "Thank you."

Giles settled himself into the rear of the car. He had revised his plan to remain in Wickham Falls for more than one day. Scrolling through his phone directory, he tapped Jocelyn's number. She answered after the first ring.

"I need you to arrange for a flight back to New York for tomorrow morning out of the regional airport." The regional airport was a shorter distance from his hotel. "And please call my mother and let her know I would like to see her tomorrow night at seven. Be certain to let her know dinner will be at my place."

"Consider it done."

"Thank you, Jocelyn."

He had asked Jocelyn to contact Amanda because Giles did not get to see his mother as often as she would like. Unlike her other son, Giles's position took him out of the country, and he wanted to tell her in person that she had another grandchild—and this time it was a girl.

And while he wanted to wait for Lily to wake up from her nap to see her again, he knew Mya needed time to accept that she would now have to share her daughter with him. Putting distance between them would also help him to try to understand why Samantha had elected not to tell him about the baby.

Had she viewed him as someone who had used her for only for sex? Did she not trust him to take care of her and the baby? Or had she denied him his parental rights because she knew he had been adamant about not wanting to marry or father a child?

There was one more person he wanted to call, but he decided to wait until after he checked into the hotel.

If Samantha hadn't told him about the baby, then he wondered if there were other things she'd sought to conceal from him. Not only did he intend to have Samantha's background dissected but also her sister's. And if anything negative about either of them surfaced, then he was prepared to bring holy hell down on Mya to secure full custody of his daughter.

Chapter 3

Giles settled into a hotel suite less than an hour's drive from a regional airport. After checking in, he changed into a swimsuit and swam laps in the indoor pool. Once he had showered and changed into a pair of walking shorts and a rugby shirt, he ordered room service.

A ringtone on his phone indicated a text message from Jocelyn:

Return flight scheduled for departure at 1:00 PM tomorrow at Tri State Airport. Ground transportation confirmed. Confirmed dinner with your mother

Giles responded with: Thank you.

He could always count on Jocelyn to simplify his life. Once he had set up the company's international division,

Giles couldn't convince his older brother to run the department with him. Patrick had declined because, as a husband and now a father of two young boys under the age of six, he claimed he didn't want to be away from his family even if it was only for a week.

Patrick also professed he preferred working with their father in the legal department to jetting off to exotic climes, leaving Giles to ponder how much longer he would be able to maintain a one-man operation. Several third-generation Wainwrights cousins were still undecided whether to come and work for the company. He had made them generous offers to come and work with him, yet they still were ambivalent about becoming involved in the real estate business.

He finished his lunch and left the tray on the floor outside the door. Walking across the room, he flopped down on the king-size bed and reached for the cell phone on the bedside table and dialed the number to Jordan's cell phone. It rang four times before going directly to voice mail. He decided not to leave a message. Either Jordan was in court or with a client. He made another call, this time to his cousin's office.

Jordan had always teased Giles, declaring they were the family outsiders. Jordan and his law school mentor had gone into partnership, setting up Chatham and Wainwright, PC, Attorneys at Law. The firm was housed in a brownstone in Harlem's Mount Morris Park Historic District. Despite his reputation as a brilliant corporate attorney, Jordan refused to work for the family business, while Giles had opted for the military rather than join the company once he'd graduated college.

"Good afternoon, Chatham and Wainwright. How may I direct your call?"

"I'd like to speak to Jordan Wainwright."

"May I ask who's calling?"

"Giles Wainwright."

"Hold on, Mr. Wainwright. I'll see if he's available to take your call."

"Thank you." He didn't have to wait long before he heard Jordan's familiar greeting.

"What's up, G?"

Giles smiled. Jordan was the only one in the family who referred to him by an initial. "I'd like to hire your firm to conduct a background check on a couple of people." A swollen silence followed his request.

"Why are you asking me when your legal department can do it?"

"I'm asking you because what I'm going to say to you should stay between us. Attorney-client privilege," he added.

"What's going on, Giles?"

He knew he had gotten Jordan's attention when he addressed him by name. Giles was completely truthful when he told Jordan everything—from sleeping with Samantha, the phone call asking him to come to Wickham Falls, West Virginia, and to the revelation that he was now the father of a seven-month-old little girl and the rights extended to him as her father.

"That's really a low blow," Jordan drawled.

Giles smiled in spite of the seriousness of the situation. "I agree. I need to know everything about Samantha Madison Lawson and Mya Gabrielle Lawson.

Both were adopted, so I don't know how far back you'll be able to go."

"I'll have the investigators begin with their adoption records and go forward from there. Is there anything you've noticed about the aunt that would make her unfit to be your daughter's mother?"

"Not really. We spent less than an hour together. Her home is clean and tastefully furnished, and she claims to have taught college-level literature."

"Does she appear financially able to raise and educate the child until she is emancipated?" Jordan asked.

Giles stared up at the ceiling. "I don't know. That's what I need for your people to find out." Although Mya drove a late-model vehicle, it wasn't in the luxury category. He also had no idea if Samantha had life insurance, and if she did, if Mya had been her beneficiary. His concern was how she was supporting herself as a stay-at-home mother.

He had called Jordan because he knew he would never divulge what Giles had just told him. However, Giles knew he owed it to his parents—his mother in particular—to let her know that they had another grandchild.

"Are you prepared to accept the results if they come back clean?"

"I'll have to accept it, but that doesn't mean I'm going to stop fighting to claim my daughter."

"I wouldn't expect you to give up," Jordan continued, "because I would do the same if I were in a similar situation. What I wouldn't do is antagonize your daughter's mother. Try to remain civil with her and perhaps she'll come around and allow you more involvement in the baby's life."

"That's what I'm hoping will happen." Giles paused. "Do I have an alternative if the background checks yield nothing? What can I use to sue for at least joint custody?"

"Your only other option would be charging her with neglect. You'll have to be able to prove that the child has failed to thrive, that she doesn't get the medical care she needs, or if you've witnessed any verbal or physical abuse. I've never handled a child abuse or neglect case, but Aziza has. Although she's well versed in the family court system, I don't want to involve her in this because she's so close to her due date. Maybe after the baby's born and if she feels up to it, I'll ask her to look into this for you."

"When is she due again?"

"October 5. The doctor says the baby could come a week before or a week after that date."

"You still don't know if you're having a girl or a boy?"

"No. We want to be surprised."

"Have you narrowed it down to names?"

"We're leaning toward Maxwell if it's a boy and Layla if it's a girl."

"I like those names."

His cousin and his wife were given the privilege of selecting names for their unborn baby, while he'd had no say in naming his daughter. Every time he thought about Samantha's deception, it served to refuel his anger.

"Look, G, I'm going to hang up because I have a client waiting for me. And don't worry about the background checks. I'll have the investigators get on it ASAP."

"Thanks, Jordan."

"No need to thank me. Talk to you later."

Giles ended the call and rested his head on folded arms. He would take Jordan's advice and not do anything to antagonize Mya because she held all of the cards when it came to Lily's future. At least for now.

What she wasn't aware of was his intent to use any and everything short of breaking the law to claim his daughter.

The following evening Giles opened the door to his apartment and waited for his mother to emerge from the elevator.

Amanda Wainwright stepped out of the car, her smile indicating she was as pleased to see him as he was her. It was a rare occasion when Giles saw his mother without a fringe of hair sweeping over her ears and forehead. Tonight she had styled her chin-length, liberally gray-streaked black hair off her face. She was conservatively dressed in tailored taupe slacks she had paired with a white tailored blouse. She was hardly ever seen in public without her ubiquitous navy blazer, Gucci loafers and the magnificent strand of South Sea pearls and matching studs she had inherited from her grandmother.

There had been a time after graduating college and before he'd joined the marines when they had rarely spoke to each other. However, that changed when Giles called to inform his mother he was being deployed to Afghanistan. After all, he'd owed it to her to let her know he would be going into combat.

That single call changed him forever. It had taken days before he could forget the sound of her heartbreaking sobs. He apologized for severing all communication with her, while she apologized for interfering in his life and attempting to control his future. He returned to the United States after his first tour, shocking his parents when they opened the door to find him in uniform grinning ear to ear. The homecoming signaled a change in their relationship. He was still their son, but he had also become a decorated war veteran.

"Hello, gorgeous."

An attractive blush suffused Amanda's fair complexion with the compliment. Giles had been truthful. His mother's stunning beauty hadn't faded at sixty-four. It was her tall, slender figure, delicate features, coal-black hair and vibrant violet-blue eyes that had attracted Patrick Wainwright II, who married her after a whirlwind courtship; a year later, they had welcomed their first child.

Amanda rested a hand on Giles's light stubble. "You are definitely your father's son. You always know what to say to make a woman feel good."

Giles kissed her forehead. "You have to know by now that I never lie." He threaded their fingers together and led her through the foyer and into the expansive living-dining area.

She pointed to the dining area table set for two. "You cooked?"

He seated his mother on a love seat and dropped down next to her. "Surely you jest," he said, smiling. His many attempts to put together a palatable meal had resulted in either over-or undercooked dishes that always ended up in the garbage. In the end, he preferred eating in or ordering from his favorite restaurants or gourmet shops.

"I ordered from Felidia. It should be here in about twenty minutes."

Amanda gave Giles a long stare. "Why did you order in? You know I love eating there because the place reminds me of a little ristorante Pat and I discovered when we were in Bologna."

"I decided we'd eat in because I need to talk to you about something."

"Please don't tell me you're going to rejoin the military."

Giles dropped an arm over his mother's shoulders and hugged her. "No. What I want to tell you shouldn't be disclosed in public."

Amanda's eyelids fluttered as the natural color drained from her face. She rested a hand over the pearls. "Please don't tell me something that's going to hurt my heart."

He shook his head. "It's something you claim you've been wishing for. You now have a granddaughter."

Giles knew he had shocked his mother when her hands trembled, but then she quickly recovered and cried tears of joy. Waiting until she was calmer, he told her everything he'd disclosed to Jordan. He left out the fact that he wanted his cousin to conduct a background check into the lives of his daughter's mother *and* adoptive mother.

Amanda sniffled as she opened her handbag and took out several tissues. "What are you going to do?" she asked, after blowing her nose.

"I'm going to take the legal route to claim my daughter."

"You claim you have visitation, so when can we expect to meet her?"

Giles recalled the designated holidays outlined in the codicil. "It probably won't be until Thanksgiving."

A crestfallen expression crossed Amanda's face. "That's more than two months from now."

"I know, Mom. I'm hoping to convince Mya to bring her before then."

"Who else knows about this?"

"Just you and Jordan," he admitted.

Amanda rested her head on her son's shoulder. "I'd rather not say anything to Pat right now, because he's probably going to go ballistic and go after this poor girl who had no idea what her sister was planning."

Giles pressed a kiss to his mother's hair. "You're right." There was nothing his father liked better than a legal brouhaha. "Then this will remain between you, me and Jordan for now." The chiming of the building's intercom reverberated through the apartment. "That's probably our dinner."

He answered the intercom. The doorman announced a delivery from Felidia. "Please send them up."

Two hours later, Giles escorted his mother to the street, waited for her to get into a taxi and stood on the curb watching as it disappeared from his line of vision.

It was as if he could exhale for the first time in more than twenty-four hours. Talking to his mother, and her decision not to tell her husband temporarily assuaged his angst over attempting to explain the circumstances of him becoming a father.

Giles shook his head to rid his thoughts of the possible scenarios Patrick could employ to make Lily a Wainwright, because he intended to use his own methods to get what he wanted. If he was able to get a judge to rule in his favor to grant him joint custody, then he would happily comply with the law to share his daughter with Mya.

The sidewalks were teeming with locals and tourists in sweaters and lightweight jackets to ward off the early autumn chill. Giles, not wanting to return to his apartment, walked along Second Avenue to Forty-Second Street, stopping at intervals to do some window-shopping before reversing direction and heading back uptown. The walk had been the antidote to release some of his anxiety about reuniting with Mya and hopefully agreeing to what was best for Lily.

The night doorman stood under the building's canopy. "Have a good evening, Mr. Wainwright."

Giles nodded and smiled. "You do the same, Raoul."

During the elevator ride to his floor, Giles mentally mapped out what he had to accomplish before returning to Wickham Falls. He knew it was time for him to give Jocelyn more responsibility if he was going to be away for any appreciable length of time. And that meant she would have to accompany him during his next trip to the Bahamas.

Mya sat on the porch, bouncing Lily on her lap. Giles had called to inform her he was in Wickham Falls and for her to expect him to arrive at her house before one that afternoon.

It had been three weeks since their initial meeting,

and she had resigned herself to accept him as Lily's father. If Sammie hadn't wanted her daughter to have a relationship with her father, then she never would've added the codicil.

She had gotten up earlier that morning to put up several loads of laundry, give Lily breakfast and followed with a bath. After dressing her, she spent fifteen minutes reciting nursery rhymes. Mya knew Lily was more than familiar with many of the words and would be able to repeat them once she began talking.

Her daughter had become quite a chatterbox when she babbled about things Mya pretended to understand, while their favorite games were patty-cake and ring around the rosy. Now that Lily was standing up while holding on, Mya would gently pull her down to the floor when she sang the line "they all fall down" in "Ring Around the Rosie."

Mya went completely still when she registered the sound of an approaching car. The vehicle maneuvering up the driveway wasn't a town car but an SUV with New York plates. And as it came closer, she noticed a car seat.

Mya held her breath when Giles got out and waved to her. He looked nothing like the well-dressed man who had questioned her late sister's decision not to grant him custody of their daughter. Relaxed jeans, a sweatshirt with a fading USMC logo and running shoes had replaced the business attire.

She rose stiffly, as if pulled up by a taut overhead wire, and waited for his approach. He hadn't shaved and the stubble afforded him an even more masculine quality.

At first, she had asked herself why her sister had put up with him, but seeing him like this, Mya realized Giles Wainwright was not a man most women could ignore at first glance. Piercing blue eyes and balanced features made for an arresting face. He was tall, several inches above six feet, broad-shouldered and appeared in peak physical condition.

Giles slowly made his way up the porch steps, stopping only a few feet from her.

"Hello again."

An unconscious smile parted Mya's lips. "Welcome back. How long do you plan to stay?"

Giles met her eyes. "I don't know. It's open-ended, so I checked into an extended stay hotel."

Her smile faded. "What do you mean by open-ended?"

"I may have to go to New York for a few days for meetings, but once they're concluded I'll be back.

Her jaw dropped. "Oh I see."

"Hopefully you do, because it's going to take a while for Lily to get used to seeing me, so I'm prepared to take as much time as necessary to bond with *my daughter.*"

His reference to Lily being his daughter was not lost on Mya. Biologically the baby was his daughter, but legally Lily was hers. "I'm not opposed to you bonding with *my* daughter," she countered, smiling. "And if there is anything I can do to speed up the process, then please let me know."

She knew she had shocked him with the offer when he gave her a long, penetrating stare. It was apparent he hadn't expected her to be that cooperative. His gaze shifted to Lily.

"May I hold her?"

"Hold out your arms and see if she'll come to you."

Giles extended his arms, and much to his surprise Lily leaned forward and held out her arms for him to take her. He smiled at the little girl looking up at him. "She looks different from when I last saw her." Her hair was longer and there was a hint of more teeth coming through her upper gums.

Mya leaned against the porch column and crossed her arms under her breasts. "I'm able to see her change even though I'm with her all the time. Right now she's teething, so she's drooling on everything." As if on cue, Lily picked up her bib and gnawed on it.

Giles shifted his attention from Lily to Mya. He marveled that a woman without a hint of makeup and wearing faded jeans and a white T-shirt and socks could appear so incredibly sensual.

"How old is she now?"

"She turned eight months two days ago."

He quickly did the math. "Her birthday is February 5?"

"Yes."

"Our birthdays are four days apart. Mine is February first."

"That's quite a coincidence." Mya turned and opened the storm door at the same time Lily let out a piercing scream. "That's her way of telling me she wants to be changed. In fact, it's time for her afternoon nap."

Giles followed Mya inside the house and sniffed the air. "Something smells good."

Mya glanced at him over her shoulder. "I'm making pot roast. You're more than welcome to stay for dinner."

He stared at the denim fabric hugging her hips and smothered a groan. Giles knew it wasn't going to be easy to completely ignore the woman with whom he would spend time whenever he came to see Lily. Everything about her turned him on: her face, body, hair, softly modulated voice with a hint of a drawl and then there was the way she stared at him. It was as if she knew what he was thinking or going to say before he spoke.

Jordan had come up with nothing—not even a parking ticket—in Samantha and Mya's background for him to use as leverage to bolster his case if and when he decided to sue her. The only alternative was to watch for signs of neglect, and watching Mya closely was definitely going to become a delightful distraction.

"I'd like that very much. Do you cook every day?"

"Yes, because I have to prepare meals for Lily."

Giles slipped out of his running shoes, left them on the thick straw mat near the door and followed Mya through the living room and up a flight of stairs to the second story. "You don't buy baby food from the supermarket?"

"No. I've heard stories about jars of baby food being recalled because of foreign objects, so I decided it's safer and healthier to prepare her food myself. I'll cook carrots, beets, spinach or sweet potatoes and then purée them to a consistency where she can swallow without choking."

"That's a lot of work."

"She's worth it." Mya stood at the entrance to the nursery. "Do you want to change her?"

Giles didn't mind holding a baby but usually drew the line when it came to changing diapers. The few times he'd changed his nephews it was apparent he had been too slow when they urinated on him. "I'll watch you do it."

Her eyebrows flickered a little. "You've never changed a baby?"

"Only boys. My brother has two sons." Giles handed her Lily.

"The fact that they're not anatomically the same shouldn't make a difference. You are familiar with the female body, aren't you?"

Giles narrowed his eyes. "That's not funny. I remember you warning me about being facetious," he added when she gave him a Cheshire cat grin.

She scrunched up her nose. "I do remember saying something like that."

Giles had to smile. His daughter's mother was a beautiful sexy tease. How different she was from their first encounter where he could feel her hostility. This was a Mya he could readily get used to.

"Everything you'll need to change her is in the drawers of the changing table." She opened and closed each drawer. "Here are diapers, wipes, lotion and plastic bags for the soiled diapers."

He stood at the changing table positioned at the foot of the crib and watched as Mya removed Lily's bib and onesie. She quickly and expertly changed the wet diaper and disposed of it in a plastic bag. "Where do you put the plastic bag?"

"There's a garbage can in the mudroom."

Giles studied the exquisite furnishings in the nursery. It was apparent Mya had spared no expense when it came to decorating the space. Green and pink were the perfect contrast for the white crib, dresser and chest of drawers. The colors were repeated in the rug stamped with letters of the alphabet with corresponding images of animals. A solid white rocking chair and footstool had covered cushions in varying shades of pink and red roses.

"Is she sleeping throughout the night?"

Mya nodded. "Now she is."

"What time do you put her to bed?"

"Eight."

He angled his head. "That should give you a few hours for yourself before you turn in for the night."

"A few," she said cryptically. Mya handed Lily back to Giles. "You can hold her while I throw away the diaper and bring up a bottle."

Giles smiled as Lily stared up at him with curious, round, clear blue eyes with dark blue centers. "Hello, princess. I'm your daddy and now that I'm here we're going to get to see a lot of each other. I have lots of plans we can do together once you're older. I'm going to teach you to swim, ice-skate and, when the time comes, how to drive. You like sports?" he asked, continuing his monologue with the little girl. "Well, if you're a Wainwright, then you'll definitely be into sports. And if you come to live with me in New York, then you're going to have to decide whether you like the Yankees or the Mets. Those are baseball teams. You don't have to choose when it comes to football because your cousin

Brandt played for the NFL. That means we always cheer for one of the New York teams. Rooting for the Rangers rather than the Islanders is a better pick since you'll be living in Manhattan. Let's see, what's left? Oh! I forgot about basketball. Your daddy is partial to the Knicks, although I also like the Nets.

"Then there's your family. Your birth certificate may list you as Lawson, but I don't want you to ever forget that you are a Wainwright. You'll probably be a little overwhelmed when everyone will want a piece of you, but not to worry because Daddy will make certain to take care of his princess. And when you're older and you want to live with me in New York, I'll make it happen. There's a wonderful school blocks from Central Park where several generations of Wainwrights were educated."

"Don't, Giles."

He turned to find Mya standing in the doorway to the nursery. "Don't what?"

"Don't promise her things that may not become a reality. I know she doesn't understand what you're telling her. And I forgot to tell you that Sammie's will states that Lily should be raised here."

Giles clenched his teeth in frustration. It was apparent Mya wasn't that ready to compromise, that she was going to hold to Samantha's mandate that Lily grow up in a town where the residents appeared reluctant to accept it was now the twenty-first century.

"Do you realize how manipulative your sister was? That she's controlling three lives from the grave?"

Mya reacted as if he had struck her across the face.

"Maybe she had a reason for setting up the conditions for how she wanted her daughter to be raised."

"What reason could that be?" Giles spat out, angrily.

"I don't know, because I wasn't aware that my sister was seeing someone until after she'd become pregnant. And even then she refused to tell me your name."

"I think we need to talk."

"What about?"

"About my relationship with your sister."

"You are so right about that," Mya said.

Giles handed Lily to Mya and stalked out of the room. If Samantha hadn't revealed the name of her baby's father, then he had to assume she had never spoken to Mya about him or their on-again, off-again liaison.

He knew he could never move forward in his quest to claim his daughter if he withheld the truth about the woman who had remained an enigma even before she disappeared from his life.

Chapter 4

Mya found Giles in the family room. He stood with his back to the French doors. "Are you going to stand while we talk?" she asked.

He took several steps and pointed to the love seat. "You first."

She sat and he folded his tall frame down on a chair opposite her. "Where and how did you meet my sister?"

Stretching out long legs, Giles stared at his sock-covered feet. "Samantha was the flight attendant assigned to first class on my flight from the Bahamas to the States. I had a connecting flight in Miami, but all planes were grounded because of severe thunderstorms. I decided to check into a hotel rather than spend hours in the airport waiting for the weather to clear. Samantha and several crew members were checking into the same hotel because they weren't scheduled to fly out again until the following day. She invited me to have drinks with her, and we agreed to meet in the hotel lounge."

"Are you saying that Sammie picked you up?"

Giles shook his head. "No, she didn't. We'd passed the time during the flight from Nassau to Miami chatting about movies, so when she suggested we have drinks, I accepted because I'd found her pretty and outgoing. She told me her parents were dead and that she was an only child. When I mentioned her Southern drawl, she said she'd grown up in a small town in what I'd assumed was Virginia."

Mya bit her lower lip to still its trembling. She wondered how many other men had Sammie told the same lie. "Why do you think she lied to you?"

Giles lifted broad shoulders under his sweatshirt. "I don't know."

"What else did she tell you?"

"She said she hated growing up in a small town and that's why she decided to become a flight attendant. And when I asked her what she wanted for her future, she claimed she hadn't figured that out. When the topic of marriage and children came up, we both agreed we definitely weren't ready for either." Giles paused, seemingly deep in thought. "After seeing her a couple of times, whenever she had a layover in New York I could detect restlessness in her. As if she was always looking for something or someone. And when I mentioned it to her, she played it off, saying she always felt more comfortable in the air than on the ground."

Mya had to agree with Giles when he talked about Sammie being restless. "That someone she was looking for was her birth mother." She told him about Samantha's mother getting into a taxi with her week-old baby and when she got out, she hadn't bothered to take the infant with her. "There were times when I suspected Sammie never really appreciated what our adoptive parents did for us. She'd complain about feeling incomplete because she'd been abandoned."

"I suppose her feeling that way wouldn't permit her to engage in a committed relationship."

Mya stared at Giles. "You wanted a commitment from her?"

He blinked slowly. "I wanted more than her calling me every couple of months to tell me she was in town and wanted to see me."

Mya frowned. "So you just wanted to see her for sex?"

"No! There were times when we were together and never made love. I'd always ask her when I would see her again because she knew her flight schedule well in advance, and her answer was 'I don't know.' We dated off and on for a little more than a year, and then it ended. One month passed and then another and after the third month, I knew it was over."

"Had you argued about something that made her angry?"

"We may have had some minor disagreements but it never escalated to an argument. Come to think of it, I did notice she would become sullen whenever I talked about my family."

"That's because you grew up with your biological mother and father and she didn't."

He sat straight. "So she punishes me by having my

child and using her as a pawn so I'll never be able to legally claim her as a Wainwright."

A shiver of annoyance snaked its way up Mya's spine. She wasn't about to let Giles attack her dead sister. "Maybe because you are a Wainwright Sammie feared you would use your family's name and money to take Lily away from her because you'd told her you weren't ready for marriage and fatherhood. In other words you'd take the baby but not the mother."

"I'm not going to lie and say I was in love with your sister, but I'll say it again that if I'd known she was carrying my baby, I definitely would've provided for them."

Mya threw up a hand. "Do you hear yourself, Giles? You talk as if money will solve everything. Sammie didn't need money because our parents made certain we would be financially secure before they passed away. They left us this house and their furniture-manufacturing company, which we sold because neither of us wanted to get involved in running a business. Sammie had two life insurance policies, and as the beneficiary I invested most of the monies in tax-free bonds for Lily's college education and whatever else she'll need to start life on her own."

Giles ran a hand over his face. "None of this makes sense."

Mya closed her eyes when she recalled the times when they recited their prayers before going to bed, and Sammie's prayer was always the same. She wanted to find her real mother. Those were the times when Mya resented the Lawsons for telling Sammie she was adopted. It would've been so easy for them to say she was their biological daughter because of the physical resemblance. But living in a small town where it was diffi-cult to hide anything made that virtually impossible.

She opened her eyes. "It doesn't make sense because you have what Sammie wanted most in life. My sister used to spend hours on the computer pouring over sites dedicated to people searching for their relatives. She told me whenever she had a layover in the Midwest she would search through local birth and death records for a woman who'd given birth to an infant girl around the time she was born. Sammie couldn't know where she was going because she didn't know where she had come from."

"Where did her mother abandon her?"

"It was in New Lebanon. It's a city southwest of Dayton, Ohio."

"What about you, Mya? You've never searched for your birth mother?" Giles asked.

"No. Because whoever she is, I know if she'd been able to take care of me she wouldn't have left me in the hospital. When people ask me about my race, I al-ways tell them I'm African-American. And if they asked whether I'm mixed race, my comeback is, isn't every-one? All they have to do is take the ancestry DNA test to find their true ethnicity."

Giles laughed. "That is so true."

Mya realized it was the first time she'd heard Giles laugh. The sound was low and soothing. "Sammie did take a DNA test and it said she had ancestors who were European Jewish, Russian and Scandinavian. She fo-cused on the Scandinavians because they'd settled in the Midwest."

Giles angled his head and smiled. "I guess that makes Lily quite an ethnic gumbo."

He sobered. "I'm glad you told me about Samantha. I think I understand her a little better now."

"Are you still upset that she didn't tell you about Lily?"

"Whether I'm upset is irrelevant. What's done is done. What you and I have to do is come to an agreement as to what is best for Lily. You have a jump on being a mother while I have to learn that being a father is a lot more than offering financial support. I will not make any decisions concerning Lily unless I discuss it with you. I did tell my mother that she has a granddaughter, so she's anxious to meet her."

"What about your father?" Mya asked.

"He still doesn't know, and Mom and I won't tell him until you're ready to come to New York."

"What if we aim for Thanksgiving?" Mya knew it was one of the holidays Sammie had designated for visitation, yet after talking with Giles she was willing to be flexible as long as he didn't threaten or put pressure on her about Lily's future.

"That'll work. That gives us at least six weeks to get used to being a family."

Mya wanted to ask Giles about his relationship with his father when she recalled his statement about fatherhood: *I have to learn that being a father is a lot more than offering financial support.*

Had his father not been a positive role model? Had he just provided financial support while relinquishing the responsibility of child rearing to his wife? She'd heard the expression *more money, more problems.* Did his father's wealth did not translate into knowing or doing what was best for his progeny?

Mya pushed to her feet. "Where are my manners? I forgot to ask you if you wanted lunch."

Giles rose in one fluid motion. "Thank you for offering, but I had a buffet breakfast before I left the hotel." He glanced at his watch. "It's time I go and check in with my office." He winked at her. "By the way, what time is dinner?"

"Six."

"I'll see you later, Mya."

Mya nodded. "Okay."

She watched as he slipped into his shoes, walked out of the house and closed the self-locking door. Giles's arrival had altered her writing schedule. She had to tweak a proposal for the next book in her series and submit it to her editor by the end of the week.

When her sister came back to Wickham Falls with the news that she was staying until she delivered her baby, Mya knew her well-ordered life would never be the same. Before Sammie's return, all she had to concern herself with was refining her lectures notes; reading and grading papers and penning novels in her spare time. And now when she had adjusted to being a full-time mother and part-time writer, she would now have to change again. This time she would have to adapt to sharing Lily with Giles.

Fortified with a cup of fresh pineapple and a cup of green tea, Mya raced up the staircase and into the office to see how much she could accomplish before Lily woke up.

Giles noticed the blinking light on the hotel phone; there were only three people who had the number for the hotel: his mother, Jordan and Jocelyn. He'd sent Jordan a text with the number to avoid Mya overhearing their conversations if the call came through his cell. He smiled. Jordan had left a message for him to call him back.

"Hey, brand-new Daddy. Are you getting any sleep?" he asked Jordan.

"Barely. My boy really has a set of lungs. He's hungry all of the time and I've told Aziza to give him a bottle in between breast feedings."

"What did she say?"

"I can't repeat it on an open line. She says she wants to breastfeed him until he starts cutting teeth. Not to change the subject, but what's going on down there with Mya?"

"So far it's all good," Giles admitted. "She seems to have softened her stance about coming to New York with me."

"When is she coming?"

"She mentioned Thanksgiving. Hopefully she'll change her mind and we'll come sooner. I found out that she doesn't need money, so that's an argument I can't use as a basis for joint custody." He told Jordan about Mya's parents leaving her and her sister the house and business. "The baby is getting bigger and more delightful than when I first saw her."

"So you like being a daddy?"

Giles smiled. "I'm getting used to it. What I really want to be is a hands-on father. I want to be there for her piano and dance recitals. I want to become involved during parent-teacher conferences and—"

"Enough, G," Jordan said, interrupting him. "I know

you resent your father not being there for you because he put WDG ahead of his family obligations. Think about it, Giles. The company is a python. It constricts and then swallows you inch by inch until you can't get out. Don't be like Patrick. Take time to enjoy your family before it's too late."

"I will." He paused. "And thanks for the pep talk."

Jordan laughed. "There's no need to thank me. You've helped me get my act together more times than I can count. Now, the next time we talk, I want you to tell me that you and your baby's mother have become one happy little family."

"We'll see," Giles said noncommittedly. "Give Aziza my love and kiss Maxwell for me."

"Will do," Jordan said.

After ending the call, Giles thought about his cousin's reference to one happy little family. That had become a reality for Jordan when he married Brandt's attorney. They were now the proud parents of a little boy. He knew Jordan wasn't just blowing smoke when he talked about taking time to enjoy being part of a family. Jordan and his law partner agreed he would take a six-week paternity leave. Six weeks.

And that's how long Giles planned to stay in Wickham Falls, and hopefully when he left to return to New York it would be with Mya and Lily.

Leaning back in the desk chair, he studied a framed print of a beach scene. The suite was a cookie-cutter replica of many others he'd checked into. While some suites were more luxurious and opulent, the overall physical design was the same. He compared the furnishings with those in the villas on the islands owned by

WDG International. With the assistance of his broker, WDG, Inc., sold several properties to the wealthy looking to live permanently on their private island, while several others were designated as vacation properties.

Reaching for the television remote, he turned on the television and began channel surfing. Viewing what he sometimes referred to as mindless TV had become the distraction to temporarily take his mind off his work. Occasionally he would get out of bed in the middle of the night to boot up his computer to input ideas for a new project, aware that he had become his father.

Patrick Wainwright II rarely shared the evening meal with his family. He left home at dawn to go into the office and occasionally returned home after everyone had retired for bed. The running family joke was when had Pat found the time to get his wife pregnant—not once or twice, but three times?

In the past, Giles never would've stayed out of his office for more than a week. Now it would be six weeks. And he was prepared to stay in Wickham Falls even longer if he was able to convince Mya that it was in his daughter's best interest to connect with her other family.

Legally, Lily was Mya's daughter, while biologically she was his. And that made her their daughter and a family.

Holding Lily against his heart and feeling the warmth of her little body had elicited an unconscious craving to protect her against everything seen and unseen.

Giles stood on the porch, peering through the glass on the storm door. He rang the bell and within seconds

Mya came into view carrying Lily on her hip. Smiling, she unlocked and opened the door.

"You're early."

He kissed her cheek. "I thought I'd come by and see if I can help with something."

His admiring gaze swept over her face, lingering on her mouth, before slowly moving down to a loose-fitting light blue blouse and navy leggings. A pair of blue ankle socks covered her feet. The first time he'd come to the house, he'd noticed Mya did not wear shoes indoors. It was obvious she was a neat freak because everything was in its place and the floors were spotless.

"Should I take off my shoes?"

"Please. Only because Lily's crawling and she puts everything she finds on the floor in her mouth. I should've warned you that jeans and sweats are the norm around here, because Lily will sometimes spit up her food or milk."

Bending slightly, he took off his slip-ons, leaving them on the mat beside her running shoes. "I'll know for the next time." He'd exchanged his jeans and sweatshirt for a dress shirt and slacks.

"Did you come to help me cook?" Mya asked.

Giles stood straight. "I can't cook. I came to babysit." He reached for Lily who extended her arms for him to take her. He pressed his mouth to her hair. "Hi, princess."

Mya stared at him as if he'd spoken a foreign language. "How do you eat?"

"I order in or I eat out."

"You're kidding me, aren't you?"

"No, I'm not. I never learned to cook. I can make coffee and toast, but not much beyond that."

Mya shook her head and rolled her eyes upward. "That's pitiful."

"What's pitiful?"

"What if you can't order in or go out? Do you subsist on toast and coffee?"

Giles winked at her. "I always have peanut butter on hand."

She smiled. "You're hopeless. Come with me to the kitchen. I have to finish making Lily's dinner."

"Should I close and lock the door?"

"You can if you want."

"Do you always leave the inner door open?"

Mya nodded. "Most times I do. Of course I close and lock it at night. Why do you ask?"

"I don't like that you live here by yourself, while your closest neighborhood is across the road."

"I always keep the storm door locked. And my closest neighbor happens to be a deputy sheriff. He'll occasionally come over to check on me and Lily."

Giles sat on a stool at the cooking island and settled Lily on his lap. "I only asked because a woman living alone can become a target for someone looking to take advantage of her." His protective instincts had surfaced, and he did not want to think of something happening to Mya or Lily.

"There's no need to worry about us," Mya said.

"I have to worry about you and Lily." What Giles didn't say was that he now regarded both of them as family, and to him family was everything.

Mya washed her hands in one of the stainless steel

sinks and then dried them on a towel from a stack on the quartz countertop. "I have a security system that's wired directly to the sheriff's office, and whenever someone rings the doorbell I see their image on my cell phone. Lastly, I have a licensed handgun and shotgun in the house, and I know how to use both."

"Damn!" he whispered under his breath. "You're a regular Annie Oakley."

"Please watch your mouth," Mya chided. "Lily may be too young to talk, but she does have ears. And d-a-m-n," she said, spelling out the word, "sounds too much like dada."

"Sorry about that. I suppose I don't spend enough time around children."

"Don't forget that you have a daughter and my pet peeve is a girl with a potty mouth."

"You don't curse?"

"I try not to. It comes from my upbringing. My Southern Baptist mama would have a fit if any of us used bad language."

Giles glanced around the ultramodern, all-white kitchen with bleached pine cabinetry and antique heart-of-pine flooring.

"Your home is exquisite inside and out."

"Thank you. I loved growing up here. It was somewhat of a culture shock when I moved to Chicago to attend college. I'd rented a one-bedroom apartment and I always felt as if the walls were closing in on me."

"You didn't like Chicago?"

"Please don't get me wrong. I loved the city, but I wasn't used to apartment living."

Giles digested this information. It was apparent Mya

would be opposed to living in New York City, despite him owning a spacious two-bedroom condominium with incredible views of the East River and the many bridges linking Manhattan with other boroughs.

"How long did you live there?"

"Seven years. I stayed long enough to earn an undergraduate, graduate and post-graduates degrees."

Giles whistled, the sound causing Lily to look up at him. "That's a lot of learning."

"It was necessary because I wanted to teach college-level courses." Her head popped up and she gave him a direct stare. "Are you an architect?"

"No. I'm an engineer. I've familiarized myself with different architectural designs since becoming a developer."

"You build in New York?"

"No. I build in the Bahamas."

Her hands stilled. "You must spend a lot of time there because you're quite tanned." She went back to slicing a beet. "I hope you're using sunblock."

Lines fanned out around his eyes when he smiled. "I didn't know you cared," he teased. "And you sound like my mother."

Her smile matched his. "That's because mothers know best." She placed the carrot and beets in a blender. "How long have you been doing business in the Bahamas?"

"Four years."

Giles told her about leaving the military to join his family's real estate company. He set up the international division after he convinced the board to extend the monies he needed to purchase three undeveloped private islands. He subsequently hired an architect to design villas and worked with an engineer to build desalination processing systems to convert ocean water for human consumption. The sale of the islands yielded a three-hundred-percent profit for the company, and he was given the green light to purchase more uninhabited islands. He now headed the division to expand their holdings to build vacation resorts on private islands throughout the Caribbean.

Mya gave him an incredulous stare. "How many more have you bought?"

"We now own twelve. But only half have been developed."

"Are there that many islands up for sale?"

"The Caribbean Sea has an archipelago of about seven hundred islands and at least twenty-five hundred cays."

"That's amazing. I never could've imagined there would be that many."

He smiled. "What's amazing is there's an extensive list of millionaires and billionaires waiting to write checks so they can own an island."

"What specs should I look for if I wanted to buy an island?" Mya asked Giles.

"Acreage, and if it's an island with a beach. Some buyers want one that is turnkey or if it has income potential. Another important factor is access. They want to know if it has an airstrip or the capability for a fly-in."

"What's the price range, from high to low, for these rich folks' playgrounds?"

He smiled. For some owners, it was a private playground. "An island of about seven hundred acres will cost about sixty-two million. A smaller one measuring two acres will go for a quarter of a mil."

"Going, going, gone," Mya intoned, grinning. "I'll take the one with two acres."

"That's two acres with nothing on it. It'll probably set you back several million to make it habitable."

She affected a sad face. "Sorry, but I'm forced to withdraw my bid due to lack of funds."

Giles caught Lily's hand when she reached for his face. "Whoa, princess. Not the eye."

"You have to be careful with her because she likes pulling hair and gouging eyes. I try to keep her fingernails cut to minimize the damage."

"Maybe she's training for the baby WWE."

"That's not nice, Giles."

"What's not nice is her trying to put my eye out." He pretended to bite on the tiny hand as he watched Mya press a button on the blender. Within seconds, the beets and carrots took on a pinkish shade. She continued blending until the vegetables were converted into hot soup. She poured it into a small bowl to let it cool.

"That's remarkable. You just made hot soup in a blender."

"Vitamix isn't your ordinary blender. It doubles as a blender and food processor. I use it to make baby food, soups, smoothies, and frozen desserts." Mya opened a drawer under the cooking island and took out a bib. "You can put her in the high chair so I can feed her."

Giles took the bib from Mya and tied it around Lily's neck. "I'll feed her. I have to learn some time," he added when she shot him a questioning look. He placed Lily in the chair and carried it over to the breakfast bar.

"I'll finish putting dinner together while you feed your princess."

"Does it bother you that I call her princess?" he asked Mya.

She made a sucking sound with her tongue and teeth. "Of course not. Not when her mother is the queen."

It took him several seconds to understand her retort. He wasn't certain whether she was teasing him, and if she was then he wasn't offended. He preferred the teasing Mya to the one who occasionally radiated hostility. He understood her apprehension that he would attempt to challenge her right to his daughter, and Giles knew it would take time before she would trust him enough not to disrupt her life or Lily's. "If you are a queen, then what does that make me?"

"A king." She held up a hand when he opened his mouth. "Our monarchy will differ from most because as king and queen we will rule as equals."

"That sounds fair to me."

"So you're willing to learn to cook?"

"Oh…" Giles swallowed an expletive. "Do I have to?"

"Yes. I'll not have you filling Lily up on processed foods because you can't put together a healthy meal. Do you want your daughter plagued with high blood pressure and elevated cholesterol levels before she's enrolled in school?"

"Damn, woman," he said sotto voce. "You really know how to pile on the guilt."

"What did I tell you about cussin'? Do I have to put out a swear jar and charge you five dollars for every time you cuss?"

"I thought it was cursing, not cussin'."

"You're in the South, so down here it's cussin'."

He executed a mock bow. "Point taken, Miss Sweet Potato Queen."

Mya stared at him and then doubled over in laughter. His laughter joined hers and seconds later Lily let out a cackle and waved her hands above her head.

Even before their laughter faded Giles was filled with an overwhelming emotion shaking him to the core. He, Mya and Lily had become a family in every sense of the word. He was a father, Mya a mother and Lily was their daughter.

Chapter 5

Mya glanced over at Giles as he attempted to feed Lily. Although the vegetable soup had cooled enough for it not to burn her mouth, Lily continue to fret.

"Why is she crying?" he questioned when her whimpers became a loud wail.

"You're not feeding her fast enough."

"You're kidding?"

"No, I'm not."

"But…but won't she choke?"

Mya set down the potato ricer. "It's puréed, Giles." She walked over and took the spoon from him. "Let me show you." She made quick work of feeding the baby, who hummed and rocked back and forth with each mouthful. "It's like eating ice cream. You taste and then swallow."

Giles's dark eyebrows slanted in a frown. "I can't believe you make it look so easy."

"That's because I know what she wants. Do you want to try feeding her dessert?"

He nodded. "I can't give up now."

Mya retrieved a jar of a peach-and-pear mix from the refrigerator and gave it to Giles. She gave him a reassuring pat on the back. "Give yourself a couple of days and you'll be a pro."

She went back to ricing potatoes, adding cream, salt, pepper and garlic butter, then whisked the potatoes until they were smooth and fluffy. She'd made them as a side dish for the fork-tender pot roast. The slow cooker, Dutch oven and pressure cooker were her favorite kitchen appliances, and she alternated utilizing all three when preparing one-pot meals.

"Hooray! We're finished!" Giles clapped his hands while Lily joined him, putting her tiny hands together.

Mya blew them a kiss. "I told you you'd get the hang of it."

Giles proudly pushed out his chest. "What now?"

"Wet a paper towel and wipe her face. She always drinks water after her meals. Please get the playpen from the family room and put her in it. I'll get her sippy cup for you."

Mya filled a cup from the fridge in-door water dispenser and handed it to Giles. She knew it would take a while for him to become familiar with the routine she had established to meet her own and Lily's needs. There were mealtimes, bed, nap and playtimes. In between, she set aside time for grocery shopping, laundry, housecleaning and preparing meals.

Time had become a precious commodity and she jealously guarded the little she had for herself.

Giles placed Lily on the floor, watching as she crawled over to a stool and attempted to pull herself up by holding on to the legs. He moved quickly when the stool tipped precariously, catching it before it toppled over. Now he knew why Mya told him to put Lily in the playpen. He put her back in the high chair, retrieved the playpen and placed it between the kitchen and dining area. Lily took several sips from the cup before tossing it aside and redirected her attention to gnaw on the gel-filled teething ring, as she babbled what sounded like *mumum*.

Giles walked over to Mya and rested a hand at her waist. "I don't know how you do it."

She tilted her chin, staring up at him, and he suddenly found himself drowning in pools of green and gold. His eyes moved slowly over her high cheekbones. He smiled when she lowered her eyes, and charming him with her demure expression.

"Do what?"

"Take care of Lily, cook and keep the house clean."

"I'm no different from other mothers, whether they stay-at-home or work outside the house. We do what we have to do to keep from being overwhelmed."

Giles splayed his fingers over her back. "Don't you know some young woman looking to make some extra money, willing to come in and help clean the house?"

"I really don't need anyone to help me clean the house. There's only me and Lily, so aside from dusting, vacuuming and cleaning the bed and bathrooms, there's not much to do. I get a lot done when Lily's sleeping."

"What's going to happen when she doesn't sleep as much?"

"By the time she's five, I'll enroll her in kindergarten."

"Do you plan to go back teaching once she's in school?"

"If I do, then it has to be locally. I'll apply for a position at the high school. All of the schools in the Johnson County school district occupy the same campus, which makes it convenient for teachers and staff whose children are enrolled there."

He leaned closer and inhaled the lingering scent of Mya's perfume. Giles felt her go stiff and then relax against his hand. "So you have it all figured out as to Lily's future."

"No, I don't. If you want to eat, then you're going to have to let me go. I need to take the pot roast out of the slow cooker. Thank you," Mya whispered when he dropped his hand.

Giles wanted to tell her that if he had a choice between eating and touching her, he would've chosen the latter. He felt more comfortable and relaxed around Mya than he had with any other woman he'd met or known. At first, he'd contributed it to her connection to Lily but after spending time with her, he realized it was the woman herself.

There were so many things he admired about her but it was her sense of loyalty that had won him over. She had willingly sacrificed her career to care for her terminally ill sister and raise her niece. And she had become the perfect mother when she put Lily's needs above her own.

Jordan had revealed that his investigators had not come up with anything in regard to a man or men in her life. There was no record of her having been married or divorced. And he wondered if she'd been involved with a man before she resigned her position at the college to become her sister's caretaker and Lily's adoptive mother.

Giles thought of Mya as a superwoman as she quickly, with no wasted effort, put dinner on the table. Along with the pot roast, carrots au jus, garlic mashed potatoes, an escarole salad with orange and grapefruit sections and red onions tossed with red wine vinegar, she also included corn bread and pitchers of chilled water and sweet tea.

"Oh my goodness," he crooned after swallowing a forkful of potatoes seasoned with a subtle hint of garlic and rosemary. "These potatoes are to die for." He raised his glass of tea. "I'm ready to enroll in cooking school."

Mya smiled. "When do you want to start?"

"What about tomorrow?"

"Okay. If you come early enough, I'll show how to prepare a traditional Southern breakfast with grits, sausage or bacon, with eggs and biscuits."

"What about lunch?"

"Lunch will be dinner leftovers. We'll vary it with pulled beef sliders. I've put away some of the mash potatoes and gravy for Lily's lunch."

Giles glanced over at Lily in the playpen biting on a rubber duck as he took a sip of sweet tea. Mya told him she preferred agave to sugar to sweeten the beverage. "What do you plan for dinner?"

"Chicken with a brown rice pilaf."

"Who taught you to cook?"

"I'm proud to say it was my mother. Mama earned a reputation as being one of the best cooks in the county. Whenever there was a church potluck dinner or PTA fund-raiser, her pies and cakes were the first to go. I used to come home after school and sit in the kitchen to do homework so I could watch her cook. The year I celebrated my twelfth birthday, she allowed me to assist her—but only on the weekends. Mama refused to let anything come before our schoolwork. She wanted me and Sammie to have careers—something she regretfully gave up after she married my father. She'd gone to college to become a math teacher but wound up keeping the books for Daddy's company after the longtime bookkeeper retired."

Giles listened, transfixed when Mya revealed how much her mother resented spending hours in an office above the factory floor tapping computer keys and writing checks. After twenty years in a childless marriage, she convinced her husband to adopt a child. Graham Lawson finally gave in and they adopted Mya.

"Before my adoption was finalized, Mama had trained a high school graduate to replace her, and at the age of forty-five, she finally become a mother. Then they adopted Sammie and years later, Mama told me that she'd felt complete for the first time in her life. By the time Mama was finally an empty nester, her perfect world crumbled when Daddy called her to say he was working late, but when he didn't come home, she called the foreman and asked him to go by the factory to check on him. They found him slumped over his desk. An autopsy concluded that he'd died from a massive heart attack."

Mya's eyelids fluttered. "Mama kept saying she had nothing to live for, while I tried to reassure that she still had her girls. Less than a year after Daddy passed, Mama died in her sleep. The doctor claimed it was heart failure, but I knew she'd died of a broken heart. She was an incredible mother and I'm certain if she was still alive she would be a spectacular grandmother."

Giles pushed back his chair and rounded the table when Mya's eyes filled with tears. He eased her up and pulled her into his arms. Everyone she loved was gone: mother, father and sister. He buried his face in her hair. "Your sister and parents are gone, but you still have a family. You have Lily."

She nodded. "I know that." Mya lifted her chin and met his eyes; her eyes were shimmering pools of green-and-gold tears.

"I promise to stay in this relationship for as long as it takes for Lily to grow up and walk across the stage at whatever college she chooses to accept her degree."

"Please don't make promises you're not certain you'll be able to keep."

Giles's hands moved up and cradled her face. "I never make a promise I can't keep."

Her hands covered his. "What if you meet a woman, fall in love and want to—"

Giles placed a thumb over her mouth, stopping her words. "Don't say it, Mya. Lily doesn't need a stepmother when she has you."

"You've lost your mind if you believe I'm going to agree to a twenty-year relationship with you just so we can raise Lily together."

His lips twisted into a cynical sneer. "What's the matter, Mama? Are you hiding a secret lover?"

A noticeable flush suffused her face with his gibe. "If I had a lover, I definitely would've married him within days of discovering you were Lily's father, because you showed your hand when you threatened to sue me for custody. And marrying the son of a local family court judge would've definitely stacked the cards in my favor."

"You were engaged?"

The seconds ticked as Giles held his breath and waited for Mya's response. How, he chided himself, had he been so self-absorbed that he hadn't considered perhaps there had been a man in Maya's life? After all she was the total package: looks, brains and poise—everything a most men would want in his woman. And he was no exception.

Mya lowered her eyes. "No. I was seeing someone for a while, but we broke up when I had to take care of Sammie."

"Why did you break it off?"

"I wasn't the one who ended it. He didn't believe me when I told him that my sister was ill. Even before that, we were seeing less and less of each other. A few times he'd go off on a waitress who'd mix up his order, or he'd exhibit uncontrollable road rage because he'd believed another driver had cut him off, and when I tried to tell him that he needed to seek counseling to manage his anger he'd accuse me of not having his back. After a while, I realized I didn't want to deal with his explosive temper and told him it was over. Four months later, he called to tell me he was in counseling and wanted to see me again. We went out a few times, but that's after Sammie returned to the Falls to tell me she was pregnant. When I told him about Sammie, he accused me of using her as an excuse to see other men. He hung up and I never heard from him again."

"Where does he live?"

"Charleston."

Giles brushed his mouth over Mya's slightly parted lips. "He's far enough away so you don't have to run into him. And if he bothers you, then he'll have to deal with me, and that's something I don't think he'd want to do."

She blinked slowly. "What would you do?"

"You don't want to know."

"I don't like violence, Giles."

"I don't, either," he retorted, "but I'm certainly not going to cut and run if he bothers you."

"Now you sound like a former marine."

"Wrong, baby. Once a marine, always a marine. One of these days I'll tell why I enlisted the Corps instead of going to work for the family business."

Lily let out a loud shriek and Giles and Mya turned to find her standing up while holding onto the mesh netting covering the sides of the playpen. "Mumum," she repeated over and over as she jumped up and down on the thick padding.

"What is she saying?" Giles asked Mya.

She shook her head. "I don't know. Usually when she wants me to give her something, she'll open and close one hand and say it. She's probably trying to say *me*."

"When is she going to start talking?"

"That all depends on the child. Some kids talk early and others wait until they're almost two and then speak in complete sentences. Lily is a chatterbox, and I'm sure that when she begins, she'll never stop."

"How about walking?"

"Now that's she pulling up and holding on, I'm willing to predict she'll be walking by herself by the time she's ten months." Mya glanced at the clock on the microwave. "It's almost time for her bath. I usually sit in the rocking chair and read to her before putting her in the crib."

Giles stared, complete surprise on his face. "You read to an eight-month-old?"

"Don't look so shocked. Haven't you heard about pregnant women reading or playing classical music for their unborn child?"

"No."

"Well, there are studies that prove that these babies usually are more alert and display more creativity than those who don't receive the same stimulation."

"What do you read to her?"

"Nursery rhymes and Dr. Seuss. It's the repetition that will make it easy for her to recognize certain words."

Giles angled his head and smiled. "That's why you're the teacher and I deal with putting up buildings while focusing on quarterly earnings and profit margins."

"Well, Mr. Hotshot Businessman, it's time I clear the table and clean up the kitchen. You can hang out with Lily until I take her upstairs for her bath."

Giles sat on a stool in the bathroom watching as Lily sat in the bathtub splashing water. Mya knelt on a fluffy mat and drew a washcloth over Lily's face and hair. She claimed it was only a sponge bath and the warm water helped Lily to relax. Once the baby was dressed for bed, Mya cradled Lily in her arms and rocked back and forth while reading *Goodnight Moon.*

He suddenly realized there was much more to parenting than writing checks to the orthodontist or tuition for private schools and colleges. It went beyond providing clothes, food and shelter. It was about nurturing and making a child feel loved. And it was the love that was priceless. He'd led men and women into combat and found that easier than being a father. His heart turned over when he saw Mya kiss Lily's head before placing her on her back in the crib.

She checked the locks on the windows and switched on a baby monitor and then placed a finger over her mouth and motioned for him to follow her. Mya flipped the wall light switch, and the night-lights plugged into several outlets provided enough illumination to move around the room without bumping into objects.

"She's down for the night."

Reaching for Mya's hand, Giles cradled it gently. "It's amazing how calm she was when you were reading to her."

"I think she likes the sound of my voice."

Giles wanted to tell Mya that her voice had a wonderful, soothing quality that he never tired of listening to. He silently applauded Samantha for choosing Mya to raise her child. He knew if he'd known of the pregnancy and his former lover had agreed to list him as the father on the birth certificate, he would've asked his mother to help him raise his daughter.

Claiming the Captain's Baby

However, there were things a woman in her sixties wouldn't be able to do for an infant that a thirtysomething woman could accomplish with ease. Amanda had raised three children with little or no input from her husband, and Giles knew it wouldn't be fair to ask his mother to take on the responsibility of raising her granddaughter.

They descended the staircase together. "I'm going to be on my way so you can have some time for yourself."

Mya laughed softly. "A man can work from sun to sun, but a mother's work is never done."

He squeezed her fingers. "I'm a witness to that." Mya walked him to the door where he retrieved his shoes. "What time do you want me to come tomorrow morning?"

"Eight o'clock is good. By that time I've fed and bathed Lily."

"Do you want me to bring anything?"

She smiled. "No, thank you. I have everything I need."

Giles knew he was making small talk because he didn't want to leave Mya—not yet. He wanted to end the evening sitting on the porch and enjoying the silence. It was something he'd found himself doing whenever he returned to his condo. He'd sit in the dark, staring out the window at the buildings across the river. That had become his time to get in touch with himself, to be still and listen to the beating of his own heart, while asking why he had survived when so many he'd known hadn't.

It was also when he questioned his purpose in life. He knew there was more than buying and selling private islands to those to whom price was no impediment. And it was when he realized he didn't see his mother, brother and sister often enough. That he spent too many hours in the office or in the air. His main concern was buying and selling land, while conferring with his Bahamian real estate broker Kurt DeGrom to work another deal. Lily had changed his life and his priorities. His daughter was now first and foremost in his life.

Resting his hands on Mya's shoulders, he leaned down and brushed a light kiss on her cheek. "Good night, my lady."

Her teeth shone whitely when she smiled. "Good night."

Mya closed and locked the door behind Giles before he drove away. She exhaled slowly as she made her way into the kitchen. It felt as if she could draw a normal breath for the first time since she opened the door earlier that morning to Giles's ring. Being around him made her feel as if his larger-than-life presence sucked up all of the oxygen in the room.

She'd always believed she had a monopoly on confidence, but interacting with Giles had her doubting herself, although he hadn't exhibited any of the hostility from their first encounter. It was as if she was waiting for the proverbial other shoe to drop. Whatever she had shared with Giles was still too new for her to lower her guard and trust him enough to let him into *her* life.

Mya knew how important it was for a girl to grow up with a father because Graham Lawson had become her father in every sense of the word. Whenever he came home, he'd called out for his girls. She and Sammie would race and jump into his arms while he spun them around and around until they pleaded with him to stop. Once they grew too tall and heavy and he more frail with age, they were resigned to a group hug.

She missed her parents but missed Sammie even more, because they were inseparable when growing up.

Their mother had given each girl her own bedroom, yet night after night, Sammie would come into Mya's room and crawl into bed with her. She claimed she was afraid to sleep alone because she was afraid of the dark. But even after Veronica installed night-lights in her younger daughter's bedroom, Sammie continued to come into Mya's room.

Sleeping together ended after Veronica offered them the opportunity to decorate their rooms because they were becoming teenagers. Along with the new furniture, each room had its own television, audio components and worktables for their computers and printers.

Sleeping separately signaled a change in Sammie, who had begun to spend most of her free time online searching for her mother.

Mya thought it eerie that her niece would share the same fate as her biological mother. As Veronica had chosen and loved her, Mya would make certain to let Lily know she had made the choice to love and raise her as her own.

Mya knew she should be in her office writing instead of sitting in the kitchen ruminating about the past as she recalled a course she had taught covering the works of D. H. Lawrence. There was something about Giles that reminded her of the characters in Lawrence's novella *The Fox*, where she compared herself and Lily to the author's Jill Banford and Nellie March, two females who live alone, while Giles was Henry Grenfield, a young man who comes to stay with them. Although Henry's presence was more psychological than physical, in the end the lives of the two females would never be the same.

Is that what's going to happen to us? Mya thought. She prayed that she had made the right decision to not only invite him into her home, but also allow him to share Lily's life as well as her own.

Chapter 6

It had taken two weeks, and the doubts Mya had about Giles proved unfounded when he seemed genuinely interested in not disrupting her life as he bonded with Lily. He was a quick study when it came to changing, bathing, dressing and feeding her, yet balked and complained that cooking involved too many steps and he didn't have the patience for measuring countless ingredients. When she reminded him that he was an engineer and had to utilize math, he said he had no interest in learning the differences between thyme, cilantro, parsley or dill. To him, they all were green leaves that did not taste the same. Mya knew it was useless to try to convince him and did not mention it again.

She had put Lily in her crib for her nap when she found Giles waiting for her in the hallway outside the nursery. He had taken her advice to wear jeans and T-shirts because he liked rolling around on the floor with Lily whenever he pretended he was a cat or dog, barking, meowing, sniffing or nibbling on her toes.

"Is something wrong?" she asked, averting her eyes from the laser-blue orbs that suddenly made her feel as if he was undressing her. It was the first time that she felt physically uncomfortable with him. She come to look for his chaste kisses when he greeted her in the morning and before leaving at night because she felt there wasn't anything remotely sexual in his motives.

"If you don't mind my asking, I'd like to know where you disappear to when Lily takes her afternoon naps."

She took his hand. She knew he was curious when she declined to join him on the porch or in the family room. "Come with me and I'll show you." Mya led him down the hall to her office. Pushing open the door, she stepped aside to let him peer in. "This is where I write."

Giles entered the room Mya had set up as a home office. Floor-to-ceiling shelves spanning an entire wall were tightly packed with books. An L-shaped workstation positioned under one window held an all-in-one computer. Framed photographs of Samantha and Mya at various ages and with their parents crowded an oak drop-leaf table. Rays of afternoon sunlight reflected off the pale green walls and dark jade carpet.

His gaze lingered on a window seat large enough for two people to lay side by side. The fabric on a love seat matched the pink-and-white floral window-seat cushions. The office had everything one would find in a break room: watercooler, portable refrigerator, a single-cup coffee maker, radio and a wall-mounted flat screen television.

He noticed a stack of pages with red-penciled proof-reader notations. "Are you an aspiring writer?"

"Not any longer."

"You're published?"

Mya laughed when he gave her a look mirroring disbelief. The woman with whom he found himself more entranced each passing day continued to astound him. There was nothing about Mya with which he found fault. Even when he'd explained he honestly had no interest in learning how to cook, she did not press him. A lifting of her shoulders communicated *suit yourself*.

"Yes."

"What do you write?"

Mya dropped his hand and selected a paperback from several on a lower shelf, handing it to him. "New adult. This is my latest novel. It will go on sale next week."

He read the back cover of the novel. It was part of an exciting new series featuring a team of twentysomething cyberspace cold-case crime solvers. "Congratulations! That's a mouthful of alliteration," he said, smiling. "How did you come up with the plot?"

"I grew up reading books from my mother's childhood, and her personal favorite was Nancy Drew. I was still in grad school when I overheard several forensic science and prelaw students discussing a mock cold case their professor had assigned the class. I recalled details of their conversation whenever I watched the Investigation Discovery channel for episodes of *Disappeared*, *Snapped*, or *True Crime*. After a while, I'd filled several notebooks with what I'd gleaned from those shows.

"I'd planned to write a novel once I retired, so in my head, the project had become my plan B. Once I joined the faculty at the University of Charleston, plan B kept nagging at me. I'd come home every night and write and before I knew it, I'd completed a novel. I created my team of cold-case crime solvers with five protagonists, three guys and two girls, who bond in a chat room but never meet in person. Once they become a crime-fighting team, they interact with one another by video conferencing, Skyping or with FaceTime. There's some subtle flirting between one guy and girl despite both being in committed relationships. I've gotten tons of email asking me to have them meet in person, but I'd like to keep their sexual tension going for a few more books."

"You must have an incredible imagination."

"It comes from being an avid reader. As a kid, I'd read any and everything. I'd sit at the breakfast table and read the cereal boxes. I read to Lily because I want her to grow up with her asking me to buy her a book rather than the latest video game."

Giles silently applauded Mya for introducing Lily to books before she could walk or talk. "How many books have you published?"

"Six. I recently submitted a proposal for the next two titles in the series." Mya told him how she'd arbitrarily selected the name of a literary agent from the internet and mailed off a letter outlining her proposed series. It took nearly five months before she got a reply with a request for Mya send her the completed manuscript. She continued to write, finishing two more novels, when she finally received a call from her agent informing her that an editor from an independent New York publisher wanted to publish her series.

Giles continue to stare at the cover. "If you're a *USA Today* bestselling author, why are you using a pseudonym?" It listed her as Hera Cooper. It was definitely the reason Jordan's investigators hadn't discovered she was also a published author.

"I'd thought it best that my students didn't know their professor was moonlighting as a writer."

"Why Hera Cooper?"

"Cooper was my mother's maiden name and Hera was the supreme Greek goddess of marriage and childbirth and had a special interest in protecting married women. She was also Zeus's wife and sister, but that's another story."

"That is creepy."

"There was a lot of creepy stuff going on in Roman and Greek mythology."

Giles dropped a kiss on her curls. "One of these days I want you to give me a crash course on mythology. I never could get the names of the gods straight. I'm ashamed to admit English wasn't one of my best subjects, and that's why I took every elective math and science course available to boost my GPA."

"Where did you go to college?"

"MIT."

"Impressive!"

Giles buried his face in her fragrant hair. He liked seeing Mya with a cascade of curls framing her face. "The University of Chicago is right up there with MIT."

"Yeah, right."

Hugging Mya and kissing her good-morning and

good-night seemed as natural to him as breathing. It just happened involuntarily. He pulled back and turned to face her. "You're beautiful and brilliant." He noticed the flush darkening Mya's face with the compliment. "Do you have any idea how incredible you are?"

She lowered her eyes. "I'm far from being incredible."

"Self-deprecating, too?" he added with a wide grin. "The day the book debuts, we'll have to go out and celebrate. The problem is there aren't too many fancy eating establishments around here."

Mya chuckled. "Ruthie's is as fancy as we get here in the Falls. It's an all-you-can-eat, buffet-style family restaurant."

Giles curved an arm around her waist. "I'd like to take you to someplace more upscale with tablecloths, a waitstaff and an extensive wine list."

"We'd have to go to Charleston if you really want fine dining. One of my favorites is The Block Restaurant and Wine Cellar. But if you want exceptional Italian food, then Paterno's at the Park is the place to eat. My other favorite is The Chop House, which has earned a reputation for serving some of the best aged steaks in the state."

"Choose the one you want and I'll call and make reservations."

Mya rested her head on his shoulder. "Have you forgotten we have a baby and no sitter?"

Giles groaned aloud. "I forgot about Lily. I suppose we'll have to wait until we get to New York where my mother will babysit her while we go out or..."

"Or what?" Mya asked.

"What if we don't wait until Thanksgiving to go New York?"

"What are you talking about?"

"Why don't we—you, me and Lily—go to New York now? We can introduce her to my immediate family before the remaining hoard of Wainwrights gather for Thanksgiving. We can also celebrate the release of your book at the same time. Perhaps you'd even want to drop in and see your editor."

"I did enough celebrating with the release of my first title when I drank four glasses of champagne and woke up the next day with a dry mouth and pounding headache. Sammie sent me a gift of a week's vacation at an all-inclusive resort in the Dominican Republic. She surprised me when she showed up on the second day. We hung out on the beach during the day and danced all night until we dropped from exhaustion."

There was silence for a moment, and then Mya spoke again. "That was one of the happiest times in our lives. It was as if we hadn't a care in the world. There are times when I still don't believe she's gone. I miss her just that much." Going on tiptoe, she buried her face in the hollow of Giles's throat. "Forgive me for being such a Debbie Downer.

"It's okay, baby. I miss her, too."

Giles's hands circled her waist, molding their bodies together. He tried to ignore the crush of her full breasts and failed when the flesh between his thighs stirred to life. He'd told himself that Mya was off-limits because he had slept with her sister, but the silent voice in his head reminded him they were sisters in name only.

Suddenly Giles felt as if he was on an emotional

roller coaster, because if anyone would have hinted more than a year before that he would be a father he would've said they were crazy. He'd told Samantha that he wasn't ready to have children, but now that Lily was here he had to ensure his daughter's future, and that meant a relationship with the child's mother.

He had committed to stay connected to a woman for the next twenty years so they could raise their daughter together, a woman who hadn't given him the slightest indication she wanted anything more than friendship. And at this point in his life he wasn't certain whether he wanted more than friendship from Mya. And if he did, then it would have to be because of her and not because she's was Lily's mother.

"There are times when I think I hear her voice even though I know it's just my imagination," Mya whispered. "I realize now that I should've gone away—anywhere for a while after the funeral, but then I had to think about Lily. I'd thought about taking her to Disney World or on a cruise, but I couldn't pull myself out of a funk to make travel arrangements."

"That's because you're still grieving."

"You're probably right."

"I know I'm right," Giles said. "What about now, Mya? Do you still want to get away?"

Easing back, she smiled. "I do if the offer to go to New York before Thanksgiving is still open?"

Giles cradled her face in his hands. "Of course."

"I'm going to ask my neighbor to pick up my mail and keep an eye on the house, and then make and freeze enough food for Lily."

"You don't have to make anything for Lily. I'll call my mother and have her buy the blender."

"Are we going to stay at your place while we're there?"

"No. You and Lily will stay with my parents, because they have a room that's set up as a nursery. Whenever my brother brings his kids over, he doesn't have to lug around a portable crib or playpen."

"How old are your nephews?"

"Three and eighteen months. I'm going to have to watch them around Lily because they are really rough-and-tumble."

"I wouldn't worry too much about our hair-pulling, eye-gouging feisty little girl. I'm sure she'll be able to hold her own against her rough-and-tumble boy cousins."

"No shit!" Giles clapped a hand over his mouth. "Sorry about that."

Mya held out her hand. "Pay up."

"I said I was sorry."

She glared at him. "And I said pay up."

Mya waited for him to reach into a pocket of his jeans and take out a monogrammed money clip. He thumbed through the bills. "My lowest bill is a ten."

"Hand it over because you know you're going to cuss again." She took the bill from his fingers and slipped it into the pocket of her jeans. "Do you cuss at work?"

Giles shook his head. "No. At least not where my assistant can hear me."

"Is it because she's a woman?"

"Yes."

"Is she pretty?"

"I'd say she is. What's up with the inquisition?"

"Just curious."

He angled his head. "Curious about what?" Giles ran a finger down the length of her nose. "You know what they say about curiosity."

"Yeah, I know. It killed the cat."

"And to satisfy your curiosity, gorgeous, there's nothing going on between me and my assistant. I took her with me the last time I flew down to the Bahamas to introduce her to the broker and when I spoke to Kurt the other day, he admitted he's smitten with Jocelyn and plans on stealing her from me."

"What did you say to him about that?"

Giles chuckled. "I told him to go for it because if Jocelyn decides to move to the Bahamas, then I would bypass him and deal directly with her, cutting him out of his commission."

"That's sounds a little cutthroat."

"All gloves are off when someone messes with my employee." Giles told Mya that he had hired and fired a number of assistants until he found everything he wanted and needed in an admin with Jocelyn Lewis. "I'll take you to the office so you can meet her."

"How long do you plan to stay in New York?"

"That's up to you, sweets. I'm electronically connected to my office, so I can be reached anywhere."

"I'd like to be here for Halloween."

"What's up with Halloween?"

"The whole town turns out to celebrate the holiday. There're games, a photo gallery where parents can pose with their children, face-painting for the kids and tailgate parties for the adults. Once the sun sets, there are hayrides and bonfires with people taking turns reading ghost stories. This year, there will also be a costume party in the church basement. The current mayor and town council have continued the tradition of Halloween as a town celebration that began more than twenty years ago to control teens who were vandalizing properties and terrorizing townsfolks."

"If we come back on the thirtieth, then that will give us about five days to hang out in the Big Apple."

Mya's smile was dazzling. "Can you stay here with Lily while I walk across the road to talk to my neighbor?"

Giles kissed her forehead. "Of course."

"I'll begin packing after I come back. I'd planned to go grocery shopping tomorrow, but that can wait until we return."

"Meanwhile I'll call and reserve a flight for tomorrow afternoon."

"Are you certain you'll be able to get a reservation?"

"Quite certain, sweets. We're going to take the company jet."

"Why do you call me that?" Mya asked.

"Sweets?"

"Yes."

Giles winked at her. "That's because you are sweet. Would you prefer I call you darling or my love?"

Mya blushed again. "Sweets will do—for now."

"So are you saying there's the possibility of you becoming my darling or my love?"

"No comment," she said, smiling. Mya returned his wink. "Later, Daddy."

Lines fanned out around Giles's eyes when he smiled. "Later, Mama."

* * *

Mya buckled Lily into her car seat on the sleek modern jet before fastening her own. She was on her way to New York with her daughter and the man who, in spite of her busy schedule, intruded into her thoughts during the day *and* at night.

She'd found Giles to be gentle, generous, patient and even-tempered—the complete opposite of the man with whom she had been involved. And if she had had any reservations as to whether he would be a good father, those doubts were quickly dashed when he had become a hands-on father in every sense of the word. Mya wasn't certain whether he was overcompensating because she suspected it hadn't been that way with him and his father.

"Tell me about your family," she said to Giles when he'd turned the white leather seat to face her. Mya wanted to know what to expect before she met the Wainwrights.

He met her eyes. "There's not much to tell. I have an older married brother with two kids and a younger sister. My father heads the legal department for the Wainwright Developers Group, known to insiders as the WDG. Dad, whom everyone calls Pat, is Patrick II and my brother is Patrick III. Patrick works with Dad in the legal department."

"What about your mother and sister?"

"My mother is Amanda. Even though she's lived in New York for forty years, she still talks like a Bostonian. She majored in art history in college and was hired by the Metropolitan Museum as a cataloguer. She put her career on hold after she married and started a family."

"Did she ever go back to the museum?"

"No, but she's still involved in the art world. She works every other weekend at a Second Avenue gallery. My sister Skye just got engaged to her longtime boyfriend a couple of months ago. My mother's freaking out because this summer, Skye gave up her position as a high school guidance counselor to move to Seattle to live with her fiancé."

"A lot of engaged couples live together to save money."

"Skye doesn't have to save money. She has a trust fund."

Mya didn't have to have the IQ of a rocket scientist to know the Wainwrights weren't pleased with Skye's choice in a fiancé. "What does he do?"

Giles frowned. "What doesn't he do? He's had a food truck business that failed. He was in partnership with some of his friends who had a moving business that also went under. Skye claims he's willing to try anything to find his niche. I try not to get involved in her life, but I did tell her his singular calling is getting his hands on her money. Sometimes my sister may let her heart overrule her head, but not her money."

"What did she do?"

"The last time I spoke to her, she said the love of her life was no longer as affectionate as he used to be because she told him she had put herself on a strict budget because she wasn't working."

"It sounds as if lover boy wants her to bankroll his next entrepreneurial venture."

"Bingo! Give that lady a cigar," Giles teased. "It's not nice, but we're all taking bets that she'll be back before the end of the year."

The pilot's voice came through the cabin instructing the crew to prepare the cabin for takeoff. Mya stared out the oval window as the jet taxied down a private runway before it picked up enough speed for a smooth liftoff. All of the furnishings in the aircraft reflected opulence: butter-soft white leather seating for eighteen, teak tables and moldings, flat screen televisions and a fully functional galley kitchen and bathroom.

She glanced over at Lily who'd fallen asleep almost immediately. It was early afternoon and her nap time. The aircraft climbed, Mya's ears popping with the pressure, and then leveled off to cruising speed.

The five-hundred-mile flight from Charleston to New York on a commercial carrier would take at least four hours, including a connecting flight, and more than eight hours by car, but their flight on the private jet was estimated to take only ninety minutes. They'd decided to forego lunch because Amanda had planned for an early dinner.

Mya's gaze shifted back to Giles, who smiled when their eyes met. His hair was longer than when she first saw him in the lawyer's office. The ends were curling slightly, reminding her of Lily's shiny black waves. Her gaze lingered on his strong mouth. "You promised to tell me why you joined the Marine Corps."

His smile vanished, replaced by an expression of stone. "I did it to spite my mother." Mya wasn't certain if he could hear her audible exhalation. "I'd dated a couple of girls while in college, but none of the relationships were what I'd think of as serious. Meanwhile unbeknownst to me, my mother was colluding with the mother of a young woman who went to high school with me to set us up. A week after graduation, Mom invited the family and some of her friends with kids who'd gone to my high school over for an informal get-together. I'd remembered Miranda as a nice, quiet girl but she wasn't someone I'd date. Everyone was posing with me for the photographer Mom had hired for the event. Two months later, I get a call from one of my cousins that he saw my photograph alongside Miranda's in the engagement section of the *New York Times*."

"Were you two dating?"

"I told you I had no interest in her. When I confronted my mother, she said she'd hoped that Miranda and I would fall in love and eventually marry and she may have also communicated that to Miranda's mother, who'd taken it to the next level. When I demanded they print a retraction, Mom pleaded with me to go along with it for a few months, and then pretend to break it off. What she didn't want to do was embarrass Miranda's family.

"Meanwhile people were calling and congratulating me on my engagement. I tolerated it for a week before walking into a recruitment office and telling the recruiter if he was looking for a few good men, then I was his man. I moved out and checked into a hotel until it was time for me to go to Parris Island, South Carolina for basic training. I'd attained the rank of captain by the time I was deployed to Afghanistan. Meanwhile I hadn't spoken to or communicated with my mother in more than six years. Not knowing whether I'd come back, I called to tell her I was being deployed and I don't remember what she said because she was crying so hard that I lost it. I told her I loved her and then hung up. That's the memory of my mother that continued to haunt me until I returned from my first tour."

Mya hadn't realized she'd bitten her lip until she felt a throbbing pain. "Did you see her when you got back?"

Giles smiled. "Yes. We had a tearful reunion. She claims I'd left a boy and returned a man. I'd put on a lot of muscle and was in peak physical condition. I signed on for a second deployment and after losing several members of my team, I decided to resign my commission. Transitioning to life as a civilian was very difficult for me."

"PTSD?"

He nodded. "It took six months and a kick in the behind from a cousin for me to seek counseling. Once I felt I was in control of my life, I purchased a condo and went to work for WDG."

Reaching over, Mya grasped his hand. "You're one of the lucky ones, Giles. There are a number of veterans from Wickham Falls who've been diagnosed with combat-related post-traumatic stress disorder. More than half the boys who graduated high school with me enlisted in the military because they couldn't find employment now that most of the mines have closed. There was a time when boys graduated or left school to work the mines like their fathers, grandfathers and even great-grandfathers."

Giles threaded his fingers through Mya's. "Do they come back?"

"A few do. Sawyer Middleton and I were in the same

graduating class. He enlisted in the army, became a software engineer, made tons of money and then came back last year to head the high school's technology department. He's now married to one of the teachers at the middle school. And there's my neighbor, the deputy sheriff, who also served as a military police officer before coming back to go into law enforcement."

"Now those are what I call success stories." Giles gave her a long, penetrating stare. "You came from Wickham Falls and you did all right."

"That's because my parents were business owners who employed at least two dozen men and women. When it came time for me to go off to college, all my father had to do was write a check. And once I graduated, I didn't have any student debt staring me in the face. I wasn't as lucky as I was blessed that I was adopted into a family that didn't have to count pennies to make ends meet.

"Many of the folks that live in the Falls are the invisible ones that live at or below the poverty line. Twice a year, the church holds a fund-raiser to help families in need. Someone may request a used car so they can get to work, or a single mother with children will ask for monies to fix a leaky roof or repair her hot-water heater. Last Christmas, an anonymous donor gave the church enough toys, clothes and shoes to fill a tractor trailer."

"That's nice."

Her eyebrows lifted a fraction. "That's more than nice, Giles. I'm going to become a donor this year because I intend to purchase at least two hundred children's books for grades one through six."

Giles sat forward. "I'll match your donation."

Her jaw dropped. "Really?"

"Really," he teased. "Let me know what else you want to donate and I'll cover it."

"You don't have to do that."

"Yes, I do if I'm going to live here."

Mya sat back, pulling her hands from his loose grip. "So you've resigned yourself to living in the Falls."

"Do I have a choice if I want to be with my daughter? And becoming an absentee father is not an option."

"No, you don't have a choice," she countered. "It's what Sammie wanted."

Mya watched a hardness settle into Giles's features as he slumped in his chair and glared at her under lowered brows. Mya had stopped questioning her sister's motives where it concerned Lily, but it was apparent Giles hadn't.

She wanted to tell him to suck it up and accept what he couldn't control, otherwise the resentment would fester like an infection. If he could forgive his mother for trying to set him up with a woman he didn't want to marry, then it was time he forgave Sammie and concentrated on making certain his daughter knew she was loved.

Chapter 7

Giles switched Lily from one arm to the other as he rang the bell to the town house that once was his childhood home. A buzzing sound answered his ring and he shouldered the door open, holding it for Mya to enter the vestibule. The instant he saw the antique table and two straight-backed pull-up chairs, he was reminded that Mya would be the first woman he would bring home to meet his parents. There were a few women that had been his plus-one for various fund-raisers where social decorum dictated he make introductions but nothing beyond that.

"You can leave the bags by the table," he directed the driver who had unloaded their luggage from the trunk of the limo. Reaching into his shirt pocket, he slipped the man a bill.

"Thank you, Mr. Wainwright."

The door closed behind the driver at the same time the one at the opposite end of the hallway opened. Amanda placed both hands over her mouth, walking toward them as if in a trance.

The tears filling her eyes overflowed and ran down the backs of her hands. "Oh my heavens," she whispered through her fingers. She extended her arms. "May I hold her?"

Giles placed Lily in her grandmother's outstretched arms. "She's heavier than she looks."

Amanda's expression spoke volumes. It was obvious she'd instantly fallen in love with her granddaughter. "She's so precious!" She took a step and kissed Giles's cheek. "Thank you for bringing her." She beckoned to Mya. "Come here, darling, and give me a kiss."

Mya approached Giles's mother and pressed her cheek to the older woman's. "Thank you for opening your home to us."

A tender smile parted Amanda's lips. "You are family. So my home is always open to you. Please come in and relax before we sit down to eat. You picked the perfect time to visit New York because we're having an Indian summer and it's warm enough for us to eat in the backyard. Speaking of food," she continued without pausing to take a breath, "Giles told me that you make your own baby food, so I got the blender you need."

"Thank you, Mrs. Wainwright."

Amanda wagged a finger. "None of that Mrs. Wainwright around here. Please call me Mom or Amanda." She wrinkled her delicate nose. "Personally I prefer Mom."

Mya nodded. "Then Mom it is."

Giles rested a hand at Mya's waist. "Go on in, sweets. I'll bring the bags."

He picked up Lily's diaper bag, grasped the handles to Mya's rolling Pullman and followed his mother and Mya down the carpeted hallway to his parents' street-level apartment.

His father purchased the three-story town house when he was still a bachelor. He renovated the entire structure, adding an elevator, and eventually rented the second-and third-story apartments. There had been a time when the entire building was filled with Wainwrights, when the younger Patrick occupied the third floor and Giles the second. They'd joked about moving out without ever leaving home.

He had just walked into the entryway when his father appeared. "Hi, Dad. I didn't expect to see you here."

"When Amanda told me about the baby, I decided anything I didn't finish at the office could wait until another day."

Giles left the Pullman next to a table with an assortment of African-and Asian-inspired paperweights. Pat talking about leaving work on his desk was a practice he should've adopted when his children were younger. Giles had lost count of the number of times his mother waited for her husband to come home and share dinner with the family, until she finally gave up and fed her children before it was time for them to retire for bed.

"So it takes another grandbaby to pull you away from your office."

Pat smiled, the gesture softening his features. Giles had to admit work was probably what had kept his father motivated. At sixty-six, his blond hair had silvered and there were few more lines around his large, intense blue eyes, while spending hours sitting at a desk hadn't taken its toll on his tall, slim physique.

Pat's pale eyebrows lifted. "Something like that. I'd like to talk to you before I officially meet your baby's mother."

Giles went completely still. There was something in the older man's voice he interpreted as censure. "What do you want to talk about?"

"Are you going to marry her?"

"Why would you ask me that?"

"Because Wainwright men don't get women pregnant and not marry them."

Giles struggled to control his temper. At thirty-six, he did not need his father to remind him of how he should live his life. "Have you forgotten that Jordan's father didn't marry his birth mother?" Edward Wainwright, Patrick's cousin, was engaged when he had an affair, an affair that resulted in a child he and his wife secretly adopted and raised as their own.

"I'm not talking about Edward," Pat countered.

"Well, he's the only Wainwright that I can recall who didn't marry his baby mama."

"I'm talking about you, Giles. Your mother tells me you have a child and when I asked if you had or were going to marry the baby's mother, she said no."

"That's because I can't marry her."

"And why the hell not?"

"Because she died, Dad! Mya is not Lily's biological mother. She's her aunt and adoptive mother." Realization suddenly dawned when Giles saw his father's stunned expression. "You thought I'd slept with Mya and got her pregnant?"

"I guess your mother didn't tell me the whole story."

Giles forced a smile. "I guess she didn't." He paused. "Now, are you ready for me to introduce you to my daughter's mother?"

Pat dropped an arm over his son's shoulders. "Lead on."

Giles and his father hadn't always seen eye to eye on a number of things, but rather than go toe to toe with him as his older brother had, Giles would walk away until cooler tempers prevailed. And what he failed to understand was why Patrick would choose to work under their father when the two argued constantly.

They found Mya in the den with Amanda bouncing Lily on her knee. He registered Pat's intake of breath when Mya rose to stand. The action was as graceful and regal as the queen she professed to be.

When Giles had arrived at her house earlier that morning for the ride to the airport, he had been temporarily stunned by her transformation. Missing was the bare face, jeans and T-shirt and socks; they were replaced with a light cover of makeup highlighting her luminous eyes and lush mouth, and a black wool gabardine pantsuit, black-pinstriped silk blouse and matching kitten heels. She had brushed her hair until there was no hint of a curl and pinned it into a chignon on the nape of her neck.

Seeing her like that had jolted him into an awareness that she had been a career woman before giving it up to become a full-time, stay-at-home mother.

Lily was laughing and squealing at the same time.

Mya had changed her and given her a bottle during the ride from the airport to Manhattan, and after spending time with his daughter, Giles was now attuned to her moods. She fretted when he didn't feed her fast enough, cried and squirmed when she needed to be changed and loved crawling around on the floor with him. She was much calmer with Mya when she sang or read to her, and whenever they were together in the rocker, it took only minutes for her to fall asleep.

Mya smiled at the tall, slender blond man striding toward her, arms extended. She noticed the only things the older man and Giles shared were height and eye color. A warm glow flowed through her when he hugged her and then kissed her cheek.

"Welcome to the family."

She smiled up at Giles's father. "Thank you, Mr. Wainwright. I'm Mya."

He kissed her other cheek. "Around here, I'm Grandpa." He eased back, his eyes moving slowly over her face. "My granddaughter has a beautiful mother."

Mya wanted to tell him she wasn't Lily's biological mother, but decided to hold her tongue and leave it up to Giles to explain their connection. "Thank you."

"Don't thank me, Mya. Thank the two people who gave you your exquisite looks."

Her smile faded. *I would if I knew who they were*, she thought. "This is Lily, your granddaughter."

Pat stared down at the baby who'd stopped laughing long enough to look up at him. "It's unbelievable." He was unable to disguise the awe in his voice. "She's the spitting image of Skye when she was a baby."

Amanda pressed her mouth to the back of Lily's head. "Speaking of Skye. I called her to tell her about Lily and she says she'll be here tomorrow to meet her niece."

A slight frown appeared between Pat's eyes. "So, that's why she asked me to buy a ticket for her to come home. I thought she'd gotten enough of that leech sucking her dry and had come to her senses and decided to leave him."

"Please, Pat. Let's not talk about that now," Amanda said softly.

Mya was grateful Amanda wanted to change the topic because the last thing she wanted was to become a witness to what had become a source of contention for the Wainwrights. It was never a good thing when parents or family members did not approve of their children's choice in a partner.

A young woman in a gray uniform and white shoes walked into the den. "Mrs. Wainwright. Dinner is ready."

Giles approached Mya and took her hand. "I'll show you where we can wash up."

She waited until they were behind the door of a bathroom off the den, then asked Giles, "Did you tell your father about us?"

He blinked slowly. "He's knows you're not Lily's birth mother, but not much beyond that. He did ask when I was going to marry you, because Wainwright men don't get women pregnant and not marry them."

Mya felt her heart stop and then start up again. "What did you say?"

"I told him that I hadn't gotten you pregnant, so that lets me off the hook about having to marry you."

She exhaled an inaudible sigh. "That's good."

His eyes grew wider. "What's good? Me not having to marry you, or you not wanting to marry me?"

Mya turned on the faucet and then tapped the soap dispenser. What did he expect her to say? That she could never conceive of marrying him? Or that she would consider marrying him but only if she found herself in love?

"It's not about me marrying you, because I haven't given it a thought one way or the other." She hadn't thought of it because something kept her from completely trusting him. She was certain he loved his daughter, yet she couldn't rid her mind that if he proposed marriage his ulterior motive would be to try and convince her to allow him to share legal custody of Lily.

Giles took a step, pressing his chest to her back. "You wouldn't do it because of Lily?" he whispered in her ear.

Mya closed her eyes as the heat from his body seeped into her hers, bringing with it an awareness of the man who had become so much a part of her day-to-day existence. She woke anticipating his arrival and felt a profound loss whenever he took his leave at the end of the day.

Giles had unexpectedly come into her life, and like the blistering summer heat that did not abate even after the sun had set, everything about him lingered: the firm touch of his mouth on hers when he greeted her, the muscled hardness of his body whenever he leaned into her, the brilliant blue eyes that seemed to know what she was thinking when she'd struggled in vain not to be caught up in the spell of longing whenever she was reminded of how long it had been since a man had made love to her.

There were nights when she woke in a panic from an erotic dream that made her press her face into the pillow to muffle the screams of pleasure as she experienced long-denied orgasms.

"No. There's no way I'm going to allow Lily to become a pawn in a relationship I'd have with any man."

"I'm not any man, Mya. I'm your daughter's father."

She nodded. "I know that. But I'd only marry you if I was in love with you."

Giles pressed a kiss alongside the column of her neck. "So you would consider me as a potential husband."

"Only if I was in love with you," she repeated.

He caressed her waist. "What do I have to do to make you fall in love with me?"

Mya rinsed her hands and then reached for a guest towel from a stack in a ceramic tray. "Just be you," she said cryptically. She dried her hands, dropped the towel in a wastebasket, then turned to see confusion freezing his features. "What's the matter?"

"What do you mean by that?"

She winked at him. "You're a very bright guy. So figure it out."

Giles caught her around the waist. "That's not fair."

"What's not fair?"

"You teasing me."

Mya stared up at him under lowered lashes. "All I'm saying is don't change, Giles. I've gotten to like you a lot. But you flip the script, then it's not going to go so well with us."

Giles's expression hardened. "Please don't compare me to your ex-boyfriend."

"I'm not. Malcolm is who he is, and you are who you are."

"Does this mean I can kiss you? Really kiss you?" he whispered as his head came down.

His mouth covered her before she could form an answer, her lips parting under the tender onslaught that left her shaking from head to toe. This kiss was different from the others because it was as if he was staking his claim. In that instant, she had forgotten all of the men who had ever kissed her as she returned Giles's kiss with a hunger that belied her outward appearance. Her hands came up and cradled his strong jaw as she tried to get even closer.

Then, without warning, it ended. Mya did not want to believe she was cloistered in a bathroom in Giles's parents' home allowing him to kiss her with wild abandon. And she also felt uncomfortable because it was the first time Giles had acted on his lustful stares. Maybe it was because he was more confident in New York being with his family, while she viewed herself as the outsider despite the elder Wainwrights welcoming her with warmth and open arms.

"Please open the door, Giles."

He released her and pushed open the door. "Wait for me."

Mya nodded. She noticed he was breathing as heavily as she, which meant they both were affected by the kiss.

She waited for him to wash and dry his hands, then followed him along a narrow hallway leading to the rear of the house. Mya smothered a gasp when he opened a door to a backyard garden with trees, bushes with late-blooming fall flowers, a man-made waterfall and tiny white string lights entwined with ivy within the framework of a pergola. A table with seating for four was covered with hemstitched linens, crystal stemware, china and brass candelabras. Pat seated Amanda after she placed Lily in a high chair between his chair and his wife's.

Giles pulled out a chair, seating Mya before he claimed his own next to her. "Don't look so worried," he whispered in her ear. "My mother has more than enough experience raising her children and now occasionally babysitting her grandkids."

Mya forced a smile. She wasn't aware her concern for Lily had shown on her face. She realized there would come a time when she would have to let go of her daughter, but knew it wasn't going to be easy.

Amanda smiled across the table. "Mya, I hope you and Giles will let Lily stay with me while you two take some time for yourselves while you're here, and I want to spend as much time with her before you go back to West Virginia."

"Of course," Mya said reluctantly, when Giles nudged her foot with his under the table.

"What about when you go into the gallery?" Pat asked Amanda.

"Not to worry, darling," Amanda crooned. "I'm taking off for as long as Giles and Mya are here. By the way, when are you going back?"

Mya shared a look with Giles. "We plan to stay until at least the thirtieth."

"Bummer," the older woman said between clenched

teeth. "I was hoping you'd stay for Halloween because I always take pictures of the kids in their costumes. Last year, both of Patrick's boys were dressed like pumpkins."

"Maybe next year," Giles said, "that is if it's okay with Mya."

Mya nodded. "We'll definitely think about it."

"Is that a promise?" Amanda asked.

"Of course," he replied.

"We'll be back again for Thanksgiving," Mya added.

"What about Christmas?"

Mya smiled. "We'll be here for Christmas."

She was actually looking forward to celebrating Christmas in New York City. It had always been her wish to eat roasted chestnuts from street vendors while strolling along Fifth Avenue to check out the gaily decorated department store windows. She also planned to have Giles take a photo of her and Lily in front of the Christmas tree at Rockefeller Center.

Amanda pressed her palms together. "You have to spend the Christmas week and New Year's with us. Christmas is when the entire family gets together for what becomes somewhat of a never-ending party. The New Year's Eve ball is always a fund-raiser. The family underwrites the cost of the food, drinks and entertainment for folks with deep pockets to donate to the year's designated charity."

Mya sat straight. "Who selects the charity?"

Giles rested a hand over Mya's. "Those who sit on the Wainwright board of directors, who all happen to be family members. This year, they selected the World Vision's water project for Kenya. We've committed to match whatever we raise for the evening."

Suddenly she saw his family in a whole new light. They were using their wealth to help make the world better for those less fortunate.

Mya's attention shifted to several waiters pushing carts with covered dishes onto the patio. She smiled as Lily babbled incessantly while patting the high chair tray. Amanda had asked whether Lily was lactose intolerant because she'd planned to blend macaroni and cheese for the baby. She confided to the child's grandmother that Lily was a joy to feed because the baby wasn't a picky eater.

"Do you eat like this every time you get together?" Mya asked Giles quietly as waiters set out the food. The table was covered with cold and hot dishes ranging from sushi, tuna tartare, daikon and carrot, lobster and crab salads to pasta with a variety of sauces and grilled glazed pork spareribs, Cornish game hens and eggplant.

"Yes." Giles picked up and held the platter of sushi for Mya. "Mom says she likes to be eclectic when it comes to planning a dinner. In other words, a little something for everyone."

"Does your mother cook?"

"Yes. In fact, she's an incredible cook—like her granddaughter's mother." Giles punctuated the compliment when he kissed her hair. "She ordered in tonight because she wanted to get the house ready for us."

His disclosure caught Mya slightly off guard. "I thought you were going to stay in your apartment."

"Not tonight. Tomorrow you can decide what you want to do."

She gave him a sidelong glance. "What's on our agenda?"

He lifted his shoulders. "Not much. I'll probably pop into the office to check in with Jocelyn, and after that, I'm all yours." Giles paused. "Maybe I'll call my cousin Jordan and see if we can stop by and see his new baby."

"I'm going to call my editor and if she has the time, we can share lunch before we go back."

"Are you guys talking about doing something together?" Amanda asked. "Because Pat and I don't mind babysitting if you want to have some alone time."

Mya shook her head. "I... I don't want to impose on—"

"Don't say it," Amanda warned, interrupting her. "It's not as if you asked us to look after her. We're offering. And once Skye gets here I'm willing to bet you won't get to see your daughter again until it's time for you to leave."

Giles draped his free arm over the back of Mya's chair. "Just make certain you don't spoil her so much that she'll be off schedule and not want to sleep at night."

Amanda glared at him. "I did raise three children, so I believe that qualifies me to look after my grandbabies."

Mya rested a hand on Giles's shoulder. "Let it go," she whispered. She didn't want Giles to get into it with his mother about Lily. She planned to give Amanda a detailed schedule for the baby's nap and mealtimes.

"Don't argue with your woman, son, because you'll only lose."

Amanda glared at her husband. "Stay out of their business, Pat."

"I'm not getting into their business, Mandy. I'm just trying to give him some sage advice."

"Advice they probably don't need," Amanda retorted.

Giles picked up a sushi roll with a pair of chopsticks. "Dad's right. I've learned not to get into it with Mya because I usually end up losing."

Mya's eyebrows lifted, questioning. "Usually?" she teased. "You always lose."

Pat grimaced. "Oh-kay," he drawled. "It's time to drop that topic."

Mya agreed when she said, "How often do you dine alfresco?"

"As often as I can," Amanda said. "Once all of the kids were gone, Pat and I talked about selling this place because it's much too big for two people."

"Do you use the entire building?"

"Not anymore. Once Patrick and Giles left, we rented the second-and third-story apartments to doctors, because New York Hospital is within walking distance. But I didn't like being a landlord, so when their leases were up, we decided to use the entire building for out-of-town friends and family. My brother and sisters have thirteen children and at least sixteen grandchildren among them. Whenever they come down from Boston, it's like summer camp with babies underfoot and kids running up and down the stairs."

Giles smiled. "Don't let Mom fool you. She loves it when the house is filled to capacity."

Amanda nodded. "He's right. When Pat and I were first married, we'd planned on having six children."

"What made you change your mind?" Giles asked his mother.

"I didn't realize how much work went into child rearing. I grew up with a nanny, so I never saw my mother frazzled or overwhelmed. And because I missed that close contact with her, I decided early on that I'd be a hands-on mother. I had your brother and you came along eighteen months later, and now when I look back, I know I was experiencing some postpartum depression. That's when I decided to wait at least five years before getting pregnant again. I felt my family was complete because I had my sons and a daughter."

"And now we have two grandsons and a granddaughter," Pat said in a low, composed voice.

Mya managed to conceal a smile when she pretended interest in the food on her plate as Amanda recalled some of the tricks her sons had played on her. They would hide in one of the many closets in the town house and wait for her to search the entire building to find them.

Amanda wiped away traces of mac and cheese from Lily's chubby cheeks. "I was almost at my wit's end when I decided to turn the tables on them. One day when they left for school, I had a workman come in and change the doorknobs on all of the closets. When they realized they needed a key to open them, it put an end to their disappearing acts. So if Lily is anything like her father, then she's going to be quite a challenge."

Mya nodded. "Thanks for the advance warning."

"I wasn't that bad," Giles said, in defense of himself.

"Not bad, just mischievous," Amanda countered. "Even though I love being a mother, it still doesn't compare to being a grandmother. You'll see, Mya, once Lily's married and has children."

"That's not going to be for a while," Mya said.

"That's where you're wrong because they grow up so fast that you'll wonder where the time went. I preach that to my son Patrick and thankfully he's taken my advice and spends a lot of his free time with his boys."

"That's something I didn't do with my kids," Pat admitted. He met Mya's eyes. "I let work consume me and by the time I left the office, my children were in bed. It was the same in the morning. I was up and out before they sat down to breakfast. I know I can't make it up with my children, but I promised Mandy that it's going to be different with the grandkids."

I have to learn that being a father is a lot more than offering financial support. Now Mya knew what Giles meant. Although his father had financially supported his family, it was the emotional support he had withheld.

"None of us grow up knowing how to parent," Mya said in a quiet voice. "We learn on the job. I've read a lot of books on child rearing, and there's no definitive blueprint for becoming the perfect mom or dad. Lily has her own little personality and there may come a time when we're going to be at odds with each other and I'm going to have to accept that. It's different with girls than boys because of hormones. Once we were teenagers, my sister and I weren't very nice to our mother or each other, but that didn't mean we didn't love one another. My mother admitted she went through the same thing with her own mother, so she waited for us to come to our senses."

Giles set down his fork. "Even though I'm a newbie

when it comes to being a parent, I have no doubt Mya is going to make me a better father."

"Don't be a fool and let her get away from you," Pat said to his son.

"Patrick!" Amanda admonished. "Why are you interfering?"

"I am not interfering. I'm just stating a fact." Pat pointed at Giles. "If you let Mya get away—"

"Enough, Dad," Giles said, cutting him off. "Mya and I will be together for a long time."

"How long is long?" Pat questioned.

"Patrick Harrison Wainwright!" Amanda said, her voice rising in annoyance. "Mind your business!"

"Stop it, Dad. Mya and I want the best for Lily, and we will do everything within our power to make certain she knows she's loved and protected."

Mya felt like an interloper when she felt tension in Giles as he engaged in a stare down with his father. She wondered if the older Wainwright felt his son had been irresponsible when he'd gotten a woman pregnant, or resentful that Lily wasn't a Wainwright.

Pat's comments cast a pall over the remainder of dinner as everyone, except Lily, appeared interested in eating what was on their plates rather than engage in further conversation. Mya was certain everyone was relieved when the table was cleared and no one opted for coffee and dessert.

Giles pushed back his chair. "I'm going for a walk. Do you want to come with me?"

Mya turned to look at Giles. "What about Lily?"

"She's going to be all right, sweets. Remember my

mother raised three kids, so she's certified to take care of an eight-month-old."

I'm going to have to learn to let go and not become a helicopter mom, Mya thought. The last thing she wanted to become was overbearing and smothering where her daughter's love would turn into resentment.

"Okay. Can you wait for me to go inside and change?"

Giles assisted her up. "Of course."

Chapter 8

Giles experienced the peace that had evaded him for years as he held Mya's hand when they strolled along Second Avenue. She had changed into a pair of jeans, pullover sweater and running shoes.

"I'm sorry about my father," he said after a comfortable silence.

"Don't apologize, Giles. Your father said what he wanted."

He glanced at her delicate profile. "And what's that?"

"He wants us together and I'm willing to bet that he also wants Lily to become a Wainwright."

"You're probably right about his granddaughter becoming a Wainwright. Dad views being a Wainwright as akin to American royalty. My great-grandfather came to this country broke as a convict. Like so many other immigrants during the turn of the century, he and his new bride shared a railroad flat on the Lower East Side with several other families. Patrick took odd jobs, while my great-grandmother took in wash to pay their share of the rent. Patrick managed to get a position as a building superintendent for several buildings on Houston Street, which allowed him to move into an apartment rent-free. Meanwhile his wife had become quite an accomplished seamstress and would occasionally sew for people in show business. They had three sons and a daughter, who died from diphtheria before her fifth birthday.

"James and Harrison knew their only path out of poverty was education. They graduated high school and enrolled in City College for a tuition-free college education. James became a teacher, while Harrison went into law. Meanwhile, Wyatt, the middle son took the opposite path of his brothers. He dropped out of school in the tenth grade and hired himself out as a bagman for a local thug running an illegal numbers operation. The police never suspected Wyatt because he looked much younger than sixteen. He made certain to stay off the streets during school hours to evade the truant officers, and after a while, he made more in a week than his law-abiding siblings because he had a gift for playing and hitting the numbers. His father gave him an ultimatum—go back to school and get a high school diploma or move out."

"Did he move out or go back to school?"

"Yes. He went back to school. I'm telling you this because I want you to know that the Wainwrights haven't always been legit."

Mya leaned into him. "Don't forget so-called robber barons used dubious means to become very wealthy men."

Giles told Mya that his great-uncle had amassed a small fortune and, with the assistance of his gangster mentor, bought a run-down tenement and renovated it. He moved into one of the apartments and rented the others to his criminal friends who used them for everything from bookmaking to fencing stolen goods. However, Wyatt drew the line when it came to drugs and prostitution. He was sweet on a young black girl who lived in the neighborhood but nothing came of it because interracial relationships were taboo at the time.

"Once he bought his second building, Wyatt decided it was time to leave his criminal past behind. He got one of his criminal cronies to buy him out and he hired Harrison to set up a corporation for his real estate business. Wyatt had become quite adept at buying abandoned properties, renovating them and selling them at a huge profit. He was flipping properties decades before it became popular. After he'd amassed enough money, he decided to build instead of renovate. He'd become the successful Wainwright son while the other two had to depend on others for their salaries. Wyatt made peace with his father and invited his brothers to join him when he set up the Wainwright Developers Group. Wyatt had yet to celebrate his fortieth birthday when he became a real estate mogul and a multimillionaire. Although he's semi-retired, Wyatt hasn't come that far from the streetwise, baby-faced gangster to family patriarch. He still has a gun in his desk drawer.

"There are times when my father forgets where the Wainwrights came from because he grew up privileged.

We all attended private schools, traveled abroad during school holidays and were expected to marry women with impeccable pedigrees. That was okay for my parents and their siblings, but my generation has, as you say, flipped the script because we marry whoever the hell we want."

Mya giggled softly. "Y'all have gone rogue."

Giles gave her fingers a gentle squeeze. "It feels good to throw off the shackles of a tradition that money must marry money."

There came another period of silence before Mya spoke again. "Is your father upset that Lily is not a Wainwright?"

"That's only part of it. My father may not have been there for many of the milestones in our childhood but there was something he relentlessly preached to me and my brother and that was making certain not to get a woman pregnant if we had no intention of marrying her. He said never to rely on a woman to prevent contraception because there was no way of knowing whether she was taking an oral conceptive or had an IUD. He said that the one thing we could be certain of was using our own condoms. His suspicions came from several of his college buddies who became fathers before they were ready when their girlfriends claimed they were on the pill, or they'd used the girl's condoms."

"Do you resent becoming a father before you were ready?"

Giles stopped in the middle of the sidewalk and cradled Mya's face between his palms. "No. I never would've met you if she hadn't been born."

Her hands circled his strong wrists. "This is not about me."

"Isn't it, sweets? It's all about you *and* Lily. You two are a package deal. I can't have one without the other."

Mya's eyes narrowed. "What do you want, Giles?"

He smiled and attractive lines fanned around his eyes. "I want you and I want Lily in my life."

"We are in your life," she argued softly. "Didn't you say we're a family?"

"Yes, but not in the legal sense. I want you to marry me."

A nervous laugh escaped Mya. "You want me to marry you so you'll have some legal claim on me and my daughter."

"Wrong, Mya. I want to marry you because you're the missing piece in my life. I'm no choirboy when it comes to women. I've slept with women I liked and some I didn't like because I needed a physical release, and I'm not very proud of that. Whenever I'm around you, I feel something I've never felt with any other woman and please don't tell me it's because of Lily because right now she doesn't figure into the equation.

"When I went into combat, I didn't know that if I survived whether I'd ever be the same. I did survive but lived in my own personal hell and was racked with guilt because I did survive when other men under my command didn't. Facing death forced me to acknowledge my own mortality and to live each day as if it was my last. I've never been in love with a woman, but if what I'm beginning to feel for you is love, then dammit, I'm willing to embrace it."

Going on tiptoe, Mya brushed a light kiss over his

mouth. "Why don't we take it slow and see where it leads."

"Is that a yes?"

She shook her head. "It's not a yes but a maybe. And because I'm an old-fashioned Southern girl, then I expect you to court me before you ask for my hand in marriage."

Giles flashed a smile, exhibiting a mouth filled with perfectly aligned white teeth. "How long do I have to court you, Miss Mountain State Queen?"

"At least six months of courtship."

He quickly did the calculations in his head. "We met for the first time in September, so next February or March seems appropriate for us to announce our engagement."

"You can't talk about an engagement when I haven't said whether I'll marry you."

"Will you at least consider marrying me?"

Mya paused before giving Giles an answer. She knew she was falling for him—hard—and she had sought to test Giles to uncover whether he wanted her as a wife because he loved her and not because she was Lily's mother. She couldn't dismiss the nagging suspicion that she had become the conduit through which he would eventually claim his daughter legally.

She nodded. "Right now I can say truthfully that I will consider it. And if I say yes, then I don't want a short engagement."

"How long do you want the engagement to be?"

"At least a year." Dating for six months and marrying

a year later would allow Mya more than enough time to know if she could trust Giles completely.

"That means we'll marry sometime the following spring."

She nodded. "Do you expect me to sign a prenuptial agreement?"

Giles released her face as his hands curled into tight fists. "Hell no! What made you ask that?"

She withdrew from him without moving when she saw rage lurking in the blue orbs and the skin drawn tight over his cheekbones. "Just checking. I don't want you to think I'm marrying you for your money."

"And I don't want you to think I want to marry you because of Lily."

Mya slipped her arm through his. "Now that we've settled that, we don't have to bring it up again."

She knew Giles was still bothered by her query because a muscle flicked angrily at his jaw. He was probably so used to women falling all over themselves to get his attention because of his name, looks and money that no doubt he believed she was no exception. And no matter how much she liked him, Mya wasn't going to allow her heart to rule her head.

There was a time when she disliked him intensely when they first met, but that was then. Now she enjoyed his company. And she never tired of watching him interact with Lily. At first, she'd believed he was drawn to the little girl because of vanity—that Lily reminded him of his sister—but after a while Mya knew his affection for the child was genuine. He had assumed the responsibility of reading to her before putting her in the crib for her nap. The few times Mya had looked in on them, she found Lily curled up on his chest asleep while he cradled her in his large hands. She had wanted to chastise him for holding her but held her tongue when she backed out of the room. That was when she had to remind herself he shared DNA with the baby and she didn't. That a judge had ruled that she was legally Lily's mother, while Giles would have to navigate the legal system to claim his daughter.

They continued walking and stopped in front of a sports bar where the doors were open and patrons were yelling at the top of their lungs. "I used to hang out here whenever I came home from college," Giles said.

She noticed his eyes were fixed on one of the many screens. "Do you want to go in?" He looked at her, seemingly shocked by her suggestion.

"You don't mind?"

Mya tugged at his arm. "Of course not. After a few beers, I'll probably scream with the others."

"I didn't know you liked baseball."

"I got into it when I lived in Chicago."

"White Sox or Cubs?"

Her smile was dazzling. "Cubbies, of course."

Giles managed to shoulder his way inside, pulling her behind through the crowd standing three deep at the bar. He managed to find a table for two in a corner near the kitchen and signaled the waiter for two beers.

"Is it always crowded like this?" she shouted to be heard over the babble of voices.

"Yes. But there's more people than usual because it's the first game of the World Series."

Even though she wasn't an avid sports fan, Mya enjoyed the camaraderie of getting together with friends and colleagues to watch an occasional game. And cheering for a particular team allowed her to get swept up in the excitement going on around her.

She had asked Giles to give her time to consider his proposal because she was still grieving the loss of her sister. And it would also take time to accept the reality that she would eventually sleep with the same man as her niece's mother.

After the second beer, she found herself caught up in the hysteria that swept through the sports bar like a lighted fuse. She watched Giles when he recognized someone from his past. There were a lot of rough hugs and back slaps before he introduced her as his girlfriend.

It was close to ten when they returned to the house, and Mya discovered she was slightly tipsy from downing two beers. "I'm under the influence," she whispered to Giles as he unlocked the front door.

"From two beers?"

"Yes."

"Either you are a cheap drunk or you don't get out enough."

Her lips parted in a lopsided grin. "Both," she slurred.

"Why don't you go upstairs and turn in while I check on Lily?"

"We'll check together." There wasn't a day since Sammie came home with the baby that Mya hadn't checked on Lily before turning in for the night.

They found Amanda and Pat sitting together in the den watching an all-news channel. Pat had his arm around his wife while she rested her head on his shoulder. Despite Amanda having to raise her children alone even though she had a husband, she had stayed with him. Was it because, Mya mused, she did not believe in divorce? Or did she fear not having a man in her life? Or was it because she loved him and accepted his shortcomings?

Giles placed a finger over his mouth when he led her in the direction of the nursery.

The nursery was set up in an alcove off the master bedroom where Pat or Amanda had easy access in the event one of their grandchildren required their immediate attention. Lily was sleeping soundly on her back in one of the two cribs. Her tiny rosebud mouth twitched as if she wanted to smile at something that had amused her. Mya's loving gaze lingered on the long dark lashes resting on rosy pink cheeks and the coal-black hair grazing her rounded forehead.

She leaned against Giles's body when he put an arm around her waist. Turning her head, she kissed his neck below his ear at the same time his fingers tightened against her ribs. They stood watching the sleeping child, and then as if on cue, they walked out of the room.

"Baby's in bed, and now it's time for Mama to turn in before she falls on her face," he said softly.

Mya giggled. "I told you that I'm not much of a drinker."

Bending slightly, Giles scooped her up in his arms. "You didn't lie about that."

She buried her face against the column of his strong neck. "I never lie." Giles carried her up the back staircase and into the second-floor bedroom Amanda had assigned her. He placed her on the bed and lay beside her.

"Do you need help getting undressed?"

Mya gave him a crooked smile. "I don't think so. I'm just going to lie here for a few minutes, and then I'm going to get up and take a shower."

Giles shifted until they lay facing each other. "What if I hang around to make certain you don't slip in the bathroom?"

"Sorry, handsome, but no thanks. If you think you're going to get a peek at my goodies before it's time, then you're deluding yourself."

Giles flashed an irresistibly devastating grin. "Please don't tell me you're going to make me wait until our wedding night before I can sneak a peek."

"Yes."

He affected a frown. "That's cruel and unusual punishment."

"No, it's not. Remember what I told you about courting me."

"What about a sniff?"

Before Mya could reply, Giles sprang up, shifted her effortlessly until she lay on her back and planted his face between her thighs. "No!" she screamed before laughing hysterically. She laughed even harder when he made growling noises like rutting bull.

"Don't make another sound," he warned, grinning, "or my folks will think something happened to you.

Mya waited for him to inch his way up her body, while supporting his weight on his forearms. Her body shook as her laughter turned to giggles. "You're incorrigible."

Giles kissed her chin. "No, I'm not. It's just when I see something I want, I go all in."

She sobered and met his eyes. Mya knew she had to

stop denying what she so obviously wanted and needed. She'd told Giles that she wanted to wait for their wedding night to make love, yet knew realistically she didn't want to wait that long. "I've changed my mind," she said in a quiet voice. "I'm not going to make you wait until we're married for us to make love. It's just that I don't want our relationship to be based on sex like yours and Sammie's."

"That's the only thing we shared because she didn't want anything else."

"Don't forget Lily," Mya reminded him. She gave him a long, penetrating stare. "You don't like it, do you, when I mention Sammie's name?"

"Why would you say that?"

"Because you get a little frown between your eyes whenever I talk about her."

"I didn't realize that," he admitted. "Maybe it's because whenever you mention her name, I'm reminded that she was your sister."

Mya nodded. "But I am *not* my sister. Sammie was complex and almost impossible to figure out but I'd learned to accept and love her in spite of her peculiar idiosyncrasies."

"It would be a sad world if we all looked alike and thought alike."

"You're so right, love. Now let me get up so I can get ready for bed."

"Where's my night-night kiss?"

Her lips found their way to his, shivering slightly as the contact sent currents of desire racing through her. Giles returned the kiss, increasing the pressure until her lips parted; his tongue searched the recesses of her mouth until she moaned as if in pain. Her tongue touched and dueled with his and ignited a fire that threatened to consume her mind and body.

"Giles," she moaned, the sound coming from somewhere she didn't know existed.

"I know, baby," he whispered against her trembling lips. He rolled off her body and stood at the side of the bed, staring at her heaving breasts. "Good night, my sweet."

Mya stared up at the ceiling and heard rather than saw him leave the bedroom as he closed the door behind him. Groaning, she turned over on her belly and pounded the mattress. Giles had only kissed her and now she was like a cat in heat. She had changed her mind about them making love because she knew she could not hold off not allowing Giles to make love to her until they were engaged, because she wanted him to want her for herself as if he'd never met Sammie or fathered Lily.

And it wasn't for the first time that she blamed herself for not having as much as experience with the opposite sex as her sister. She'd dated a few boys in high school, but none reached the point where they were intimate. It was in her second year in college that she had her first serious relationship with an adjunct lecturer from a nearby college. He was older, divorced and responsible for awakening her dormant sexuality. They slept together for two years until he secured another position out of the state. It was another three years before she dated again. But it lasted less than four months before she called it quits.

After she returned to Wickham Falls and was appointed to teach at the college, she finally accepted Malcom Tate's invitation to have dinner with him. She had been reluctant because they worked together. She enjoyed his company because he was closer to her age and they had a lot in common. The exception was temperament. She was composed while he was volatile and that did not bode well for a future together.

Mya closed her eyes and willed her mind blank. So much had happened in the past year that she needed a daily journal to record the events: she'd become an aunt, buried her sister and become a mother, and now she had committed to share her life and future with her daughter's father. The million-dollar question was: what's next? She wasn't in love with Giles but with time she knew she would come to love him.

She opened her eyes and slipped off the bed. She had to get up and shower before falling asleep in her clothes.

Mya woke the same time as she did every morning. Her internal clock indicated it was time for her to get up. She completed her ablution in record time because she wanted to be up and dressed before Lily woke.

She made her way down the staircase to the wing of the house with the master bedroom. The door was closed. When Giles mentioned that his parents had installed a nursery in their home, she did not think it would be within their bedroom. Mya knew she would have to wait to see Lily.

Her sock-covered feet were silent on the gleaming parquet floor when she walked down a wide hallway and peered into exquisitely furnished rooms. Paintings, wall hangings and fragile vases validated Giles's claim that his mother had earned a degree in art history. The spaces were reminiscent of rooms in museums with priceless objets d'art. She lingered outside one room with tables and curio cabinets filled with obelisks and sculptures and carvings of Egyptian cats, jackals and crocodiles. She walked down a hallway with framed prints of impressionists, cubists and modern artists and turned into a large gourmet kitchen.

Mya swallowed a gasp of surprise when she saw Pat and Giles sitting together in a breakfast nook. She did not know why, but she hadn't expected them to be up so early. It was only 5:45 a.m. Giles wore a white T-shirt and jeans, while his father was dressed for work. She could not pull her eyes away from Giles's muscular upper body. His clothes had concealed a man in his prime and in peak conditioning.

"Good morning," Mya said cheerfully.

Giles jumped up. Apparently she had startled him. "Good morning." He approached her as she entered the kitchen. He cupped the back of her head and brushed a kiss over her parted lips.

Easing back, she nodded to Pat. "Good morning, Grandpa."

Pat lifted his cup of coffee in acknowledgment. "Good morning. You're quite the early bird."

"I get up early to take care of Lily."

"You don't have to do that with Mandy hovering over her like a mother hen." He patted the bench seat next to him. "Come sit down. Giles, please make her a cup of coffee. I was talking to Giles about Mandy and I taking Lily to the Bronx Zoo today, and he said I'd have to ask you. I plan to go into the office this morning for a couple of hours, then come back and pick up Mandy and the baby. We keep a stroller, car seat and a baby carrier on hand, so transporting her shouldn't be a problem. Mandy says she's going to make her food and store it in a bag that will keep it warm, along with bottles of milk and water."

"If you want my permission, then you have it." Taking Lily to the zoo was a way for them to bond with her. "What do you have planned for tomorrow?"

Pat flashed a sheepish grin. "We were talking about possibly driving up to Boston to introduce Lily to Mandy's brother and sisters. I have a feeling she wants to show her off," he said under his breath. "Skye's scheduled to arrive today, so we'll wait and see if she wants to come with us."

"If you go to Boston, Dad, then that's not going to be a day trip," Giles said as he walked to the breakfast nook carrying a mug of steaming hot coffee. He set the mug on the table. "Coffee with a splash of milk and one sugar for the pretty lady."

"That's what I told your mother. But she says if we hire a driver, then we can do it in a day."

Mya stared at the liquid in the mug. Lily had become somewhat of a novelty to the Wainwrights and she realized they wanted to spend as much time with her before she went back to Wickham Falls. She ignored the anxiety tightening the muscles in her stomach when she thought of not seeing her baby for more than twenty-four hours.

"You can keep her overnight if you want."

Pat's face lit up like the rays of the rising sun. "Bless you, my child."

Giles sat down next to Mya and combed his fingers through her unbound hair. "What do you want to do today?"

She shivered slightly from his light touch when his finger traced the outline of her ear. "Other than a little shopping, I'm open to whatever you want."

"I'd like to take you into the office to meet Jocelyn. After that, you can shop until you drop."

"Who's shopping?" Amanda asked. Bending slightly, she placed Lily on the floor and the little girl crawled over to Mya.

"I am." Mya scooped Lily off the floor. Amanda had given Lily a bath, combed her hair and secured a lock of hair atop her head with a narrow white ribbon. "Good morning. Your grandma made you look so pretty with that ribbon in your hair."

Amanda smiled. "You don't know how long I've waited to put a ribbon in a little girl's hair."

Giles stood up and kissed his mother. "Something tells me you're partial to girls."

Pinpoints of color suffused her fair complexion. "That's not true. I love my sons as much as I love my daughter, but it's different when it comes to dressing little girls."

Giles kissed her again. "Just teasing. Do you want coffee?"

"Yes, please." Amanda sat down next to her husband. "Do you want to eat breakfast here or do you plan to grab something at the office?"

"If it won't be any trouble, I'd like to eat here."

Amanda patted the shoulder of his crisp white shirt. "Of course it's not any trouble."

Mya waited until Giles brought his mother's coffee before handing off Lily to him. "I'm going to help your mother fix breakfast."

Amanda appeared surprised by her offer when she said, "You really don't have to help me."

"But I want to. I'm not used to sitting around doing absolutely nothing."

"That's because you don't know how to relax," Giles interjected.

"That's because mothers aren't allowed to relax," Amanda countered. She took a sip of coffee and stared at Mya over the rim. "Because you've pierced Lily's ears, I have a set of earrings I'd like to give you for her. And once she turns sixteen, she'll inherit the pearls and matching earrings my grandmother gave me for my sixteenth birthday."

Mya was slightly taken aback with the generous offer. She'd noticed the magnificent strand of South Sea pearls and matching studs Amanda wore the night before. "Don't you want to give the pearls to your daughter?"

Amanda slowly shook her head. "There's a little wicked tale attached to the baubles. My grandfather died suddenly, leaving my young and attractive grandmother a very eligible widow. After a respectable period of mourning, men came calling on her. She went out with some and rejected a number of others. What she suspected was that most were after her money. So she decided to test them. In other words, put your money where your mouth is. She told each of them that her birthday was coming up and she wanted jewelry as a gift. Some gave her earrings and others broaches. There was one gentleman in particular who'd asked her father what was her favorite jewel. He told him pearls. And not the ordinary cultured pearls but the golden South Sea variety.

"The potential suitor paid someone to sail to Tahiti and bring him back enough thirteen millimeter pearls for a necklace and earrings. It took nearly four months but when he presented my grandmother with the pearls, she decided he was the one. They were married a year later and she gave him six children—all boys. I was her only granddaughter, so I inherited all of her jewelry. I've put aside some for Skye, and the rest I was saving for my granddaughter."

Mya knew Amanda loved talking about her family and there was no doubt she had many, many more stories to tell. "Lily's a very lucky little girl."

"After breakfast, we'll go through the jewelry and you can pick out what else you want for Lily."

Pat cleared his throat. "I hope you save some for Patrick because he and Bethany may change their minds and have another baby. And it could be a girl."

Amanda shook her head. "That's not happening because Bethany told me she's done having children. I didn't press her about it, so I'm assuming she's either having or had a procedure so she wouldn't get pregnant again."

Sitting in the kitchen and talking was something Mya missed with her family. Her father would come home and vent about his workmen or customers who changed their minds after he'd designed a table or a headboard. Then it was her mother who updated everyone with news from home about a relative who'd been caught cheating on his wife or a wife cheating on her husband. Mya never thought of it as malicious gossip but idle chatter because there wasn't anything else to talk about. Occasionally they would discuss politics and the fact the country was going to hell in a hand-basket as it had over the past two hundred years. What Graham and Veronica sought to do was shield their daughters from local gossip, but as they got older what they heard from their classmates they never repeated to their parents. Their peers whispered about girls who'd slept with every boy on the football team, and several underage girls who'd sought to hide their relationships with older men, and then there were the boys and girls who were gay—rather than come out they waited until graduation to leave Wickham Falls to escape the taunts and harassment to live openly with a same-sex partner.

And nothing had changed when Sammie came back to the Falls to live and people began noticing that she was putting on weight. Once her condition was evident, folks wanted to know who the father was. Both she and Sammie were mute because her sister wasn't the first single mother in Wickham Falls and she definitely would not be the last.

Mya joined Amanda at the cooking island as they selected the items needed to make breakfast for their men.

Chapter 9

Mya stared at the emerald-cut ruby ring surrounded by a double halo of flawless blue-white diamonds set in twenty-four carat gold on her left hand. Amanda had insisted she wear it because the blood-red stone was the perfect match for her golden skin tones.

"I can't take it."

"You can and you will," Amanda insisted. "That ring belonged to my mother but she hardly ever wore it because she didn't like red. And the gold made her pale skin look washed-out."

"It's magnificent."

Amanda smiled. "I agree." She pressed her palms together. "Now let's see what else is in this so-called treasure trove I can give away."

Mya was in awe when Amanda handed her a pair

of diamond earrings for Lily. They totaled a carat, set in platinum and the accompanying appraisal certified they were flawless.

"I think Lily and I are good for now," she said when Amanda selected a diamond bracelet. "Why don't you wait until she's older when she can really appreciate the sentimentality. Then she can say Grandma gave me this ring for my tenth birthday or this necklace for my high school graduation."

Amanda nodded. "You're right."

Mya hugged the older woman. "I'll always remember today because of the ring."

"So will I, because it is the day I got my second daughter." She pulled back. "I get on Pat about interfering in his kids business only because I don't want him to make the same mistake I did when I tried matching Giles up with my best friend's daughter. He punished me in the most severe way possible when he disappeared for years. No one in the family knew where he was, and there was a point when I didn't know whether he was dead or alive. I had no idea he'd joined the military until he called to let me know he was being deployed. It was that day I swore I would never meddle in my children's lives again. Pat and I are not happy with the man Skye has chosen to live with, but I refused to say anything to her. When she's had enough, she'll leave him. There is one thing I know about the Wainwrights. They are survivors."

Amanda was right. Sammie had died so that Lily would survive. And not only was Lily a survivor but Mya knew she was also a survivor. She watched

Amanda lock the box and return it to a wall safe behind a framed Rembrandt reproduction.

"Art students would love your home."

"You're probably right. I had a photographer approach me with an offer to photograph the house for a slick architectural magazine but I turned him down. Some of the pieces are originals and many are copies, and I don't want to invite thieves who use the most devious ways to break into someone's property. It was only after I became an empty nester that I decided to turn the house into somewhat of a museum. Whenever the grandkids come over, I simply close the doors to the rooms with the art. I've catalogued and have every piece appraised, and I've indicated in my will who gets what. I will not have my children fighting one another over material items."

Mya wanted to tell Lily's grandmother that she and Sammie hadn't had that problem. Their parents had divided everything they owned evenly. Amanda was candid when she said there had been a time when she'd had a live-in housekeeper, but now she valued her privacy, and the housekeeper only came in two days a week and whenever she hosted a get-together.

Mya nearly doubled over in laughter when she saw Lily crawling along the carpeted hallway to get away from Giles, who was on all fours crawling after her. Piercing screams rent the air as Giles pounced on Lily and pretended to gobble her up. Pressing her back against the wall, Mya moved past them and took the staircase to her bedroom.

Mya emerged from the en suite bath after brushing her teeth to find Giles sitting on a chair bouncing Lily on his knees. "You better be careful juggling her like that before she barfs on you."

Giles lifted several strands from Lily's moist forehead. "That's all right. My princess can do anything she wants." He glanced up, his gaze lingering on her hand. "Where did you get that ring?"

She held out her hand, fingers outstretched. "Your mother gave it to me. She said it belonged to your grandmother."

Giles dropped a kiss on the back of her hand. "It's beautiful."

"I agree."

"She also gave me a pair of diamond earrings for Lily, but she won't be able to wear them until she's older."

"Mom loves giving gifts. You'll discover that when we come back for Christmas."

Mya knelt near the chair, her eyes meeting Giles's. "Are you going to miss not living in New York?"

Giles pressed his forehead to Mya's. "What I'd miss is not being with you and Lily. I could live anywhere as long as we're together. Dad and I had a very candid talk earlier this morning about what it means to be a father. His father was a workaholic and Dad followed in his footsteps. I hadn't realized how much I resented my father not being around for dinner until I shared this morning's breakfast with you and Lily. Night after night, I'd watch my mother hold back tears when she stared at the empty chair at the opposite end of the table waiting for my father because he was always running very late. One night, Patrick had had enough when he raised his voice to Mom and told her that she was deluding herself if she expected her husband to share dinner with his family. That must have been a wake-up call for her because she never waited for him again."

"Lily and I will not eat with you whenever you leave on business."

"Not if you travel with me. I'd like you to apply for a passport for Lily, so when we fly down to the Bahamas, she can come with us."

Mya stared at him, momentarily shocked with his offer of wanting her to accompany him on a business trip. However, a silent voice nagged at her that he'd offered because he didn't want to be away from Lily. If not, then he could've suggested they leave the baby with his parents until their return.

"How long do you normally stay?" she asked when she recovered her voice.

"It can be two days to more than a week. Meanwhile, you and Lily can have the run of the resort."

"Does it belong to WDG?"

Giles rubbed their noses together. "Yes. You're now unofficially a Wainwright because you just called Wainwright Developers Group WDG."

She smiled. "That's because I've heard you refer to the company as WDG, and it's also stamped on the sides of the jet."

"You don't miss much, do you?"

"Nope."

Giles glanced at his watch. "I'm going to my place to get dressed, and when I come back, we'll leave to go shopping"

"Do you live far from here?"

"No. I'm about twenty blocks away and closer to the river. I'll take you there before we come back tonight."

"When is your sister coming in?"

"Her flight is scheduled to touch down around one this afternoon. Dad has already arranged for a car to pick her up. She'll be jet-lagged for a few days, then watch out. If you think Lily's a squealer, then you have to hear Skye. It's ear-shattering."

Mya extended her arms. "Give me the little squealer. I'll be dressed and ready by the time you come back."

Mya stood in the private elevator with Giles as the car rose swiftly to where WDG occupied the entire top floor in the Third Avenue office building. Giles had informed her that although WDG owned the building, the company leased office space to other businesses on the other twenty-six floors, and space on every floor of the high-rise structure was filled to capacity.

His attire harked back to the time when she'd first encountered him in Preston McAvoy's conference room. The dark gray suit, white dress shirt, royal blue silk tie and black wingtips reminded her he was a businessman who bought and sold multimillion-dollar properties with the stroke of a pen. She eschewed entertaining negative thoughts, yet she couldn't rid her head of the fact that Giles would become disenchanted living in Wickham Falls, that if they married he would somehow concoct a scheme where they would have to live in New York.

"You look very nice."

Mya inclined her head. "Thank you."

She had packed several outfits she had deemed business attire. When many instructors and professors favored jeans and running shoes, she had opted for pantsuits and conservative dresses. Today, she had selected a black lightweight wool sheath dress with a matching hip-length jacket. Sheer black nylons and a pair of leather-and-suede booties were in keeping with the favored ubiquitous New York City black. The elevator opened to doors with the company's name etched in silver across the glass.

Resting his hand at the small of Mya's back, Giles swiped a key card and when the light changed from red to green, he pushed it open. The receptionist sitting behind a mahogany counter smiled at him. The screen on the wall behind her displayed the time, temperatures and headlines of countries from around the world.

"Welcome back, Giles."

He returned her smile. "Thank you, Linda." Giles escorted Mya up three stairs to an expansive space covered in pale gray carpeting spanning rows of glassed-in offices with the names and titles of the occupants.

"Nice views."

He nodded. "I agree, but occupying a space enclosed by glass has its advantages and disadvantages. There're times when I find myself staring out the window daydreaming." Giles nodded and greeted employees he rarely saw because he didn't spend much time in his office. His fingers tightened on Mya's waist. "My office is at the end of the hall."

"Where are your father's and brother's offices?"

"They're in what everyone refers to as the West Wing. Legal, accounting and cyber security are thought of as the heart of the company, while all of the other departments are its lifeblood."

"How many people do you employ?" Mya asked.

"The last count was thirty-eight. We have a number of real estate agents based in upstate New York, Massachusetts, Connecticut, New Jersey and as far south as D.C. They come into the office the second Friday in the month for a general meeting, while the board meets the first Monday of each month."

"Do they expect you to attend those meetings?"

"I just got special dispensation from my uncle Edward to participate using videoconferencing because of Lily. It's a perk all Wainwrights are afforded whenever there's a new baby."

"I suppose it pays to be a Wainwright around here."

Giles pulled her closer to his side. "You've got that right." He wanted to tell Mya that doors would open and Lily given full discretionary privilege if she was Lily Wainwright rather than Lily Lawson.

He opened the door and was met with a bright smile from Jocelyn sitting in an alcove outside his private office. "Hello, boss. Thanks for holding it down," Giles said teasingly.

Jocelyn's smile got even wider. "I had the world's best teacher."

Giles turned to Mya. "Mya, I'd like you to meet Jocelyn Lewis, the third woman in my with life whom I cannot live without. Jocelyn, Mya Lawson."

Jocelyn extended her hand and Mya took it. "It's a pleasure. Giles told me about you and your precious daughter." She pointed to the ruby on Mya's left hand. "Your ring is beautiful."

The skin around Mya's eyes crinkled in a smile. "Thank you." She patted Giles's shoulder. "And thank you for keeping my man sane. He says you're invaluable." Jocelyn lowered her eyes with the compliment.

Giles could've kissed Mya at that moment. He liked the comment about him being her man. "Are there any updates since our last email?"

"No. But I'm expecting a call from Kurt this afternoon about the Pederson deal. As soon as I hear anything, I'll update you."

"Thanks, Jocelyn. I'm going to see my father before we leave. You know how to reach me."

"She is very pretty," Mya said once they were far enough away so Jocelyn couldn't overhear them. Jocelyn's demeanor indicated she was older than Mya, but she felt envious of the woman's flawless complexion. Her chemically straightened hair, parted off-center, ended at her jawline, and there was a subtle hint of color on her full mouth while the only allowance she made for eye makeup was mascara.

"Jealous, sweets?" Giles teased.

"Should I be?"

"Never. Remember, I'm committed to you until Lily graduates college."

"What happens after that?"

Giles stopped, nearly causing Mya to lose her balance. He pulled her over into an area with a low table cradling a large fern growing in a painted glazed pot. "What do you mean by what happens after that?"

"Will we still be together?"

His brows lowered in a scowl. "What do you think?"

Mya stomped her foot. "Why are you answering my question with a question?"

"Because you're not making sense, Mya. What do I have to do or say to convince you that I'm just not in this for Lily? Even if you decide not to marry me I'll buy a house in Wickham Falls and come to see Lily everyday so she can grow up knowing that I'm her father."

Mya felt a fleeting panic grip her until she found it hard to breathe. She didn't want to lose Giles, because she needed him, needed him for more than a physical craving that grew stronger with each passing day. She needed him to love her and to restore her faith in men; after dating Malcolm, she still harbored a fear that she would become involved with another Jekyll and Hyde.

She found Giles even-tempered and soft-spoken, yet she sensed he could be unrelenting and uncompromising.

His expression changed, softening when he saw indecision in her eyes. "You've reminded me that you're not your sister, and I have to remind you again that I'm not your ex-boyfriend. What you see is what you get."

A trembling smile flitted across her lips. "You just read my mind."

"Let's hope you can't read mine because it would be rated triple X right about now." His eyes made love to her face before they moved lower over her chest. "Damn, woman. Do you know that you're sexy as hell?" he whispered in her ear.

Mya swatted at him. "Shame on you," she chastised, "talking dirty in the middle of a hallway where anyone can come by and hear you."

"There's a company policy about gossiping. One infraction and you're canned."

"That's a little severe."

"Spreading gossip is not only malicious but a form of bullying, and around here, that's grounds for an immediate dismissal. Come with me, baby. I want to introduce you to my brother."

Mya felt more in control when she followed Giles into an office next to his father's. The blond head popped up when the occupant realized he wasn't alone.

Patrick Wainwright stood up and winked at her. "So you're the woman who has my brother stuttering every time he mentions your name." He rounded the desk. "Come and give me a hug."

The resemblance between Giles and Patrick was remarkable enough for them to be twins. The only difference was the color of their hair. Patrick was fair and gorgeous and Giles dark and dangerous. Mya found herself in Patrick's arms as he lowered his head and kissed her cheek.

"It's nice meeting you, Patrick."

He pulled back, holding her at arm's length. "I must admit my little brother has exquisite taste in women."

"Stop flirting with my woman or I'll tell your wife."

Patrick cut his eyes at Giles. "Nice try. You know my wife wouldn't believe anything negative you'd say about me." He lifted Mya's left hand. "Is that what I think it is?"

Mya smiled. "Yes. It's your mother's ring."

"Does this mean you and my brother are engaged? She shook her head. "No." Even though she was vacillating about whether she wanted to marry Giles, deep down inside it was something she wanted more than any else thing in the world. She had always grown up believing she would fall in love, marry and have children. She wanted a family of her own and to share all of the wonderful things her parents had given her.

The few times she and Sammie argued it was when Mya accused her of being selfish and ungrateful because their adoptive parents had given them what their biological parents hadn't been able to. She tried to make her sister see the flip side of their lives where they could've grown up living in squalor where hunger was commonplace instead of a rarity. They'd known kids they'd gone to school with who, if it hadn't been for free lunch or food stamps, they would have been malnourished.

Patrick kissed her on both cheeks. "Dad told me about Lily and I can't wait to meet her. I know my boys will happy to know there's another cousin they can play with. It's going to be a while before Jordan's little boy will be underfoot."

"You know Lily is the only princess among these young princes," Giles bragged.

"No shit," Patrick drawled. "We'll have to wait and see what Brandt and Ciara have."

"Ciara's pregnant?" Giles asked his brother.

"I don't know, but the last time I spoke to Brandt, he said they were going to get a jump on starting a family because he wants a football team."

Giles grunted. "There's no way Ciara's going to agree to having eleven kids."

"By the way, how many kids do you guys plan to have? I mean if you do decide to marry," Patrick blurted out.

Mya shared a look with Giles. They'd talked about marriage but not about whether they would have children together. Suddenly she felt as if she'd been put on the spot because she was wearing Amanda's ring. Patrick had assumed she and Giles would eventually marry, and wondered how many more Wainwrights would come to the same conclusion. "We'll probably have another two," she said after a noticeable pause.

"Why stop at three?" Patrick questioned. "Why not round it out and have four?"

Giles dropped an arm over Mya's shoulders. "Mya and I would like to wait until Lily's walking and talking before we go back to changing diapers."

"I hear you, my brother." The phone on Patrick's desk rang. "I'm going to have to take that call. It's nice meeting you, Mya. If the family doesn't get to meet you and Lily before you guys go back to West Virginia, then it's Thanksgiving for certain."

Mya noticed Pat's office was empty when they retraced their steps to the elevator. "I hope folks don't assume we're engaged because I'm wearing your mother's ring," she said once they stepped into the car.

Giles crossed his arms over his chest. "People will always draw their own conclusions. Once we're officially engaged I'll buy you a ring."

She held out her hand. "What's wrong with this ring?"

"Nothing. I just believe a woman should have her own ring."

"If my birthstone was a ruby rather than a pearl, I would definitely consider a ruby."

"When's your birthday?"

"June 12."

"The month for weddings and graduations." He reached for her hand when the doors opened. If they married on her birthday, then he would have no excuse for forgetting their wedding anniversary. "Are you ready to go shopping now?"

Mya smiled. "Of course."

"Do you know where you want to shop?"

"Yes. I researched online and discovered a few shops on Madison Avenue that carry the labels I like."

"I hope I don't come to regret this," Giles mumbled under his breath.

"I heard that, sport."

"I wanted you to, sweets. Are you the type of woman that has to try on a dozen dresses and then decides to buy the first one she tried on?"

Mya rolled her eyes at him. "I'm not even going to dignify that with an answer."

Giles waved his hand and whistled sharply between his teeth to flag down a taxi. The driver came to a screeching stop at the curb. Giles opened the rear door and allowed Mya to enter, then slid onto the seat next to her. He gave the driver their destination and the driver took off as if he was racing in the Indy 500.

Mya huddled closer to Giles. "I hope we'll get there in one piece."

He buried his face in her hair. "New York City taxi drivers are notorious for weaving in and out of traffic."

She closed her eyes. "Let me know when we're there."

Mya found a boutique that carried the designs she favored. Several salesladies fussed over Giles as he sat in a comfortable chair in the seating area and was given green tea and sliced fruit while he watched a wall-mounted flat screen television.

It was too early for cruise wear, but the salesperson said they still had some items in stock from the beginning of the year. She wanted a few outfits for when she went to the Bahamas with Giles. Mya preferred shopping in specialty shops because of the individual service and there weren't endless racks of the same mass-produced dresses and blouses.

It took more than an hour for her to try on dresses, jackets, slacks, blouses, shorts and several swimsuits. When the assistant helping asked if she wanted her boyfriend to see her in anything, Mya told her no, because she wanted to surprise him. She wasn't certain whether Thanksgiving and Christmas were semiformal events for the Wainwrights so she chose several dresses that she deemed appropriate. Mya thought about asking to see formal wear for the New Year's Eve fund-raiser, and then changed her mind. She decided to wait until they came back for Thanksgiving to shop for a dress. It would signal the beginning of holiday shopping and she knew she would be able to select something appropriate for the event.

"I suppose that's it," she said to the assistant who'd help her into and out of garments.

The woman smiled. "I'll take these up front while you get dressed."

When Mya emerged from the dressing room, she found Giles at the register as the cashier rang up her purchases. He pushed her hand away when she handed him her credit card. "Put *that* away," he ordered between clenched teeth. He took it from her fingers and slipped it into his shirt pocket when she hesitated. "I'll give it back later."

He turned back to the cashier, offering her a friendly smile. "Could you please have someone deliver these to my apartment?"

The clerk glanced at the card he'd given her. "Of course, Mr. Wainwright. Is it all right if we deliver it tomorrow because deliveries for today are already out on the van?"

"Of course." He plucked a business card off the counter and jotted his name and address on the back.

The woman glanced at the address. "It should arrive before noon."

"No problem. Let the driver know he can leave it with concierge." He signed the receipt and returned the card to a case in his jacket's breast pocket. "Let's go, sweets. I don't know about you but I'm hungry enough to eat half a cow." He whistled for a taxi that sped by without stopping. "I'm going to order something and have it delivered to the apartment. What do you feel like eating?"

Reaching into her hobo bag, Mya took out a pair of sunglasses to shade her eyes against the glaring autumn sun. "Half a cow," she said, deadpan.

He splayed his hand over her hips. "You could use a little more meat in this area."

"I have enough, thank you." She wrapped her arm around his waist under his suit jacket. "Thank you for paying for my clothes."

Giles frowned. "There's no need to thank me, Mya. Whenever we're together, I don't want you to go into your wallet for anything. And I repeat—*anything*."

"Oh, that's how it's going to be?"

"No. That's how it is."

Mya decided it was futile to verbally spar with Giles. Most times it accomplished nothing so she mentally accepted his mandate that he would pay for whatever she needed when they were together. After all, it was his money and he could spend it however he wished.

Chapter 10

Mya sat on the balcony outside Giles's bedroom staring out at water views while enjoying the most delicious chicken piccata with a side dish of broccoli in garlic and oil she had ever eaten. And throwing caution to the wind, she had accepted a glass of rosé to accompany the meal. She had shed her dress, jacket, nylons and booties in exchange for one of Giles's long-sleeved shirts.

She closed her eyes for several seconds and turned her face up to the warm sun. "This is wonderful." She opened her eyes to find him watching her. "How often do you sit out here and have your meals?"

His lids came down, concealing his innermost thoughts from her. "Not enough. Whenever I sit here, it is usually to clear my head." A faraway expression swept over his features. "This is what I call my therapy place. When I first bought this condo, I would sit out here for hours until nature forced me to get up. At that time I was in a very dark place."

She recalled him admitting to experiencing post-traumatic stress disorder. "What about now?" she asked in a quiet voice.

He blinked as if coming out of a trance. "I'm good. Very good." Giles pointed to her half-empty wineglass. "Do you want more wine?"

She placed her hand over the top of the glass. "Please no. I'm surprised I'm having it when I'd gone down for the count after two beers."

"I do happen to have a bed where you can sleep it off," he teased.

Mya glanced over at the king-size bed with a massive dark gray quilted headboard. "I just might take you up on your offer." She patted her belly over the shirt. "Right now I'm as full as a tick on a dog's back."

Throwing back his head, Giles laughed. "I'm going to have to get used to your regional expressions."

"Like, if the creek don't rise, or she was madder than a wet hen."

"Exactly."

"Once you spend some time in the Falls, you'll become familiar with all of the expressions. I…" Her words trailed off when Giles's cell phone chimed.

He picked it up and read the text message. "My sister decided not to come. She says she'll see you and Lily at Thanksgiving."

"Is something wrong?"

Giles shook his head. "I don't know. Half the time I wonder what she's going through with that clown. I hope and pray he's not abusing her because it won't go well for him. My father is a laid-back dude, but don't mess with his little girl because he can more dangerous than Uncle Wyatt."

"Do you think she would put up with a man abusing her?"

"Skye is a throwback to a flower child. She believes in peace and live-and-let-live. She feels guilty that she was born into money when there're so many people that are hungry and homeless. When I suggested she donate her trust fund to charity, she said she's wary of charities because the money will usually pay for administrative salaries rather than for the earmarked need."

"Why doesn't she set up her own charity? That's what Sawyer Middleton did when he donated almost a million dollars to update the technology lab at the school. Not only does he head the charity, but he's also responsible for overseeing the project. If she's a guidance counselor, then she can set up a counseling center for kids with emotional issues. And if she's really ambitious, she can add a tutoring component and hire teachers looking to supplement their income to help students needing extra help with their schoolwork. I'd be willing to volunteer to help kids struggling with English."

Giles leaned back in his chair and pressed a fist to his mouth. "I think you've got something there. I'll be certain to mention it to Skye. She'd fit right in living in Wickham Falls because she's so unpretentious."

"There you go," Mya drawled. She pushed off the chair. "I'm going to accept your offer to take a nap before we go back to your folks' place."

"Leave the dishes. I'll put everything away."

She walked off the balcony and into the bedroom. Pulling back the white silk comforter, she slipped under a sheet and lightweight blanket. "Are you going to join me?" she asked Giles when he entered the room balancing plates along his forearm.

"Later."

Giles wanted to ask Mya if she had lost her mind inviting him to share the bed with her. Did she trust him that much not to try to make love to her? Then he had to remember she would be the first woman to sleep there, because every woman he'd slept with since returning to civilian life had been in a hotel. It was as if the condo was his sacred sanctuary and he didn't want to defile it by having sex with different women. And sex was what it had been. He had never allowed himself to feel anything other than hormones calling out to one another for a physical release.

Giles didn't need a therapist to tell him he would've continued to live his life by his leave: spending hours in his office, traveling to the Caribbean and waiting for women to call him, if it hadn't been for Mya and Lily. He had made it a practice never to call a woman but waited for them to call him.

He put away the food and stacked the dishwasher. Spending time with Mya had enhanced his domestic skills. She'd shown him how to load and operate the dishwasher, washing machine and dryer. The last bastion for him to scale was learning to cook. Although he had balked, Giles knew eventually he would have to make an attempt.

He returned to the bedroom, slipped off a pair of

walking shorts, leaving on his boxer briefs, and got into bed with Mya. Her back was turned to him. "Are you still awake?"

"Yes. I'm not as sleepy as I am relaxed."

He kissed the nape of her neck. "Good." A pregnant silence ensued, and he felt her suddenly go stiff. "What's the matter, sweets?"

"I was just thinking about Sammie sleeping here with you."

"She never slept here with me." Mya turned to face him, and he told her about the suite at a Chelsea boutique hotel where he conducted his affairs. "I pay for the suite every month even if I didn't use it. Something wouldn't allow me to bring a woman here."

Mya rested a hand on his cheek. "Until now."

He smiled. "Yes. Until now." Giles pulled on a curl that escaped the pins in the chignon. "There are times when I need you to be patient with me if I become somewhat overbearing. I suppose it comes from giving orders and expecting them to be followed without question."

Her fingernail grazed an emerging beard. "Did you enjoy the military?"

"I did because it was strictly controlled, regimented, and I needed discipline at twenty-one." Giles met her large, slightly slanting, catlike gray-and-green eyes. "I'd grown up believing as a kid of privilege I could do whatever I wanted and the hell with everything else. I went to a private school where infractions at a public school would've resulted in a suspension or expulsion, but because our parents were doling out the big bucks for tuition or bestowing substantial endowments, we got away with things that would've been questionable by law enforcement. Like a lot of teenagers, we drank, smoked weed, had sex with girls willing to give it up, and a few kids ended up in rehab because they got hooked on crack or heroin.

"I was an above-average student and was accepted by several top universities but in the end, I chose MIT. I continued to drink and smoke weed, but I'd become discriminating when it came to sleeping around because I knew I wasn't ready to deal with an unplanned pregnancy. My senior year signaled a change when I stopped hanging out as much and stopped drinking and smoking altogether. I managed to graduate with honors and Wyatt, who was at the time WDG's de facto CEO, asked me to join the engineering department."

"What did you tell him?"

"'Ask me again in three months and I'll give you my answer.' I was burned-out and needed that time to recharge. That's when my mother decided that her youngest son needed a steady girlfriend."

"Is that when your mother tried to set you up with Miranda?"

Giles nodded.

"But you were so young to think about settling down with a wife."

"I know that and you know that, but people in particular social classes are always looking for their children to make a proper match, much like an arranged marriage in some cultures. Once I discovered the subterfuge, I enlisted in the branch of the military with the toughest basic training. I met the initial requirements for officer eligibility and worked and studied harder than I ever had in my life to graduate Officer Candidate School. It was when I was mentally, physically and morally at my best."

Mya cradled his face. "You've come a long way from that weed-smoking, skirt-chasing and binge-drinking boy to a man Lily will grow up to be proud of."

"And I swear if I find some pimply faced, pothead cretin sniffing around my daughter, I'll snap his head off and roll it down the street like a bowling ball."

Mya's laugh was low, throaty. "Why do men always talk about hurting a boy if they come around their daughter?"

"That's because we know what we've done to some man's daughter."

"It's called karma and payback."

Resting an arm over her waist, Giles pulled Mya closer until her breasts were flattened against his chest. "Karma is a very nasty girl."

"That she is."

Those were the last words she mumbled before Giles registered her breathy snoring. He had done something with Mya he had never done with another human being and that was to bare his soul. His parents never knew of his drinking and drug use either because he'd become so adept at concealing his destructive behavior or they were in denial, unable to believe their so-called model son was less than perfect.

"I love you."

Giles knew Mya couldn't hear him, yet he felt compelled to say what lay in his heart. He loved everything about her: her loyalty to her sister, willingness to sacrifice her career to take care of her sister's child and her feistiness when she refused to back down when he challenged her.

He was aware of her reluctance to share her life and future with a stranger and he was willing to wait however long it would take to convince her he wanted her as his wife with or without Lily. Mya had accepted the responsibility of raising his child with or without him, while offering him an alternative to a lifestyle where he had become so self-absorbed that his only focus was doing what made him happy.

Wickham Falls would not top his list of places to live and retire; however, he found himself looking forward to living in the Louisiana low-country style house with a woman and child that had him planning for their futures.

Giles's breathing deepened, and after a while he joined Mya in the comforting embrace of Morpheus.

Mya held Lily to her chest as she paced back and forth on the sidewalk while she waited for Pat to retrieve his car from the indoor garage. A freezer chest with jars of baby food and bottles of milk and water, a carry-on with Lily's diapers and clothes, a portable crib and a car seat sat on the curb.

"You are becoming quite the traveler," she crooned. "First you visited the Bronx Zoo and now you're going to Boston." Lily cooed and patted Mya's face with her small chubby hands. "You have tons of cousins so I want you to be on your best behavior when they meet you. We can't have them thinking you have no home training." She went completely still when she detected the familiar scent of Giles's aftershave and the warmth from his body as he came up behind her. His moist breath feathered over her ear. "I was just giving your daughter a pep talk about behaving."

He laughed softly. "She's my daughter when she misbehaves and your daughter whenever she's a good girl?"

Mya smiled. "You said it and I didn't."

"Isn't that what you implied, Mama?"

"Not in the least, Daddy."

Giles rested a hand on Mya's shoulder and he leaned over to blow Lily an air kiss who pulled at her hand-knitted hat in an attempt to pull it off. He gently brushed her hand aside. "Don't, princess. Once you get into the car, I'll take your hat off."

Mya reached up and adjusted Lily's hat. "We're going to have a problem once winter arrives because she doesn't like wearing hats or socks."

"That's because she's a free spirit."

"You won't think she's that much of a free spirit when she comes home from college in bare feet, one side of her head shaved and a boyfriend with a braided beard trailing behind her. And the first words out of her mouth will be, 'But, Daddy, I love him!'"

"And Daddy will throw him in a Dumpster where he belongs."

Tilting her chin, Mya scrunched up her nose. "Why so violent?"

"I'm not going to let anyone mess over my baby girl. Here comes Dad."

A black Lexus SUV maneuvered up along the curb and came to a complete stop as the hatch opened. Mya continued to hold Lily as Giles stored everything in the cargo area and then placed the car seat on the second row of seats. He returned to take Lily from her arms.

Mya gave her a kiss and then turned and walked back into the house. She didn't know why but she felt as if she was losing her baby, even though she had a responsibility to let Lily know she had a large extended family. What Mya feared was that as Lily grew older, she might eventually lose her to the Wainwrights.

Amanda, carrying several bags, found her sitting on a chair in the entryway. She was dressed for traveling: cropped khakis, pullover sweatshirt, running shoes and a cap bearing a Yankees logo.

"We're going to take good care of your baby."

Rising to her feet, Mya flashed a smile she didn't feel. "I know you will."

"I'll call Giles to let him know we've arrived safely."

She hugged her future mother-in-law. "Safe travels, Mom."

"Thank you, darling."

Mya was standing in the same spot when Giles returned and closed the door.

"What's the matter, sweets?"

"Nothing."

Giles didn't believe Mya. She looked as if she was struggling not to cry. His fingers curved under her chin. "She'll be back tomorrow."

Mya nodded. "I suppose I'll have to get used to sharing her."

"Remember, you're sharing her with her family."

"I know that."

"If you know that, then why the long face?"

"I really don't want to share her, Giles. When Sammie put her in my arms and made me swear an oath to love and take care of her baby, I interpreted that to mean she wanted me and not you, Amanda or Pat to be responsible for her. Now this is the second time that I've allowed someone else to assume that responsibility, and if you think I'm being selfish, then just say it."

Giles searched her upturned face, his heart turning over when her eyes filled. "You're not selfish, Mya. You're just being a mom. You've been with Lily every day of her life, and when you wake up, you look for her and it's the same at night when you get her ready for bed. But today is different because someone else will put her to bed and do all of the things for her you would normally do. Her grandparents taking her away for a day or two is preparing you for a time when Lily will leave for a much longer period of time. Maybe it will be sleepaway camp or an out-of-state college."

"I can't even think that far ahead."

"Neither can I, but we both know it's going to come. You've been rehearsing for your role as Mommy for eight months, while I just got the part as Daddy, so it's going to take us time before we really master our starring roles in this production based on parenting. Characters may come onto the stage for a brief moment before disappearing and others may become major supporting characters that remain on the stage until the final curtain comes down. We are the protagonists and my parents and the rest of the Wainwrights are the major supporting characters. They're not going to leave the stage, Mya. They're going to become a part of Lily's very existence because that's what Samantha wanted when she added the codicil. She wanted Lily to know who her biological father was and connect with his family because that's what she'd wanted for herself."

Mya rested her head on his shoulder. "Thanks for the pep talk. You're going to be an incredible father."

He buried his face in her curls. Giles wanted to tell Mya that he wanted to a good father and an incredible husband. "Now that we don't have to concern ourselves with a babysitter, I'd like to make good on my promise to take you out to dinner to celebrate the release of your latest book."

"Where are we going?"

"I have a few places in mind."

"Should I wear something nice?"

Pulling back, Giles smiled. "Yes." He still hadn't decided where he would take her but he wanted to make the night a special one.

"I bought an outfit yesterday that may be appropriate. But..."

"But what?"

"I need shoes and accessories."

Shaking his head, Giles rolled his eyes upward. "More shopping?"

"I don't need you to come with me."

"Do you know where you're going?"

She laughed softly. "I'm not going to get lost, Giles. I've downloaded a maps app on my cell and if I want to find a particular store, then I'll just Google it."

"I suppose you'll do okay in the big city."

"Just okay? Remember I lived in Chicago for nearly seven years."

Giles wanted to tell Mya that even though Chicago was a big city, it still wasn't New York City with its five boroughs and countless neighborhoods. "While you're shopping, I'm going to visit a cousin. I'm going to give you the keycard to my apartment and leave instructions with the doormen to let you into the building. Meanwhile, I'm going to call a few places to see if we can get a reservation for tonight."

"Maybe I'll stop and get a mani-pedi." She ran her fingers through her hair, frowning when she rubbed the curls between her thumb and forefinger. "And if I have time, I'll try to get my ends trimmed."

"I'll give you my charge card in case you run out of money."

"You gave me back my card and I have enough of an available balance to cover what I need to buy."

"I want you to take it anyway and buy whatever you want. In fact, keep it. I'll call the company and have them overnight me another one."

"You may come to regret that decision."

Giles winked at her. "I don't think so, sweets."

Mya returned his wink with one of her own. "Do I have a spending limit?"

"There is no spending limit."

Her expression changed, amusement crumbling like an accordion. "You're kidding?"

"No, I'm not." One of the many perks of having a Black Card was no spending limit. He knew it would take Mya time to adjust to the changes in her life once they were married. She would not have to concern herself with standing in line at airport terminals to take a commercial flight because a single phone call would give her direct access to a private jet. She would no longer stick to a budget when it came to managing household expenses, and if she wanted a new car, she wouldn't have to negotiate with the dealer for discounts on optional features.

"Okay."

His eyebrows lifted questioningly. "Just okay?"

"Yes. I can't think of anything else to say."

Threading their fingers together, Giles brought his hand to his mouth and brushed light kisses over her knuckles. "Have fun shopping."

Her smile began with a slight parting of her lips before moving up to her eyes, and Giles felt as if he was staring into a misty gray pond with delicately floating water lilies. "Thank you."

He kissed the back of her hand again. "There's no need to thank me because there isn't anything I wouldn't do to make you happy."

"I am happy, Giles. Happy that you're Lily's father and happy that you're in both of our lives."

She eased her hand from his loose grip, turned on her heel and headed for her bedroom. Inviting her to come to New York with him signaled a change in Mya. She appeared less tense, with the exception of agonizing over not having Lily with her 24/7.

When he'd introduced her to his friend in the sports bar, the word girlfriend had come out unbidden, and despite her wanting to wait until next spring to announce their engagement, he had begun to think of her as his bride-to-be. When she had asked him to court her, Giles knew the tradition of a man dating a woman for a specific period of time before proposing marriage had come from her traditional mother's Southern upbringing.

Giles regarded Mya as a small-town girl with big-city sensibilities. She could navigate a city with a population of millions, but it was her small town roots that surfaced when she preferred spending hours cooking to eating at a restaurant. She said grace before every meal, kept the tradition of making Sunday dinners the most important meal of the week, and whenever she sat at her computer, it was to pen her novels and not post messages to her friends on various social media groups.

Giles did not want to fool himself into believing that relocating from New York to Wickham Falls would be without angst. He would miss going into his office, interacting with WDG employees and sitting in on meetings with department heads and the board of directors. He wouldn't be able to pick up the phone and make dinner plans with his mother or join Brandt or Jordan at baseball and basketball games. The only constant would be the flights to the Bahamas, and the upside to that was the probability of Mya and Lily accompanying him.

His life had become a series of highs and lows. He'd graduated college with a degree in engineering but within months, he'd turned his back on his family when he'd enlisted in the Marine Corps. He'd taken to military life like a duck to water when graduating as an officer and rising to the rank of captain. But after facing and cheating death twice, he wasn't ready to challenge it again when he resigned his commission and returned to life as a civilian, unaware it would become the darkest period of his young life. And in reconciling with his mother, facing his post-wartime demons and joining WDG, he'd become the phoenix rising from the ashes to soar and come into his own as the head of the company's international division.

Giles smiled as he exhaled an audible breath. His life was good and he predicted it would become even better once he, Mya and Lily became a legal family.

Chapter 11

Jordan Wainwright opened the door and pulled Giles into a rough embrace. "I'm glad you came over because right about now I need some serious male bonding."

Giles studied his cousin. The brilliant attorney looked different. His dark hair was close-cropped and instead of being clean-shaven, he now sported a short beard. Giles noticed there were dark circles under Jordan's large hazel eyes. He'd earned a reputation as a champion for those less fortunate, and many of the residents who recognized him on sight had dubbed him the Sheriff of Harlem.

"You now have your son to bond with."

Jordan blew out a breath. "I love my boy to death but all he does is cry, pee, eat and sleep. Then he wakes up only to repeat the cycle."

Giles smiled. "That's what babies do. And as a new dad, you have to sleep when they sleep or you'll end up falling on your face."

Jordan led the way into the maisonette. He and his wife divided their time between their Manhattan duplex facing Central Park and a house in Westchester County. "Do you want anything to eat or drink?"

"Why? Did you cook?"

Jordan flashed a wide grin. "I'm learning. Zee told me if I'm going to hang around the house for six weeks, then I should learn to put a meal on the table."

"How's it going?"

"I made chicken with dumplings last night. She gave me an A, so if you want to sample leftovers, I'll heat up some for you."

"No, thanks. I'm good." Mya and his mother had prepared a buffet-type breakfast.

"Sit down and take a load off your feet," Jordan said as they walked into the living room. "Zee's upstairs feeding Max."

Giles sat on a butter-soft leather chair. He'd always liked Jordan's apartment because of its proximity to the park where he had an up-close-and-personal view of the changing seasons. However, for Giles it had one drawback: the noise of traffic along Fifth Avenue. His condo, high above street noise and the pollution from nonstop vehicles along the FDR Drive, was his sanctuary, a place where he decided who came and went.

Mya had been the first woman, other than his female relatives, he had invited in. And she was the only woman to share his bed

Jordan stretched out long legs and crossed his feet at

the ankles. "Sleep has become a premium around here. By the way, do you sleep when your daughter sleeps?"

"Not really. Whenever Lily takes her afternoon nap, I usually hang out on the porch reading or relax in the family room watching television." Giles didn't tell Jordan it was a time Mya jealously guarded whenever she retreated to her office to write.

"What about at night?"

"I don't sleep over."

A slight frown creased Jordan's forehead. "I thought you and the baby's mother were getting closer."

"We are." Giles candidly told Jordan everything that had transpired since he left New York to move into the extended stay hotel so he could see Lily every day. "I've gotten her to agree to consider announcing our engagement sometime next year, but even that is tenuous. She wants us to date before we take what we have to another level."

Smiling, Jordan tented his fingers. "In other words, you're not sleeping together."

"We did share a bed but nothing happened. Our relationship is different from boy meets girl, boy likes girl, and then they fast-track their relationship from platonic to intimate. Right now, Mya and I are still in the platonic stage."

Jordan angled his head. "I'm going to ask you a question, and you don't have to answer it if you don't want. Are you in love with her?"

"Yes," Giles replied without hesitation. It was the easiest question he'd ever had to answer. "I've never been in love before so what I'm feeling for her has to be love. I say that because she's the first woman I've known whom I want to see every day. I like that she can be serious and teasing at the same time. I love her strength, intelligence and her devotion to Lily. And I admire the sacrifice she's made to give up her career to raise her niece."

Jordan chuckled under his breath. "She sounds quite remarkable."

"She is. And on top of that, she's gorgeous and sexy."

Jordan sobered. "When you called me, I thought you were going to bring your daughter so we could meet her."

"I would have if she wasn't on her way to Boston to meet her grandma's people."

"Are they flying up?"

"No. Mom and Dad decided to drive."

Jordan went completely still. "Your father took time away from the office to go on a road trip?" Giles nodded. "But he never takes off. Only when he's sick. Which my father says isn't often."

Giles had to agree with his cousin. Jordan's father, Edward, was now CEO, and there was an ongoing joke throughout the office that Pat was looking to replace Edward once he announced his retirement. Giles knew his father did not want to take over the reins as head of the company. He loved heading the legal department. Pat was single-focused, a workaholic, a perfectionist and a control freak. Patrick told him that their father tended to micromanage everyone and everything in the legal department, and that's why Giles knew he could never work for his father.

"Dad took one look at Lily and it was like he'd become a different man. And because he isn't a first-time grandfather, I'm willing to bet having a granddaughter is the reason for the change. I remember my mother mentioning that he took off for two weeks when she had Skye, compared to leaving the office to drop Mom off at the hospital once she went into labor with me and Patrick and then going back to the office. Once she came home with his sons, he hired a nanny to help her out because he claimed his work was piling up and he didn't want to fall behind."

"Are you saying my uncle has a soft spot for girls?"

"What else can it be?" Giles saw movement out of the side of his eye and stood up when he saw Aziza descending the staircase cradling her son in her arms. "Hey, beautiful."

"Don't talk the talk if you can't walk the walk, playa," she teased.

Giles winked at his cousin's wife. "My playa certification expired once I discovered I had a daughter."

"When Jordan told me you were dropping by, I thought you were bringing your daughter and her mother."

Aziza Fleming-Wainwright sat on the love seat next to her husband and then placed the infant in his arms. The new mother wore a white man-tailored shirt over a pair of black leggings and had styled her shoulder-length dark hair into a loose ponytail. When Jordan had introduced Aziza as his fiancée, Giles hadn't been able to resist staring at the tall, brown-skinned, slender woman with large, round dark eyes in a doll-like face with a hint of a dimpled chin. And when she'd smiled at him, he'd been completely enthralled with her.

Aziza's connection with the Wainwrights began

years before she met Jordan. Their cousin Brandt had been and still was her client whenever she reviewed his NFL contracts and now his business projects. Jordan confided that he'd had to work hard to convince Aziza to marry him because she had been burned by a disastrous first marriage.

"She's on her way to Boston because my mother wants to show her off to her relatives."

Jordan chuckled. "Aunt Mandy must be over the moon now that she has a granddaughter."

Giles nodded, smiling. "You're right about that." He told Jordan and Aziza they probably wouldn't get to meet Lily and Mya until Thanksgiving. "We'll be back again for Christmas and stay until after the New Year."

"You guys are welcome to spend a couple of nights with us," Aziza said.

"I'll definitely run it past Mya." Giles was certain Mya would probably want to hang out with Jordan and Aziza because they all were around the same age. "Who are the designated babysitters for New Year's Eve?" he asked Jordan.

"My sisters Chanel, Stephanie and Keisha have volunteered to monitor the childcare center."

A suite in the Wainwright family mansion had been transformed into a permanent nursery with cribs, youth and bunk beds. Another area had been set aside as a playroom rivaling those at some fast-food restaurants.

Soft grunting from Maxwell garnered everyone's attention. The infant had inherited his father's swarthy complexion and his mother's features. Sparse dark hair covered a perfectly rounded little head.

Jordan wrinkled his nose. "I think somebody needs to be changed."

Aziza reached for her son. "I'll do it."

Waiting until Aziza took the baby upstairs, Giles asked Jordan, "You don't change diapers?"

Jordan rubbed a hand over his bearded jaw. "Not if I don't have to." His hand stilled. "You change diapers?"

Giles nodded. "I've been certified as a Mister Mom. I've learned to diaper, feed and bathe Lily."

"There's no doubt you've earned your Daddy certification. I took off six weeks to help Zee around the house. We still use the cleaning service, but there's laundry and cooking. Now that I no longer have a live-in housekeeper I've learned to operate the washer and dryer and fold clothes. Instead of going to the supermarket, we now order online and have the groceries delivered." Shaking his head, Jordan blew out a breath. "I can't even begin to imagine what a single mother has to go through caring for her new baby and keeping her house in order and still remain sane. And those who make it look easy are definitely superwomen."

Giles knew exactly what Jordan was talking about. Before he'd stepped in to help Mya with Lily, she had done it all. "I hear you, cousin."

Crossing his arms over his chest, Jordan gave Giles a prolonged stare. "How are you adjusting to life in the country? Have you traded your luxury SUV for a pickup with a gun rack?"

"That's not funny, man. When I first got there, I was ready to cut and run, but now I can't wait to get back." He held up a hand. "Don't get me wrong, Jordan. I love New York but I think of Wickham Falls like finding an oasis in the desert. It's where I'm able to feel at peace with myself and everything around me."

"Maybe it has something to do with your new family."

"Maybe," he conceded. "Or maybe it goes beyond Mya and Lily. There are times when it's so quiet I can hear crickets in the daytime. Wickham Falls looks like a picture postcard with mountains, forests, waterfalls and white-water rapids. Once Lily's older, I'm going to teach her to swim in a lake rather than in a pool. I want to take her fly-fishing and white-water rafting. And because we live in a rural area, I'll also teach her to handle a rifle and a handgun. And of course whenever we come to New York I'll take her to most of the sporting events."

"So it looks as if you have your future all mapped out."

"Not really. Those are just some of the things on my wish list. I…" His words trailed off when his cell phone vibrated in the back pocket of his jeans. Rising slightly, he retrieved the phone and answered the call. It was a store calling to ask if his charge card was missing or stolen. "No, the card isn't stolen. I gave the card to Miss Lawson for her use. Thanks for calling." Giles ended the call. "Sorry about that. I gave Mya my charge card and a store clerk thought she'd stolen it."

"What you need to do is apply for one in her name."

"I've already done that." He'd called the credit card company earlier that morning and requested an additional card for an authorized user. Giles glanced at his watch. He stood up. "I have to head out now because I have a three o'clock appointment with my barber."

Jordan pushed to his feet. "I know you have your itinerary planned out in advance while you're here, so I guess we'll see you guys for Thanksgiving."

"You bet." Giles's parents were hosting Thanksgiving, while Jordan's parents had assumed the responsibility of planning Christmas. He hugged Jordan again before taking his leave. "Kiss Aziza and that beautiful boy for me. I'll see you guys next month."

Giles left the maisonette, walking east to Lexington Avenue where he hailed a cab to take him downtown. He'd called a former high school classmate who recently opened an intimate restaurant with a piano bar on a quiet block between First and Second Avenue and within walking distance of his Sixty-Second Street apartment. He knew Mya was in a funk because it was the first time since Lily came home from the hospital that she hadn't been there with and for her, and Giles hoped eating out and listening to music for several hours would help to lift her dark mood.

If Mya entertained doubts as to whether Giles would approve of her outfit, they vanished completely when she walked into the living room to find him waiting for her. He stared at her as if she was a stranger as he slowly rose to his feet. She held her hands out at her sides.

"I hope I'm not overdressed."

Giles blinked once. "Oh my... I... I don't," he stuttered, seemingly unable to get the words out. He cleared his throat. "You are beyond perfection."

She'd chosen to wear a sleeveless, high-necked, mid-calf, ruby-red, lace sheath dress with an attached black underslip. Black silk-covered, four-inch stilettos and an evening clutch completed her elegant look. A stylist had trimmed the ends of her curly hair just above her shoulders; each time she turned her head, the loose gold-streaked curls moved as if they'd taken on a life of their own.

He headed toward her, and Mya recognized lust shimmering in the depths of his electric-blue eyes at the same time a shudder of awareness eddied through her. At that moment, she felt an intense physical awareness that was frightening and palpable.

Giles leaned into her. "You smell and look good enough to eat."

Mya was helpless to stop the swath of heat that began in her face before slowly moving to her chest and even lower. She knew it had been a long time since she'd made love with a man, yet she did not know if she wanted that man to be Lily's father. Not before she sorted out if what she was beginning to feel for him was love or simply a need that reminded her she was a woman who'd denied her femininity for far too long.

"I think we'd better leave now before we're late," she lied smoothly. Mya knew if they lingered, then she would beg Giles to strip her naked, take her into the bedroom and make love to her.

Giles picked up his jacket off a chair and slipped his arms into the sleeves, and then handed Mya her black cashmere shawl. He waited for her to wrap it around her shoulders before reaching for her hand and leading her out of the apartment and down the hall to the elevator.

She averted her eyes as he continued to stare at her during the ride to the lobby. It was the first time since meeting Giles that she wasn't as comfortable and confident with him, and she attributed her uneasiness to the realization that her pretense of keeping him at a distance was nothing more than a smoke screen for her true feelings: she was in love with Giles Wainwright.

Although she had stopped thinking of him as her sister's lover, Mya was still attempting to sort out if Giles wanted her for herself and not just because she was Lily's mother. And whenever she thought about Sammie adding the codicil to the will, she wondered if her sister wanted her and Giles together because she probably knew how much family meant to him. Mya had witnessed for herself that the bond between the Wainwrights was strong and invincible. They'd embraced her as if she had given birth to Lily, and before Giles's sister postponed her travel plans, Skye had been ready to drop everything to fly across the country to meet her niece.

It was as if her life had come full circle: she had been adopted by a couple who had given her everything a child could want or need, and now years later, she had adopted a baby and she and Lily were now a part of a large family who would give her daughter everything she could want or need.

"What are you thinking about?" Giles asked, once the car stopped at the lobby.

"Lily."

"What about her?"

"How blessed she is to have a big family."

Giles tucked Mya's hand into the bend of his elbow as they exited the elevator car. "Her blessings came from Sammie sacrificing her life to give birth to a healthy baby, and the second from having you as her mother."

"You're saying that because you're biased."

"No, I'm not. Seeing you with Lily has allowed me to see women and mothers in particular in a whole new light.

"Even though my mother grew up with nannies and live-in help, she didn't want the same for her children because she claimed she saw her nanny more than her mother. I remember her and Dad arguing constantly about having a resident cook and live-in housekeeper. In the end, Mom compromised when she allowed for a cleaning service to come in twice a week to clean the townhouse. She claimed she felt uncomfortable with having strangers living in her home with her children."

"I agree with her," Mya said. "Our house isn't *that* big that I can't maintain it." Although the house where she'd grown up was larger than many of the homes in Wickham Falls, it wasn't ostentatious. When her father hired an architect to design the house, he'd planned on having at least four children. The plans included two full baths, a half bath, five bedrooms that included the master bedroom on the main level with easy access to the veranda.

Graham had insisted on woodburning fireplaces and window seats in every bedroom, and a fireplace in the living room. The architect had divided the downstairs space into three zones: the front for two formal rooms for entertaining and dining, to the rear was the family room and kitchen with an eating area off the outside porch, and the third was the main-floor master bedroom suite.

Then there was the flower garden because Graham knew how much his bride-to-be loved tending her rose garden. He'd hired a landscape architect to create a garden on the one-acre property with flowers, trees, ornamental grasses and aromatic herbs. Every Saturday morning after breakfast, Veronica could be found in her garden, weeding and pruning her collection of hybrid roses. Now a landscaping crew came every week beginning in the spring to mow the grass and maintain the garden until early November when the flower beds were covered to protect them from wildlife foraging for food during the winter months.

Giles smiled when Mya said *our house*. It was apparent she had begun to think of them sharing a future where they would eventually live under one roof. "Our house is perfect for a couple with at least two or three kids. I'd like Lily to have a brother or sister before she turns two."

She shot him a questioning glance. "Please don't tell me you're planning for the next baby even before Lily begins walking."

Giles nodded to the doorman as he escorted Mya across the marble floor to the street. "I'm going to turn thirty-seven in February, and I don't want to find myself out of breath running after a toddler when I'm forty-five."

"There are a lot of men who have kids in their forties and fifties."

"I'll be fifty-five when Lily's eighteen and by that time, I will have earned membership in the silver fox club. And I don't want my six-year-old embarrassed when his friends ask if I'm his grandfather."

"How many kids do you plan to have? And have

you selected the woman who will agree to bear your children?"

Giles stopped in midstride, nearly causing Mya to trip and fall. He caught her, holding onto her arm to steady her. "Did you think I was thinking of someone other than you?

She blinked slowly, reminding him of an owl. "I don't know what to think, Giles. I can't understand why you continue to make plans for us without talking to me first."

Giles felt properly reprimanded. He knew Mya was right because he hadn't had to think of anyone else but himself until now. He was single-focused when it came to securing Lily's future and he figured Mya would just go along with whatever he proposed. Unknowingly he had become his father, micromanaging Mya's life and expecting her to agree with his decisions.

He cradled her face between his hands. "I'm sorry, sweets. I've spent so many years doing what I want that it's going to take some time for me include others in my decision-making."

Mya's eyes clung to his. "You can make all of the decisions you want when you're at your office, but at home you're going to have to discuss things with me before we can compromise on anything that impacts our future."

"Yes, boss."

She lowered her eyes. "I'm not your boss."

"You think not," Giles teased. He pressed a kiss on her fragrant curls. "Let's go before we lose our table."

They continued to the corner and waited for the light to change. "I'm sorry, Giles."

Giles registered raw emotion in Mya's apology. "What are you sorry about?"

"I didn't mean to bite your head off, but I don't want you to forget that we're not even engaged and meanwhile you're talking about having more children. I'd believed I would raise Lily as a single mother. That I could be mother and father, but now I know I was deluding myself when I recall my own childhood. As a child, I loved coming home from school to find my mother in the kitchen preparing the evening meal. But the highlight of the night was when my father arrived because he'd open the door and yell in a perfect Ricky Ricardo imitation, 'Honeys, I'm home.' I thought he was just greeting my mother but he kept calling for his honeys. After a while, I knew he wanted me and Sammie, too. Then all of us would have a family hug and Daddy would say how much he loved his girls. That hug said more than words. It meant we were a family and nothing or no one could break that bond. That's what I want for you, me and Lily."

"And that's what we'll have. A bond that will last all of our lives." An expression of triumph and satisfaction showed in Giles's eyes.

Chapter 12

Mya, holding onto Giles's hand, slowly made her way down a flight of stairs to Dewey's Hideaway, a below-street-level restaurant. She didn't know what to expect but it definitely wasn't the grotto-like eating establishment with the only illumination coming from a wood-burning fireplace, a backlit indoor waterfall, dimmed recessed lights and the candles on nearly two dozen tables positioned close together to maximize space. Most of the tables were filled with diners, as the soft sound of the pianist playing show tunes competed with conversations and the distinctive rattling of serving pieces and plates.

"How did you find this place?" she whispered to Giles when she saw the hostess coming in their direction.

"A friend owns it." Giles smiled at the young woman

with neatly braided hair. "I have a reservation for two. The name is Giles Wainwright."

Picking up two menus, she lowered her eyes, then stared up at him through eyelash extensions. "Please come this way."

Mya didn't miss the flirtatious glance the woman directed at Giles. She seated them at a table not far from where a gleaming black concert piano sat on a raised platform. The hostess removed the Reserved sign from the table and walked away with an exaggerated roll of generous hips.

"How often do you come here?" Mya asked, as she folded her shawl over the back of her chair.

"Not often enough," answered a deep baritone.

Her head popped up while Giles came to his feet. She stared at a tall black man with a black bandana covering his head, chef's jacket and black pinstriped pants with Dewey's Hideaway and D. Dewey, Executive Chef stitched on the tunic over his heart. Giles and Dewey thumped each other's back in greeting. Mya found herself smiling when the two men began talking at once.

"I didn't want to believe it when my sister told me G. Wainwright made a reservation for two."

Giles pumped Dewey's hand. "Who did you think it was?"

"Your brother Patrick. When he calls to make a reservation, he identifies himself as P. Wainwright. He and his wife eat here at least once a month. She likes our mac and cheese with truffle oil." He winked at Mya. "Aren't you going to introduce me to your beautiful lady?"

Cupping Mya's elbow, Giles helped her come to her

feet. "Darling, this is Darryl Dewey, proprietor, chef and all-around good guy. Dewey, Ms. Mya Lawson."

Mya extended her hand to the handsome man with a complexion reminiscent of whipped chocolate mousse. The skin around his dark eyes crinkled in a perpetual smile. "It's a pleasure meeting you, Dewey."

Dewey kissed the back of her hand. "No, Mya. It's my pleasure to meet you." His eyes lingered on her left hand. "I don't know if your fiancé told you, but we go way back as far as the first grade."

"No, he didn't, but I'm certain he's going to fill me in," she replied. It was apparent Dewey thought the ring was an engagement ring.

"You guys can order on or off menu." He pounded Giles's shoulder. "I have to get back to the kitchen because we're down one chef tonight. I have your number, so I'll be in touch."

Mya sat down again. "Please don't tell me you two spent more time in the principal's office than you did in the classroom?"

Giles shifted his chair until they were seated side by side. "Wrong, sweets. Although we were best friends, we were also very competitive when it came to grades. When we graduated, Dewey's GPA beat me by one-tenth of one percent. He enrolled in New York University as a business major and, after graduating, went into investment banking. Dewey said although he made tons of money he hated it because his real passion was cooking. One day, he walked away from his six-figure salary and applied to the Culinary Institute of America to become a chef. He bought this place two years ago and now he's living out his dream."

Mya placed her hand over Giles's. "Are you living out your dream?"

A mysterious smile tilted the corners of his mouth. "I am. Before I met you, my sole focus was on work, and the harder I worked, the more I was able to convince myself that I didn't need or want anyone to share my life." He pressed his forehead to hers. "Meeting you has proven me wrong. Not only do I want you but I also need you."

Mya closed her eyes, too stunned to cry. Men had told they needed her, but they were glibly spoken words they believed she wanted to hear. She felt his hand shake slightly under hers and in that instant she was aware of the power she wielded over Giles. That he'd shown her vulnerability for the first time.

"I need you, too." Her voice was barely a whisper. "I need you to love and protect me and our daughter. When you go away on business, I'll be counting down the days until you return. And I want every subsequent homecoming to be as special as the first one. I know you want more children, but I want to wait and give Lily time to experience being an only child. I also need to warn you that I can be stubborn when—"

"Enough, Mya," Giles admonished softly. "You don't have to try and convince me that you're not perfect because no one is."

"Not even you?" she teased.

"Above all, not me." Cradling her jaw, he brushed a kiss over her mouth. "And I'll try and make certain every homecoming is more special than the one before it. We'll talk about you, me and Lily when we get home."

She nodded. "Speaking of home, I'd like to suggest you give up your hotels and move in with your *fiancée* and daughter so we can begin living as a family. I'll fix up one of the bedrooms for you."

Giles pulled back, his features deceptively composed. "Are you serious?"

A slight smile softened her lips. "Very serious. You no longer need your love shack and you can stop polluting the environment driving between your hotel and Wickham Falls."

"Consider it done." Giles shifted his chair to sit opposite her, while resisting the urge to pump his fist. It was obvious Mya was willing to consider sharing her life and future with him. He did not tell her that he hadn't renewed the Chelsea hotel suite reservation for the month of October. Once he discovered he'd become a father, he realized he couldn't continue to have sex with arbitrary women to slake his sexual frustration. It had become a wake-up call that not only had his life changed, but he had to change.

Some of the guys with whom he'd attended college had planned to marry their girlfriends and start a family. They found it odd that he never mentioned having a special woman or marriage. At the time, giving up his bachelor status had not been an option. He had not wanted to be responsible for anyone but himself. However, fate had a way of altering his well-ordered lifestyle when he unknowingly became a father. Even the best-laid plans were known to go awry.

The spell that Mya had unknowingly woven wrapped

him in a cocoon of peace. The newfound joy was shattered when a waiter came to take their drink order.

It was as if any and every other woman Giles had dated ceased to exist as he shared nearly ninety minutes of eating, talking and listening to live music. The four-course meal began with a toast to her latest novel and followed with a salad of bitter chicories paired with crisp lardoons, toasted pine nuts and crumbled feta tossed with red wine vinegar and extra-virgin olive oil; the salad was followed with an appetizer of baked clams and entrées of marinated grilled skirt steak and shrimp scampi with side dishes of macaroni and cheese and linguine with garlic and oil. Their waiter had suggested sparkling white peach sangria as a cocktail, which had become an excellent complement for the expertly prepared dishes.

"Are you under the influence?" Giles asked Mya after she'd drained her wineglass. He noticed she did not take a sip of the wine concoction until after she'd finished the first two courses.

She smiled and the flame from the flickering votive cast flattering shadows over her delicate features and highlighted her hazel eyes with a golden glow. "Surprisingly, no. Maybe it's because I ate first." She touched the napkin to the corners of her mouth. "I see why your sister-in-law orders the mac and cheese. It's insanely delicious."

Giles wanted to tell Mya that she was insanely beautiful in red. Her palomino-gold skin reminded him of liquid gold, and his mother had chosen wisely when she gave Mya the ruby and diamond ring. As a young boy, he would watch his mother go through the jewelry she had inherited from her grandmother and meticulously select what she wanted to wear for a luncheon with her friends or a formal event with her husband. He remembered his elderly grandmother telling him that while some women in her social circle collected wealthy husbands, she preferred priceless jewels. He wondered if Mya would continue the tradition of giving the ring to their granddaughter.

Giles shook his head. He did not want to think of Lily marrying and making him a grandfather. At least not for a long time. He wanted to watch her grow up from infant to toddler, to young girl and teenager and finally a woman. He wanted to be there to cheer her successes and comfort her during disappointments. An unconscious smile crinkled the skin around his eyes. And more important, he wanted to be the role model for the man she would eventually chose as her husband and partner for life.

"What are you smiling about?" Mya questioned.

"I was just thinking about Lily making us grandparents."

"Bite your tongue, Giles. She's still in diapers, meanwhile you have her having babies."

He sobered. "You know it's probably going to happen one of these days."

"I know, but there's still so much I want to do with her before she's a woman."

Reaching across the table, Giles held Mya's hand. "And you will." He winked at her. "Are you ready for coffee and dessert?

"I don't think so. I am stuffed. The next time we come back to New York, we have to eat here again. Tell your friend that he's a gastronomical genius."

Releasing her hand, Giles signaled the waiter for the check. "I'll definitely let Dewey know you give him an A." He settled the bill, leaving a generous gratuity, and escorted Mya out of the restaurant.

She moved closer to his side. "It's really getting cold. Wearing lace in late October without a coat isn't very bright."

He looped an arm around her waist, sharing his body's heat. "It's chilly because we're not far from the East River." Her dress reminded Giles of the song "The Lady in Red." Raising his right hand, he whistled for a passing taxi.

"I think I can make it back to your place before turning into an icicle."

Giles opened the rear door to the cab when it maneuvered up to the curb. "We're not going back to my place. I figured we'd spend the night at my parents' house. I don't want you staying there alone and I want us to be there when Mom and Dad bring Lily back. My father always gets up early and is usually on the road before sunrise."

He did not tell Mya that if they did spend the night in his condo, he did not trust himself not to try to make love to her. And more important, he did not have any condoms on hand and he didn't know if Mya was using birth control.

Mya huddled close to him in the back seat. "I called my editor and was told she's in Europe for a book fair."

Giles buried his face in her hair. "Maybe you'll get to see her when we spend the week here between Christmas and New Year's."

"I doubt that. Publishing usually goes on hiatus that week. I'll probably hook up with her sometime next spring."

Meeting her editor in person was not a priority for Mya. Having Giles live with her was. She'd told him that she wasn't raised to shack up with a man and now she was going against what she'd been taught once she invited Giles to move in with her and Lily. Living together would offer her a glimpse into the life she would share with a man who'd roared into her life like a tornado that had touched down to sweep up everything in its path. Her emotions were strewn everywhere and once the twister was gone, she was left craving his touch, his kiss and wanting to know how it would feel to have him inside her.

"Speaking of spring," Giles said after a pregnant silence, "I know I'm fast-forwarding almost two years, but do you want a spring or summer wedding?"

"I'd like a late-spring wedding. It can get quite hot and uncomfortable in the summer."

He went still, and then his head popped up as he met her eyes. "You want to get married in Wickham Falls?"

"Of course."

"Is there a venue large enough to accommodate our family and friends?"

Mya nodded. "We can hold the ceremony and reception in a hotel off the turnpike or interstate."

"Would it bother you if I hire a wedding planner?"

She gave him an incredulous look. "Of course not. Did you think I would object?"

"I don't know. You've ragged me enough about not checking with you when making decisions that affect both of us."

Mya lowered her eyes. "You would remind me of that."

"Only because I don't want you to think I'm trying to run your life. I'd like to hire Signature Brides. Even though they're based in New York, I'm certain they would like to add another Wainwright wedding to their long list of high-profile weddings. They were responsible for coordinating my cousin Jordan's wedding and now they're involved in planning Brandt's destination wedding."

"You can hire them. All I want to do is show up and enjoy our special day."

"Would you like to become a June bride?"

She smiled. "Yes."

Giles retrieved his cell phone from the breast pocket of his suit jacket and tapped the calendar icon. "Your birthday falls on a Sunday. Would you like to share your anniversary with your birthday?"

She buried her face against his neck. "Of course not. It will give me an excuse to celebrate not once, but twice."

"And I don't have an excuse that I forgot our anniversary."

Mya laughed softly. "Something tells me that you don't forget much."

"Not when it comes to you."

* * *

Mya stared through the glass of the French doors. She'd returned to Wickham Falls in time to join in the town's Halloween festivities, while counting down the days when she, Giles, and Lily would return to New York for Thanksgiving However, the weather had conspired against them.

The house would've been as quiet as a tomb if not for the tapping of frozen rain against the roof and windows. She was mesmerized by the ice coating the branches of trees and a carpet of white turning the landscape into a Christmas card winter scene.

But it was still four weeks from Christmas, and the plan to go to New York to share Thanksgiving with the Wainwrights had been cancelled because of ice and snow storms ravaging the East Coast from North Carolina to Maine. Flights were grounded and states of emergency had been declared by governors in all of the affected states.

She felt the warmth from Giles's body as he stood behind her. There were times when she marveled that he could enter a room so silently that she would look up and finding him standing there. He had moved into the house and into the master bedroom. To those who saw them together, they were a normal couple with a child, but behind closed doors, they shared everything but a bed.

His arms circled her waist as he pressed his chest to her back. "You're not writing today?"

Mya closed her eyes and rested the back of her head against his shoulder. "I don't feel like writing."

"Do you have writer's block?"

"No. I revised my schedule because I thought we were going to New York this weekend."

"I was looking forward to it, too. So it looks as if we'll have our own Thanksgiving here."

Turning in his embrace, Mya went on tiptoe and brushed a kiss over his parted lips. "I have so much to be grateful for. I never could've imagined being this contented. And you're responsible for that."

Giles affected a half smile. "Only because I love you."

"Not as much as I love you."

He eased back, staring at her as if she had spoken a foreign language. "What did you say?"

Mya knew she'd shocked him, because it was the first time she'd admitted what lay in her heart. "I love you, Giles Harrison Wainwright, and right now I want you to take me to bed so I can show you how much I love you."

Giles blinked once. "I don't have any condoms with me."

"You don't need condoms, darling. I'm on the pill."

Giles knew Mya could feel the runaway beating of his heart against her breasts. He and Mya had been living together for nearly a month, and during that time, he had been reluctant to seduce her in an attempt to get her to agree to sleep with him. He hadn't thought of himself as an overly patient man but somehow she'd proven him wrong when he decided to wait—wait as long as it would take for her to come to him of her own free will.

Bending slightly, he swept her up in his arms and, taking long, determined strides, headed for the rear of the house and the master bedroom. Giles placed her on the king-size bed and lay beside her. He threaded their fingers together. "Are you certain you're ready for this?"

"Yes."

Moving over her while sitting back on his heels, Giles's hands searched under the hem of her T-shirt, massaging the tight flesh over her ribs before moving up to cover her breasts. Her breathing deepened as he slowly and methodically undressed her, and then himself. There was enough light coming through the windows to make out her eyes. Her steady gaze bore into his as he lowered his head and kissed her mouth.

Giles wanted Mya because he found her sexy, sexier than any woman he had ever met. That he wanted her because he knew he couldn't have Lily without her. And that she unknowingly had cast a spell over him, bewitching him with her poise and beauty. She challenged as well as seduced him, and instinctively he knew he could grow old with her.

She extended her arms and he went into her embrace. Placing his hands under her thighs, he parted her knees with his and eased his erection inside her. She gasped once, and then moaned and writhed in an ancient rhythm that needed no prompting or tutoring.

The impact of their lovemaking matched and surpassed the ferocity of the ice storm lashing the countryside with its fury as Mya ascended to heights of passion she had never experienced before. She sought to possess Giles as he did the same with her. Her sighs from experiencing multiple orgasms had not faded completely when Giles reversed their positions. Burying her face against the column of his strong neck, she kissed him under his ear at the same time he growled deep in his throat and caught the tender flesh at the base of her throat between his teeth, leaving a visible imprint of his claim. She savored the lingering pulsing of his hardness inside her.

Her fist pounded the pillow beneath his head. "Why did you wait so long?"

Giles frowned up at her. "Wait for what?"

"To make love to me."

"I can't believe you'd say that," he drawled. "If you'd given me the slightest hint that you wanted me to make love to you, I would've had you on your back a long time ago."

She smiled. "I suppose that means we'll just have to make up for lost time."

Giles winked at her. "You've got that right, sweets."

Two weeks before they were scheduled to fly to New York for the Christmas week Mya felt as if her fairytale world had suddenly imploded.

The fear and uneasiness she'd managed to push to the recesses of her mind had suddenly had resurfaced. The man with whom she had fallen love, made love with every chance they got, and looked forward to sharing her daughter and their future with had deceived her.

She had just put Lily down for her nap and walked into her office only to overhear Giles on his cell. The door was slight ajar and she heard Giles talking to someone. Her step faltered when she heard him mention Lily's name. Her heart stopped, and then started up again when he said, "Her name should be listed as Lily Hope Lawson-Wainwright. Yes, Wainwright."

Mya didn't wait to hear anymore. She made her way down the staircase to the kitchen at the same time she tried to slow the runaway beating of her heart. What she'd suspected all along had become a reality. Giles had wined and dined, wooed, courted and proposed marriage because it was the only way he could claim his daughter. She glared at him when he walked into the kitchen.

"Hi, sweets. I thought you'd be upstairs writing."

"I don't feel very much like writing. Not after over-hearing your conversation."

An expression of confusion settled into his handsome features. "What are you talking about?"

"Lily Hope Lawson-Wainwright," she spat out. "How dare you go behind my back and –"

"Stop it, Mya!" Giles said, interrupting her. "It's not what you think."

"It's not what I think but what I overheard."

"Why were you eavesdropping?"

Mya's temper flared. "Eavesdropping? In my own home?"

He managed to appear contrite. "Maybe I used the wrong word."

"You're damn right you did." Giles moved closer at the same time she slipped off the stool, putting more distance between them. "Don't touch me." She held up a hand. "And please don't say anything because right about now I'm ready to lose it."

A muscle twitched in Giles's jaw. "Suit yourself." Turning on his heel he walked out of the kitchen.

Mya closed her eyes, willing the tears welling up behind her lids not to fall. How could she have been so blind? The silent voice had nagged at her not to trust Giles, but unfortunately she had ignored it when time and again Giles made decisions without first consulting her. She was not his employee or soldiers under command where he issued orders and expected them to be followed without question. It had been a while since she had to remind Giles that legally he had no claim on Lily, and it was apparent that he had forgotten that fact.

Chapter 13

"I can't believe we had to wait until New Year's Eve to meet you for the first time."

Mya smiled at Giles's cousin's wife. She never would've guess that Aziza Fleming-Wainwright was the mother of a three-month-old. A black off-the-shoulder gown clung to the curves of her tall, slender body. "I don't know, but every time Giles and I plan to come to New York it's as if the weather conspires against us. First, an ice storm for Thanksgiving and then a blizzard with nearly two feet of snow for Christmas."

Temperatures in the northeast had gone from below freezing to mid-fifties and within days mounds of snow had begun to melt.

What she did not say was her relationship with Giles had gone from frosty to icy. They had become polite

strangers living under the same roof, while Lily continued to thrive. She was walking, holding on to objects to
keep her balance and had begun calling Giles 'Da-da.'

When Mya arrived earlier that afternoon she'd found
the suites in the four-story, gray-stone mansion spanning a half block on Fifth Avenue filled with several
generations of Wainwrights, and she hadn't seen Lily
once Amanda discovered her granddaughter was in the
nursery with the other young children.

There was a soft knock on the door before it opened
and a young woman wearing a black backless gown
with a full skirt swept into the room. Her chemically
straightened hair was styled in a loose, curling ponytail. Mya knew without introductions that she was Ciara
Dennison, Brandt's fiancée. During their first visit to
New York Giles had pulled up several family photographs on his computer and given her an overview of
each person. Mya had teased him about the two, very
pretty African-American women definitely adding a
bit of color to the overwhelming number of Wainwright
blonds.

The diamond ring on Ciara's left hand caught the
light when she held out her arms to Mya. "All of the
guys were whispering about how beautiful you are, and
I just had to come and see if they were blowing smoke,"
she said with a wide grin. "Girlfriend, you are stunning!" She drew out the word in two distinct syllables.
"I'm Ciara."

Mya pressed her cheek to Ciara's. "And I'm Mya."

Aziza rested her hands at her waist. "I'm certain

when people hear your names, they probably think of the two female singers."

Mya laughed. "I'd starve to death if I had to sing for a living."

Ciara patted her hair. "I'd probably do a little better than you because I can carry a tune."

Her clear brown eyes sparkled like newly minted pennies. "It looks as if we sister-girls are batting a thousand when it comes to scooping up these fine-ass Wainwright men."

"I second that," Aziza drawled.

Mya had to agree with the attorney and psychiatric nurse. Even if their men weren't Wainwrights, Jordan, Brandt and Giles were the heroes women fantasized about when reading romance novels. "Excuse me, but I have to see Giles about something." Lifting the skirt of her chocolate-brown strapless gown, she walked out of the suite.

Turning on her heel, she made her way down the wide carpeted hallway to the curving staircase leading to the great hall. The mansion was decorated for the season: live pine boughs lined the fireplace mantel as a fire blazed behind a decorative screen. Lighted electric candles were in every window, and the gaily decorated, twelve-foot Norwegian spruce towered under the brightly lit chandelier suspended from a twenty-foot ceiling. Many of the more fragile glass ornaments on the tree were purported to be at least two hundred years old.

The ball was in full swing with formally dressed men and women eating and drinking, and many couples were dancing to a live band. Someone tapped her shoulder, and she turned to find a young man with brilliant green eyes in a deeply tanned face smiling at her. "May I have this dance?"

Mya returned his smile. "Of course."

"Who are you here with, beautiful?" he whispered in her ear as he spun her around the marble floor.

"Giles Wainwright."

"It's just my luck you would be connected to the folks hosting this shindig."

The song ended and Mya barely had time to catch her breath when she found herself dancing with another man. This one held her too tight as he couldn't pull his eyes away from her chest. When she pleaded thirst, he led her to the bar and waited until she asked the bartender for a club soda with a twist of lime.

"How about another dance?"

"Dude, how about finding another woman to dance with." Mya turned to find Giles glaring at the man. "Move along," he added when her dance partner hesitated and then walked away.

"What's the matter with you?" Mya asked between clenched teeth. "Have you gone and lost your mind?"

The coldness in Giles's eyes reminded her of chipped ice. "You have the audacity to ask me what's wrong when I'm forced to watch you disrespect me when you flirt with every man salivating over your chest."

"Disrespect! You have a nerve to talk to me about—"

Giles's fingers curled around her upper arm. "Come with me. We don't need to air our problems in front of everyone."

"Problems? I don't have a problem. You're the one with the problem," she said as they wove their way through the throng and out of the ballroom. Mya followed Giles to an area near the elevator. She was too angry to acknowledge he looked magnificent in formalwear.

Holding onto her shoulders, Giles gave her a death-stare. "What the hell was that back there?"

"Nothing!" she spat out. "A couple of men asked me to dance and I saw nothing wrong with dancing with them. Now if you're going to go off every time I talk to a man, then I don't think we should be together."

"What do you mean that I'm the one with the problem?"

"You have a problem being truthful, and I'm angry with myself because I allowed you to lure me into a trap where you can get legal custody of Lily and change her name by marrying me."

"If you hadn't shut me out I would've told you about my conversation with my cousin. I was talking to Jordan about setting up a trust fund for our daughter."

Mya blinked as if coming out of a trance. "She doesn't need a trust fund because I've set aside monies for her future."

"Why is it always what you want for Lily, Mya? Can't you just this once include me in the equation. Lily's not only your daughter but *our* daughter. I know I can get ahead of myself when it comes to planning her future, but from now on I again promise to talk to you first before making *any* decision about her."

Mya smile mirrored relief. Giles wasn't planning to change Lily's name. "And I'll be certain to remind you of that in case you forget."

"You can do anything you want to me, but promise me you won't shut me out again."

"I'll think about it."

"While you're thinking about it I need to do this." Giles lowered his head and brushed a light kiss over her mouth.

She bit down on her lip as she fought back tears. "I'm sorry, babe, for not trusting you." She took a step and curved her arms around his inside his tuxedo jacket. "Can you forgive me?"

Giles cradled her chin, his eyes making love to her. "Of course I forgive you. But can you forgive me for going Neanderthal on you?"

"Yes. Now kiss me again before we go back."

Giles needed no further urging when he lifted Mya off her feet and kissed her with all the passion he could summon for the woman who'd stolen his heart. "What do you say we go upstairs and have a quickie before everyone rings in the New Year?"

Mya shook her head. "Don't you ever get enough?"

Throwing back his head, Giles laughed loudly. Before their heated confrontation, they had made love nearly every night. "As long as I can get it up, I'll never get enough."

Mya looped her arms through his. "Let's go back before folks come looking for us." Midnight would signal a new year where she could look forward to marrying a man who had promised to love and protect her and their daughter all the days of their lives.

Eighteen months had sped by quickly and Mya would celebrate not only her birthday but also her wedding day. She'd chosen Giles's sister Skye to be her maid of honor and Aziza and an obviously pregnant Ciara as her attendants. Giles had selected Jordan as his best man and Brandt and his brother Patrick as his groomsmen.

Mya had asked her future father-in-law to give her away and he appeared visibly overcome with emotion when he nodded mutely. The weather had cooperated. Bright sunshine and afternoon temperatures were perfect for a garden wedding.

She touched the diamond necklace Giles had given her for a wedding present following the rehearsal dinner.

The owners of Signature Brides had arrived two days ago to make certain the tent was scheduled to be up for the ceremony and coordinate with the hotel's banquet manager for the reception. There had been a steady stream of Wainwrights checking into the hotel over the past three days. Some of the men were talking about returning in the fall to go hunting. A few of her colleagues from college were also in attendance.

She adjusted the flowing skirt of her gown with white lace appliqued flowers and a trailing train. A pale pink belt with silk roses matched the underslip. In lieu of a veil, she had selected to wear pink and white rosebuds in the chignon on the nape of her neck.

The string quartet played a Mozart concerto as Skye, Aziza and Ciara processed down the white carpet with their partners. The entire assembly under the tent rose to their feet with the familiar strains of the "Wedding March."

Mya and Pat shared a smile before she turned her attention to the man waiting to make her his wife. She was smiling from ear to ear when he winked at her. She counted the steps that would take her to his side. He reached for her hand even before the judge asked, "Who gives this woman in marriage?"

"I do," Patrick announced loudly, as a ripple of laughter came from those under the tent.

Mya did not remember repeating her vows or when Giles placed a wedding band on her finger. However, she did recall his long and passionate kiss when the judge told him he could kiss his wife.

When they turned to face those who'd come to witness their nuptials, Mya smiled at Lily who squirmed to escape Amanda's hold. "Daddy!" she screamed, extending her arms for Giles to take her.

Not only was she walking but she was also talking. A photographer and videographer captured the image of Giles holding his daughter while he curved an arm around his wife's waist. He had given Mya the necklace for a wedding gift, while she'd handed him a gaily wrapped box with a copy of Lily's birth certificate with a note that it was time to amend the certificate so their daughter could legally become Lily Hope Wainwright.

When Giles had walked into the lawyer's office what now seemed eons ago, he never knew how his life would change. It was better than he could have ever imagined. He'd claimed his baby and a woman whose love promised forever.

* * * * *

COMING NEXT MONTH FROM

H HARLEQUIN®

SPECIAL EDITION

Available July 16, 2019

HSECNM0719

SPECIAL EXCERPT FROM

HARLEQUIN

™

SPECIAL EDITION

*To give the orphaned triplets they're guardians of the
stability they need, Lulu McCabe and Sam Kirkland
decide to jointly adopt them. But when it's discovered
their marriage wasn't actually annulled, they have
to prove to the courts they're responsible—
by renewing their vows!*

Read on for a sneak preview of Cathy Gillen Thacker's
Their Inherited Triplets,
the next book in the
Texas Legends: The McCabes *miniseries.*

"The two of you are still married," Liz said.

"Still?" Lulu croaked.

Sam asked, "What are you talking about?"

"More to the point, how do you know this?" Lulu
demanded, the news continuing to hit her like a gut punch.

Travis looked down at the papers in front of him.
"Official state records show you eloped in the Double
Knot Wedding Chapel in Memphis, Tennessee, on
Monday, March 14, nearly ten years ago. Alongside
another couple, Peter and Theresa Thompson, in a double
wedding ceremony."

Lulu gulped. "But our union was never legal," she
pointed out, trying to stay calm, while Sam sat beside her
in stoic silence.

Liz countered, "Ah, actually, it is legal. In fact, it's still
valid to this day."

Sam reached over and took her hand in his, much as he had the first time they had been in this room together.

"How is that possible?" Lulu asked weakly.

"We never mailed in the certificate of marriage, along with the license, to the state of Tennessee," Sam said.

"And for our union to be recorded and therefore legal, we had to have done that," Lulu reiterated.

"Well, apparently, the owners of the Double Knot Wedding Chapel did, and your marriage was recorded. And is still valid to this day, near as we can tell. Unless you two got a divorce or an annulment somewhere else? Say another country?" Travis prodded.

"Why would we do that? We didn't know we were married," Sam returned.

Don't miss
Their Inherited Triplets *by Cathy Gillen Thacker,*
available August 2019 wherever
Harlequin® Special Edition books and ebooks are sold.

www.Harlequin.com

HSEEXP0719

SPECIAL EXCERPT FROM

HQN™

*Read on for a sneak peek at
the first funny and heart-tugging book in Jo McNally's
Rendezvous Falls series,* Slow Dancing at Sunrise*!*

"I'd have thought the idea of me getting caught in a rainstorm would make your day."

He gave her a quick glance. Just because she was off-limits didn't mean he was blind.

"Trust me, it did." Luke slowed the truck and reached behind the seat to grab his zippered hoodie hanging there. Whitney looked down and her cheeks flamed when she realized how her clothes were clinging to her. She snatched the hoodie from his hand before he could give it to her, and thrust her arms into it without offering any thanks. Even the zipper sounded pissed off when she yanked it closed.

"Perfect. Another guy with more testosterone than manners. Nice to know it's not just a Chicago thing. Jackasses are everywhere."

Luke frowned. He'd been having fun at her expense, figuring she'd give it right back to him as she had before. But her words hinted at a story that didn't reflect well on men in general. She'd been hurt. He shouldn't care. But that quick dimming of the fight in her eyes made him feel ashamed. *That* was a new experience.

A flash of lightning made her flinch. But the thunder didn't follow as quickly as the last time. The storm was moving off. He drove from the vineyard into the parking lot and over to the main house. The sound of the rain on the roof was less angry. But Whitney wasn't. She was clutching his sweatshirt around herself, her knuckles white. From anger? Embarrassment? Both? Luke shook his head.

"Look, I thought I was doing the right thing, driving up there." He rubbed the back of his neck and grimaced, remembering how sweaty and filthy he still was. "It's not my fault you walked out of the woods soaking wet. I mean, I try not to be a jackass, but I'm still a man. And I *did* offer my hoodie."

Whitney's chin pointed up toward the second floor of the main house. Her neck was long and graceful. There was a vein pulsing at the base of it. She blinked a few times, and for a horrifying moment, he thought there might be tears shimmering there in her eyes. *Damn it.* The last thing he needed was to have Helen's niece *crying* in his truck. He opened his mouth to say something—anything—but she beat him to it.

"I'll concede I wasn't prepared for rain." Her mouth barely moved, her words forced through clenched teeth. "But a gentleman would have looked away or…something."

His low laughter was enough to crack that brittle shell of hers. She turned to face him, eyes wide.

"See, Whitney, that's where you made your biggest mistake." He shrugged. "It wasn't going out for a day hike with a storm coming." He talked over her attempted objection. "Your *biggest* mistake was thinking I'm any kind of gentleman."

The corner of her mouth tipped up into an almost smile. "But you said you weren't a jackass."

"There's a hell of a lot of real estate between jackass and gentleman, babe."

Her half smile faltered, then returned. That familiar spark appeared in her eyes. The crack in her veneer had been repaired, and the sharp edge returned to her voice. Any other guy might have been annoyed, but Luke was oddly relieved to see Whitney back in fighting form.

"The fact that you just referred to me as 'babe' tells me you're a lot closer to jackass than you think."

He lifted his shoulder. "I never told you which end of the spectrum I fell on."

The rain had slowed to a steady drizzle. She reached for the door handle, looking over her shoulder with a smirk.

"Actually, I'm pretty sure you just did."

She hurried up the steps to the covered porch. He waited, but she didn't look back before going into the house. Her energy still filled the cab of the truck, and so did her scent. Spicy, woodsy, rain soaked. Finally coming to his senses, he threw the truck into Reverse and headed back toward the carriage house. He needed a long shower. A long *cold* one.

*Don't miss
Jo McNally's Slow Dancing at Sunrise,
available July 2019 from HQN Books!*

www.Harlequin.com

Love Harlequin romance?

DISCOVER.

Be the first to find out about promotions,
news and exclusive content!

Facebook.com/HarlequinBooks

Twitter.com/HarlequinBooks

Instagram.com/HarlequinBooks

Pinterest.com/HarlequinBooks

ReaderService.com

EXPLORE.

Sign up for the Harlequin e-newsletter and
download a free book from any series at
TryHarlequin.com.

CONNECT.

Join our Harlequin community to share
your thoughts and connect with other
romance readers!
Facebook.com/groups/HarlequinConnection

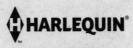

HARLEQUIN®

**ROMANCE WHEN
YOU NEED IT**

HSOCIAL2018

Reward the book lover in you!

Earn points on your purchase of new Harlequin books from participating retailers.

Turn your points into **FREE BOOKS** of your choice!

Join for FREE today at
www.HarlequinMyRewards.com.

Harlequin My Rewards is a free program (no fees) without any commitments or obligations.